Peter Sykes served as a consultant surgeon for _ _ _ _ _ the medical director of an NHS Trust. In 1998 he led the group that won the UK Medical Management Team of the Year Award. During the final three years of his career, he was involved at a national level in the control of quality of surgical services.

Now retired, when he is not writing, he spends his time gardening, golfing, enjoying the company of his grandchildren and occasionally grumbling that 'Things ain't what they used to be'.

****

This novel is a sequel to 'The First Cut' published in 2011 which described young Doctor Lambert's misadventures, both medical and romantic as he was thrown, bewildered and unprepared, onto a busy surgical ward.

'A very entertaining and thoughtful read'

Simply Books (twice named Independent Bookseller of the Year)

'A comedic yet heartfelt realisation of life as a young doctor ..... constantly encouraging you to read on.'

Nursing Times

Behind The Screens at the City General Hospital

Peter Sykes

Published by New Generation Publishing in 2013

Copyright © Peter Sykes 2013

First Edition

www.newgeneration-publishing.com

 **New Generation Publishing**

This book is a novel; it is not literally true. Some characters owe a little
to patients and doctors I have known, but none of them are real.
Similarly, events described are fictitious.

This book is dedicated to health care workers everywhere.

May care and compassion be their constant companions.

All author royalties from the sale of this book will be shared equally between East Cheshire Hospice, Macclesfield and St Ann's Hospice, Stockport.

I wish to thank Edward Vickers and Sean Butler for valuable assistance with the cover design. Steve Linnell of Linnell Illustration created the cartoon character and similarly gave his time and expertise free of charge. I am grateful also to Julie Mann who typed the original manuscript and to my wife Jane for her patience and for supplying innumerable cups of tea.

Above all, I thank the many patients that it has been my privilege to serve for giving me the inspiration to write this book.

Group photograph courtesy of Rex/ITV Features

Chapter One

3rd September 1969

Paul emptied the cubicles in order; cubicle one, cubicle two, cubicle three. Then back to cubicle one. It may be imagined that it was boring, but it wasn't. Each cubicle held a new patient, a different problem and a fresh challenge. Already that day he had removed a peanut from the nose of a three-year-old girl. Her elder brother had placed it there in a vain attempt to control her fit of sneezing! He had treated a builder who had dropped a lump hammer on his foot. Foolishly, he had left his steel capped boots at home and gone to work wearing open toed sandals! He had applied a plaster cast to a lad whose ankle had been broken in a 'friendly' game of football; at least it was supposed to have been a friendly match. Later, there had been an office worker with indigestion, a housewife who had cut her hand whilst filleting fish and an elderly man with concussion sustained in a road traffic accident. It had been a typical shift in the casualty department. Fortunately none of the patients had been seriously injured and Paul had managed to treat them all without calling for senior advice.

It was now two in the morning. He was sitting in the office, sharing a well-earned pot of tea and some hot buttered toast with the nursing sister when staff nurse popped her head round the door. She had a huge grin on her face.

"I've just put a patient into cubicle three," she said above the background noise. "She's got abdominal pain."

The drunk whose head wound had just been stitched was groaning, as he stumbled towards the exit, assisted by one of the night porters. A young woman, who had swallowed a handful of sleeping tablets in a futile attempt to convince her boyfriend of her undying love, was sobbing gently in an adjacent cubicle. She had suffered the ignominy of having her stomach pumped out. Paul was tired. It had been a long day. He had been hoping that no more patients would arrive and that he would be able to snatch a couple of hours sleep before morning. There was nothing remotely amusing about having to attend to yet another patient.

"And what's so funny about that?" he asked.

"You'll find out when you see her."

"Is it urgent or can I finish my mug of tea?"

"I really don't know." The staff nurse was laughing. "It's difficult to say."

It was clear that there was something about the patient in cubicle three that she found highly entertaining. It didn't sound as if the problem was sufficiently urgent for Paul to interrupt his snack, but curiosity got the better of him. He went to discover what it was that staff nurse found so amusing.

Patients from all walks of life attended the City General Hospital's accident department; injuries and illness having no respect for social class or status, but this particular lady looked distinctly out of place. She was about 70 years of age and stoutly built. She was sitting primly to attention; knees and ankles clamped tightly together. On her head she wore what appeared to be a home knitted woollen tea cosy, decorated with a bold and colourful floral design. A large string of multicoloured glass beads hung round her neck over her cardigan, which again was hand knitted and matched her hat. A heavy tweed skirt, a pair of thick woollen socks and walking boots completed her outfit. With her round gentle face and grey hair, matching whiskers on upper lip and chin, she reminded Paul of the maiden aunt who visited his family home each Christmas when he was a child. Her hugs and kisses were tolerated only because they were followed by the gift of a large, crisp, white five pound note which his father promptly confiscated, *'for safe-keeping'*. On her lap she held a wicker basket covered with a tea towel. Paul thought that she would have looked more at home attending a village craft fair on a Saturday afternoon, than a city centre casualty department in the small hours of the morning. She didn't appear to be in any pain or distress; indeed she looked sheepish rather than ill.

Paul introduced himself, sounding irritated. His first impression was that this lady had no need to attend casualty, or to waste time which he would preferred to spend tucked up in a nice warm bed.

"Hello, I'm Dr Lambert. I believe you've got some tummy ache."

She looked embarrassed and sounded apologetic.

"No," she said. "Actually I haven't, though I confess that's what I told the lady at the reception desk. If she had known what I really wanted, she would probably have thrown me out. And I do so desperately need to see you. The truth is there's nothing the matter with me at all. It's Kitty."

Gently she took the tea towel from the basket and revealed a large, but distinctly unhappy looking cat, which was lying on a pad of heavily blood stained cotton wool. The cat mewed in a weak and pitiful way as she stroked it lovingly.

"Look," Paul said defensively. "I'm not a vet. I don't know anything about cats."

8

"I know you're not a vet," she said softly, "but you have studied medicine; you must have some ideas."

It was obvious that she was genuinely concerned about her cat and was pleading for some assistance. Paul was tempted to end the consultation there and then, rather than making any further enquiries. He was well aware that the more involved that he became, the more difficult it would be for him to extricate himself from the situation. There was a bed and the prospect of sleep waiting for him when the cubicles had been cleared. There was no need for him to be concerned about a cat. His responsibility was to care for humans not animals. It was however the look in her eyes, begging for help, that made him weaken.

"What do you think is the matter with it?"

"Not 'it', Doctor. Kitty is female and I think she must be pregnant. I know I should have taken her to the vets long ago to get her doctored, but I couldn't bear to think of Kitty having an operation. I thought that if she was kept indoors and I kept a close eye on her, this wouldn't happen."

Knowing how cats love to wander the lonely streets at night, Paul considered this to be highly optimistic.

"And what makes you think she might be pregnant?"

"Well, she has been trying to make a nest in the back room and has been 'yowling' something terrible. It has been so bad that I've had complaints from the neighbours and now Kitty is in a lot of pain. I suspect she's in labour and I can't bear to see her suffer."

Tears filled her eyes as she lifted the large tabby out of the basket, placed the basket on the floor, then sat with the cat on her knee, gently stroking the fur on the back of its neck and making soft cooing sounds.

"Look," Paul said desperately, still looking for an early exit strategy, "I really don't know anything about cats. When I was a lad at home, I had a couple of white mice and a budgerigar. And there was a time when my father kept chickens in the back garden, but we never had a cat or a dog."

With tears now rolling down her cheeks, she reached for Paul's hand and pleaded. "But you will look at her for me, won't you, Doctor? She's so weak and lethargic now and she has lost such a lot of blood. I'm afraid that she's going to die."

It was a request that was impossible to refuse, so crouching down beside Miss Mullins, for that was the lady's name, Paul took the cat in his arms. It failed to react in any way to being handled by a stranger. It just lay still, with eyes glazed, its head lolling weakly from side to side. The cat's abdomen was swollen, which suggested that it could be pregnant, and from time to time its whole body went rigid and then quivered, as if it was experiencing a spasm of pain. And despite having no knowledge of feline anatomy, Paul could see that Kitty was bleeding from an orifice that he assumed to be the vagina.

Paul recognised that he was out of his depth, that this was a situation that he was unable to resolve on his own. Despite having treated thirty or more human patients during the course of the day without recourse to assistance, he needed help with this veterinary case. However he most certainly could not risk waking the surgical registrar, to whom he would normally turn for advice and guidance on a diagnostic problem. Wondering whether, by chance, there might be someone in the department who knew more about pregnant cats than he did, he lifted Kitty back into her basket, covered her with the tea towel and then asked Miss Mullins to accompany him to the office.

Bill Makin, the medical registrar was there, together with the casualty sister. They were chatting with a couple of ambulance men, who were enjoying a break whilst waiting for their next call.

"Does anybody know anything about pregnant cats?" Paul asked as he ushered Miss Mullins through the door. The question was something of a 'conversation stopper' but immediately George, one of the ambulance drivers, a rotund, ruddy-faced man in his fifties, expressed interest.

"Yes, I do. I've kept cats for years. Indeed I breed them. It is a hobby of mine."

"Excellent," Paul replied, much relieved, "because I've got a rather unhappy moggy here that seems to be struggling in labour."

Quickly George took a concise clinical history from Miss Mullins that would have done credit to any medical practitioner. He ascertained that in the last few days, as well as 'yowling' and attempting to create a nest, Kitty had lost interest in food, had been anxious and restless and had spent many hours licking her belly and perineum.

He took a look at the abdomen and confirmed that she was indeed in labour. He then voiced concern that this had lasted significantly longer than the three hours that was normal for a cat, adding that the bleeding was much heavier than he had previously witnessed. He obviously shared Miss Mullins' anxiety about the matter.

"For some reason the kittens are not coming through as they should," he said. "There must be a blockage of some sort. I really think this cat ought to be seen by a vet."

"Or by an obstetrician," Bill Makin remarked. "I've already been on the telephone to St Margaret's Maternity Hospital earlier this evening about one of our cases. My old pal, David Winterbourne is on duty there. He and I used to be students together. We'll send Kitty there. He's sure to know what to do. I'll give him a ring."

It was the nursing sister who spotted the obvious flaw in this plan.

"You really can't send a cat to a maternity hospital, even if she is pregnant," she protested.

"Of course I can," replied the registrar. "I've known David for years, he won't mind in the least."

"And we can run her there," said George, knowing that St Margaret's was only half a mile away. "We're not doing anything at the moment; just sitting here twiddling our thumbs waiting for the next call to come through."

Bill Makin reached for the phone and rang his friend. The casualty staff were able to hear one end of the conversation.

"I'm sorry to trouble you twice in one evening David," he said, "but I'm afraid that I have another patient here. She's pregnant for the first time and I need your advice. It's a bit complex. As you know, I'm not an expert in obstetrical matters but I have a sneaking suspicion that this may be a multiple pregnancy. She's in labour; probably has been for four or five hours now, and she's started to bleed quite heavily. She's in a lot of pain and really doesn't look at all well. I would be grateful if you would take a look at her."

There was a pause but those in the office could imagine what was being said at the other end of the line, even though they couldn't actually hear it.

"No, she's not one of your patients."

Another pause.

"I'm afraid that she's had no antenatal care whatsoever. This is the first time anybody has realised that she's pregnant. I think that she's been a little secretive about it."

There was a longer pause. "Yes, I know. Some people blame the schools, others blame the government but personally I think poor parenting has a lot to do with it. There is no shortage of contraceptive advice available these days, is there? Mind you, I don't think she's the most intelligent of patients. I suspect that she's the sort that just can't say 'no'."

Another pause, shorter this time.

"No, I haven't remonstrated with her; I'll leave that to you. But I think I should warn you, she's a bit woolly headed. I very much doubt that she will understand. Her mother is with her though. She seems quite sensible and may be able to keep an eye on things in the future."

Another pause.

"Look, David, I'm a chest physician. Anything below the belt is a 'no go' area for me. In my speciality, we don't go delving or diving into deep dark holes. I wouldn't know where to find the cervix, let alone say whether it was dilated.

Another pause.

"OK and thanks for agreeing to take her. She's called Kitty by the way. I'm not sure what her surname is. She will be coming by ambulance and I'll have her with you within twenty minutes. Thanks David. It's very good of you."

Bill smiled as he continued to listen.

"Yes, fair enough. I owe you one. I'll buy you a drink next time we meet. Good night and thanks again." Then as an afterthought he added, "Oh and David, perhaps you would let me know how things turn out."

He turned to face the group who had been listening intently to the telephone conversation. Everyone realised that he had failed to inform his friend that the patient was a cat.

"David says he's sick and tired of silly young girls who get themselves pregnant and then are so ashamed that they hide themselves away, thinking that they can cope all on their own but who then turn up in labour having had no antenatal care at all. When he has sorted Kitty out, he intends to give her a good telling off."

He turned to the ambulance men.

"Are you sure you're able to take Kitty to St Margaret's? I wouldn't want you to get into any trouble."

"Of course we're sure," said George. "Nobody at Ambulance Control is going to know anything about it, because it's not going to get recorded in our log. We'll have her there in two ticks."

George picked up Kitty and the basket, his colleague took Miss Mullins by the arm and they started towards the door.

Miss Mullins turned, a grateful smile on her face. "Thank you all so much. You really have been most kind."

"It's been a joint effort," David replied, "and our pleasure. I hope all turns out well."

Work in the casualty department continued but two hours later Miss Mullins was back. Carrying her basket with great care, she had made the return journey from St Margaret's, albeit this time on foot. She looked overjoyed, beaming from ear to ear, bursting to tell what had happened.

"I just had to let you see."

Gently, she placed the basket on a chair, then lifted a corner of the towel and showed everyone her beloved cat. Kitty was now lying contentedly in the basket, tenderly licking three tiny balls of fur that were snuggled up to her belly, their eyes closed. She handed sister a letter.

"This is from the doctor at St Margaret's. He was just as kind as you were."

Sister opened the envelope.

'Dear Casualty Staff,' it read. *'You were quite right. This was indeed a multiple pregnancy; triplets in fact. But all has turned out well. As you see, mother and babies are all fine despite the lack of antenatal care. To avoid further problems, I have taken the liberty of giving Kitty's 'mother' some contraceptive advice.*

Kind regards,

David.'

Chapter Two

1st August 1969

One month earlier, at 8 am on the 1st August 1969, Paul strolled cheerfully along the corridor to the Surgical Five male ward. It was his first day as a senior house officer (SHO) at the City General Hospital and he was retracing the steps that he had taken three years earlier as a young doctor. That day, fresh out of medical school, he had been as nervous as one of Kitty's kittens. Apprehensive of the challenges facing him, he had been desperately concerned about his ability to cope. In fact, all his fears had been fully justified. It had quickly become apparent that he was totally unprepared for the role of junior house officer; the twelve months apprenticeship that all doctors had to serve before they were permitted to 'practice' unsupervised on the great British public. With the benefit of hindsight, Paul now recognised that the other house officers, all of whom had started at the same time, had been equally ill equipped for the job, though this had been of little consolation to him at the time. His ignorance of ward routine had caused him considerable embarrassment. He had felt himself to be an outsider, an encumbrance, as he observed the student nurses as they worked easily and efficiently around him. Though significantly younger than he was, they were far more familiar with basic patient care. Five years at university had taught him a great deal of medical theory but little of medical practice. As a medical student, he had been taught how to elicit a patient's history, the story of their illness. He was well versed in clinical examination and diagnosis. He was conversant with the appropriate treatment of a wide variety of conditions; from measles to malaria and from scurvy to scarlet fever. But he had learned nothing of practical procedures or hospital routine. He knew the cause of tuberculosis and toxoplasmosis but had never put a catheter into a patient's bladder or an intravenous line into their arm. He understood the difference between tetanus and tetany, and knew the life cycle of the tapeworm but did not know how clinical specimens were transported from the ward to the laboratory. He knew about blood groups and rhesus factors but did not know how to order blood for transfusion, or what safety checks were required before the blood was administered to the patient. Paul and his fellow house officers, finding themselves so ill prepared for life on a busy hospital ward, had invited the consultants to arrange an induction programme for future medical graduates. Paul wondered whether this advice had been heeded and whether such training now existed. Two new house officers would be starting on the Surgical Five unit alongside him on this very day. Paul hoped they would be better prepared than he had been, though no doubt they would be just as nervous. He remembered the advice and encouragement that Mr Khan, the experienced Surgical Five registrar, had given him when he had been the 'rookie' on the ward and he made a silent vow to do what he could to support the new housemen (they were always referred to as 'housemen', regardless of their sex!)

Although three years had passed, Paul recalled vividly the confrontation he had had with the ward sister on his very first morning as a doctor. Sister Ashbrook had belittled him in front of her nurses, refusing him access to the ward office as she chatted with the night staff before they went off duty. She was a slim, dark haired woman with sharp features and a sharper tongue. She ran her ward efficiently but held firmly to the belief that junior doctors had been created for no other purpose than to make life difficult for her nurses. She had refused to acknowledge that Paul was no longer a medical student; that he was now a qualified doctor, appointed to work alongside her on the ward. She had insisted that the office was '*her*' office, rather than the clerical base for *all* ward personnel. Although Paul had painful memories of that first encounter he was much more confident now. Having worked on the ward previously, he knew the staff and was familiar with the routine. He understood how the two consultants liked their patients to be managed and was aware of their idiosyncrasies. Sir William Warrender, the older of the two, was tall and distinguished with his straight back, silver hair and genial face. Always the perfect gentleman with exemplary dress and manners, he was coming towards the end of an illustrious career. The hospital's benevolent senior surgeon, he was respected by the staff for his gentle manner, wisdom and experience. He was also much appreciated by his patients for the detailed explanations that he offered about their medical conditions. These though were a considerable test of patience for the members of his team who had heard them many times before! He had thoroughly enjoyed his own surgical training and delighted in reminiscing about days gone by, relating longwinded accounts of events he had experienced as a junior doctor. As a result, his ward rounds lasted twice as long as those of other consultants, as he told and retold his seemingly endless fund of stories. Now approaching retirement, he was gradually slowing down and becoming more hesitant, particularly when working in the operating theatre. The junior doctors, ever observant, had commented on his slight tremor in a sketch that they had performed at the hospital's annual Christmas show.

To the tune of *'My bonny lies over the ocean'*, they had sung:

Sir William's a mighty fine surgeon,
he tackles his patients with zeal,
his tremor makes speed none too easy,
as fast as he cuts them --- they heal.

Perhaps the words were a little cruel, but there was more than an element of truth in them!

Leslie Potts, the junior consultant, was quite a different character. He was a bluntly spoken, irascible man; a difficult taskmaster with a short fuse. Paul would renew his acquaintance within the next hour, when Mr Potts came to undertake his twice-weekly ward round.

As he rejoined the unit, no longer the newly qualified doctor or the most junior member of the team, Paul had the confidence that comes with experience. Quite apart from the time he had spent previously on Surgical Five, he had been employed for a year at the Middleton, a busy hospital in the south of the city. He was familiar with the preoperative management of common conditions and knew how to treat postoperative complications. He had performed many minor surgical operations and was looking forward to enhancing his manual skills and performing more major procedures. No longer did he feel inept or in awe of the nurses when working on the ward. He now had experience of working alongside many different ward and theatre sisters; Sister Ashbrook being the only one with whom he had ever had a difficult relationship. Paul decided that this was a good opportunity to make a fresh start. He was determined not be intimidated or dominated by her this time.

Turning the corner to enter the ward, it was immediately apparent that Sister Ashbrook was up to her old tricks. A young man wearing a brand new white coat was sitting outside the office door. He looked forlorn and apprehensive, like a naughty schoolboy outside the headmaster's room, waiting for six strokes of the cane.

Paul introduced himself. "I'm the new SHO, starting work today. You must be the house officer."

"Yes," he said, "Richard Hill. Newly qualified I'm afraid. It's my first day as well but I'm not at all sure what I'm suppose be doing."

Richard was a tall, slim, fresh-faced young man who, without doubt, would prove attractive to many of the young nurses with his athletic appearance, blond hair and clear blue eyes. Paul thought that he would not normally be short of confidence but on this occasion he looked nervous and self-conscious. His fingers slipped periodically to the pager in his top pocket, to check that it was still there; as if to assure himself that he really was a qualified doctor. He was probably proud to be carrying it right now; it was a symbol of his medical qualification and status. But within a few weeks he would come to hate it. It's demanding shrill 'bleep' would interrupt his routine, providing him with extra work throughout the day. Equally he would come to loath the bedside phone that would call him from his bed during the night, resulting in a chronic tiredness that eroded morale and induced a state of physical and mental exhaustion.

"Come on," Paul said, "I'll introduce you to Sister Ashbrook."

"I've already met her. She says I have to wait here until the nursing handover is finished."

"Nonsense, Richard. She tried exactly the same thing on me when I started as a houseman. It's a little game of one-upmanship that she plays. You will quickly learn that she gets up to all sorts of tricks. She likes to prove that nursing sisters are superior to house officers."

"But I was told that it was wise for newly qualified doctors to befriend their ward sisters and to seek their advice. At medical school we were advised to be guided by them and that in return, they would do what they could to help. I don't want to upset her on my very first morning."

"Generally that's true," Paul replied. "Certainly it's true of 95% of nursing sisters and most certainly true of Sister Rutherford, on our female ward. You will find her extremely helpful, but unfortunately, it's not true of Sister Ashbrook. Come on. I'll take any flack that she throws at us. We'll go into the office together and I'll introduce you."

Richard looked apprehensive as Paul knocked on the door but he followed meekly as he led the way into the office.

The daily 'handover' was taking place. The nurses who had watched over the patients during the night were reporting to the oncoming day shift. Sister was sitting behind her desk, a cluster of nurses around her; a mother hen with her brood. All the nurses wore dresses which were 'colour coded' according to their seniority. Student nurses wore green; staff nurses wore light blue and Sister was in navy blue. The dresses extended below the knee, a broad white belt emphasising the waist. The sleeves were short and ended in fluffy, elasticated white cuffs around the upper arm. A white cotton headdress and matching pinafore apron completed the uniform, the apron being so heavily starched, that holding a nurse in your arms was as romantic as embracing a cardboard box and as frustrating as sucking a chocolate wrapped in silver foil!

"Good morning, Sister Ashbrook," Paul said as he breezed in.

She looked up and scowled.

"Oh, Dr Lambert it's you. I suppose it is still *'Doctor Lambert'* and not *'Mister Lambert'*?

Paul smiled at the subtle insult. She was implying that he had not yet passed the postgraduate examination to become a Fellow of the Royal College of Surgeons and therefore was still not entitled to be addressed as *'Mister'*. Paul had been very pleased when he had passed the final medical school exam and had become *'Doctor Lambert.'* But if one day he fulfilled his ambition and became a Fellow of the Royal College, he would revert to *'Mister Lambert'* and be even more delighted. 400 years ago, doctors representing the established medical profession had ostracised those who had started to perform surgical procedures, deriding them and insisting that such activities had no place in reputable medical practice. They had pointedly referred to them in a derogatory fashion as *'mister'*, to infer that they were not proper doctors at all. With the passage of time, as the benefits of surgery became apparent, the term *'mister'* stuck and indeed has now become a badge of honour amongst surgeons. It crossed Paul's mind to enquire whether she was still *'Sister'* Ashbook and not *'Senior Sister'* Ashbrook but thought better of it. There was little to be gained by crossing swords with her on his first morning back.

"Yes Sister, still *'doctor'*, I'm afraid," he replied. He then introduced Richard, commenting that he was sure that she would welcome him onto the ward with open arms and make him feel at home!

With Mr Potts due to arrive for his round in less than an hour, they collected some clinical records from the notes trolley, left the office and went through the double doors onto the ward.

"We're both new," Paul explained, "so let's try to get to know a few of the patients before the boss arrives."

Mohammed Khan, with whom Paul had enjoyed an excellent relationship when he had been the junior houseman, joined them. At that time, he had been the registrar but had finally been appointed as senior registrar. For many years he had been overlooked for promotion despite his experience, research papers and seniority, having been overtaken by less well-qualified English graduates. As one of the more enlightened consultants had once observed to Paul; *'Perhaps his face doesn't fit for some reason'*. Although nominally Paul had been supervised and trained by the consultants, in practice Mohammed, who was known throughout the hospital as 'Mo', had been the one who had helped him most. He had showed Paul how to manage the daunting workload and how to perform practical procedures; indeed he had been

18

the one who had guided him through his first appendix operation. Paul was particularly grateful for the support Mo had given when he had suffered a crisis of confidence; when he had doubted his ability to cope with the responsibility of caring for patients during a ninety-hour working week. Essentially he was the one who had helped Paul to survive those six exhausting months, when the joy of fulfilling his vocation had been reduced to the simple satisfaction of performing his duty; when nights on call were no longer approached in eager anticipation of exciting new experiences but with irritation and apprehension.

When Mo was promoted a most unusual event had occurred. A female trainee had been selected to replace him. She was an Oxford graduate called Victoria Kent. She was the first such appointment in the city. Unfortunately since she had yet to take up her post, the unit would be short staffed for the next couple of weeks. Paul was eager to renew her acquaintance. Their paths had crossed when he had worked at the Middleton Hospital. He held Victoria in high regard, impressed by her clinical knowledge and work ethic. She too had set her sights on a career in surgery but in truth, the odds were heavily stacked against her. Achieving consultant status in surgery was tough enough for men but with the prejudice that existed, it was very much harder for women.

In due course Mr Potts arrived. It was the first time that Paul had seen him for three years, but he had changed little. Perhaps slightly less than average height and stockily built, he was aged between forty-five and fifty. Paul remembered the familiar well tanned face, recalling that he had a yacht and spent much of his spare time sailing. As before his hair was well oiled and swept back, though now perhaps a little greyer than before. His face, with its furrowed brow, usually held a tense expression. With dark challenging eyes and a tight mouth that rarely smiled, he gave the impression of a man who did tolerate fools gladly - nor indeed did he! He held himself straight, like an officer on parade, with his shoulders back and his chest thrust forward. Wearing his immaculate suit he was an impressive, some might say, a daunting figure. Seeing him again, reminded Paul of some of his other characteristics. He compensated for his lack of inches with a huge ego. In the operating theatre he was an exhibitionist, always keen to demonstrate his knowledge and technical ability. Paul also recalled his impatient manner, his short fuse and quick temper. His staff needed to be on their toes, whether assisting him in theatre, or working alongside him on the ward. Anyone who did not live up to his high standard was liable to get a verbal lashing, unless of course, they happened to be an attractive young nurse or a female doctor with a pretty face and a shapely ankle. He had the reputation of being a 'ladies man', never failing to select the most glamorous of the female graduates to work as his house officer.

Formal introductions were made and Mr Potts welcomed Paul back to the ward with a brisk handshake. He said a polite *'Good morning'* to Richard Hill.

"You will be working primarily for Sir William, I presume," he said to Richard. "Do you happen to know where Dr Webb is? She is the other house officer who will be working for me. It would be a shame if she were to miss her first ward round. I was expecting her to be here to brighten up the ward."

No one knew the answer to this question, so Richard was despatched to contact her, his first job as a doctor. It was an early illustration for him that the most junior member of the team, though medically qualified, was expected to perform a wide variety of non medical tasks, everything from brewing the tea, to running to the laundry for a clean pair of theatre trousers for his consultant!

The ward round began, Mohammed Kahn presenting each patient to his consultant in a succinct fashion. Mr Potts' communication skills were poor. It was frequently said that he preferred his patients to be asleep, anaesthetised in theatre, rather than awake on the ward! He tended to stand at the foot of the bed rather than at the bedside, speaking in a hushed voice to the attendant doctors and nurses, rather than addressing his patients with whom he rarely established eye contact. If a patient's progress was satisfactory and no change in their management was required, Mr Potts would merely nod towards the head of the bed, say *'good'*, then turn his attention to the next patient. It was unusual for more than two minutes to be spent at any one bedside and the result of Mr Potts' brusque manner was that rapid progress was made down the ward. Inevitably patients felt excluded from these consultations and it was left to the houseman to return later to explain the decisions made. The junior doctors had to hope that the patient would agree to whatever operation the consultant had decided to perform! The ethos was that Mr Potts knew what was best for his patients.

Five or six patients had been seen in this way, when a low 'wolf whistle' emanated from a man in one of the beds near the entrance to the ward. Richard was returning, accompanied by a stunningly beautiful young woman, presumably Dr Webb. Although Paul was by nature attracted to a shapely female figure, it was not his habit to *'look her up and down'*. He believed it appropriate to view the fairer sex with the respect that they deserved. Subconsciously though, on this occasion his visual assessment of her began with her ankles then swept upwards, possibly because of the noise that her black high-heeled shoes were making on the polished linoleum floor, as she tripped down the ward. She had long, shapely, stocking-clad legs, a hemline that finished well above the knee, a pristine white coat that must surely have been shortened to match the length of her skirt and a sheer white blouse, barely thick enough to safeguard her modesty. The blouse sported a neck line sufficiently low to be dangerously distracting to young male patients and a severe hazard to any elderly gentleman with a high blood pressure. Her shoulder length blond hair was beautifully groomed and her make up immaculate. She held her head high, like a model on a catwalk, as she wiggled confidently down the centre of the ward, between the two lines of beds. She was clearly aware of, and pleased with, the impression she was creating. The male patients looked on with undisguised appreciation. Paul exchanged a glance with Mo who closed his eyes in mock horror. Two of the nurses giggled quietly.

Paul noted the expression on Sister Ashbrook's face and knew instinctively that there was trouble ahead. Without doubt, she would give this new house officer a hard time. When he had been the houseman, she had been tough on him; she would be even tougher and rougher on Dr Webb. Matron's regulations with respect to nurses' uniforms were strict. Nurses' dresses were sealed with a collar around the neck and finished well below the knee. Hair had to be worn 'up' and covered with a neat cap. All cosmetics and jewellery were strictly forbidden. Richard had been perfectly correct when he had suggested that it was in the best interests of house officers to keep on the right side of their ward sister. The nursing sister, if she chose, could help a house officer enormously. She could remind him of things he had overlooked, demonstrate how to perform practical procedures and undertake many of the jobs that fell in the interface between nursing and medical duties. She could give advice on ward routine, inform him of the consultant's preferences and could resuscitate him periodically with strong sweet tea and biscuits.

However, a ward sister was not obliged to do any of these things. She could find herself too busy to produce a chaperone when one was needed, she could be tardy in producing instruments needed for practical procedures. If she chose to be particularly vindictive, she could interrupt the house officer's work by 'bleeping' him frequently and unnecessarily. Sister Ashbrook knew all of these tricks and a few others as well.

Mr Potts looked delighted as Dr Webb joined the group.

"I'm so pleased to see you, young lady," he beamed. "I was just saying to the rest of the team, that we were missing you."

Then to the world in general, he added. "This is Dr Elizabeth Webb, our new house officer. It will be wonderful to have a little glamour on the ward to add some sparkle to the day." The remark seemed certain to increase Sister's antipathy to the poor girl!

Paul wondered whether she had any idea of the stressful and exhausting six months that lay ahead of her; months that would become quite intolerable without the full support of the nursing staff; support that would certainly not be forthcoming from Sister Ashbrook! No doubt her mind was already working overtime, devising schemes to cut this new house officer down to size.

Mr Potts laid his hand loosely on Dr Webb's shoulder. A frown crossed Richard's face, the significance of which Paul was slow to appreciate.

"I may call you Liz, mayn't I?" he remarked.

"Of course you may, Mr Potts," Dr Webb replied sweetly. "I do apologise that I'm just a moment or too late this morning."

"Not to worry at all, my dear. We did actually start a few minutes ago but you haven't missed much. No doubt Khan will be able to fill you in with the details in due course." This was a different Mr Potts to the irascible surgeon for whom Paul had worked a few years before. Had he been late for a ward round, his reward would have been a stinging rebuke, to embarrass him, not only in front of the patients, but also in front of his medical and nursing colleagues.

"Now," Mr Potts continued. "We must get on with the ward round. Liz, you stick close to me and you'll learn a lot."

No sooner had the team moved to the next bed, than Paul's pager sounded. It was a call asking him to go to the casualty department to attend to an emergency. With some reluctance he asked Mr Potts' permission to leave. He would have been fascinated to continue to observe the interaction between Mr Potts, his glamorous young house officer and Sister Ashbrook. But for the moment that would have to wait. There would be ample opportunity to see how things developed in the coming months.

Chapter Three

The patient in the casualty department was a pleasant 26-year-old woman called Helen Seddon, who asked little more of life than to support her husband, be a good mother to her two young children and to keep a tight rein on the household budget. She was in severe pain and it was obvious from the moment that Paul entered the cubicle that she was extremely ill. She had a classical story of bowel obstruction, the symptoms of which may easily be imagined by considering the result of a blockage of any other sewage pipe. Nothing comes out of the bottom end, and the pipe then 'backs up' until it overflows at the top. Her constipation and foul vomiting were accompanied by severe griping pains and loud gurgling noises; the result of spasms of her bowel as it attempted to squeeze food passed the blockage. As a result of the vomiting, Helen was severely dehydrated. She needed fluid replacement by intravenous infusion as a matter of urgency. Her appendix had been removed six months previously, so Paul considered that the most likely cause of her obstruction was internal scar tissue, though he knew that this would only be confirmed by a surgical exploration. He thought it was unlikely to be due to anything sinister in such a young woman.

Paul explained to Helen that although she would need some xrays to confirm the diagnosis, she would almost certainly require an operation later in the day.

"Are you sure it's necessary for me to stay in hospital?"

"Yes, it is. And you will need to remain with us for at least a week after the surgery."

On hearing this news, Helen's first thoughts were not for herself but for her husband and her children.

"We are not a wealthy family," she explained. "My husband works in the market. He starts very early in the morning. I do part time cleaning work in the evenings to make ends meet. It will be very difficult for my husband to stay at home with the children. It's the summer holidays now so they are not going to school."

Since there were no family members or neighbours available to take care of the children, Paul spoke with the almoner to arrange some domestic help, then phoned the female ward to ask them to prepare a bed for the new admission.

In the afternoon he was scheduled to work in the out patent clinic, but during the course of the session slipped away to review Helen and to look at her xrays. Sister Gladys Rutherford, the sister on the female ward, met him with open arms and a welcoming smile. In her mid 50's, motherly and plump, she was everything that Sister Ashbrook was not. Warm, friendly and caring, she was a superb ward sister, loved by her patients, appreciated by her nurses and respected by the consultants. The junior doctors thought she was perfect. Always helpful, particularly to new house officers, she guided them through their early difficult months and was always prepared to revive them when they were weary, with mugs of hot tea and words of encouragement. Whereas there was always a degree of tension in the air on Sister Ashbrook's male ward, here the atmosphere was calm. Yet despite the relaxed ambience, discipline was strict and the nursing care was of a high standard. No one sought to take advantage of her good nature.

She gave Paul a big hug and planted a kiss on his cheek.

"I heard a rumour that you were coming back. It's lovely to see you again."

"It's great to be back. Just like old times."

"How long has it been?"

"Nearly three years, Sister."

"And what have you been doing with yourself."

Paul gave her a brief resume of the posts he had held since he saw her last.

"No, Paul," she scolded. "I didn't mean your academic career, though I'm glad you're still studying surgery. I meant your social life." Then with a twinkle in her eye, she added, "As I remember, you were very friendly with one of our nurses; Kate Meredith."

"You have a good memory Sister." There was an awkward pause.

"Well?"

"Well I'm afraid it didn't work out, mores the pity. Somehow or other we drifted apart. I'm afraid that I spent too much time working and then Kate's mother was taken ill. Kate gave up her nursing career and left the hospital to care for her. The last I heard, she was engaged to be married. Apparently she is going to become a farmer's wife in the Lake District. Indeed she may already be a farmer's wife for all I know."

Sister Rutherford must have heard the bitterness in Paul's voice, for she placed a caring hand on his arm.

"I am sorry to hear that, Paul," she said softly. "Kate was a lovely person and an excellent nurse. It's a great shame she's left the profession. So there's no little lady in your life at present?"

"No, I am afraid not."

Even though three years had passed, thoughts of Kate still caused Paul's heart to ache. He had truly loved her. She was not one to stand out in a crowd. Not the tall willowy figure of a model, or the face that you might see gracing the front cover of a glossy magazine. But to Paul she was just perfect, with her healthy complexion, blue eyes, soft brown curls and lips that broke readily into a warm smile; lips that Paul had kissed when he had held her in his arms. Kisses willingly returned in equal measure. The memories that continued to haunt him remained sharp and painful. And Sister was right; with her gentle and caring personality, she would have made a superb nurse. Paul could still picture her working on the ward; a trim figure, neat in her nurse's uniform, her voice quiet, her manner calm, never appearing to be rushed, yet purposeful in everything she did, exchanging a word of sympathy here and a gesture of reassurance there. Paul had thought that Kate had loved him too. It had been a cause of great sadness and deep regret to him when she had left to care for her mother. Their romance had died and with it Paul's dreams of a life spent together. Although he had dated several girls since, he could not forget Kate.

The truth was that at school and even during his medical training, he had never felt completely at ease in the company of the fairer sex. Envious of his contemporaries who found no difficulty in conversing freely with a pretty girl, Paul recognised that he was shy. When introduced to a young lady, he became tongue-tied, self conscious and unable to think of anything to say. The likely explanation for his reticence was that as one of three brothers who had attended a single sex school, there had been few opportunities for him to engage with members of the opposite sex. Then later, for financial reasons, he had attended the medical school in his home city. When lectures were over for the day, his fellow students were able to relax and socialise in the university's bars and lounges or in the halls of residence, whereas Paul had to commute back to his parent's home some fifteen miles away, a daily train journey of over an hour.

But all this changed when he met Kate. With Kate, he felt relaxed and comfortable. She was the only girl with whom he felt completely at ease. With Kate he could talk openly and would share ideas and thoughts that he would normally have kept to himself. They shared the same interests; music and walking and together they had spent many happy hours tramping the hills of the neighbouring Peak District. When Paul's duty roster allowed, they would set off early in the morning, sandwiches and water in a rucksack, and spend the day walking the heather clad moors, enjoying the fresh air and taking in the magnificent scenery before relaxing in a country pub for a drink and a meal. They had been more than good friends, though never lovers. Kate had been very special to Paul and it had broken his heart when she had left. His hopes for the future dashed, he had thrown himself into his job, working long days on the wards and in theatre, and studying surgical textbooks and research journals when his duty roster allowed. But still he could not forget Kate.

With patients waiting to be seen in the outpatient department, Paul had an excuse to end a conversation that had become painful for him.

"Sister, I'm afraid that I must keep moving. I've just slipped out of the clinic to see Helen, the young woman who has been admitted with a bowel obstruction. She will probably have to go to theatre later."

By chance, Mo entered the office at that moment and together they went to review their patient. Fortunately, Helen now looked a little more comfortable, thanks to some fluid replacement and a generous dose of morphine. The x-rays confirmed the diagnosis of bowel obstruction but the blood tests indicated that Helen remained dehydrated. Mo decided that it would be wise to give more fluid before an operation was undertaken and therefore said that the exploratory surgery should be deferred until later in the day.

It was not Surgical Five's day to admit emergencies. Paul and Mo had only become involved with Helen because she had previously been a patient of Mr Potts. They would have been perfectly entitled to ask the 'on call team of the day' to operate on her, but that was not the way things were done on their unit. They felt an ongoing responsibility for their patients and Mohammed, who had removed Helen's appendix less than a year before, was keen to perform the operation. Being single, unattached and with nothing arranged for the evening, Paul happily agreed to assist.

"Do you think Dr Webb would like to come along and watch?" he asked Mo as they left the ward.

"It wouldn't be a bad idea to ask her. It will probably be helpful for her to scrub up and assist us, before she is faced with the challenge of assisting Mr Potts."

***

That evening Paul joined the crowd of newly qualified house officers as they ate in the doctor's 'mess', the residency that was to be their home for the next six months. They sat around the large communal dining table chatting nervously, reflecting on their first day as practising doctors. Paul felt a considerable sympathy for them. At this early stage, they had yet to realise just how arduous their jobs would be, how difficult it was to make the transition from medical student to doctor, or how jaded they would become as they tried to cope with the never ending stream of tasks which would be delegated to them. Spotting Richard Hill and Liz Webb sitting side by side, he took the opportunity to speak with them, suggesting to Liz that she might be interested to join Mo in the theatre to witness Helen's operation. She immediately looked dismayed.

"Richard and I were planning to go out this evening for a drink to celebrate having survived our first day as doctors," she said, looking to her fellow house officer for support.

Her response indicated that she completely failed to understand the responsibilities of her job.

"I'm afraid that won't be possible," Paul said. "As Surgical Five house officers, one of you is required to be in the hospital, available to the patents on our wards, continuously for the next six months, from now until the 1st February next year. One of you can leave the hospital if you like, but not both of you at the same time."

"But I thought we would hand over our patients to the Surgical Three staff for the evening. Surely they are 'on call' tonight," she protested, shocked at what she had just heard.

"They are indeed 'on-call' until tomorrow morning and therefore both of their house officers need to remain in the hospital. Together with the Surgical Three registrar, they will be responsible for the surgical emergencies that arrive through the night but I'm afraid that we can't hand our Surgical Five patients to them. They simply couldn't cope if they had to cover the patients on our wards as well as staffing casualty, covering their own wards and caring for new admissions. If you read your contract, you will find that it states that one of you has to be in the hospital at all times, day and night for the next six months. Didn't you realise that?" There was a long pause during which neither Liz nor Richard replied.

"I'm sorry to be the bearer of bad news," Paul added.

"No," she said finally. "I didn't realise that."

Paul was amazed at this response, as were many of the other newly qualified doctors around the table, who obviously understood better than Liz what was expected of a house officer.

"You don't need to come to the theatre tonight if you don't wish to. It's entirely up to you. Mo and I can manage perfectly well on our own. But we thought that you might be interested to watch. I presume you have 'scrubbed up' in theatre before?"

"No," she said. "I haven't."

This was another astonishing admission. How could she possibly have studied for five years at medical school and never have 'scrubbed' for an operation?

"In that case," Paul said emphatically, "it will definitely be to your advantage to come to theatre and practice 'scrubbing up', before you have to 'scrub' to assist Mr Potts. He will expect you to be familiar with theatre routine." He thought it best not to add that he had a short fuse and didn't suffer fools gladly!

He was dismayed at the way the conversation had developed. Liz, the glamorous new house officer, clearly had no idea of what was required of her. Paul was quite prepared to help her, to show her the ropes whilst she settled in. He was also certain that Mo would be generous with his time and advice, just as he had helped Paul when he was newly qualified. But it was obvious that Liz faced a steep learning curve. Unless she tackled this with enthusiasm and determination, the job would quickly overwhelm her. Again Paul kept these thoughts to himself but hoped that she would come and watch Helen's operation later that evening. 'Scrubbing up' required practice and attention to detail. The theatre staff would happily instruct medical students and nurses how to do it, although they probably wouldn't expect to have to teach a qualified doctor.

Paul thought that it was highly unlikely that Liz would cope with life as a junior hospital doctor and, as it transpired, his fears were quickly confirmed.

Chapter Four

At eight o'clock that evening, cheerful and relaxed, Paul walked to the theatre to assist Mo as he performed Helen's operation. Although a number of the theatre nurses were new, the theatre sister and senior staff nurse remembered Paul from his previous time at the City General. They greeted him like a long lost friend. The operating theatre, old fashioned even by the standards of the 1960s, was just as he remembered it. The theatre itself was quite small but it had four large alcoves, each having a different function. On one side was the 'preparation' area, where trays of sterile instruments were stored on formica shelves, each specific for a particular operation and individually labelled. Adjacent to it was the 'scrub up' area with its long metal, waist high trough, surmounted by three pairs of elbow taps. Opposite were the 'sluice area' where dirty instruments were washed and the alcove occupied by the two autoclaves. The larger autoclave, used to sterilise several trays of instruments at a time, was a polished steel cylinder six feet long and three feet across with a circular pressurised door at one end, akin to the door on a submarine's torpedo tube. The smaller autoclave, a quarter the size of its neighbour, was used to sterilise small individual items, such as instruments inadvertently dropped, or very occasionally thrown by an irascible surgeon, during a procedure. Whenever opened, the autoclaves belched clouds of steam making the working environment hot, humid and oppressive.

Maintaining a pleasant temperature during surgery was further compromised by the theatre's position, situated as it was on a south-facing balcony. A major part of the theatre roof and the end wall consisted of glass, effectively turning half of the room into a conservatory. At the height of summer, the temperature frequently rose above eighty degrees, despite attempts to reduce it by 'white washing' the glass on the inside and hosing cold water across the outer surface. In winter, the problem was to keep the room sufficiently warm. Many a patient, having lain virtually naked on the operating table for an hour or two, was returned to the ward shivering from the cold.

Paul was happy to be back in the theatre where he had started his surgical career and was looking forward to assisting Mo at Helen's operation. Had he been in a strange theatre, or working alongside a new surgeon, he might have felt anxious, afraid of creating a poor first impression but back in these familiar surroundings, he was completely at ease. He looked around to see whether Dr Webb had followed his advice and come to scrub; but it seemed that she had not.

Dressed in 'theatre greens', loose fitting cotton tops and cotton trousers secured with a pyjama cord around the waist, Paul and Mo scrubbed their hands from fingertips to elbows, then donned their gowns and surgical gloves. The abdomen was painted with an antiseptic solution, sterile drapes were placed around the proposed operation site and Mo made his initial incision. As soon as the abdomen was opened, the obstructed loops of bowel, bloated to three times their normal size, their walls tense, pink and moist, mushroomed up through the wound like an inflated bicycle inner tube. Mo immediately asked Sister for warm damp flannel swabs to cover and protect them for the duration of the operation.

It was at this moment that the theatre door opened and Liz appeared, still wearing her mini skirt, short white coat and stiletto heels. Sister immediately spotted this inappropriately attired intruder. Scrubbed at the table, unable to deal with the situation herself, she turned to her staff nurse.

"Nurse, go and ………"

But she needed to say no more, for the staff nurse had also seen Liz and was already shepherding her back through the door, to prevent any further contamination of the theatre environment.

"Who on earth was that?" Sister asked.

"That's our new house officer, Dr Elizabeth Webb," Mo replied.

"Oh, Is that so?"

"I'm afraid that she hasn't visited an operating theatre before," he added. "I think it would be helpful if she were to scrub up and join us at the table. There might be some unfortunate consequences if her first experience was when Mr Potts was operating."

With a surgical cap covering her forehead and a mask concealing her nose and mouth, little was visible of Sister's face, but the frown lines that appeared around her eyes suggested that she wasn't overly happy with this proposal. However she voiced no objection.

Mo's initial objective, to identify the site of the obstruction, proved difficult. As soon as one 'balloon like' loop of bowel was laid to one side, another sprang out of the abdomen obscuring the view. The loops wriggled like an angry snake as the bowel spasms continued their attempt to overcome the blockage. And extreme caution was required. The wall of the gut was thin and under such tension that it could easily have been ruptured had it been handled roughly. Such an event would have been a disaster. Highly toxic bowel content would have spilled within the abdomen, dramatically increasing the chance of death. Mo however, handled the bowel with great care and as more and more loops were lifted out through the wound, it eventually became possible to see some collapsed empty gut beyond the point of obstruction.

Out of the corner of his eye, Paul saw Liz re-enter the theatre accompanied by Staff Nurse. She was wearing one of the nurse's standard utilitarian theatre smocks, a garment designed to be both shapeless and sexless. Her long blond hair had been bunched beneath a theatre cap, though odd strands hung down untidily around her neck. On her feet she wore white rubber boots which appeared to be a couple of sizes too large. Loose on her feet, the heels dragged noisily along the floor as she walked. She looked significantly less glamorous than she had when making her first dramatic appearance on the ward!

Mo looked up and spoke quietly to Sister.

"Sister, would you mind if Dr Webb were to scrub and come to the table? It will be good practice for her but I think that she will need to be supervised."

"No, I don't mind, provided of course, that she scrubs correctly."

Mo called across to Liz. "Dr Webb, I suggest that you scrub up and join us. Then you'll be able to observe exactly what we're doing. If you watch as the operation is performed, it will give you a good appreciation of the symptoms Helen has suffered this last week. It will also help you to understand how her post operative care should be handled." Paul noted that he had failed to mention the main reason for getting Liz to scrub up; which was to learn how to do it correctly before she had to do it with Mr Potts watching!

Sister turned to her Staff Nurse.

"Dr Webb is going to join us at the table. Supervise!" Her voice was stern. "And supervise carefully," she added. "This will be the first time that she has scrubbed. Keep a very close eye on her and make sure that she does it properly. We must not compromise the sterility of this procedure." There was a strong emphasis on the words '*very close eye*'.

"I will," Staff Nurse replied, smiling as she spoke, and there was something about the smile that suggested that she was going to enjoy her task of supervision.

Although still quite junior, Paul was already beginning to make judgements about the technical skills of the surgeons with whom he worked. Sir William was a safe and competent surgeon. He operated slowly with what, at times, seemed excessive caution, checking and double-checking sutures and bleeding points. Even simple procedures could be quite protracted and just occasionally his patients experienced side effects as a result of the long anaesthetics and, as previous residents had noticed, he did have a slight tremor. Leslie Potts was a much faster, slicker operator, but was prone to get flustered if things

31

did not proceed smoothly. Then he tended to shout, to blame his assistants and, albeit on rare occasions, toss instruments onto the floor. Of all the surgeons Paul had seen, it was Mohammed Khan whose technique he admired the most. When Mo was operating, the area being dissected was always clearly displayed, bleeding was kept to a minimum, the tissues were handled with great care and no matter how urgent or hazardous the procedure, he maintained a calm demeanour. Paul found it particularly educational that it was Mo's custom to give a running commentary to those assisting him as he worked. This also helped the scrub nurse to know which instrument to hand to him at each stage of the operation.

Over Mo's shoulder, Paul was able to watch events in the scrub up area. Liz was scrubbing her hands with antiseptic soap, using a hard-bristled brush, for the requisite three minutes, under the eagle eye of the Staff Nurse. She was instructed to scrub carefully under her long manicured nails and to concentrate particularly on the sides of her fingers and the web space between one finger and the next. Paul noticed however, that Liz was not scrubbing her forearms and was still wearing a watch. Sister noticed this too, caught Staff Nurse's eye, then silently tapped her left wrist with her right index finger. In response Staff Nurse nodded and smiled but said nothing either to Sister or to Liz.

When all the distended bowel loops had been laid to one side, the cause of the obstruction was identified. There was a strong cord of scar tissue, looking like a short length of thick white string, lying across the bowel, compressing it and completely blocking it. A quick snip of the scissors was all that was required to release this band and relieve the obstruction. Immediately, gas and liquid stool poured through into the collapsed bowel beyond. However the short length of bowel that had been lying directly beneath the scar tissue was deep purple in colour and considerably bruised.

Across in the scrub up area, Liz had decided that the statutory three minutes of scrubbing had elapsed and she turned to pick up a theatre gown. It was at this point that Staff Nurse informed her that she ought to have removed her watch. Liz looked daggers at her but had no option but to remove the offending article, thereby contaminating her clean hands. Scowling, she began the scrub up process again. Perhaps Staff Nurse's behaviour had not been above reproach but Liz's error had been absolutely basic. It was born out of ignorance and Staff Nurse knew that all medical students were supposed to visit theatre as part of their training long before they qualified as doctors.

Mo looked at the damaged bowel thoughtfully.

"We have to decide whether it's safe to leave this tiny length of crushed bowel or whether it would be wiser to remove it. It's been compressed so tightly and for so long that I'm not sure that it's still viable. We'll wait and watch it for a few minutes, to see if it recovers."

Although he had said *'wait and watch'*, Mo carefully wrapped the damaged bowel in warm moist swabs, then crossed his arms on his chest and started to chat, asking Paul of his experience whilst working at the Middleton in his previous job. He was particularly interested to know how much practical surgery Paul had been allowed to perform.

"I was pleased at the amount I was able to do, and happy with the supervision and training that I was given."

In fact, Paul had performed quite a variety of surgical procedures, including operations for ruptures, varicose veins and piles and had also assisted at numerous major operations. Staffing levels were thinner in the peripheral hospitals than they were at the City General and as a consequence, trainees gained more practical experience.

As they were chatting, Liz completed the second scrubbing of her hands, this time including her wrists and forearms, which she then dried quite correctly on the sterile paper towel provided. Staff Nurse showed her the bin into which the towel was discarded and then indicated that she should step forward to pick up a gown. Unfolding and donning a surgical gown is difficult and requires practice. The surgeon is required to remove the gown from its sterile wrapper and then unfold it, all the while holding it away from his body, to prevent it coming into contact with any non-sterile surface. It is then necessary to wriggle into the gown's arms, then to stand still whilst an assistant pulls the gown up over the shoulders and ties a series of cords at the back, from the neck down to the level of the buttocks. The surgeon is usually male, the nurse typically female and the manner in which this task is performed has been known to convey many a silent message from nurse to surgeon, unseen and unsuspected by any other member of the theatre staff. A rough tug of the gown on to the shoulders with no contact between female hand and male skin has a totally different significance to the lightest featherlike caress of fingers on the nape of the neck!

Liz's first two attempts to don a gown had to be abandoned as she allowed it's outer sterile surface to touch her cotton shift but on her third attempt, her gown having been safely tied at the rear, she inadvertently allowed it's cuff to touch the shelf as she reached for a packet of surgical gloves. She was therefore instructed to remove her gown and in doing so, she inevitably desterilised her hands. Liz was directed back to the scrub up unit where she once again commenced a three-minute scrub! It was like watching a game of snakes and ladders in which there are no ladders and every snake leads right back to the starting square. Liz's face, or as much as one could see of it behind her mask, was a picture of suppressed fury. Paul felt sympathy for her but knew that she was learning two important lessons. Firstly, how to scrub up proficiently for a surgical procedure and secondly, that nurses knew a great deal more about practical procedures than she did.

Meanwhile, Mo was taking a second look at the area of bowel that had been crushed. He had waited five minutes to see if it would recover but even so, it still looked distinctly unhealthy and he therefore informed Sister of his intention to remove it. With no undue haste and without spilling even the slightest drop of bowel content, he removed the damaged length of bowel and then sutured the open ends together, thereby restoring the continuity of the intestine. He checked that all swabs and instruments had been removed from the abdomen and started to close the wound.

By this time, Liz had successfully re-scrubbed, re-gowned, and her final task was to put on her gloves. She didn't know what size of gloves would fit her, so Staff Nurse opened a packet of size seven and a half, realising that gloves that were a little on the large side would slip over the fingers more easily than gloves that were too small. She also demonstrated to Liz how to dust her hands with the drying powder before attempting to don the gloves. Unfortunately, Liz spilled most of the powder on the floor, and as anyone who has attempted to apply Marigold gloves when washing the dishes knows, it is almost impossible to put rubber gloves on to wet hands. As a result, Liz struggled to get her fingers into the gloves, the empty tips of which fell over in flaps like rabbit's ears. Eventually, after battling with each finger in turn and muttering barely audible curses under her breath, she achieved her objective. Mo was just inserting the last suture into the skin and preparing to apply a surgical dressing to the wound, when Liz, now successfully gowned and gloved, tentatively approached the operating theatre table. As she did so, the final disaster occurred. Her mask slipped down off her nose and without thinking, she pushed it back into place with her sterile gloved hand. In doing so, she slid down the longest snake on the board and was dumped once again at the starting point. For a moment she looked as if she about to cry but instead she turned venomously on her tormentor.

"Damn you," she shouted at the Staff Nurse. "You've done all that out of spite." Then she added, "I need a drink. Make me a cup of coffee."

For a moment, there was silence, tension like static electricity in the air. A sudden flash of fire lit up in Staff Nurse's eyes and there was movement behind her mask as her mouth opened to respond.

34

"I'll make the coffee," Paul said quickly. "Do you want one too Sister, and how about you Staff Nurse?"

"Yes, I'll have a coffee," Mo said out loud. "Milk and one sugar, please."

Then quietly he added, as an aside to Paul, "Quite the diplomat, aren't we? Clearly Dr Webb needs a little advice, but don't worry, I'll have a quiet word with her when I have finished here. You go and make the coffee."

When Helen had been safely returned to the ward, the nurses, no doubt because of Liz's outburst, declined to join the surgeons for a drink. They chose instead to remain in the theatre, to tidy away the dirty gowns and instruments, wash down the table and prepare for the next day's operations. As Liz drank her coffee in sullen silence, Paul entered the details of the operation in the surgical register and wrote an account of the procedure in Helen's notes. Meanwhile, Mo prescribed pain relief and night sedation, and wrote instructions for the observations that would be undertaken by the ward staff through the night. He then turned to Paul.

"Would you mind slipping to the ward to check that Helen is alright while I have a word with Dr Webb?"

Paul took the hint and left Mo alone with Liz. Mo proceeded to tell her, in the quiet and constructive fashion that was typical of him, that nurses were vital members of the team and had a great deal of practical experience that she had yet to acquire. They should not be considered subordinate to the medical staff, particularly by newly qualified doctors fresh out of medical school. He hoped that she would heed the lesson, knowing that her life on the unit would become exceedingly difficult if she continued to regard the nurses as the doctor's hand maidens.

As Paul left the hospital that evening, he reflected on his first day back at the City General.

Liz was an obvious concern. His first impressions were that she was totally unsuited for life on a surgical unit. The house officer was a key member of the surgical team. He or she was the doctor that spent most time with the patients. The houseman was the one who made sure that all the prescriptions were written, that all the blood samples had been taken, that the results of the investigations were available for ward rounds and that all the drips were running smoothly. The houseman had to ensure that the patients' questions were answered, that the 'consent for operation' forms were signed, that the operation lists were prepared and circulated to the wards, that blood was available for those who needed transfusion and that relatives were kept informed about the progress of their loved ones. There were a thousand and one jobs for them to do and, in truth, scarcely enough hours in the day in which to do them. The house officer was the lubricant that kept the surgical unit going and a good relationship with the nursing staff was vital. A successful house officer needed to be cheerful and hard working, to be well organised and to be a good communicator. But he also needed to be humble enough to act occasionally as a nurse, a porter or a domestic, or to make the coffee or tea. Paul did not think that Liz had these attributes and doubted that she would acquire them in the weeks to come. Perhaps her intelligence, combined with a pretty face and fine figure had enabled her to rise above such menial tasks in the past, but a haughty attitude would cut no ice with the nurses on the ward or in the theatre. If Liz was to survive, she had to accept that she was the most junior member of the medical team and had to recognise that she had much to learn from the nursing staff. Relations between the doctors and nurses on Surgical Five had always been excellent. That was one of the factors that made working there so pleasant; the last thing the unit needed was a doctor-nurse confrontation. But Paul was also concerned for himself. As the next most senior doctor, it would fall to him to cover her tracks, to correct any errors or omissions that she made. A reliable and conscientious house officer would make Paul's job significantly easier but a house officer who was a liability, would add significantly to his workload.

In other ways though, he felt that it had been a good first day back. It had been pleasant to renew old acquaintances, all of whom, (with the possible exception of Sister Ashbrook), had made him welcome. Particularly he was pleased to be working once more alongside Mohammed Khan. They had already re-established the easy relationship they had enjoyed three years previously. The highlight of the day though, had undoubtedly been Helen's operation and had reinforced in him the attraction, the seduction, of surgery. She was only a young woman, just twenty-six years of age, the mother of two young children. She had presented with a condition which, had it been left untreated, would certainly have resulted in her death within 72 hours. Yet Mo with his intervention, identifying and relieving the blockage, had reversed that process. All being well, Helen would now make a smooth convalescence. The operation that he had performed and at which Paul had assisted, had quite literally saved her life. Doctors in many branches of their profession are able to relieve suffering and to eliminate disease but there was a drama and immediacy about surgery that Paul found almost addictive. It was participating in surgical procedures like this, and a desire to acquire such technical skills for himself, that drove Paul to continue his career in surgery.

Chapter Five

Within a week, Liz cracked. No longer the tall, confident young doctor, patrolling the wards with poise and glamour, Paul found her crying in a corner of the office, her head in her hands, her mascara smudged and with tears rolling down her cheeks. Although her superior attitude towards the nurses and her lack of preparation for her first job had contributed hugely to her situation, Paul felt a great deal of sympathy for her. He remembering only too clearly the difficulties that he had encountered, early in his own medical career. Not wishing her to be seen by other members of staff, particularly by the nursing staff, he escorted her back to the sitting room in the doctor's residency.

From his own bitter experience, Paul knew that life as a medical student and life as a young doctor were vastly different and that the transition from one to the other could be traumatic. Medical students owe it to themselves to make the most of the opportunities that they have been given. They need to study diligently for the various examinations that have to be negotiated, but they have no other responsibilities. They have the freedom to enjoy hobbies, to play sport, to relax with friends in the evenings and at weekends and, most important of all, they have the opportunity for uninterrupted sleep, a blessing not appreciated until it is denied. Masters of their own time, they are able to study at their own pace and convenience and can balance their work with pleasurable social activities. Overnight, when they become junior hospital doctors, they carry a formidable workload and bear significant responsibility. They face the challenge of being the 'new boy' in an alien environment. They are unfamiliar with practical procedures and ignorant of ward routine. They lose the ability to manage their own timetable and are at the beck and call of the patients, nurses and their senior medical colleagues. However, by far the most significant trial is the loss of sleep that results in a debilitating chronic tiredness. Liz and Richard had arrived on the 1st August. Since then, one or other of them had been 'on call' for every minute of every day and would remain so for the next six months. They were required to be available to the patients on the ward for prolonged periods, up to 36 hours at a time. They would often be on their feet, working from 8.30 in the morning until 10 or 11 at night. The 'bleep' from their pager would disrupt their routine by day and the shrill ring of their bedside telephone would disturb their sleep at night. It was tough, there was no doubt about that and there was no escape from the unrelenting workload.

With the lounge in the residency to themselves, Paul invited Liz to share her problems. Her words tumbled out in a rush as she unburdened her troubles to him.

"I'm going to quit." she wailed, tears pouring down her face. "I can't stand any more of this. I have to get out."

"Tell me more," Paul prompted, despite knowing exactly how she felt, for there had been numerous occasions when, as a house officer, the workload had threatened to overcome him. Worse still, there had been times when he had been consumed with self-doubt, certain that his lack of knowledge and his inexperience was putting patients at risk.

"I just can't cope," Liz cried, handkerchief to her eyes. "There simply aren't enough hours in the day to perform everything that is expected of me. Each morning I try to plan my day, try to organize my workload, but eight or ten hours later, there are more jobs waiting to be done, than there were when I started. By the end of the day, I'm so exhausted that I can scarcely drag one foot in front of the other. How am I expected to make decisions and be effective when I'm as tired as this? Sooner or later I shall make some dreadful mistake, perhaps prescribe the wrong drug and one of my patients will die. I've not had an uninterrupted night's sleep since I started and I haven't done my night as a casualty officer yet. I'm dreading it."

She was referring to the arrangement that required house officers, once a fortnight, to work through the night as the casualty officer, in addition to performing their normal duties on the ward. The hospital only employed dedicated casualty officers from 9am until 5pm on weekdays. For the houseman, it meant working during the day on the ward, continuing through the night acting as the casualty officer, (snatching an hour or two of sleep if the flow of patients allowed), then working the following day back on the ward. In truth, it was a highly unsatisfactory, indeed dangerous arrangement. Not only were the doctors treating the victims of major accidents extremely tired, they were also incredibly inexperienced.

"And how is Richard coping?" Paul asked.

"Not well, but a lot better than me. It's not fair though. He gets a lot of help from the nurses but they hate me. They obey you and they obey Mr Khan, but they never do what I tell them to do. In fact, I'm sure they go out of their way to ignore or disobey me. And Sister Ashbrook is an absolute bitch. She is always giving me extra work, then refusing to offer me any help when I need it. At times she is actively obstructive."

Paul knew it was necessary to do some plain talking. Inadvertently she had put her finger on one of the major problems. She wanted to 'tell' the nursing staff what to do. Mo 'asked' them, prefacing the request with 'would you mind' or 'when you have a minute'. There was a subtle but important difference. Sir William was prone to make a similar observation about the relationship between doctors on the ward and those in the support departments such as radiology and pathology. *'When we're working on the wards,'* he would ask, *'why do we speak of 'ordering' blood tests or xrays? Surely we should explain why we need the test and 'request' our colleagues to perform it for us.'*

"Look," Paul began, "firstly, whatever you do, you must not quit. You've studied for five years at university to get where you are today; years that will be wasted if you resign after only a few days in the job. I suggest that we sit down with Richard tonight. We'll look at the workload to see what can be done to make things a little easier. But whilst I have you on your own, there are a couple of things you need to understand, things that Mo may already have mentioned when he spoke with you after Helen Seddon's operation the other day. Doctors and nurses need to work as a team. The ward can't function without the doctors, but neither can it function without the nurses, or for that matter without the ward orderly, the domestic or the porter. It isn't wise to *'tell'* a nurse what to do, it is better to *'ask'* them with a *'please'* and a *'thank you'*. In fact, it's best to regard the sisters and staff nurses as being significantly senior to you. Their training may not have been as long as yours but it was practical and ward based. They are experienced; they understand ward routine and are familiar with all the procedures. They know how to deal with common surgical problems because they've seen them all before. And they know how Sir William and Mr Potts like their patients to be managed. They understand exactly what is expected of them in any given situation."

There was some other advice that Paul felt reticent about offering but knew it had to be said. He also believed it was advice that was best given whilst they were on our own.

"Look," he said, "I feel awkward about saying this, but there's something else that you need to think about. The nurses have to wear their uniforms strictly in accordance with Matron's rules and regulations. Flat shoes, no makeup, no jewellery, skirts to be worn below the knee. I can't claim to be an expert in the vagaries of the female mind, but I don't think they take kindly to miniskirts, high heels and plunging neck lines."

"But I like to look nice," she protested. "I want to be smart and professional when I'm working and it does seem to be appreciated by the men on the ward."

"That's probably true and no doubt it raises their blood pressure as well but surely you can see that it will be resented by the nurses. If you take my advice, you'll dress more soberly in future and as a bonus, if you wear flat heels, I'm sure that your feet will be more comfortable at 11 o'clock at night."

In offering this advice, Paul felt positively middle-aged! It amused him to think how his mother, always traditional in her views, would have laughed if she could have heard him.

Liz though, looked unconvinced. She offered no response. Paul had tried to give the message gently and constructively, hoping it would be taken in the right spirit but only time would soon tell if it would be heeded.

***

That evening Paul sat down with Richard and Liz and explained to them the *'facts of hospital life'* and gave them some practical tips on how to cope. It was exactly the same advice that he had been given three years earlier by Mohammed Khan, when he had been in their situation.

"The houseman on a ward," he began, speaking bluntly but honestly, "is the medical *'dog's body'*, the lowest of the low. I'm afraid that you are at the bottom of the pecking order. You may imagine that you have been appointed to the hospital as a doctor. You have, but you are the most junior member of the team. You have your medical duties to perform but, from time to time, you are expected to be a nurse, a porter, a secretary, even a cleaner. I'm afraid that's the way the system works. That's how it worked when I was a house officer and that's the way it's likely to remain, until we get some more enlightened consultants. Frankly, it's best to accept it, since the system is not about to improve. Don't try to buck against it. The system is entrenched and you won't change it."

There was another matter that Paul wanted to clarify, to confirm a suspicion that had been forming in his mind, since first meeting Liz and Richard,

"Tell me; are the two of you special friends? Are you a couple?"

Richard and Liz exchanged a hesitant glance and there was a pause before Liz replied. "Actually Paul, Richard and I are going out together, in fact we are engaged. We thought it best not to tell too many people on the unit, but we're actually planning to get married at the end of our house jobs."

Paul laughed. "Well if the two of you are engaged to be married, this should be excellent training for you. If you can survive the next six months working together without falling out, you should have a long and happy union. Well then, acting as your marriage guidance counsellor, let me explain what you can do to make life a little easier for yourselves.

Each evening before going to bed," he advised, "visit the wards and try to anticipate what might occur in the night that could result in the nurses having to disturb you. For example, make sure that all your patients are written up for night sedation and for pain relief. There is nothing more irritating than being woken from your own sleep and having to get out of your nice warm bed, and then walk to the ward to prescribe a sleeping pill for a patient; especially when you realize that with forethought, you could have prescribed it before you retired! Also check that all the drips are working, and that the nurses know which drips need to be replaced if they stop running and which may be left until the morning. You can also arrange that one of you takes the night calls for both wards, instead of covering one ward each. Then at least you will be able to enjoy undisturbed sleep on alternate nights."

Paul also listed some tasks that could be delegated to the medical students, pointing out that this experience was actually beneficial for them, since it helped prepare them for the role of house officer when their time came. But, most of all he stressed, particularly for Liz's benefit, the importance of working in harmony with the nurses. Many of the tasks on the ward fell in the interface between medicine and nursing and could be undertaken by members of either profession. Most nurses recognized that the house officers worked much longer hours than they did, and if there was a good team spirit on the ward, they would be sympathetic and do what they could to ease the doctors' load.

"Sister Rutherford on the female ward seems reasonable enough," Liz said, "but Sister Ashbrook is horrible to me. She never misses an opportunity to bleep me or to find fault. And she delights in criticizing me in front of the nurses. She acts as if she's the doctor and I'm just one of her junior nurses."

"Remember what I said earlier about the role of doctors and nurses," Paul replied. "Thinking of a nurse as a doctor's handmaiden does not create a good team spirit. Treat the nurses with respect and you will find them extremely helpful."

He had to admit though, that Sister Ashbrook was an exception to the rule and that life for the junior doctors would be considerably easier if she had a kinder attitude towards them. But he added, "You will find that she's not perfect. From time to time she oversteps the mark. Maybe your time will come."

Little did he realize though, when speaking those words, quite how soon that would be.

The next day, Paul was busy working in Sir William's outpatient clinic, when the strident sound of his pager interrupted him. The nurse who was chaperoning him took a message on his behalf. She soon returned looking anxious.

"It's Dr Webb on the phone. She says there's a patient on the ward who's bleeding and that she needs help. She seems to be in a bit of a panic but it does sound urgent."

"All right. Tell her that I'll be there within a couple of minutes."

Paul excused himself from the patient, then dashed up the stairs and ran along the corridor to Surgical Five. Liz was waiting for him at the entrance to the ward. He made a mental note to speak with her about that later. If a patient was bleeding, she should be at the bedside starting resuscitation, organizing a blood transfusion and inserting an intravenous line. This was an example of the deficiencies of medical school training. Students gained an excellent theoretical knowledge enabling them to pass their examinations, but often lacked an understanding of the priorities of medical management.

Liz looked terrified. "It's Mr Mills," she said. "He's pouring blood from his rectum."

The name meant nothing to Paul.

"Who is Mr Mills?"

"He's a patient who came in today, only in his 40's. He's known to have a stomach ulcer."

"But it's not our admitting day. Why have we admitted an emergency with a bleeding ulcer?"

"No," Liz replied," the anxiety clearly evident in her voice. "He's not an emergency admission. He was admitted from the waiting list. I was checking that he was fit enough for his operation tomorrow. I did a routine rectal examination and found that he was bleeding profusely."

By this time, they had arrived at Mr Mills' bedside. Paul had expected to find him pale, cold and sweating, gasping for breath, collapsed on the bed with a racing pulse and a desperately low blood pressure. In fact, he looked to be a perfectly healthy middle-aged gentleman.

"He doesn't look as if he's lost a lot of blood," he said. "What's his pulse and blood pressure?"

"Oh, I haven't done that yet." Liz replied.

Inwardly Paul groaned. It was easy to see why the nurses hadn't taken to her. It wasn't just her attitude and appearance; they would quickly have realized that she wasn't a good doctor. If Mr Mills was bleeding, monitoring his pulse and blood pressure was basic medicine. Every nurse learned that within a week of arriving at the hospital. This was an omission that could not be ignored.

"Don't you think that you should have taken the blood pressure?" Paul observed, perhaps a little too severely.

Immediately he regretted it, as tears welled up in Liz's eyes.

"All right. Let's set that aside for the time being. Perhaps you would like to take Mr Mills' pulse and blood pressure now. He appears to be pink and comfortable. He doesn't look as if he's lost a lot of blood."

These investigations proved to be entirely normal. Feeling the need to rebuild Liz's confidence, Paul invited her to relate the patient's clinical story.

"Mr Mills has had indigestion for many years," she said. "It tends to come and go but recently it has been present most of the time. It's been very troublesome and has caused him to lose a lot of time from work. He's tried all the usual bland diets and medicines but nothing seems to help and he has now started to vomit. That's why he has come into hospital. His operation is planned for tomorrow."

"And has he had any bleeding from the ulcer before?" Paul asked.

"No."

"But you say he's bleeding now."

"Yes he is – heavily."

Paul frowned. This did not fit at all. Heavy bleeding would inevitably result in 'shock'. The patient should be cold, pale and sweaty.

"Is this just a splash of blood on the surface of the stool, or mixed throughout?" he asked, knowing that a little surface blood would probably just mean piles.

"No," she said. "The whole stool is bright red."

To Paul, this seemed incompatible with the pink healthy man who was sitting, looking relaxed, in the bed in front of him, but who was beginning to wonder what all the fuss was about. The rectal tray was still sitting on the bedside locker and the obvious way to resolve the mystery was for Paul to inspect the stool himself. Mr Mills did not look particularly pleased at the prospect of a further examination but turned on to his side in preparation without complaint. Two minutes later as Paul withdrew his finger; he was able to inspect the stool on the plastic glove. Immediately he relaxed and smiled. This was not the characteristic red of fresh blood, but subtly different, as if a red dye had perfused through the stool. He knew exactly what it was, not due to any academic brilliance; simply that he had seen it before. It was an appearance that every experienced surgeon recognizes but something rarely recorded in surgical textbooks.

"That's not blood," he said to Liz. "Ask him what he ate for his dinner last night."

"Lamb, potatoes and vegetables," Mr Mills said in response to Liz's enquiry. "My wife cooked a lovely shoulder of lamb. She said it might be the last good meal I had for a week or so, with me having an operation."

Paul needed to prompt him. "And the vegetables that you ate were........?"

"Beetroots, doctor."

"Beetroots fresh from your own garden?" Paul suggested.

"Well from the allotment actually, Doctor. I never have much luck with carrots or peas. The carrots get infested with flies and the mice eat all the peas but the beets and the parsnips always do well. My wife serves the beets with a tasty white sauce. They're always delicious, tender and sweet. I can't resist them."

Liz looked tearful again. "So it's not blood then," she said. "Look, Paul, I'm sorry to have troubled you...."

"Don't worry, it's an easy mistake to make and I only know because I've seen it before. You're not the first to make that mistake and you won't be the last. In truth, you were right to seek advice. As a doctor, if you are worried about a patient, you should never hesitate to seek help. Better to ask for assistance unnecessarily, than fail to ask for it, when it's needed."

Returning to the outpatient clinic, there was much for Paul to ponder. Liz had not seen a stool discoloured by beetroot before, so it was reasonable for her to be concerned. And she had sought advice, which was good. However, not to have taken the patient's pulse and blood pressure and not to be starting resuscitation whilst waiting for him to arrive, was inexcusable. It was clear that she would need close supervision. Theoretically, this was Mr Potts' responsibility. He was her consultant; the person who, in due course, would be asked to state whether she was sufficiently competent to be registered with the General Medical Council and allowed to work unsupervised as a doctor. But in practice, as her immediate superior, it fell to Paul to cover her back. It appeared, though, that if he were to be overcritical, or perhaps merely honest about her performance, she would simply burst into tears.

After lunch, the team congregated in the office, waiting for Mr Potts to arrive for his twice-weekly ward round. On these occasions, there was always a slight tension in the air. Whereas Sir William could be relied upon to be relaxed and benevolent, Mr Potts was unpredictable.

Sometimes he would be in a good mood; full of *bonhomie*, charming and witty but more often, for no apparent reason, he was taciturn and irritable. Furthermore, his mood could change abruptly if something or someone displeased him. Woe betide any junior who crossed him at such a time.

Fortunately, on this occasion, he was in one of more genial moods. He greeted the team with a smile, and then paid a pretty compliment to Liz on her appearance, Paul's advice on appropriate dress having been completely ignored! Liz smiled sweetly and said a polite, '*Why, thank you Mr Potts*' but in the background Sister Ashbrook's face hardened.

The first patient had a simple hernia, which presented no risk to the young man's life but caused him some pain and interfering with his job.

"Suppose a man has discomfort walking," asked Mr Potts looking at Liz, "perhaps from a rupture such as this, or maybe from arthritis of the hip, at what stage would you offer him surgery?"

"Perhaps when he was only able to walk a mile or so," she replied, tentatively.

"A very reasonable suggestion my dear, but not quite what I was looking for." Mr Potts turned to Paul, raising an eyebrow.

"Well, Sir," he responded. "You have to accept that surgery and anaesthesia are not without risk, and operations are not always 100% successful, so perhaps a couple of hundred yards."

Mr Potts said nothing though it was obvious from his slight frown that he did not agree with this answer. He turned to Mohammed Khan.

"There isn't a precise answer, Sir. It depends upon his lifestyle."

"Exactly," said Mr. Potts. "It depends upon his lifestyle. A retired seventy year old who drives a car and spends his evenings relaxing in the pub, perhaps playing darts or dominoes, doesn't need to walk very far. He wouldn't need surgery, even if he could only walk fifty yards. However it would be justifiable to operate on a postman who could walk several miles, since without an operation, he wouldn't be able to do his job. But you are right, Lambert, when you say that not all operations are successful. Sometimes I think that we surgeons are the victims of our own success. Results from surgery are getting better all the time and patients are beginning to expect relief from all their symptoms and a complete cure for every disease. It is important for them to understand that this is not the case. No surgical procedure is uniformly successful. The reality is that occasionally patients will be worse off after their operation than they were before. And of course, some operations result in the patient's death. This should be discussed before the surgery is performed. Too often though, doctors avoid telling patients unpalatable truths.

"And that applies to nurses too," he said turning to Sister Ashbrook. "How often do you hear a nurse with a large syringe and needle in her hand, say to a patient *'just a little scratch, it won't hurt'*? Whenever I've had an injection, it has hurt like hell. Mind you," he continued, changing tack, "patients don't always remember everything you tell them. A little while ago, in the outpatient clinic, Sister Jenkins and I ran a little experiment. At the end of every consultation, I told each patient three things about their condition. I then arranged for Sister to interview them as they left the hospital a few minutes later. Believe it or not, on average, patients only remembered one of the three things that I had mentioned to them. The study was published in the College Journal," he added proudly. "I recommended that information for patients should be written down, so that they may refresh their memory at home, when they are less stressed."

"That really is most interesting, Mr Potts," volunteered Liz, somewhat unnecessarily.

"You're welcome, Liz," replied her boss with a smile and the touch of his hand on her shoulder.

They had been at the patient's bedside for ten minutes or more but Liz was right. The exchange between Mr Potts and his staff had been both interesting and educational. The junior hospital doctors received no formal teaching. Theirs was a traditional apprenticeship. They worked alongside the consultants, watching, listening and learning whilst on duty. As undergraduates at medical school, they had received formal lectures and attended tutorials. Now as postgraduates, they extended their knowledge by private study. They digested advanced textbooks and research journals as and when time allowed. But in no way did this prepare them to be practising surgeons. 'Surgical wisdom' such as this, was not to be found in any surgical textbook. It could only be gained with experience, by working alongside the consultants on the wards, in the outpatient clinics and in the theatre.

In due course, they arrived at Mr Mills' bed, the patient who had been admitted for an operation on his stomach ulcer. To Paul's surprise, he saw that intravenous fluid was running through a drip into his arm. He couldn't understand why. Surely Liz had believed him when he had reassured her that the discoloration of the stool was simply due to beetroot.

Liz introduced the patient to Mr Potts, describing Mr Mills' symptoms, detailing the length and severity of his indigestion and adding that he had recently started to vomit and lose time from work. Mr Potts nodded to the patient and said that his operation was planned for the following morning. He was about to move to the next bed when

Sister Ashbrook interrupted.

"Mr Potts, Dr Webb has omitted to tell you an extremely important bit of information. Mr Mills is actually bleeding from his ulcer at the moment. I did inform Dr Webb about it earlier but it seems that she thought that she knew best. She has ignored me and decided not to take any action. So I took it upon myself to put up the drip and to arrange for some blood to be ready for transfusion later today." She looked hard at Liz, a self-righteous look on her face and then added, "I do think it unfortunate when a newly qualified doctor cannot listen to her experienced ward sister."

The last remark seemed unnecessarily pointed, but if Sister Ashbrook had indeed informed Liz that she thought that the patient was bleeding, Liz, in turn, had clearly not told her ward sister that the discolouration of the stool was due to beetroot and not to blood. The antagonism between houseman and nursing sister was getting unpleasant and unfortunately had started to impinge on patient care. A drip had been placed, quite unnecessarily, in Mr Mills' arm. A bit of friendly rivalry between doctors and nurses was not a bad thing, indeed it made for a good relationship, but there was a danger that this confrontation might get out of hand. Paul expected that Liz would immediately counter by saying that Mr Mills was not bleeding but for a moment she hesitated and looked uncertain. She glanced at Paul enquiringly, as if needing reassurance and confirmation about the beetroot. Paul was about to explain the situation to Mr Potts, hoping to defuse the tension that had arisen, when Liz suddenly regained her confidence.

"That's because it isn't blood, it's staining from beetroot. Mr Mills has an allotment and ate home grown beetroot last night. He doesn't need a drip and he doesn't need a transfusion." Her face was stern, her voice sharp and the words were aimed like bullets at Sister Ashbrook.

Mr Potts glanced at the two women, who were now glaring angrily at each other, two cats hackles raised, bristling for a fight. He seemed to find the situation amusing.

"Well, I wonder who's right," he said with a smile. "There's only one way to find out. Sister, would you please ask one of your charming nurses to fetch the rectal tray."

Mr Mills however, looked far from happy.

"Not again," he protested. "It's not pleasant having someone's finger thrust up your backside. And it's been done three times today already!"

"Just relax. This won't be in the least uncomfortable," Mr Potts replied, ignoring the advice he himself had given not five minutes before, about telling little white lies to patients. He donned an examination glove, put some lubricating gel on his index finger and made the fourth rectal examination that the patient had endured that day. Withdrawing his finger, he looked carefully at the colour of the stool. Then, holding the soiled glove on high, his forefinger raised like an umpire confirming a batsman's fate, he glanced in turn at each of the warring women. He paused, deliberately prolonging the tension, enjoying holding the two antagonists in suspense. With a huge grin on his face, he delivered his verdict.

"Definitely beetroot," he announced. "Well done, Liz, well done indeed."

Liz's features relaxed into a triumphant smile. Sister Ashbrook looked furious.

"Thank you Sir," Liz said. Then, without so much as a glance in Paul's direction, she added, "I knew it wasn't blood. That's why I saw no need for a drip."

Paul was incensed. It was outrageous that Liz should claim to have made the correct diagnosis. She too had believed Mr Mills was bleeding, and worse, had panicked at the prospect. He tried to catch her eye to convey his feelings to her, but she studiously avoided his gaze.

Mr Mills then proceeded to add to Sister Ashbrook's distress by declaring, "I tried to tell Sister that the doctors had said it wasn't blood but she wouldn't listen. She just dashed off firing instructions at her nurses."

Then Mr. Potts made the situation even worse.

"I'm sorry about the examinations Mr Mills, but we've sorted it out now and it's nice to know that we have a bright young doctor working for us. Not only bright but pretty as well. Congratulations Liz." Momentarily he slipped his arm around her waist. "I can see you will make an excellent house officer. Better luck next time, Sister," he added over his shoulder, already walking down the ward to see the next patient.

The whole episode had amused him immensely and he remained in an effervescent mood for the rest of the round, but Paul was far from happy. When he had worked on Surgical Five previously, there had been a great camaraderie amongst the staff. It had been one of the strengths of the unit and had made the hard work and long hours tolerable. Certainly Sister Ashbrook had frequently tried to get 'one up' on the junior doctors, but there had never been this animosity. Liz's attitude to Sister Ashbrook was worrying. She had deliberately embarrassed her ward sister in front of the medical staff, but more importantly in front of her own nurses. And it had been wrong for her to take the credit for knowing that the coloured stool was due to beetroot. Only a few hours earlier, Paul had advised her to be a team player, told her that doctors and nurses needed to work together, but here was clear evidence that his advice was being blatantly ignored. Sister Ashbrook was not one to take such humiliation lying down. Without doubt she would want her revenge and there would be ample opportunity for her to obtain it. She was an experienced ward sister. She had been in charge of the ward for at least five years; she knew every trick in the book and a few more besides. Liz had been qualified for just one week; she was a complete novice. She had been exceedingly foolish to make such a powerful enemy.

And Paul foresaw another problem. A shadow had crossed Richard's face when Mr Potts had slipped his arm around his fiancée's waist. There was clearly trouble ahead. Mr Potts was known to be a ladies' man and he appeared to have 'taken a fancy' to Liz. Paul felt that she was quite old enough and, no doubt, experienced enough, to look after herself. How she reacted to the personal attention that she was receiving from her boss was none of his business but it was important that the relationship between the two house officers was good. They needed to support each other, to share the workload, and to be flexible when arranging off duty and nights 'on call'. The patients would suffer and Paul's workload would increase if they ceased to cooperate. Regrettably it appeared that life on Ward Five in future was not going to be as harmonious as it had been previously.

Chapter Six

Liz and Richard were 'housemen', a term denoting their contractual requirement to reside in the hospital. Paul, as a senior house officer (SHO), had to provide his own accommodation as were those employed at the more senior grade of registrar. Many SHO's and registrars were married, as often as not to nurses! Generally they rented flats or had lodgings in the city and were only to be found in the doctor's residency as dictated by their duty roster. For convenience, Paul lived in a flat in the hospital grounds some three hundred yards from the surgical wards. The rent was reasonable, it reduced the time and expense of travelling to work and meant that if he felt lazy, or exhausted from prolonged periods on duty, he had no need to cook for himself. Meals were available in the residency, or 'doctor's mess', as it was generally known. Being single, he frequently gravitated to the warmth and friendship to be found there, even when off duty.

The residency was a modern two-storey building connected to the old Victorian hospital by a covered corridor. It served as home to the twenty or so housemen. It also provided *'on call'* accommodation for SHO's and registrars when they were required to be on duty overnight, as Paul was every fourth night and fourth weekend. The rooms were simply furnished, with a chest of drawers, desk, wardrobe and a bedside table upon which stood the dreaded telephone. All the doctors came to loathe the phone. It was the bane of their lives; summoning them back to care for their patients at all times of the day or night. There was a pleasant communal lounge; a largish room, around which were scattered a number of easy chairs and settees, most of which looked as if they had come from the local charity shop. All had food stains and were pock marked with cigarette burns. A bar was situated at one end. Beer and soft drinks were available twenty four hours a day, seven days a week, yet the only time that Paul saw anyone the worse for wear, was on the rare occasions when the residents held a party. The bar was self-service, an honesty book being provided for residents to record their drinks. Surprisingly, at the end of every month, when bar bills were settled, there was never a shortfall.

Meals were provided at a huge table in the dining room by loyal catering staff. They 'mothered' the doctors, chiding them if they rushed their meals, or failed to eat a balanced diet. They always ensured that wholesome food was available, and recognised that the unpredictable nature of their duties meant that the doctors were not always able to take meals at the appointed time. A snooker room and a television lounge added to the facilities, although the long hours on duty meant that they were not much frequented. The residency was an important feature in the lives of the housemen. It was a haven in which to shelter from the hectic life on the ward, a place where young people thrown together in difficult circumstances developed a camaraderie, much as develops in an officer's mess in the armed forces; a place where lifelong friendships were forged.

A couple of weeks later, on a Saturday evening when Paul was not 'on duty', but was nonetheless relaxing in the residency, he was surprised to be contacted by the hospital switchboard. Normally, such a call would only be justified in the rare event of a major incident in the city, such as a rail disaster or catastrophic industrial accident. It was Tony, the friendly telephone operator. Dr Makin, the registrar covering the medical wards, wanted to speak with Paul and Tony asked if he was prepared to take the call.

"Sorry", Paul replied, "but I'm not on duty at the moment. Its Surgical Three's admitting day. You need to contact their SHO, Roger Watkins, or if he's not available, their registrar."

"Yes, I know that," Tony replied apologetically, "but I've have been trying to contact Roger for an hour or more and I'm afraid that I haven't been able to locate him. The batteries in his bleep may have gone flat. Mind you, knowing Roger, he may well have taken them out and thrown them away."

"Then please ring round the various departments where he might be. He must be in the hospital somewhere."

"I've already tried just about everywhere. I've bleeped him and phoned his room. I've tried the Surgical Three wards, as well as their theatre and the casualty department but without success. He seems to have disappeared into thin air."

"Then what about their registrar?" Paul asked.

"I located him easily enough," Tony replied. "He's operating on an emergency, but he's going to be tied up in theatre for a couple of hours and I'm afraid Dr Makin's patient does sound quite urgent."

Paul sighed. Being available for 80 hours a week was bad enough without working on your weekends off. "In that case I suppose I'll have to take the call. You'd better put Dr Makin through."

Bill Makin apologised profusely. "I'm sorry to trouble you, Paul. I know you're not 'on call', but I would be grateful if you would see a lady on Medical Three for me. She's 85 years old and was admitted with a chest infection. That's responding well to treatment but I'm worried about her belly. Roger saw her yesterday and thought she might have a minor bowel infection, but she's significantly less well today. Her temperature has gone up, she's getting a lot of pain in her abdomen so there must be something brewing there, but I'm dammed if I know what it is."

"Fine. Tell me her name and I'll go and see her ".

Despite it being a Saturday evening, Paul had nothing special planned and wasn't too unhappy about being asked to undertake a consultation on the medical ward, although being so easily available to cover unforeseen staff shortages was a consequence of living on the hospital campus that he had not anticipated. There has always been a friendly rivalry between physicians and surgeons, each deriving a sense of satisfaction if they are able to resolve a problem that has confounded their colleagues. Physicians are experts in chest and heart problems but have little experience of abdominal disorders, or indeed of maternity problems, as Bill Makin had acknowledged when confronted with Miss Mullins' pregnant cat! Surgeons on the other hand, see such patients on a daily basis. With three years experience of dealing with abdominal complaints, Paul was familiar with the symptoms and signs they produce and was able to make the correct diagnosis in the majority of cases. Given reasonable luck, he would be able to resolve this patient's problem and have bragging rights over the physicians for a week or so.

Mary Murphy was a mother of five, grandmother of thirteen and was obese, cheerful and garrulous. In medical practice, as in other walks of life, there are some folk to whom you immediately take a liking, with whom you have an affinity and others who are better kept at arm's length. Such impressions are usually formed at first encounter and once made rarely change. Paul found that Mary belonged in the former category. Time passes slowly for patients in hospital and they are generally happy to spend time chatting. The medical staff on the other hand, rarely have time for small talk. Their conversations are usually confined to the exchanges necessary for enquiry into the patients' medical problems. On this occasion however, with only Mary to see, Paul was quite content to sit and chat.

As a doctor Paul was privileged to be able to enquire, not only about a patient's symptoms, but also about their background; their family, their employment and hobbies, which may be both interesting and educational. With little prompting, Mary was happy to talk freely about herself in a way that would have been foreign to Paul, who was naturally reserved and rarely spoke about himself.

"'Tis my chest doctor, sure 'tis my chest," she said. "No doubt due to all those cigarettes I smoked when I was young and foolish. I really should have known better." She spoke in a strong Irish accent, coughing and wheezing as she went. "Mind you, I didn't smoke 'til I left home. There was scarcely enough money to put potatoes in the pot in those days, let alone to buy cigarettes."

"And where was home?" Paul asked.

"Ballybunion, Doctor, on the west coast of Ireland, where the mighty Shannon reaches the sea," she replied, before going on to speak of her background.

She had left home at the age of seventeen because there was no work available locally and hers had been an extra mouth to feed. She had travelled to Liverpool, enrolled as a student nurse and served in various hospitals in the days before the National Health Service. Eventually she became the senior sister of a medical ward in a Lancashire cotton town.

"So you're a trained nurse?"

"Sure I was, until I retired that is. But that was 25 years ago. Times have changed since then of course."

"And what do you think of modern nursing?"

Paul had expected her to reflect on the changes in nursing practice that had occurred over the years; the development of antibiotics, modern anaesthetics, renal dialysis and surgical developments, such as transplantation, but she didn't. She looked round surreptitiously before replying, checking that she wasn't being overheard.

"Today's nurses are sloppy," she said, "and they have little discipline. I tell you Doctor, they wouldn't have lasted two minutes on my ward. When they're making beds or serving meals, they chatter amongst themselves about their boyfriends and what they plan to do when they next get off duty. They're not as interested in the patients as they should be and they really don't know what hard work is. When I was a student nurse, we worked a ten-hour day, six days a week. And there isn't the same attention to detail. In my day, matron visited the ward every morning and woe betide any sister whose ward was not spick and span. All the beds had to be straight, even the wheel castors had to be in line. And the poor patients were expected to sit to attention, no matter how ill they were! Matron inspected the nurses too. Collars and cuffs had to be starched, headdresses had to cover every last wisp of hair and shoes polished so that you could see your face in them."

At that moment one of the nurses walked by, her hemline two inches below the knee.

"And nurses were not allowed to show even a glimpse of ankle, lest it distract the doctors," she added primly, with a sniff of disapproval.

Paul smiled at the earnest expression on her face. Perhaps it was ever thus, each generation intolerant of the lifestyle of the next. There was a pause in the conversation and he took the opportunity to explain why he had come to see her.

"The doctors on this ward are physicians; experts in diseases of the chest and heart but they don't get a lot of experience in abdominal problems. That's why I have come to see you. I work on the surgical wards."

"Does that mean that I need an operation, Doctor?"

"Not necessarily," Paul replied. "It depends very much on what's going on inside your tummy. Hopefully it's something that will settle down without an operation. We would prefer to avoid an anaesthetic because of your chest infection."

"Another doctor came to see me yesterday. Was he a surgeon too?"

Paul looked at her clinical record and saw the notes made by Roger.

"Yes, he was," he replied.

Paul prompted her to speak of her abdominal troubles and Mary started to describe the symptoms that she had experienced. Unfortunately her story was vague, little more than some generalized discomfort, some nausea and slight disturbance of her bowels. It gave little clue to the source of her troubles.

However, when Paul examined her abdomen, he was concerned to find that Mary was quite tender and a little distended; features that, according to the notes, had not been present the previous day. The swelling raised the possibility that Mary might be developing a bowel obstruction. It was not as marked as Paul had seen on his first day in this job, but whereas Helen Seddon had been young and her obstruction had proved to be due to simple scar tissue, Mary was in her eighties. At this age, cancer of the bowel would be the most likely cause.

Paul was aware though that his examination was incomplete. The advice that Sir William had drummed into him as a house officer echoed in his head. *"Young man,"* he would say, *"the examination of the abdomen begins in the groin and ends in the rectum. If you don't put your finger in, sooner or later you are bound to put your foot in."* If Paul had heard him say that once, he had heard him say it a dozen times. Roger's records, however, made no mention of either examination. Paul exposed Mary's abdomen again. The examination of the groin wasn't pleasant. Her obese abdomen hung down in a fold over her fleshy upper thigh and the groin skin crease had not seen the light of day nor, Paul suspected, any soap and water for many a long month. The skin there was moist, excoriated, and smelled unpleasantly. Careful examination however, revealed no abnormality.

The next job was the rectal examination and Paul needed to find the tray, which held the examination gloves and lubricant gel. Unfamiliar with the ward, he went in search of a member of the nursing staff to tell him where the tray could be found. The ward sister was in the office writing reports, a cup of tea at her side.

"I am sorry to disturb you, Sister, but if it's not too much trouble, could you tell me where I can find the rectal tray. I need to do an examination on Mrs Murphy".

Sister looked up and Paul recognized a familiar face but certainly not a welcome one. It was Sue Weston. His heart sank as memories of their previous encounters flooded into his mind. Now a nursing sister, it was Sue, who as a staff nurse, had marched brazenly into his *'on call'* room, on the pretence of bringing him an early morning cup of tea after his overnight shift in the casualty department. She had been a siren in nurse's uniform, although not a uniform worn in the manner that Matron's regulations prescribe. With the top three buttons of her dress undone, she had made herself comfortable sitting on the side of Paul's bed, her ample bosom displayed for his indulgence. She had made it emphatically clear to an inexperienced, shy young doctor, that she was available. She was the type of girl who confused and frightened men such as Paul with her blatant sexiness, the more so, since according to the hospital grapevine, she was what was known, as a 'good time girl'. The truth is that she scared the life out of him and she knew it. She had teased him about it ever since, whilst reminding him periodically that she would welcome a liaison should he forego his principles and enjoy life more. More than once she had said to him *'Life is for living, love is for giving',* usually adding, *"and I'm an exceedingly generous girl."*

"Hello Paul." The voice was just as Paul remembered it, throaty and seductive. "So you've come back to the City General have you? I must say it's very nice to see you."

"Hello Sue."

"Ah, so its *'Sue'* now is it, not *Sister Weston*. I can see that I'm finally making some progress," she said, her eyes twinkling.

Determined as he was to cut out any casual conversation and to get on with the examination of his patient, it was impossible for Paul not to notice Sue's generous mouth and her hour glass figure, emphasized by the tight belt worn round her waist.

"I've come to see Mrs Murphy to try to sort out her abdominal problem," he said as formally as he could. "Perhaps you would tell me where I could find the rectal tray?"

"That really is a shame, Paul. I had hoped you had come especially to see me, but perhaps another time. Now that you're back in the hospital, I'm sure there will be plenty of other opportunities for us to get together, to enjoy each other's company and have some fun."

"The rectal tray, please Sister, if it's not too much trouble." Paul repeated, trying to instil coldness into his voice, though conscious that his pulse was racing and his face was flushed.

It was obvious from the smile on her face that she knew exactly what effect she was having.

"All right Paul, but you really are a disappointment to me. You and I could have such a good time together if I could only persuade you to relax. Life shouldn't be all work and no play you know. And fancy calling me *'Sister'*. I thought you and I were on first name terms. Helping you to find the rectal tray is certainly not too much trouble. You know I would do *anything* for you".

The emphasis on the word *'anything'* was unmistakable. Such a remark made between friends might be considered a tease, part of harmless meaningless banter, but knowing Sue's reputation, Paul realised that these were not empty words. He knew that she was a predatory female. She was not particularly pretty with her rather coarse skin, large mouth and her forward manner. Yet at one and the same time, he found her both repulsive and desirable, for there was an earthy sexiness about her and he was painfully aware of being physically attracted. Others of his sex would have regarded her as an 'easy lay', and accept what was clearly on offer without any sense of guilt or shame, but Paul's instinct was to flee, to exit the room as rapidly as possible.

In response to Paul's request, a ward sister might be expected to direct a visiting doctor to the relevant cupboard, or to delegate a junior nurse to collect the tray. But this was no ordinary sister. She led Paul personally to the storeroom, allowed him to enter first, and then closed the door behind them. Alone in the room with her, Paul felt trapped, his sense of anxiety heightened. Opening a cupboard, she passed him the metal tray, but as he took hold of it, she held on to it for a second or two longer than was necessary and their hands touched. A thrill of excitement, or was it pure panic, spread through Paul's body. Their eyes met and a slow seductive smile crossed her face.

"One day, Paul, one day." She spoke the words quietly, almost as if she were talking to herself, making herself a promise.

With the tray in his hands, in his haste to get away, Paul forgot to say *'thanks'* as he ran out of the room, back to the safety of the open ward and Mrs. Murphy's bedside.

It may be imagined that a rectal examination is not the most agreeable job for a doctor to perform, but Paul had undertaken the task so frequently that his personal emotions ceased to be involved. He recognised that it was not the most pleasant or dignified of procedures for a patient either but fortunately Mary, as a retired nurse, knew what to expect. To his dismay, Paul found a hard unyielding mass. In a lady of this age, it was almost certain to be a rectal cancer; a diagnosis that would explain her symptoms. The consequences were worrying. Removing the tumour would require major surgery under an anaesthetic, and since Mary still had a chest infection, this would carry a grave risk to her life.

Paul knew that a telescopic inspection was needed to confirm the diagnosis as a matter of some urgency. Any delay would allow the obstruction to become more marked, causing a further deterioration in her condition. It might even result in the bowel bursting which would undoubtedly prove fatal. Mary though, was not Paul's patient. He was seeing her on behalf of the Surgical Three team, so after explaining that a telescope test would be arranged, he took his leave of her. Then, carefully avoiding Sue Weston in the ward office, he went to find the Surgical Three registrar. After explaining how he came to be involved in Mrs Murphy's care, Paul shared his findings and concerns with the registrar who agreed to take over Mary's future care.

Since his involvement with the case was now over, Paul returned to his hospital flat but keen to know how Mary fared and to find out whether his diagnosis was correct, he resolved to keep himself informed of her progress. This was a laudable, well-intentioned resolution. Little did he know that it was destined to lead him onto the horns of an impossible ethical dilemma, one that was subsequently to threaten his entire career as a surgeon!

Chapter Seven

Responsibility for emergency admissions was shared between the surgical units, though Surgical One, being a specialist unit was exempt. The Surgical Five team were *'on call'* each Thursday and every fourth weekend. On these 'admitting' days, it was their responsibility to care for surgical emergencies. These could be accident cases that arrived in casualty, urgent referrals from general practitioners or acute problems that arose elsewhere in the hospital. It was a daunting workload. Since the weekend encompassed Friday, as well as Saturday and Sunday, it meant that once a month, Paul lived in the hospital from nine o'clock on Thursday morning until five on Monday afternoon, as indeed did the two house officers, Liz and Richard. This hundred hour spell of duty could be extremely exhausting since it was rarely possible to enjoy an undisturbed night. Usually sleep was disrupted by one or more calls, resulting in a visit to the ward or the casualty department. Should a patient require emergency surgery, virtually a whole night's sleep could be lost. At such times, there was a real danger that chronic tiredness would result in some catastrophic error. The junior doctors were particularly concerned that should a disaster occur, the authorities would make no allowance for the extreme fatigue caused by these unacceptably long hours of duty.

There was therefore, a general sigh of relief that when Mohammed Khan was promoted, Victoria Kent arrived without undue delay to fill the registrar post that had fallen vacant. Paul had worked alongside her in his previous post at the Middleton Hospital and held her in high regard. Mo's promotion had been long overdue, but he had now reached the penultimate step on the surgical ladder. After three or four years in his new post, he would be eligible to apply to be a consultant, though this would almost certainly be in a district general hospital. The appointment of an 'overseas' surgeon to a teaching or university hospital was as likely as snow in Saudi in summer. In truth though, he would make an excellent consultant. He was a sound clinician, a good teacher and when operating, he was the best technical surgeon that Paul had seen.

Victoria was battling against another well-established prejudice. 50 years previously, the medical staff at the City General Hospital had been exclusively male, as the portraits of past consultants on the walls of the main corridor bore testament. Women still comprised only a tiny proportion of consultants in the NHS. Some had made the grade in peripheral hospitals in less competitive specialties, such as radiology and anaesthetics, but there were no female consultant surgeons in any of the hospitals in the city. It was suggested that the training was too demanding for women. Certainly surgical training was exacting and arduous. Few achieved consultant status under the age of 40. The need to work long and unpredictable hours and the requirement to live in the hospital periodically, made a social or family life outside the hospital difficult. Yet academically, women were just as capable as men. They were equally dexterous and just as able to undertake technical surgical procedures. In general, they were probably better communicators than their male counterparts, (Paul thought that they couldn't possibly be worse than Leslie Potts), and certainly they were more caring and sympathetic. Part time training was not available, so any woman who wanted to pursue a career in surgery had either to stay single, or to have a very supportive spouse. This sentiment though applied equally to men, since the wife of a male trainee similarly had to tolerate her husband's long and unpredictable hours and periodic absences.

Paul would have been loath to admit that he had any sexual prejudice, but in truth, before meeting Victoria, he had wondered if she might be a tough hirsute 'hockey type', with a flat chest and a booming voice. Such irreverent thoughts however, were quickly dispelled when he met her. Of average height, she had a natural fresh complexion, devoid of any makeup, which made her look younger than her 28 years. With her hair worn short in a practical fashion and wearing clothes that were comfortable and discrete, she was accepted without question by the nursing staff. She had warm brown eyes and an engaging smile that quickly put the patients at ease. The more Paul saw of her as he worked alongside her, the more he liked and admired her. Unassuming, without any airs or graces, she was thoughtful and quietly spoken, yet her words were chosen with care. On the ward, she was thorough; she never gave the impression of being hurried or in a rush. In the theatre, she took great care with every procedure. She handled the tissues gently and avoiding excessive bleeding or bruising. As on the ward, she worked quietly without any fuss, bother or histrionics. And she particularly enjoyed working in casualty, supporting and advising the housemen, assistance which they greatly appreciated.

Life in the accident department was always busy but there were a number of occasions when the department was truly chaotic; days which staff preferred to avoid. One such was New Year's Eve, another was St Patrick's Day. The Irish Club was situated half a mile north of the hospital and the Shamrock Club half a mile to the south! There was also the day on which 'derby matches' were played between the city's two first division football teams and unfortunately the first such match of the season chanced to fall on Surgical Five's admitting day. Richard was scheduled to work from five pm 'til nine pm, but Liz would then take over and work through 'til nine the next morning. This shift, known to the residents as the 'graveyard slot', would be the occasion when Liz acted as the casualty officer for the first time. As SHO, it would be Paul's job to support her. He was not relishing the prospect, especially as she had already told him how much she was dreading it.

A crowd of 50,000 was expected to attend the match. The teams had been first and fourth in the division the previous season and there was inevitably great local rivalry between the two sets of football supporters. It was not unknown for running battles to develop on the streets around the ground, before and after the match. Although the police would be out in force, it was likely that some would require medical attention before the night was over.

With the kick off scheduled for seven thirty, the first casualty arrived at about six pm. He was a lad of about sixteen years of age, called Pete. He was wearing a blue and white United shirt, was clearly the worse for drink and had been stabbed in the chest. Richard phoned Paul and asked for advice, aware that inspection of the short skin wound gave no indication of the depth of penetration, or the nature of any internal injury. Together they listened to his story, sadly a common one. Pete had been roaming the streets all afternoon with his mates, drinking steadily and looking to cause trouble. The group had encountered some of the opposing fans, Pete referred to them as '*the enemy*', in one of the city's main squares. Mutual verbal abuse had led to a scuffle, then someone had pulled out a flick knife and Pete had been stabbed in the left side of his chest. His main concern was revenge; he was '*effing and blinding*,' threatening to murder the next Rovers fan he met. The casualty sister had wisely placed him in the end cubicle so that he could be isolated should the next casualty attendee be wearing Rover's colours! Fortunately his clinical condition was good, it seemed unlikely that the blade had injured the lung, or the heart but none-the-less, commonsense demanded that he should have a precautionary chest x-ray.

Paul had seen plenty of stab wounds in the past and knew that the outcome for both victim and assailant was very much in the lap of the Gods, this being particularly true for stab wounds to the chest. When the blow is struck, the blade will either strike a rib or alternatively penetrate the space between the ribs. If the knife hits bone, the victim comes to no serious harm and merely needs a couple of stitches in the skin wound. Only rarely will such an injury come to the attention of the police or the courts. However, should the blade chance to slip between

61

two ribs, it may puncture the lung or worse, penetrate the heart, in which case the victim may die rapidly from torrential haemorrhage. The assailant then faces a murder charge and the prospect of life imprisonment. It is purely a question of chance. Fortunately in this instance, Pete's x-ray was normal. Richard inserted a couple of stitches in the skin wound and the patient went home with the advice that he should keep better company in future. Not that it seemed likely that he would follow such advice!

Thereafter, Richard and Paul saw a variety of minor injuries, mainly cuts and bruises, though none connected with the derby football match that was being played less than a mile away and was destined to end in a goalless draw. At nine o'clock, Liz arrived to begin her first casualty duty. Paul was in the office snacking on tea and toast with the nursing staff but Liz did not go to join him. Instead she attracted Richard's attention, took him by the arm and led him into one of the patient cubicles. There they engaged in a long and earnest conversation; Liz looking wide-eyed and agitated, Richard doing his best to calm her. Ten minutes elapsed before Liz, looking very apprehensive, joined Paul. Whilst aware that she had made a poor start to her medical career and was clearly not a good team player, Paul was not unsympathetic to her situation. Having been qualified as a doctor for only a couple of weeks, she would be first 'on call' throughout the night for accidents and surgical emergencies for a population of approximately half a million people. Paul would work alongside her until the waiting room had been cleared, usually about one in the morning. Since there was only one bed in the department, he would then go to his room in the residency, leaving Liz on her own. If the flow of patients allowed, she would grab some sleep as and when she could. Paul would be able to join her within five minutes if she needed advice or assistance, but she faced a daunting challenging night. She was expected to commence the initial treatment of patients, some of whom might have life threatening injuries. Furthermore, in the event of a major road accident, multiple casualties might arrive with very little warning. Fortunately, she would be supported by some long-standing and extremely competent nurses. They were accustomed to working alongside new and inexperienced house officers and were always willing to advise and offer practical help. However they did not relish the first few weeks in August. Supervising the new recruits involved them in additional work and required extra vigilance.

"Hi, Liz." Paul greeted her in a manner that was somewhat more cheerful than he felt. "It's good to see you. I take it you gained some familiarity with the casualty department when you were a student?"

There was a long pause. "No I didn't."

Yet another disappointment, but since she had not bothered to learn how to scrub up in theatre either, Paul was not altogether surprised.

"Surely you were attached to one of the surgical units during your training?"

"Yes I was. Surgical Three."

"Did you never come to casualty when it was Surgical Three's admitting day?"

"No, I didn't know we had to."

Paul felt angry. As a student she had obviously been both lazy and foolish. Medical students, during their training, were attached to one of the surgical units for a ten-week period. Each unit was responsible for staffing the casualty department every fourth day. Attendance records were not kept, but since students graduated to be house officers, it was expected that they would take the opportunity to see all aspects of a houseman's work; not merely turn up for the short formal teaching sessions that were held in office hours on weekdays. Liz's failure to familiarise herself with life in casualty meant extra pressure for her and additional work for Paul.

"In that case," he said, barely managing to hide the irritation that he felt, "we'll start by seeing the first few cases together. It will give you a chance to meet the staff, to become familiar with the department and hopefully it will help you to settle in."

In his heart, however, he knew that this was wildly optimistic. With her lack of preparation, her ability to upset the nursing staff and her nervous disposition, it was inevitable that she would find casualty duties extremely tough. She had a long and difficult night ahead of her.

For the next two hours, Liz followed Paul round like a lost sheep. As they saw each patient, Paul took the history, performed the examination and explained how the patient was to be managed. Liz's only contribution was to record the consultation on the patient's casualty card. Frequently he invited her to ask questions but none were forthcoming. She was content simply to act as a scribe. One patient had a minor skin laceration and needed a couple of stitches. Liz was forced to admit that she had never inserted a skin suture during her training and this had to be demonstrated to her. Later in the evening, Paul suggested that she saw some patients on her own, but in every case, having recorded the history and examined the patient, she expected him to make the diagnosis and decide on management. Her lack of confidence and her inexperience worried him intensely. It was clear that she was simply not equipped for the task that lay before her. Partly this concern was selfish. As the next senior officer, Paul recognised that many nights of lost sleep awaited him as he covered her deficiencies.

At about eleven pm, it was a surprise to find that the nurses had placed three boys, all wearing United's colours, in a single cubicle. Paul was about to hustle two of them back to the waiting area, telling them that the cubicles were for patients, not for friends but it was as well that he didn't. It transpired that all three had been injured in the football stadium, where they had been treated by the St John's Ambulance Brigade, before being transferred to hospital by ambulance. Amazingly, they all had identical injuries to the wrist. Two of the lads had bandages on one wrist, but the third had strapping on both his wrists. Paul was fascinated to know how these injuries had been caused. The boys explained that to avoid their view of the match being obstructed by men standing in front of them, it was their custom to get to the ground early, and then to stand immediately behind the wall that separates the spectators on the terraces from the players on the pitch. At one particularly exciting moment in the match, the crowd behind them had surged forward and had tumbled down the steps of the terracing onto their backs, crushing them against the wall. They lads had been resting their hands on the top of the wall and their wrists had been forced backwards, over extending the joint. This was an intriguing mechanism of injury and Paul wondered whether it had been recognised previously. He made a mental note to research it in the medical library when time allowed. If it hadn't already been described, it might make an interesting report for an orthopaedic journal that would look good on his CV and improve his career prospects.

All the wrists were swollen, deformed and clearly broken, a fact that was confirmed on xray. The next step was to reduce the fractures under anaesthetic. But since the lads were not starved and the injuries did not require emergency treatment, their wrists were restrapped, they were given pain relief and told to re-attend with their parents the following morning.

No sooner had these three boys been sorted out, than another interesting patient arrived; one who was to prove the source of great merriment for the staff during the following week. Jimmy McMillan was a milkman from Glasgow, who had travelled south to attend his brother's wedding. A typical Scot, wiry of stature with a good head of red hair, he was extremely patriotic. He couldn't understand why his brother should want to take an English girl as his bride. He observed that there were more than enough pretty girls in Scotland that his brother could have married.

"I canna' understand the lad. There's many a bonny Scots lass that would have wed him. He'll nae be happy with a Sassenach wife, pretty though she may be. But he's made his own bed. He'll have to lie in it!"

Nonetheless, this had not stopped him enjoying the lunchtime reception that followed the marriage or the drinks that flowed freely thereafter. When the wedding festivities were over, Jimmy and a few of his mates had drifted to one of the local pubs and continued to celebrate late into the evening. Then disaster struck. He had been nursing a groin hernia[1] for several months, and was waiting to have it repaired at the Infirmary in Glasgow. He had been advised that should the rupture became painful or enlarged, he should lie down and ease the protruding swelling back into the abdominal cavity where it belonged. He had undertaken this manoeuvre successfully on a number of occasions but in recent weeks, the hernia had become increasingly troublesome and pushing it back had become more difficult. As a result, it had started to disrupt his job as a milkman and had necessitated some time off work. When the rupture had become painful after the wedding, he had foolishly ignored it. He had continued to celebrate with his friends, possibly because he was enjoying good company or, more likely, because the many pints of beer that he drunk had soothed the pain and caused him to forget his doctor's advice. Stand, sit or lie, he could not now persuade the swelling to return to the abdomen and he was in agony.

Standing scarcely five feet in height, Jimmy was slimly built with a jockey's physique. However, the most striking thing about his appearance was not his height or ginger locks, but his upper body. As a milkman he had physical job. It required upper body strength to load heavy crates onto the back of his milk float every morning but he also undertook weight training in the gym, and fought as an amateur boxer. His chest and shoulder muscles, especially his pectoral muscles, were remarkably well developed. He was proud of his physique and consequently wore his shirt with the top three buttons open, displaying his muscles to maximum effect. A thick gold chain bearing a large gold medallion encircled his neck, enhancing the appearance but most noticeable of all was his tattoo. Across his upper chest, in bold letters two inches tall, there was emblazoned a single word; '**CELTIC**'. It was a blessing that he had managed to avoid the marauding United and Rovers supporters who were still causing mayhem in the city!

Examination revealed no hint of any chest or heart trouble but this active young man did have one major health problem. He had a severe

---

[1] Hernia/rupture; a defect in the abdominal wall through which the contents of the abdomen protrude.

form of diabetes, a condition in which the blood sugar levels are raised due to a lack of the hormone insulin. Diabetes is a common ailment, the vast majority of sufferers having a mild form of the disease which develops in patients over the age of fifty. Treated with tablets and diet, it rarely causes major problems. The more severe form of the disease develops at a younger age and requires injections of insulin. There is a danger of unpleasant side effects, notably loss of consciousness, if the blood sugar rises too high or falls too low. Jimmy had a particularly nasty form of diabetes and needed to inject himself with large doses of insulin twice a day.

When Jimmy dropped his pants to allow Paul to examine him, the hernia was an impressive sight. The size of an orange, it was tense and painful. Jimmy clearly needed to be admitted, so Paul asked Liz to arrange for his transfer to the ward. She returned however with the news that there were no empty beds; Jimmy would have to stay in a casualty cubicle overnight. Paul assumed that Jimmy would have an emergency operation that night. That was the standard practice for such cases. But when he spoke with Victoria, she surprised him by suggesting that the surgery be deferred until the next day. She explained that his would have the advantage that the anaesthetic and surgery could be undertaken when the laboratory was open, making monitoring of Jimmy's blood sugar levels much easier. She also wanted to try one or two tricks to see if the hernia could be reduced without surgery. She asked Paul to sedate the patient, to relieve his pain, and then let him sleep on a couch with his head well below the level of his feet.

As the evening progressed, Paul continued to work alongside Liz but periodically slipped into Jimmy's cubicle to review the situation. On each occasion though, thanks to the sedative that he had been given and the beer that he had consumed, he was sleeping peacefully and snoring gently. By two thirty, with no patients waiting to be seen, it was time for Paul to return to the residency to try to get some sleep but before doing so, he took a final look at Jimmy and his rupture. Jimmy now chanced to be awake and Paul decided to try to reduce the hernia manually. Victoria's plan worked like a dream. With the patient now sedated, pain free and relaxed, the rupture slipped easily back into the abdomen. Jimmy was delighted and announced his intention to leave the department forthwith and to return to the accommodation that he and his pals had rented for the night. This course of action was clearly unwise. He had been sedated, his diabetes was poorly controlled and if he stayed at the City General, he could have his hernia repaired within the next couple of days. An intemperate Scot, Jimmy announced that he wasn't at all sure that he wanted *'to be cut by any old English surgeon'* saying that he preferred Mr Angus McDonald to operate on him in Glasgow. However when reminded that he was currently losing time off work, didn't know how quickly his hernia would be repaired in Glasgow and that in the meantime, he was at risk of further episodes of pain, he was persuaded to remain.

Although pint sized, Jimmy had a big personality. He was quick-witted, cheeky, even cocky at times. The nurses in casualty found it impossible to resist the temptation to chide him about the state of Scottish football. England had recently won the World Cup, and the impressive tattoo on his chest invited comment. But Jimmy was in no way abashed and defended his Celtic heroes vehemently.

"Aye," he said. "England may have done well in the World Cup but you watch out for Celtic in the next few years. You can keep your Arsenals, Tottenhams and Manchester Uniteds. Celtic will be beating them all within a couple of years. We've a new manager and a string of young players, all local lads; Tommy Gemmell, Billy McNeill and Jimmy Johnstone. Mark those names well; you'll hear a lot of them in the next few years. Two years ago, Celtic won every competition that they entered, and that included the European Cup. That's when I had this tattoo done on my chest. They're getting better season by season."

He stuck out his chest to display the tattoo in its full glory. "My father was a Celtic man before me, I shall be a Celtic man 'til the day I die and if I ever have kids, they will be Celtic supporters too."

"I thought Rangers were the only decent football team in Glasgow," Paul said to tease him. It would be an understatement to say that his response was uncharitable. It was in fact unprintable.

With the surgical cubicles and the waiting room finally empty, Liz and Paul sat with the nursing staff in the office, having a well-earned cup of tea and some hot buttered toast; the usual *'pick-me-up'* for weary hospital staff when matron was not around. Although tired, Paul was pleased that the evening shift had produced some interesting cases. Liz though was tense and anxious. They both knew that the time had come for Paul to depart, to leave her on her own to care for any patients who presented during the rest of the night. A bed was available for her in the department but Paul knew it was unlikely that she would sleep well. When he had been a house officer, he had found it extremely difficult to sleep when on duty in casualty. Unless absolutely exhausted, he would lie awake worrying whether he could cope with whatever emergency might arise. Then later, having attended to a patient, would find it impossible to sleep, his mind reflecting on his diagnosis and treatment, concerned that he had made some catastrophic mistake and that the patient would suffer, even die, as a result. Paul often felt that having a little more self confidence would give him greater peace of mind. But would that make him a better doctor? Surely a patient is better served by a doctor troubled by a degree of self doubt.

He reassured Liz that the nursing staff were very experienced, had seen numerous new house officers come and go, and that they would offer her every possible assistance. He also stressed that if she had any problems, she should call him; that it was better to call too often, than not to call when help was needed. With that he left her, walked through the empty corridors to the doctor's mess and bedded down in his own room, dreading to think how many times she would disturb him during the night. She would probably need advice about every single patient that attended! It seemed that he had hardly got to sleep when the telephone rang, though the clock on the bedside cabinet told him that forty minutes had elapsed since he had left the department. Logic suggested that it would be Liz, but it wasn't. It was the casualty sister, sounding concerned.

"Do you happen to know where Dr Webb is?" she asked.

"No I don't. I'm tucked up in bed and she's certainly not with me! Isn't she in casualty?"

"No, she's not. She seems to have disappeared."

"I suppose it's possible that she's been called to one of the wards, though the staff there ought to know that if they need a doctor tonight, they should call Richard."

"I've rung both the male and female wards and she's not there."

"Have you tried theatre?" Paul asked, though he knew full well that there was no earthly reason why she should be there.

"Yes, and I've tried her room as well. No one seems to know where she is."

"Have you got a doctor in casualty?"

"No, we haven't and obviously we must have one."

Paul groaned. Life on a surgical unit was tough enough when everyone was present and pulling their weight, but it would become a nightmare if members of the team went absent without leave.

"In that case, I suppose I shall have to come down, but please, do keep bleeping Liz. She must be somewhere in the hospital."

Arriving in casualty, Paul asked how Liz had seemed in the short time that she had been on her own.

"Well, we didn't see much of her. You remember that when you left, there were no patients waiting to be seen, so Dr Webb announced that she was going to go to sleep in the duty room. Shortly afterwards, when a patient arrived with a twisted ankle, we called her but she wasn't there. And the bed hasn't been slept in either. She must have slipped out of the department without anybody noticing. Goodness knows where she is now."

This was unacceptable. There were some circumstances when it was justifiable to leave the department when on duty, but to disappear without informing anybody was unforgivable. Paul realised with dismay that the only available solution was for him to complete the night shift on Liz's behalf. Quickly he arranged for the patient with the ankle injury to be strapped, told him to return in the morning for an x-ray and then, furious with Liz, he bedded down in the hot and airless room that was allocated for the casualty doctor. As it happened, he slept reasonably well, only being disturbed once to see a drunk with a head injury who felt the sharp edge of his tongue. He merely required observation by the nurses until he could be properly assessed, when the effects of the alcohol had worn off.

The next morning, after a refreshing shower and a quick breakfast, Paul hurried to the ward in time for Mr Potts' round. Mo had already completed his own review of the patients, checking to ensure that their progress was satisfactory and that there had been no change in their condition during the night. It was a matter of personal pride that he was always well informed about the patients. He hated his boss to identify a problem that he had overlooked, and with Mr Potts' unpredictable nature, and his habit of berating his junior colleagues in front of the patients and nurses alike, Mo was keen to have all the relevant facts and figures at his fingertips.

At 9.30 the medical team were waiting for Mr Potts to arrive when Liz walked in. This was a different house officer to the one they had known previously. Gone were the bright lipstick, eye shadow and the rose tinted cheeks. Gone too, Paul noticed with some satisfaction, were her high-heeled shoes. Without any of her usual make up and with her hair seemingly unbrushed, she no longer looked the glamorous young model. She looked tired and worn. Polite greetings were exchanged and then Paul waited, expecting an explanation for Liz's absence from casualty the night before, but none was forthcoming. It became obvious that Paul would have to broach the subject himself.

"The Casualty Sister contacted me last night, Liz, because you disappeared from the department. She was left without any medical staff and she had no idea where you were."

"Yes. I'm sorry about that Paul but I was taken ill. I developed a migraine."

"But Sister rang your room and there was no reply. She couldn't find you anywhere."

"I'm afraid I was too ill to answer the phone."

This was not acceptable. If a member of staff, for whatever reason, was unable to perform their duties, they had a responsibility to arrange cover, or if that was not possible, to let somebody know of the problem. Paul looked to Mo for support and guidance.

"Look Dr Webb," Mo said gently but firmly. "I'm sorry if you were unwell, I trust you have now recovered but if for any reason, any reason at all, you need to go off duty, you must let someone know. It's a question of patient safety."

"But I was genuinely ill," protested Liz.

"Maybe, but I doubt that you were too ill to inform Sister or to make a single telephone call to Paul," countered Mo. Liz looked sullen but did not comment further.

There could be no doubt that the life of a house officer was difficult. The hours were long, the duties exacting, the responsibilities a burden. Looking back, Paul remembered all too well, times when he had doubted his ability to complete the six-month term. There had been occasions when quitting the job had seemed an attractive option. Staffing levels were thin; there was very little slack in the system. If someone went on holiday or was absent through sickness, the workload did not slacken, it merely fell on the shoulders of the rest of the team. Paul suspected that this might not be the only time that Liz, for whatever reason, would be unable to complete her duties. It was obvious that she was not coping and he decided to discuss the matter with Mr Potts at the end of the round.

Further debate was forestalled by Mr Potts' arrival and the ward round commenced without delay. The consultant round was by far the most important part of the weekly ward routine. This was the time when each patient's clinical problems were discussed and definitive decisions made on their management. Which investigation will lead to the correct diagnosis? Should the patient be treated with medication, or with surgery? And if surgery is required, which operation is likely to yield the best results? For the round to be efficient and effective, the consultant needs to have access to all the information upon which these decisions are based and it was the responsibility of the junior staff to have all this data to hand.

It was customary for one of the juniors to introduce each patient to the consultant. If Sir William were conducting the round, he would listen to his trainee's account, but then take time to question the patient for himself, hearing their story in their own words. He also performed his own clinical examination. This personal attention was much appreciated by the patients, though not by the medical staff who often felt that their own assessments were not trusted. Sir William would then explain the situation to the patient in great detail. For the junior doctors, who had heard the same explanations many times previously, this was frustrating since they all had a multitude of jobs waiting for them when the consultant's round was finished. By contrast, Mr Potts made his decisions based entirely on the information that had been presented to him by his junior staff and accordingly it was vital that this was absolutely accurate and correct.

On this occasion, because Liz had been absent from the preliminary round, Mo volunteered to present the cases. Mr Potts was in his usual brusque mood. He didn't spend more than two minutes with any patient. Helen Seddon, who had made an excellent recovery from the operation to relieve her bowel obstruction, *was* dismissed with a single sentence: *"we will see you in the clinic in four weeks"*. The only patient that Paul introduced to Mr Potts was Jimmy. Having been involved in his care through the night, he was the one most familiar with his condition. Paul suggested that the rupture should be repaired during his present admission, to prevent any chance of another painful episode such as the one that had occurred at his brother's wedding. Mr Potts only comment was *'right'*. Although Jimmy was sitting with his pyjama jacket widely unbuttoned, flaunting his gold medallion, his rippling pectoral muscles and his CELTIC tattoo, Mr Potts made no comment, much to Jimmy's disappointment. As he commented afterwards, *'I thought it was we Scots that were supposed to be the dour ones.'* The entire ward round was completed in less than forty minutes and at no stage did Mr Potts exchange more than a handful of words with any of his patients.

When the round was over, it was customary for the team, together with the ward sister, to retire to the office to discuss any problem cases over a drink, out of earshot of the patients. This allowed a more open discussion than was deemed possible at the bedside and was helpful and educational for the junior surgeons. On this occasion though, Mr Potts did not enter the office, but remained in the corridor outside.

"Aren't you coming in for a cup of tea or a biscuit, Mr Potts?" Sister asked.

"Not today, thank you, Sister." he replied. Then turning to Liz he said, "My secretary tells me that you wanted to have a word with me."

"Yes please Mr Potts, if that's convenient."

"Of course it is, my dear. I have to say you do look a little tired. I hope Khan and Lambert haven't been working you too hard."

"I confess I do feel very tired, Sir. Indeed that is what I'd like to talk to you about," she replied, with a *'please come to my rescue – I'm a helpless female'* look on her face.

"Well come and have a coffee with me in my office and we'll see what can be arranged."

With that, he put his arm across Liz's shoulder and guided her down the corridor. Richard looked on grim faced, clearly not appreciating the consultant's familiar attitude towards his fiancée, whilst Mo and Paul exchanged glances, wondering what the outcome of their meeting would be. It was obvious that Liz was not coping with the workload and needed some support. But would she admit that she had deserted the casualty department in the middle of the night? Would Mr Potts offer her guidance and advice as to how to manage the workload better? Would he appoint an extra pair of hands to give her some assistance, or would Mo, Victoria and Paul be expected to undertake extra duties? They were soon to find out.

Chapter Eight

Jimmy was entirely at ease on the ward whilst waiting for his operation. He settled into the hospital routine without difficulty, never missing an opportunity to 'chat up' the nurses, with whom he became quite a favourite. He even tried, albeit unsuccessfully, to charm Sister Ashbrook. Since there was no reason for him to be confined to his bed, he took it upon himself to undertake his own ward rounds. He thoroughly enjoyed talking to the other patients, criticizing whichever team they happened to support, belittling English football in general and regaling anyone prepared to listen, of the exploits of his beloved Celtic football team. He was constantly cheerful, with an outgoing and optimistic personality. He made himself useful by helping the nurses to serve meals to bed bound patients, and happily assisted in tidying away the trays and dishes afterwards. He ran errands for less mobile patients, even slipping out of the hospital from time to time to visit the local betting shop on their behalf.

The day arrived when Paul was scheduled to assist Mr Potts as he performed a list that included Jimmy's hernia repair. Jimmy had objected violently when instructed to remove the gold chain and medallion that were so prominently displayed round his neck. He had only agreed when it was explained to him that the diathermy machine, which was used during surgery to coagulate bleeding vessels, applied an electric current to the body, which would cause a burn at the site of his chain. This would not only be painful but would also cause a scar and disfigure his tattoo.

Paul met Mo in the theatre at 8.30 ready to start the mornings operating list. For most surgeons, it is the time spent in theatre that they find particularly enjoyable, and as Paul became more experienced and his technical ability developed, he too gained the greatest satisfaction from operating. He was very conscious of course, that operating on a fellow human being was a huge responsibility. The patients have entrusted themselves to the surgeon. They rely on his knowledge of anatomy, his understanding of their disease, his experience and his manual dexterity to treat them in an intensely personal way. The surgeon must be meticulous in everything he does, since his skill, or lack of it, determines the patient's outcome. A successful operation can save a patient's life. Failure may lead to his death. Intense concentration is required throughout the procedure. Paul was also beginning to appreciate that when operating, a surgeon may experience a wide spectrum of emotions. If an operation went well, he could be filled with a sense of satisfaction and pride. But should the outcome for the patient be unfavourable, which he knew could occur from time to time even in the best surgical hands; he could experience self-deprecation, even guilt and be rewarded with yet more sleepless nights. There was much truth in the old surgical adage that 'a surgeon needs the eye of a hawk, the hands of a lady and the heart of a lion'.

When Mr Potts arrived to start a list of operations, he liked the first patient to be anaesthetised, with the abdomen already opened. He was not particularly interested in the routine of opening and closing a wound. He wanted everything to be ready for him to perform the detailed intra-abdominal part of the procedure. Entering the Surgical Five theatre was like taking a step back in time. The Middleton Hospital, where Paul had worked previously, had a brand new, purpose built theatre suite, shared by all the surgical teams in the hospital. Within the suite, there were four theatres, each with a marble floor, tiled walls and stainless steel 'scrub up' unit. Each had a huge, circular, state of the art 'theatre lamp' over a modern, electrically operated, theatre table. By contrast, Surgical Five's theatre was archaic; a museum piece. It had changed little in the 70 years since it had been built. It was cramped; the walls a kaleidoscope of colours where the plaster and paint work had been patched on numerous occasions. The table was adjusted manually, by metal handles that projected from the sides at odd angles. There were several pieces of adhesive tape, of various shapes and sizes, on its rubber mattress, evidence of the financial necessity to repair, rather than replace.

Paul and Mo were scrubbing their hands at the sink in preparation for the first case, an operation to remove the gall bladder of an elderly lady called Phyllis Stephenson, when Mr Potts put his nose around the theatre door. He was wearing his city suit and shoes; not setting the best example to junior nurses and doctors! Sister frowned but felt unable to make any comment. Mr Potts caught her expression, knew exactly what had caused it, but just smiled at her and said "Good morning, Sister dear," in his most charming voice. Then he called across to Paul.

"Lambert, is Dr Webb here?"

"No Sir."

"That's good. I'd like to have a quick word with you before she arrives."

Paul stepped back from the scrub up unit, dried his hands on a paper towel and joined Mr Potts in the changing room. In every theatre in which he had ever worked, there had always been two changing rooms. How the female changing area was arranged he had no idea, but the male changing room was always communal. As a trainee, he found it disconcerting to see his consultant boss undressing, but had yet to meet a surgeon who was in the slightest way bashful. The memory of one rather short, fat and hairy surgeon for whom he worked at the Middleton was indelibly printed on his mind. The surgeon was an excellent and enthusiastic teacher but the only one who insisted that all personnel should change all their clothes, even their underwear, before entering the theatre. Paul recalled being instructed at length on surgical technique whilst the consultant stood stark naked, his arms flailing like the conductor of a symphony orchestra, other appendages wafting in unison, as he emphasised the various points he was making. Paul remembered the episode vividly; though has long forgotten what he was being taught at the time!

"Ah Lambert," Mr Potts said. "There you are. I've a little favour to ask of you."

Paul had a premonition of what was about to be suggested and unfortunately was not mistaken.

"Dr Webb seems to be having a little difficulty settling in. She seems to be struggling with the workload and I thought you might like to help her out."

There was a pause, but as before, Paul knew exactly what was coming and once again his instinct proved correct.

"She seems to be finding the accident room duties particularly difficult. I wondered if you could see your way to cover her for the time being."

"You mean working alongside her to show her the ropes, Sir."

"No, I mean taking her place, deputising for her so that she can catch up with her sleep. The poor girl seems dead on her feet."

Mr Potts had asked politely enough, but they both knew that Paul was not in a position to say 'no', even though he would have been within his rights to do so. Being first 'on call' for casualty was the houseman's task. It was not in Paul's job description. But as his consultant, Mr Potts was all-powerful. He held Paul's future career in his hands. If Paul declined to help, he could say goodbye to continuing his surgical training.

"Perhaps an alternative would be to appoint a short term locum, Sir?" Paul suggested, more in hope than in expectation.

"That might be possible," Mr Potts replied thoughtfully, "but it would be an additional expense. We would struggle to get a suitable candidate and whoever was appointed would not be as familiar with the unit as you are. Don't worry; it shouldn't be for too long."

"And just how long will this arrangement last?" Paul asked.

"I'm not sure. We will have to see how it goes and see how Liz copes."

Whilst enlisting Paul's assistance, Mr Potts' voice had been quiet, his manner considerate, but now he reverted to his normal forthright tone. "Well, Lambert, I think you had better get back to join Khan in theatre. He will be needing an assistant. Thank you for agreeing to help."

It was clear that the conversation was at an end and that Paul was dismissed. He hadn't actually agreed to cover Liz's casualty duties. His agreement had simply been assumed. Resentful and angry, he returned to the theatre, scrubbed up and joined Mo at the table. Mo had already opened the abdomen and was waiting patiently, his arms across his chest, for the boss to arrive.

"Is Mr Potts coming?" he asked.

"He's just changing," Paul said bitterly. "He'll be here in a minute," and sure enough Mr Potts breezed in.

On the ward, Mr Potts was dour and taciturn, a man of few words. He conducted his ward rounds quickly, scarcely speaking to his patients at all, making it necessary for the junior doctors to return later to communicate the decisions that had been made. But in theatre, he came to life. He was the leading player, the star of the show. When operating he became expansive, verbose and indeed 'theatrical'. Not for him the shapeless green cotton 'pyjamas' worn by the rest of the staff. He wore a tailored, blue cotton suit, tied a white crepe bandage around his head to act as a sweatband, and wore one of the newly designed surgeon's lamps, a modification of the original miner's lamp, on his forehead. Paul envied him his confidence, although he knew from having worked with him before, that occasionally his self-assurance was misplaced. Different surgeons operate at different speeds. Sir William was slow, methodical and excessively cautious, checking and double-checking every stage of an operation but despite his slight tremor, he was an extremely safe surgeon. By contrast, Mr Potts was much faster. He was actually technically superior to his senior colleague, but once or twice, Paul had seen him get into trouble, causing unnecessary bleeding when he had been a little over confident, or perhaps a little too casual, when dealing with a large blood vessel. He had always retrieved the situation satisfactorily, but for a moment there had been anxiety in his voice, and the reason for his sweatband had become apparent. In the event that Paul needed an operation, and be in a position to choose his surgeon, he would have selected neither of the consultant surgeons but the senior registrar, Mo Khan. Paul had seen him perform numerous operations and had the greatest admiration for his surgical ability. Anatomical structures were always clearly displayed and blood loss was kept to a minimum. All procedures were performed meticulously and even though there never appeared to be any haste, all were completed in good time. Paul found it educational to note the differences in technique between the three surgeons, but it was Mohammed that Paul tried to emulate.

When Mr Potts entered the theatre, there was a subtle change in the atmosphere. Prior to his appearance, the staff had been working conscientiously but in a relaxed fashion. No one was being casual, everyone had been performing their duties correctly, but they were at ease with themselves and with the other members of the team. The arrival of the boss introduced an edge that had not been there previously. The occasional conversation and repartee between staff lapsed, everyone being careful not to do anything, or say anything, that might upset Mr Potts for they knew that his cheerful, effervescent mood could change abruptly.

"Right," said Mr Potts. "What have we got here? I see you have the gall bladder nicely exposed and the guts tucked out of the way, Khan. Nothing else of note in the rest of the abdomen, I suppose?"

"No Sir. I've had a good look round and all the other organs appear to be healthy."

"Fine, then let's tackle the gall bladder. It looks a bit angry. She's obviously had a lot of trouble with these gallstones over the years."

At this moment, Liz walked into the theatre and started to scrub up. She was displaying her charms to maximum effect, having selected a surgeon's shirt that was a couple of sizes too small for her, rather than the utilitarian smock that the nurses wore. But with three surgeons already present, a further assistant was completely unnecessary. Indeed it would make life more difficult for the nursing sister who, with more bodies around the table, would have greater difficulty passing instruments to Mr Potts.

"I don't think that we need another pair of hands Liz," Mo said.

"Nonsense," Mr Potts interjected. "The more the merrier. It will be useful for her to see some gallstones and it will help her to understand the patient's symptoms. Reading about surgery in textbooks is no substitute for seeing it in practice."

Although this was undoubtedly true, Paul's mood darkened. Only ten minutes before, Mr Potts had asked him to undertake Liz's casualty shifts, to prevent her from becoming overtired. Yet now he was wasting her time in theatre, when her duties lay on the ward. She wasn't scheduled to come to theatre. Paul wondered whether she had come of her own accord, or whether Mr Potts had specifically requested her attendance. If so, it was inconsiderate. There was no one else to perform the ward work for her; those tasks would simply be waiting for her when she finished in theatre. If she wasted a couple of hours in the morning watching Mr Potts operate, she would simply finish work two hours later than was necessary in the evening.

Seeing Liz arrive, Sister immediately directed a member of her staff to ensure that she scrubbed up satisfactorily, which fortunately she did. Gowned and gloved, she approached the operating theatre table, unsure what she should do, or where she should stand.

"Ah ha," said Mr Potts. "Here's the lovely lady. Come and stand next to me Liz, then you will get a good view of the master at work. It isn't every day that you get the chance to stand at God's right hand. Lambert, you go round and stand next to Khan. Liz, come a bit closer, then you'll see exactly what's going on. If there's anything you don't understand just ask. I'll be pleased to explain."

The operation recommenced. Mr Potts identified the duct which carries bile to the duodenum, and then divided the artery which supplies blood to the gall bladder. He was in a buoyant mood and started chatting as he worked.

"I see from the newspaper that there was a little trouble after the derby football match recently, Lambert. Did we treat many of the casualties here?"

"Yes, we did," Paul said, and took the opportunity to describe the lads whose wrist injuries he had treated. He asked if Mr Potts thought the cases might be worth reporting in one of the surgical journals.

"Yes, I think they would," he said. "It's interesting, it's topical and the editors are always looking for light-hearted articles that make easy reading. How would you plan to go about it?"

"Well I thought I would investigate whether such injuries have occurred previously, when there have been local derby matches. That would tell us whether such injuries were common or not. It would mean reviewing the records of people who had attended casualty on the days when there had been large crowds at football matches."

"Excellent. Do that and let me know what you learn. I'll help you to write the article, if you like."

"That's very kind of you Sir," Paul said appreciatively. Since he had little experience of writing articles for learned journals, Mr Potts experience would be invaluable.

"I wonder if such injuries occur at rugby matches," mused Mr Potts.

"That would mean searching through the records of hospitals which are situated near to rugby grounds," Paul said. "We don't have large attendances at rugby matches here."

"True," said Mr Potts, "mores the pity. Spectators who follow rugby are totally different characters to the aggressive thugs who watch football. I really can't see why people get so excited about soccer; rugby's the real game you know."

"Did you used to play, Sir?" asked Liz.

"Yes, my dear, I did. I've always enjoyed sport; athletics, rugby and now golf." He nodded at the anaesthetist. "Tom Lester and I both play golf regularly, though I usually get the better of him. I had a lesson from the club professional the other day. He adjusted my grip a fraction, to correct the slight fade that I had developed. I'll hit the ball even further now." To Sister's annoyance, he helped himself to a pair of long handled forceps from her tray, took half a step backwards and demonstrated his new grip and swing, narrowly missing the large theatre lamp situated above the table as he did so.

Sister scowled. "Perhaps you would be kind enough to hand that instrument back to me," she said, severely, unable to keep the tone of reproof from her voice.

Mr Potts winked at the anaesthetist. "Come, come, Sister," he said. "Relax. Just having a bit of fun," then, returning to the table and to his original theme, he added, "fortunately, I seem to be a natural sportsman and I do keep myself fairly fit."

Not true, Paul thought. Although of stocky build, he might well have been quite athletic as a young man, but Paul had observed him in the changing room. Mr Potts had clearly put on an inch or two around his waist in recent years.

"Now Liz," he said, addressing the houseman as he grasped her hand and guided it into the surgical wound, "the gall bladder is a little freer now and if you squeeze it carefully, you can actually feel the gall stones within it."

Liz fingered the gall bladder delicately.

"Oh, how thrilling," she remarked, her eyelashes fluttering above her surgical mask.

"Right," said Mr Potts. "We'll just whip the gall bladder out and we shall be through." Then, reverting to his previous topic of conversation, he added, "I used to play cricket as well to a good amateur standard. I was always a clean striker of the ball." Paul saw Sister place both her hands protectively across her surgical tray, obviously afraid that Mr Potts was about to demonstrate his prowess with another of the instruments. "By the end of the season, I was usually top of the batting averages. In the good old days, when I was training in London, there was a 'Juniors versus Consultants' cricket match every summer. I always managed to score plenty of runs. It was great fun and the nurses used to enjoy watching their heroes at play. I bowled quite well too -

took the wicket of my consultant chief once. As I remember, it was a fast straight ball that knocked his middle stump right out of the ground. He didn't like that at all. The following year, I thought it wise to bowl him some gentle deliveries to feed him a few soft runs before I took his wicket." He laughed heartily at the memory. His junior staff smiled politely behind their masks.

The germ of an idea entered Paul's head.

"Do you think the consultants here could raise a team, Sir?" he asked.

"You mean a match against the residents? That sounds like a challenge. What an excellent idea." Mr Potts thought for a moment. "I suspect we could raise six or seven and we could rope in a few of the local GP's to make up the numbers. But certainly, if you arrange it, we'll take you on. We shall be far too strong for you of course. But we'll happily give you a quick thrashing to keep you in your places," he added with a grin.

As he spoke, he freed the gall bladder from the liver, lifted it out of the abdomen, and held it aloft, like a team captain holding up the winner's trophy.

"Mrs Stephenson will be a new woman without those gallstones. It will make her feel ten years younger."

"Catch, Sister," he said and with a flamboyant flourish, threw it to Sister, failing to notice the few drops of bile that splashed down the front of her gown and the angry look on her face. Sister though, caught the gallblader neatly in the kidney dish that she had been holding in anticipation.

"Did you see that, Lambert. There's a good slip fielder there if you should need one."

With the part of the operation that interested him now complete, he turned to his senior registrar. "Right Khan, I want you to come with me to the medical wards. Apparently, there's a man there with a swelling in his armpit that the physicians want us to sort out. You might as well come too Liz, since he will probably end up on our ward within a day or two. Close up for me Lambert, and don't forget to put a drain down to the site of the gall bladder. If she gets a collection of blood or bile in the abdomen, I shall blame you," he added with a laugh.

For the last half hour, there had been too many surgeons at the table. But with the departure of Mr Potts, Mo and Liz, there were now too few; Paul having been left to close the abdomen on his own. Fortunately Sister understood his dilemma and offered to assist, in addition to performing her duties as the scrub nurse. As instructed, Paul placed a soft rubber tube to act as a drain, so that any ooze of blood or bile that occurred after the wound was closed would be led to the surface. If fluid was allowed to collect in the abdomen, it usually caused a serious infection. Then he sutured the muscle layers, the subcutaneous fat layer and finally the skin before applying a dressing to cover the wound.

"Mr Potts seems to have taken a shine to his new house officer," Sister remarked, no doubt aware of the consultant's reputation as a ladies' man.

Paul smiled. "Yes, he does, although I suspect she is well able to take care of herself. In any case, she's engaged to Richard, the other house officer. No doubt he will be there to protect her if necessary."

"So Richard's engaged is he?" Sister inquired. "That's going to disappoint a couple of my nurses."

The next patient on the list was Jimmy McMillan, the Glaswegian milkman. Although Paul hadn't specifically been asked to perform his operation, it was clear that this was what Mr Potts expected. Not that this caused Paul any concern. Thanks to his training at the Middleton Hospital, he had performed many hernia repairs, albeit under supervision, with someone more senior at his side.

In principle, learning to operate is similar to learning to drive a car. Firstly, the driver has to know the local geography and plan the route to his destination. He may use a map as a guide. The map for the surgeon is Gray's definitive textbook of anatomy, comprising 1500 closely typed pages of anatomical detail but whereas driving on a road is two-dimensional, the surgeon operates in three dimensions. When a road and a railway intersect, the driver is not required to remember which crosses over the top of the other, but where two or three anatomical structures meet, the surgeon does need to know which one lies in front and which behind. The learner driver has to find the correct line to take when approaching a roundabout or a right turn and similarly, the surgeon needs to learn, through tuition and practice how to avoid the blood vessels and nerves that stand in his way, damage to which could leave his patient with a permanent disability. On the roads, the motorist has signposts and street names to direct him to his destination but the surgeon is not so fortunate. Textbooks of anatomy illustrate arteries in red, veins in blue and nerves in yellow, but in reality, they are not colour coded and the surgeon has to identify these structures by their texture, position and shape.

The driver has to anticipate dangers that he may encounter along the way; the child hidden behind the parked car, or the elderly wobbling cyclist. Similarly the surgeon needs to be aware of potential hazards, particularly the dangers posed when structures do not lie in their natural position, perhaps due to a congenital abnormality, or when appearances are altered by disease or vital structures are obscured by scar tissue. When his landmarks have been obliterated, the surgeon must allow extra time and be especially cautious, like the motorist when driving in fog when the visibility is poor.

Thanks to his training, Paul felt ready, indeed pleased, to accept the challenge of performing Jimmy's operation on his own. He knew that if, by chance, he encountered a problem, Victoria and Mo were both in the hospital and would willingly come to assist. There was however, an extra factor to consider. Jimmy was a severe diabetic and as such, was subject to an increased risk of infection. Infection, either in the wound, or more seriously within the abdomen, would cause pain and delay Jimmy's discharge from hospital. Paul's dissection would need to be meticulous and maintaining sterility was vital. He knew that it would not be wise for him to operate without an assistant, and with considerable reluctance, he 'bleeped' Richard. Liz was with Mr Potts seeing a patient on the medical ward and if Richard came to theatre neither of the house officers would be tackling the workload on the ward. It would make a long hard day for the housemen even longer.

In the few weeks since he had joined the unit, Paul had come to like Richard. He was a conscientious, easy going and uncomplaining young man. He worked hard, often doing more than his fair share of the house officer's duties, as he covered for Liz, with whom he seemed besotted, though for the life of him, Paul couldn't understand why. Paul considered that she was manipulative; someone who expected her good looks and fine figure to open doors for her and ease her way in life. He thought that she would be more at home as a debutante working the London society scene, looking for a benevolent millionaire to marry, than working as a junior hospital doctor. She appeared to be out of place and out of her depth on a busy surgical unit. Richard also had a boyish sense of humour and when the theatre nurses saw and commented on Jimmy's impressive tattoo, Richard smiled. "I think we could have some fun with that," he said.

At the time, Paul was too busy preparing himself for the challenge of Jimmy's operation to seek clarification of Richard's intentions, though these became all too obvious during the next couple of days. Fortunately the procedure went as planned and no particular problems were encountered. Paul found the defect in the muscles through which the hernia had protruded, he was able to close it with strong sutures and, fifty minutes later, he was applying a dressing to the wound.

Whilst undertaking the surgery, concentrating intently, he had been a member of a close knit team of anaesthetists, nurses and technicians, all working with a common aim. He had enjoyed the experience. His previous anger that Mr Potts expected him to perform Liz's casualty duties had vanished, to be replaced by a tremendous sense of satisfaction. Jimmy had experienced a great deal of discomfort from his hernia. It had interfered with his job, and the episode that had resulted in his admission to hospital, had been life threatening. Provided that he now made a good postoperative recovery, he would be cured and it had been Paul's involvement, working as part of a skilled professional team that had achieved this. The warm glow induced by successfully completing an operation was like a drug; it was addictive. Paul was aware of course, that surgery could induce other emotions. There were times when concerns over his own ability and limited experience caused him anxiety. But he was still at a stage when he was able to call for assistance if problems arose. It was reassuring to know that the final responsibility for the patient was not his. He often wondered though, what it must feel like to be the consultant, the most senior member of the team, the one who 'carried the can'.

As the theatre sheets were removed, Jimmy's tattooed chest was once again exposed and as he was lifted onto a trolley and wheeled to the recovery area, Richard followed, a twinkle in his eye.

"I'm just going to have a look at that tattoo," he said over his shoulder.

Paul walked back to the 'scrub up' area to take off his gloves and remove the gown that was held in place by tapes tied down the back. As often as not, one of the nurses would assist with this, particularly if one of the ties had become knotted. As Paul pulled off his gloves and threw them into the bin, he felt the ties being loosened and a gentle hand was laid on his shoulder. A quiet voice spoke.

"Hello Paul."

It was a voice that he immediately recognised; a voice that made his heart jump, a voice that brought wonderful memories flooding into his mind. He turned, half in and half out of his theatre gown.

"Kate," he said, surprise and delight in his voice. Instinctively, he reached out and for a second held both her hands in his. Then, just as quickly, he released them, aware that the action was inappropriate, that they were in company.

"I'm so pleased to see you," he stuttered. It was the most enormous understatement. Not a day had passed in the last two years when he had not thought of her, had not wished that she were still at his side, had not regretted that they had drifted apart. Without conscious thought, he glanced at her left hand. There was no ring and again his heart jumped. For a moment he was elated. Then reality brought him crashing back to earth. Nurses were not allowed to wear rings, indeed not allowed to wear any jewellery at all when on duty, especially in theatre. The absence of a ring held no significance whatsoever.

"Where on earth did you spring from?" he asked.

"I've been back in the hospital for a couple of months now. Matron agreed to let me complete my training here. I've been working on the medical wards, but I started in theatre yesterday."

A hundred thoughts raced through Paul's head. When last he had heard, Kate was engaged to a young farmer called Peter. Was she still engaged? Perhaps she was now married.

"I had no idea that you were back at the hospital," he said, "What a lovely surprise." This was another huge understatement. His every instinct was to sweep her into his arms and hug her.

"I heard you had returned to the City General and hoped we would meet." Her voice was quiet and sincere.

Seeing her again reminded Paul of all the good times that they had spent together. She was gentle, kind and considerate. When he was with her, he felt at ease and content with the world. She soothed him when he was tired and irritable, cheered him when he was down. She gave him the confidence to believe in himself. When she was at his side, he felt ten feet tall. When they had worked together on the wards, he had admired her calm unhurried manner and her ability to put patients at ease, with a smile here and a gentle word there. At weekends they had climbed high mountains in the Lake District, gazed together at the panorama of fields and lakes laid out below them and then shared quiet evenings in cosy country pubs. And all the while, he had thought that this was the girl he would marry, the girl with whom he would share his life. But then they had parted; Kate to return home to care for her sick mother, Paul to continue with his surgical training with its demanding, impossibly long hours.

"Perhaps we could have a drink together, catch up on old times." he said.

"I should like that," Kate replied, "I should like that a lot." Her words were spoken with genuine feeling and filled him with hope.

The theatre sister, ever watchful, observed them chatting.

"Nurse Meredith," she called, not unkindly. "The morning list is over. We need to prepare for Sir William's list this afternoon. The theatre table needs cleaning, the floor needs mopping and the laundry skip needs emptying."

Paul wanted to reach out and embrace Kate, but of course he couldn't. Instead he turned and walked to the surgeon's room to write an account of the operation in Jimmy's notes, but there was a lively spring in his stride and his pulse was racing.

Was she free to resume their relationship? Did she have the feelings for him that he still had for her? Or was she now a married woman? Paul desperately needed to know how things stood between them and resolved to meet with her at the first possible opportunity.

Chapter Nine

After his operation Jimmy was confined to his bed, to prevent any strain being placed on the sutures that had been used to repair his rupture. When Paul went to review him, he was surprised to find a gaggle of nurses at his bedside. He went to investigate. He wanted to make sure that there wasn't a problem, either with the operation that he had performed or with Jimmy's diabetes. However, the nurses appeared relaxed; indeed they were teasing him about his Glaswegian football team. Jimmy was enjoying being the centre of attention. He was sitting in bed, his pyjama jacket unbuttoned as usual, displaying his fine physique; the gold chain and medallion having been restored to their rightful place alongside the tattoo of which he was so proud.

On closer inspection, the cause of the nurses' good humour was apparent. Whilst Jimmy had been anaesthetized, somebody, Paul presumed it to be Richard, had used an indelible marker pen and had taken liberties with the tattoo. Unable to see the upper part of his own chest, Jimmy was happily oblivious to Richard's handiwork. The result of the alteration was undeniably amusing but Paul felt a twinge of anxiety. Mr Potts was not known for his sense of humour. He held traditional views about a patient's right to be treated with respect and dignity. There could be unpleasant consequences if he took exception to this light-hearted prank.

Over the next couple of days, the tattoo caused much amusement and, as a result, Jimmy became something of a celebrity. The ward staff commented on it whenever they gave him his meals or dressed his wound, as did other therapists, such as dieticians and physiotherapists. As word of the tattoo spread on the hospital grapevine, porters went out of their way to pass by Jimmy's bed, to chat to him about the Celtic football team, but nobody informed him that his tattoo had been compromised. Jimmy loved his football. He knew a great deal about English clubs, including the two first division sides in the city, and there was much genial banter about the relative merits of teams north and south of the border. However the conspiracy of silence amongst all who spoke with him continued and he lapped up the attention, in complete ignorance of the real reason for the interest in Celtic.

When the time came for the next consultant ward round, there was a general concern that Mr Potts might *let the cat out of the bag* and that if he did, Jimmy, despite his good nature, would not be amused. He might prove to have a short Scottish fuse and cause a scene or make a formal complaint. In particular, Mo was anxious that Mr Potts might consider that making one of his patients the butt of a joke was disrespectful, that Richard would be punished, and that he, as the most senior of the 'junior' doctors, would be reprimanded for allowing the matter to continue.

When Mr Potts arrived, Mo took the opportunity to remind him of the Scottish milkman whom he had met a few days earlier; the one who had been reluctant to entrust himself to an English surgeon. He proceeded to confess that liberties had been taken with the tattoo that the young man sported on his chest and that, to date, the patient was unaware that an alteration had been made. Mr Potts listened carefully, but did not ask in what way the tattoo had been changed, nor did he request the name of the individual responsible. However frowning ominously, he gravely reminded the team of their responsibilities, stating that all patients should be treated with the respect that they would expect themselves if the situation were reversed. He said that he would have to see the tattoo before deciding what action to take and declined to give an assurance that he would not inform the patient that the tattoo had been altered,

In due course the team arrived at Jimmy's bed. Jimmy had his pyjama jacket open to the waist as usual. Although Mr Potts could not have failed to see Richard's graffiti, he made no comment upon it but, in a manner unfamiliar to him, he enquired diligently about the patient's progress. He inspected the wound and even looked at the diabetic chart that had been kept to check that Jimmy's sugar levels were satisfactory.

Diabetes was monitored according to the level of sugar in the urine. A sample was tested every four hours and a variable amount of insulin was prescribed; the greater the concentration of sugar in the urine, the larger the dose of insulin injected. The disadvantage of this method was that the urine could have rested in the patient's bladder for several hours. Thus, the amount of insulin given was linked to the sugar level at the time the urine was formed, not when it was passed. This meant that there were some occasions when the dose of insulin injected was not appropriate for the current requirements. Fortunately Jimmy's chart showed that his diabetes was well controlled, so Mr Potts instructed that Jimmy be allowed to return to his normal diet and to his usual daily insulin injections. He then addressed the patient.

"I'm pleased to see you're making good progress but you will need to stay with us for a little while until you become mobile. I'll review you again in a couple of days and decide when you can go home. All in all though, you are making a good recovery"

"Aye Doctor," Jimmy replied. "We have good healing flesh north of the border."

Paul was reminded of one of Sir William's favourite anecdotes. '*If a wound heals well*', he would say, '*the patient takes the credit and comments on his 'good healing flesh'. But if it fails to heal or becomes infected, the surgeon is deemed responsible and the patient asks, 'What has gone wrong with your wound, Doctor?*'

Mr Potts started to lead his entourage towards the next bed, but then appeared to change his mind. He turned and spoke again to Jimmy.

"So you decided to trust an English surgeon after all, did you?"

Jimmy, slightly more subdued than usual, faced with the senior surgeon and his retinue of doctors and nurses, answered politely.

"Och, I was only joking with young Dr Lambert. I'm grateful to you for doing the operation. If I'd gone back to Glasgow, I shouldna' been able to work and would still be awaiting my operation. But now, thanks to you, I've put it behind me. I'm feeling grand and raring to go."

"Actually, I didn't perform the operation for you. You have Lambert to thank for that and he seems to have done a good job. The wound is healing well and the repair looks good and strong. So you approve of the way we do things in England, do you?" he asked.

There was a moment's pause. Was he about to spill the beans?

"Oh definitely," said Jimmy.

"Well I hope nothing happens before you go home to make you change your mind."

Mr Potts, having spent more time chatting to this one patient than he normally did on an entire ward round, smiled and moved on. There was a collective sigh of relief from the doctors and nurses accompanying him. He had clearly decided that Richard's handiwork was no more than a bit of harmless fun.

It was inevitable that Jimmy would eventually become suspicious that so many people stopped, grinned and made comments about the Celtic football team when they passed his bed. Slowly but progressively, a doubt built in his mind until finally, he was forced to the conclusion that something must be wrong with his tattoo. Ultimately, there came the moment when he could bear the uncertainty no longer. Unable to see the upper part of his chest and not possessing a hand mirror, he got out of bed and limped slowly down the ward clutching his groin wound, to reduce the pain that resulted from movement. In the washroom he stood in front of the long mirror. To his horror he read Richard's handiwork. The tattoo read **CELTIC 0 RANGERS 3**

Afterwards Paul reflected that it was episodes such as this that enlivened hospital life and made the long hours, hard work and disrupted nights tolerable. In years to come, it would be totally unacceptable to have such a joke at a patient's expense. It might be considered a physical assault on their person or judged to be psychologically distressing. It could result in a demand for counselling or in legal action and compensation! The European Court of Human Rights might even express concerns about racial abuse, given all the banter there had been about Scotland and Scottish football teams. As it was Jimmy, after a few expletives and curses about the staff in general and about Richard in particular, (after he had discovered who was responsible), saw the funny side of the escapade and thereafter thoroughly enjoyed his celebrity status. As before, he wore his pyjama jacket open and flaunted his physique, medallion and tattoo but only after he had persuaded the nurses to remove the offending extra letters with methylated spirits!

***

In surgery, as in other branches of medicine, nothing can replace experience. No matter how many textbooks or academic journals are read, more is learned from seeing a wide variety of patients, by observing their symptoms, and watching how they response to treatment. Because Paul spent so many hours on duty, he was able to monitor patients from the time of their admission, to the moment of their discharge. He frequently grumbled about the long hours and the heavy workload but recognised that his training would have been jeopardized had he only seen patients for eight hours before handing over their care to a new team. He knew that opportunities to learn were missed if a patient was seen, a diagnosis suggested but the doctor then remained in ignorance of the outcome, not knowing if his diagnosis proved to be accurate. Paul had seen Mary Murphy, the delightful Irish lady on the medical ward just once whilst covering for Roger, his colleague who had 'gone absent without leave'. He was eager to learn whether his diagnosis had been confirmed. A couple of days later therefore, he rang the medical ward and was told that Mary had been transferred to the care of Professor Butterworth. Breathing a sigh of relief that this would save him the dubious pleasure of another encounter with Sue Weston, he went to the Professor's ward to investigate. He wanted to know whether the lump he had felt in her back passage had indeed been a tumour and if so, what had happened subsequently. Had she had an operation and how had she coped with the surgery and anaesthetic, given her age and bad chest?

Finding the notes in the office, he flicked through them to find the most recent entry. Sorry though he was to discover that Mary's telescope test had confirmed that she had cancer, he was pleased to read that the tumour had been successfully removed and that no spread of the disease had been found. If she was able to convalesce without complications from her chest or heart, there was the prospect of a complete cure. Mentally he gave himself a pat on the back and felt pleased for Mary. She wouldn't have enjoyed the surgery but at least, she was now on the mend and hopefully would make a full recovery. She was a warm and friendly soul and Paul had enjoyed talking to her.

Paul was just about to replace her notes, when his eye fell on the entry immediately prior to the operation. Signed by Roger, his opposite number on the Surgical Three unit, it gave a detailed assessment of Mary's condition, including a rectal examination, in which the finding of a tumour was recorded. Initially he thought this examination must have been performed after Mary had been transferred to the surgical ward, but no – it was alleged to have taken place on the medical ward, prior to her transfer. Furthermore, Paul's own record of seeing the patient had disappeared. His reaction was one of anger. Roger was claiming to have performed a rectal examination on Mary and was now taking the credit for Paul's diagnosis. What he had done was unethical. The patient's clinical record was a legal document. It was unlawful to alter it in any way. Paul sat looking at the notes for some time, at first almost unbelieving, but it was true. His entry had been removed and replaced by this fictitious one. Presumably Roger thought that having handed Mary over to their unit, Paul would not bother to follow her up and that his dishonesty would go unnoticed. Paul wondered whether the Professor's registrar would realize what had been done. He had known that the switchboard had been unable to locate Roger that evening. He also knew that Paul had assessed Mary on the medical ward and suggested a diagnosis of rectal cancer. It was as a result of Paul's conversation with him, that he had visited the medical ward himself to perform the telescope test. Presumably the registrar had not seen the alteration in the record and Roger was planning to shield it from him.

Much troubled, Paul wondered what action to take. The easiest thing was to do nothing. After all, the patient had suffered no harm. She had been to theatre, her surgery had apparently gone well and she was now said to be making a good recovery. On the other hand, this was an unlawful act by a dishonest colleague and should be reported. But to whom? Officially he presumed it should be reported to Roger's boss, the Professor. But would he believe Paul's story? How would he react to Paul telling tales against a member of his own team? There might be dangers if he went down that road, yet equally it didn't seem right to let the matter pass. In a state of indecision, he went in search of Mo Khan.

Although not a consultant, he was approachable and had always been a most helpful source of advice when Paul had worked on the unit previously. He never failed to offer words of wisdom. Paul found him chatting to Victoria in the ward office and told him what had happened. As always, Mo listened carefully to the full story before making any comment.

"Quite a conundrum," he commented. "Are you asking me if you should report Roger to the Professor or to Sir William?"

"I suppose I'm asking if I should report the matter at all, or just leave things as they are. I don't want to be seen as a trouble maker."

Mo thought for some time before replying.

"As you say, it's not at all straightforward. In situations like this, the care and safety of the patient is the primary concern but in this particular case, no harm has resulted. There's no doubt that the correct thing to do is to report the matter and it wouldn't really matter if you reported it to the Professor or to Sir William. But as you suggest, there are potential dangers."

"I appreciate that," Paul replied, "but I'm angry that Roger has taken credit for my work and I'm also concerned about his behaviour. It's a criminal offence to make alterations to a patient's official record. The notes may be used as evidence in court cases. They are supposed to be factually correct. It doesn't seem right to let it pass. This may not be the first time Roger has behaved like this, and if it is not reported, it may not be the last. I think I'll speak to Sir William. I know him better than the Professor. He has old fashioned values and can be relied upon to be fair minded."

"Not so fast Paul. I've met a situation similar to this before. I was working in a hospital in the Midlands, before I came up North. My consultant had told the registrar to give a patient some antibiotics before an operation to prevent infection. The registrar may have forgotten or perhaps considered that it wasn't necessary, but in practice, he failed to write the prescription. Subsequently, the patient did get a very severe infection. It almost overwhelmed him because he was old and frail. In the end he did survive, although he had a long and stormy time in hospital. The registrar realized his omission and wrote up the antibiotics retrospectively. He then altered the charts to make it appear as if the nurses had given them to the patient. He was reported to the consultant by one of his colleagues, the ward sister as it happened. Unfortunately, it was the sister who had reported him, who came off worse. The registrar denied the offence, and it became a question as to whose word was to be believed. Essentially the consultant would have preferred to turn a blind eye to the incident. I think he wished that he hadn't been told and didn't want to '*rock the boat*'. Regrettably the sister, honest though she had been, got a reputation as a troublemaker. Shortly afterwards, she was moved off the unit while the registrar subsequently got promoted."

"But why should I get into trouble for reporting it?" Paul demanded.

"Because Roger will probably deny it and you may be accused of trying to upstage him."

"What do you mean upstage him?"

"Well, you are both senior house officers, but I think he has a little more experience than you."

"Yes," Paul said. "He's one year senior. He qualified a year ahead of me."

"Soon enough then, you will both be applying for registrar jobs. As your senior, one would expect him to be promoted before you. You might be accused of attempting to eliminate him from the competition, to improve your own chances."

"Yes, I can see that," Paul admitted. "So what should I do?"

"I'm afraid Paul, that must be your decision, but do think very carefully before you start creating waves."

Victoria meanwhile, had been sitting at the desk writing up a patient's history. She had heard the entire conversation but, like the wise old owl, had listened carefully but said nothing. Paul turned to her.

"Have you any thoughts on the matter, Victoria?"

She paused before replying. "I confess that I haven't encountered a situation like this before, but my instinct is to report the matter. As you say, the patient's record is a legal document. If, for any reason the management of the patient were to be the subject of a legal case, it would be used as evidence in court and assumed to be an honest and accurate account."

"And to whom would you report it?" Paul asked.

"To the Professor. The patient is under his care and Roger works for him."

That evening, back in his flat, Paul reflected on what had been said. Mo's advice had been equivocal. He had declined to suggest a clear course of action, but had clearly warned that reporting the matter might lead to unpredictable consequences. Victoria had been clear in her own mind but it was easy for her to suggest approaching the Professor. She wouldn't be the one who might suffer some unfortunate reaction. The Professor chaired most of the appointments committees for surgical trainees. Paul doubted that it would be wise to risk crossing the most influential surgeon in the city; the one who could greatly affect his prospects of promotion. In the end, he decided to do nothing, but was left feeling angry that Roger had taken credit for his diagnosis, and frustrated that such unethical behaviour should go unnoticed and unpunished. Unnoticed that is, unless the registrar on the Professorial unit chanced to see the notes and realized what had happened. Paul rather hoped that he would. But then he was left wondering whether, faced with the same ethical dilemma, the registrar too would turn Nelson's eye.

***

Two days later, as Mr Potts had predicted, Jimmy was up and about on the ward and his daily insulin injections had recommenced. His GP in Glasgow had been contacted, arrangements had been made for a district nurse to remove his sutures and an appointment organised for follow up at his local hospital. Jimmy was to be discharged the following day and, once again, was undertaking his own ward rounds, now saying a cheerful '*goodbye*' to the many friends that he had made during his stay in hospital.

Paul was in the residency enjoying his lunch, when his pager sounded with its urgent tone. A patient had collapsed on the male ward, would he attend immediately. All sort of thoughts flashed through Paul's mind as he ran to the ward. *Which patient has collapsed? Will it be someone I already know or a patient I've never seen before? What has caused the collapse? Will I be able to diagnose the problem and know what action to take?* The troubling thought '*could I in some way have been responsible for the problem?*' flashed through his mind! Paul wondered whether all doctors were afflicted with such moments of doubt or was it just those who were naturally introspective. It was a constant source of amazement to him that so few doctors develop stress induced stomach ulcers. Arriving breathless on the scene two minutes later, Paul saw that the drama was unfolding adjacent to a bed half way down the ward on the left hand side. It was Jimmy's bed and it was Jimmy who had collapsed. He was lying on the floor, cold and lifeless, his pyjama jacket inevitably wide open. He was in full view of all the other patients. Sister Ashbrook was on her knees, bouncing on Jimmy's chest, applying cardiac massage. A senior staff nurse, also on her knees by Jimmy's head, was administering mouth-to-mouth respiration. A student nurse had a collection of heart monitor leads in her hand and was struggling to place these on Jimmy's chest, though hampered by Sisters' ongoing cardiac massage.

Emergency resuscitation was an exercise regularly practiced by both junior doctors and nurses, and Sister had matters organized exactly as described in the official manual. The patient was on a hard surface, in this case on the floor, so that compression on the chest squeezed the heart and forced blood to circulate round the body. Had the patient been lying on a soft mattress in bed, cardiac massage would have been ineffective, since pressure on the chest simply pushes the patient bodily into the mattress. The whole patient then bounces back in a rather alarming manner and no compression of the heart results. Sister Ashbrook, in exemplary fashion, had both hands, left on top of right, over Jimmy's breast bone and was pumping rhythmically at a rate of one every second. After every ten pumps she paused to allow the staff nurse, her mouth on Jimmy's, to blow twice to inflate his lungs. Another nurse rushed up with the emergency drugs trolley, and was promptly dispatched by Sister to get the defibrillator and to call the anaesthetist. All the while, the scene was being witnessed in shocked silence by the other patients on the ward, every one of them horrified at what had happened to this lively and likeable young man who had become such a favourite, such a celebrity, on the ward. He had been the life and soul of the party and, until a few moments earlier, had been cheerfully bidding farewell to his new found friends.

Sister had assumed charge of the situation and spoke to Paul as soon as he arrived. "Jimmy has had a heart attack, Dr Lambert. Take over the cardiac massage from me. I need to apply these ECG leads and see what the heart tracing is doing. We may need to defibrillate him. I've called for the anaesthetist so that we can intubate him and ensure the airway."

All the while Jimmy remained ominously still. He was pale and bathed in sweat.

Paul felt that something was wrong. It would be most unusual for a slim man in his early 30's to suffer a massive heart attack, even if he were diabetic. An alternative explanation would be that a blood clot that had formed in his legs, then travelled to his lungs but again this seemed unlikely. Although comatosed, Jimmy was sweating and neither of these diagnoses caused that. He bent down and felt carefully at Jimmy's neck.

"Stop everything you're doing for a second," he said.

He felt carefully for the carotid pulse in the neck and was fairly certain it was present. Sister began pumping Jimmy's chest again.

"Hold everything," Paul repeated, "I want no movement at all".

He felt again and was now absolutely certain that there was a pulse. It was faint but it was definitely there. This wasn't a cardiac arrest at all. What was it that Sir William was always drumming into his staff? *Common things occur commonly.'*

"Stop everything that you're doing," Paul instructed. "No more cardiac massage, no more ventilation."

He dashed to the treatment room and picked up the largest syringe he could find, and filled it to the brim with the solution that he wanted. In less than a minute, he was back at Jimmy's side, to find that Sister had recommenced cardiac massage and Staff Nurse was again giving mouth-to-mouth resuscitation. He needed to find a vein and he needed to find it fast. If this were not possible in one of the veins in the arm, then an injection would have to be made directly into the large femoral vein in the groin. He held his breath, slid the needle through the skin and fortunately, despite Jimmy's collapsed condition, found a vein at the first attempt. He injected the entire content of the syringe as quickly as possible. All the while Sister was kneeling over Jimmy, pummelling his chest and Staff Nurse, her lips on Jimmy's, was blowing into his lungs.

The effect of the injection was dramatic. Within thirty seconds, Jimmy was semi conscious and thrashing violently with both arms and legs. One wild, uncoordinated swing of his right arm caught Sister Ashbrock full on the chest and knocked her over backwards. She lay helpless, like a tortoise on its back, arms and legs flailing in the air. Staff Nurse, who was performing the artificial ventilation, fared little better. She got a mouthful of spittle, followed by a mouthful of invective and was then tossed bodily to one side, joining Sister on the floor. As she fell, she collided with the resuscitation trolley which tumbled on top of her, scattering oxygen masks and tubes, syringes and needles, drugs and dressings over a wide area. The student nurse, believing that Jimmy had come back from the dead, ran screaming from the ward adding to the pandemonium. Within a minute, Jimmy was sitting up, conscious but confused, screaming abuse at the top of his voice; at Sister, her nurses, indeed at the entire English population. Language was heard that had never been heard on the ward before, all in the broadest of Glaswegian accents.

Paul stood up, well pleased with the result of his actions. He admired the scene laid out before him. Jimmy was in the centre, conscious if a little befuddled, berating everything and everybody around him. Sister and Staff Nurse lay in heaps, struggling to regain their feet, not to mention their dignity and composure. The entire contents of the emergency trolley lay scattered around on the floor. Two young nurses, who had been watching the resuscitation from the sidelines, stood totally bewildered by the events that had unfolded before them, events that, without doubt, would be the talk of the Nurses Home for many weeks to come. Paul wasn't altogether unhappy that every patient on the ward had witnessed the entire episode. In fact, he felt a rather smug. He realized of course, that this was not a particularly honourable emotion, but in the circumstances considered it to be justified!

Slowly Sister Ashbrook sat up, then rose unsteadily to her feet, taking a few seconds to straighten her dress and her crumpled apron. She retrieved her cap, which had ended up on the floor a couple of yards away. She placed it on her head and secured it in position.

There was a long pause.

"What was in that syringe?" she asked.

Paul shouldn't have smiled, it was wrong of him to do so, but he simply couldn't resist it.

"A strong sugar solution," he said. "Jimmy's diabetic. He was in a diabetic coma. If you recall, he has just resumed his insulin injections. He probably hasn't started to eat as much as normal yet, so his blood sugar will have fallen."

He was on the verge of saying *'as Sir William regularly reminds us, common things occur commonly'* but thought better of it.

Sister Ashbrook looked steadily at him for a moment or two and then said quietly, "Thank you, Dr Lambert. Well done."

They were words that Paul never thought he would hear from the Sister who constantly strove to belittle the junior doctors. She had been the bane of Paul's life when he had worked on her ward as a newly qualified house officer.

Then she turned away and was her normal self again. She began firing instructions at her nurses in her usual brisk fashion. "Get Mr McMillan back into bed. Give him a hot sweet drink and something to eat." She turned to another of her nurses. "Tidy up this mess on the floor." To a third, "Ring the anaesthetist and tell him that he's no longer needed."

Once again she was the sister in charge of her ward. She had regained her composure and was acting as if nothing untoward had happened.

Undoubtedly Sister Ashbrook had suffered an embarrassing setback in the ongoing battle for supremacy that she waged with the junior medical staff. For Paul it was a significant milestone, for although she never mentioned this incident or Jimmy McMillan ever again, it did change his relationship with her in a subtle way. No longer did he feel any need to justify his actions to her. He recalled what Mohammed had once said of his relationship with her, *'I can't say that we like each other but we do have a respect for each other.'* That summed it up nicely and Paul felt that he too had won Sister's respect.

Chapter Ten

For Paul, meeting Kate had been a delightful surprise, especially as she had seemed pleased to see him and had agreed so readily that they should meet socially. However the knowledge that she had been engaged to Peter haunted him. She would presumably be a married woman by now, possibly even having a family of her own. Two long years had elapsed, since he had heard any news of her. Much would have happened in that time. Paul felt that in all probability, she would now regard him simply as an old friend, someone from her past with whom it would be pleasant to reminiscence about days gone by. Yet she had agreed to an outing, he didn't dare think of it as a 'date', with someone to whom she had once been close, an 'old flame'. Would she have done that, if she had a husband to consider? And if she was married to a northern hill farmer, why was she now back at the City General resuming her nursing career? Perhaps there was a chance that she was still single after all. Desperate to find out, Paul had suggested that they share a quiet meal in a country pub, believing this would give them a chance to chat and to catch up with all that had happened since they last met. He clung to the possibility, daring to dream that he might discover that she remained unattached.

It was agreed that Paul should pick Kate up from the Nurses Home at 7 pm the following Wednesday evening, an arrangement that evoked many memories. It had been in the shadow of the trees adjacent to the Nurses Home one Saturday night, that they had shared their first kiss. It had been no more than a peck on the cheek, after Paul had walked her home on their first date. What a disaster that had been. The evening had followed his overnight duty in casualty. He had been on his feet for much of the night and had worked on the ward, both the day before and the day after. He was so exhausted that in the warmth and comfort of the cinema, he had fallen asleep on her shoulder, only waking when the audience stood at the end of the film for the National Anthem. At the time she had forgiven him, then teased him about it afterwards, and their friendship had blossomed. Six months later though, she had left the hospital, to return home to care for her sick mother. Abandoning her nursing career had been a huge sacrifice for her. She loved nursing. Care and compassion came naturally to her. She had been a wonderful nurse, so comfortable and at ease when moving between the sick patients on the ward. Later Paul had moved to the Middleton Hospital. His contract there required him to be resident on alternate nights and alternate weekends. When not on duty, he caught up on his sleep and studied for his exams and as a result, they had drifted apart. Paul had been devastated when she left and ever since, had regretted not making more of an effort to travel to see her, despite the distance between them.

Yet surgery was a hard taskmaster. Anything less than 100% commitment was not good enough. Some of Paul's contemporaries were married, but he knew of at least two marriages that were on the rocks, simply because a happy married life and a successful training in surgery were virtually incompatible. The sacrifices demanded by a career in surgery were great, not just for the trainee but for his wife and for any family that he had. To be a good surgeon, you had to put your patients first. Perhaps that is why so many surgeons' wives are doctors or nurses themselves. It would be difficult for someone not familiar with hospital life to understand, or be prepared, to make the necessary sacrifice. The Dean of the Medical School in the first lecture that he had given to Paul and his fellow students, when they had arrived eager and fresh faced from the sixth form at school had advised them to look after themselves. He warned them that the rate of divorce amongst doctors was three times the national average, as was the rate of alcoholism and the rate of suicide!

Wednesday arrived. Paul's timetable for the day involved accompanying Sir William on his ward round in the morning, then performing a short list of minor operations under local anaesthetic in the afternoon. He expected to be through by five pm and unless there were any unforeseen emergencies, he would be finished in plenty of time to meet Kate in the evening. Already he felt restless and anxious, hoping desperately that the evening would be a success and that he would discover that Kate was still single. To work alongside her in the hospital, knowing that she was tied to another, would be worse than not having met her at all.

By 8.30 am, he was on the ward, quickly checking that there had been no significant change in the condition of any of the patients overnight. It was important to be up to date and to be able to give the consultant all the information that he required to make clinical decisions. Although particular events occurred to distinguish one day from the next, there was a basic rhythm to the activities undertaken, that influenced the atmosphere on the ward as each day progressed. The day for the patients began at 6.30 am when they were awakened by the night staff. Those who were bed bound would freshen up with soap, water and a hot flannel provided by the nurses. Patients who were mobile would wander down the ward to the washrooms. Others might pull the sheets over their heads, hoping to steal an extra half hour of sleep, only to be disturbed by the clanging of the breakfast trolley, as the porters wheeled it onto the ward. Hospital meals were served early; breakfast at 7 am, lunch at noon and the evening meal at 6.00 pm; a timetable dictated by the priority given to clinical activities.

Ambulant patients, perhaps six or eight in number, ate breakfast at a table set in the middle of the ward. Others missed breakfast, possibly because they were being starved for theatre, or because they had just had their operations and their stomachs needed to be rested. The remaining patients were served in their beds by the nursing staff, which allowed valuable time for the 'old fashioned' nursing skills of observation, communication and reassurance.

Breakfast over, there was a pause in the daily routine, as the nursing 'handover' took place in the office; the night staff reporting the progress of each patient to the staff who would care for them during the day. Meanwhile a nursing auxiliary or enrolled nurse remained on the ward and kept a watchful eye on the patients.

Shortly after 8 am, the hustle and bustle of ward routine resumed. Housemen and registrars arrived to take a quick look at their patients, either in preparation for a consultant round or before dashing off to theatre or to the outpatient clinic. The 'handover' complete, the nurses flooded out of the office; the night staff going gratefully to their beds in the Nurses Home for a well earned rest, the day staff to start the day's work; student nurses to clear away the breakfast dishes and to freshen sheets and pillows, qualified nurses to attend to drips and dressings and staff nurses to unlock the drugs trolley and to walk round the ward, bed by bed, dispensing medication to patients as prescribed by the medical staff.

Gradually the ward became a hive of activity as other hospital staff arrived; porters to take patients to x-ray or to theatre by wheel chair or in their beds; physiotherapists to bully patients into early ambulation or to force them to cough to clear their chests of phlegm; cleaners to move each and every bed to the centre of the ward whilst they washed and scrubbed the linoleum floor, dieticians to advise patients with special dietary requirements and the almoner to assist patients with financial or social problems.

Promptly at 9.30, Sir William arrived, immaculately dressed in a dark grey city suit, white shirt with starched collar and a sober tie. As always, a single rose, grown in his garden, adorned his jacket lapel. He was a bachelor. His home was the lodge to the mansion, long since demolished, in whose grounds the hospital had subsequently been built. As usual, Sister Ashbrook invited Sir William to have a cup of coffee before embarking on his round and as usual, Sir William politely declined, stating that it was important that he attended to the patients first.

There was an expectant hush as Sir William strode through the double doors to enter the ward, accompanied by his retinue of doctors and nurses. Taking up the rear, like a mother with a pram, Richard, his house officer, pushed the trolley containing the patients' notes in time-honoured fashion. All the patients now sat quietly in their beds, apprehensive of the forthcoming consultation, many questions in their minds. *What did my investigations show? Am I to have an operation and when is it to be? What did you find at my operation, was it anything serious? Am I making a good recovery? Are my problems likely to return in the future?* And the question that was important to them all. *Please tell me when can I go home?*

Different questions in the minds of individual patients, each question so important to their health and well being, perhaps even pivotal in the life of the person concerned, all to be answered in the next few moments. Except that not all the questions had definite answers. *We're still waiting for the results of your tests. Sometimes patients with your problem never have any more trouble, but unfortunately a few do. We will have to wait to see how well your wound heals, before we will know when you can go home.*

The consultation was not held on a level playing field. The patient was in a strange, often frightening environment, anxious and ill, lying or sitting in bed and wearing only nightclothes. The consultant, by contrast, standing, fully clothed, totally familiar with his surroundings, supported by his staff and armed with his medical training and his knowledge of the patient's illness. In these circumstances, few patients completely understood or recalled what was said to them. This was particularly true after Mr Potts' brisk ward rounds during which little or no communication with the patient occurred. But even after Sir William had taken time to give a detailed explanation using every day language, his staff would frequently find that the patient had failed to grasp exactly what had been said. An important task for the junior doctors was to give fuller explanations when required.

The atmosphere on Sir William's round was strikingly different to that on Mr Potts'. Mr Potts' manner was brusque and impatient. Any error by his staff was picked upon and criticised. By contrast, Sir William was quietly spoken and had a relaxed manner. The nursing and medical staff always did their very best for Sir William and his patients but if, by chance, there should be some mishap or oversight, Sir William was patient and understanding. He would draw out any lessons that needed to be learned, in a helpful and constructive fashion.

The team arrived at the bed of a 15-year-old boy called David

Langley, who had been admitted with belly ache and loose stools. He had spent the previous weekend at the seaside with his parents and had eaten a hotdog bought from a roadside vendor. He was not particularly ill and Paul had made a confident diagnosis of gastroenteritis and had expected him to recover quickly. Although David's bowels had settled, his pain had continued, indeed it had become more severe. Sir William listened as Paul related this story, then proceeded to take a full history himself and followed this with a thorough examination of David's abdomen. Finally he stood back.

"Lambert," he said. "I think this young man may have appendicitis."

Paul was surprised, for although he had considered this diagnosis, he had thought it unlikely. Sir William went on to explain.

"When you have seen a lot of cases of appendicitis, you come to realise that some symptoms are more reliable than others. One very reliable symptom is loss of appetite. If a patient has retained a good appetite, they rarely have appendicitis but if, like David, they have completely gone off their food, appendicitis becomes much more likely. The other is a change in the position of the pain. Appendicitis causes a pain that starts around the umbilicus but then moves to the right. If this occurs in a patient who has also lost their appetite, then appendicitis is highly likely."

"So you think David has appendicitis and should have an operation, Sir?" Paul asked.

"Yes, I do."

Paul felt awkward having missed such an important diagnosis, but Sir William, gentleman that he was, quickly offered comfort and reassurance.

"You mustn't blame yourself, Lambert. People think that it's an easy diagnosis to make, but appendicitis can present in many different ways and I'm only suspicious here because I've been dealing with appendicitis for 40 years. Besides," he added with a smile, "we don't know yet that it is appendicitis. We shall only find out when we operate."

But of course, Sir William was right. Victoria took David to theatre that afternoon and removed an inflamed appendix.

For Paul and for the others accompanying Sir William on his round, it was an important lesson and Paul was pleased that David had been one of Sir William's patients. Had he been a patient of Mr Potts, he would still have learned the lesson, but in words that would have been harsh and critical, and painful to receive in front of Sister Ashbrook and her nurses.

Much as the staff liked and admired Sir William, there were times when they wished that his ward rounds were not so protracted. Much time was spent communicating with patients, which, of course, they greatly appreciated. Less welcome though, by both patients and staff, was the fixation that he appeared to have on his patient's bodily functions, which also added considerably to the length of his rounds. Aware of the risk of constipation after surgery, he never failed to ask his patients if they had moved their bowels after their operations, and if they had not, he took steps to ensure that they did. Not only did he prescribe suppositories, he insisted on inserting these himself. *'No-one should be too proud or too senior to undertake the humblest of tasks on a surgical ward'* he would say, as he thrust his finger into his patient's anus and inserted a couple of suppositories. It was an important lesson for his students and one that had paid dividends for Paul when treating Mary Murphy. He did however feel sorry for the patients since, whatever their age or gender, they had their bottoms exposed and their suppositories inserted in front of the entire group of doctors and nurses. When Paul had been on the unit previously, to help time pass more quickly, a sweepstake had been organised to estimate the number of suppositories that Sir William would insert during his round. With the stake set at sixpence, this had provided excellent entertainment for a number of weeks. Unfortunately this pleasant diversion came to an end when Sister Rutherford informed Sir William what was going on. She strongly disapproved, considering it to be disrespectful to her favourite consultant. Luckily, Sir William had taken it in good heart and there had been no unpleasant repercussions. Subsequently, when a sweepstake on the duration of Sir William's rounds developed, care was taken to keep Sister Rutherford in the dark. Regrettably though, this pleasant pastime also had to be abandoned, when stakeholders found various ways of cheating, often engaging Sir William in long unnecessary conversations, unrelated to the patient's problems.

Even without surreptitious manipulation, Sir William was easily distracted from clinical matters. He would happily share his views on current political issues, local history or, worse, start to reminisce about his own student or early surgical days. In these circumstances, it was his registrar's responsibility to guide the conversation back to clinical matters as quickly as possible. However, if trainees concentrated on what Sir William was saying, there was much to learn, for although he was not as up to date with his academic reading as Mr Potts, Sir William taught *'surgical common sense and surgical philosophy'*. These were matters not recorded in textbooks but which resulted from a lifetime spent with patients. He taught when to be aggressive, when to be conservative and perhaps most important of all, when it was better not to operate at all, but to leave things to nature. Working alongside such an experienced practitioner, his staff greatly enhanced the basic knowledge that they had acquired as undergraduates at medical school. He taught that taking a patient's history was not an exact science, one of the difficulties being to judge the severity of a patient's symptoms. *'Some patients are stoical,'* he explained. *'They will tolerate pain, whilst others, who have a lower pain threshold, will find the same pain quite unbearable. You will know from observing your friends and acquaintances, that some people occasionally get a cold but never have 'flu', whereas others take time off work with 'flu' three or four times a year, but never have a simple cold.'*

He taught that it was inevitable that during a surgical career, mistakes would be made and that when this happened, it was natural to be concerned and anxious. *'Without such feelings you will never be a good doctor,'* he would say, *'but the important thing is to learn from your mistakes and to make sure that they don't happen a second time'.*

There was humour on Sir William's rounds too. Having seen all the male patients, he led his team to the female ward, where he was introduced to an elderly spinster called Esme Morris. She had been admitted for a bowel operation. A tiny bird like figure, less than five feet tall, with very little flesh on her bones, she looked as if she would be blown over by the slightest breeze. As always, Sir William embarked on a detailed explanation of her treatment but on this occasion struggled because of Esme's profound deafness. The curtains were pulled around the bed, but although cotton screens provide visual privacy from the eyes of other patients, they don't prevent conversations being overheard, particularly if the dialogue is being conducted in loud voices. Esme was not only elderly but also very frail and chesty. Sir William was keen to stress to her the importance of early physiotherapy and ambulation after her operation. There was good reason for this, for the incidence of chest infections and blood clots in the legs is much reduced if patients are mobilized quickly. Sir William tapped Esme's legs.

"I want you to get these legs moving after your operation."

"What did you say, Doctor?"

"I said get these legs moving after your operation," he shouted.

"Yes, Doctor, if you say so."

He got hold of Esme's hands and waved them vigorously in the air. "And get these arms moving as well."

"Say that again, Doctor. I can't hear you?"

Again Sir William shouted back. "I want you to get these arms of yours moving after your operation."

"Yes, Doctor."

"And I want you to take some nice big breaths."

"You'll have to speak louder, Doctor?"

Sir William's voice boomed across the ward, as he tapped the front of Esme's chest.

"Nice big breaths."

Esme cackled back at him, her voice shrill and penetrating, "I'm not as big as I used to be Doctor. The boys used to say I was a real big bonny girl in the old days. But I'm surprised at you, being a doctor and saying such a thing."

Sir William, the gentlemanly bachelor, blushed to the roots of his silver hair and there were gales of laughter from the unseen audience behind the screens.

A few days later, Sir William's conversation with Esme was, once again, to provide entertainment, not only for the doctors and nurses but also for all the patients in the vicinity.

Esme had successfully survived her colonic surgery and inevitably Sir William wanted to know whether her bowel activity was returning to normal.

"Have you passed any flatus yet?" he asked.

"What's that you say, Doctor? You'll have to speak up."

"Have you passed any flatus?"

"Sorry I can't hear you," replied Esme. "I'm a bit deaf you know."

"Have you passed any wind yet?" said Sir William louder than before.

"I still can't hear you, Doctor."

"Have you farted?" roared Sir William at the top of his voice.

Esme laughed and shouted back, "No Doctor, it must be one of you."

Sir William roared with laughter and was so amused that he actually forgot to perform his routine with the suppositories.

When Sir William had completed his round and left the ward to have a cup of coffee and a chat in the office, there was an audible sigh of relief from the patients. Whispered conversations began, inevitably each patient more eager to pass on their own news, than to hear about their neighbour's.

"My operation's tomorrow."

"They're waiting for the results of my tests."

"They still don't know what it is, but they think it's something quite rare."

"It's the infection in my wound that causing the temperature."

"Thankfully, I can go home tomorrow."

The consultants ward round inevitably produced a number of extra tasks; dressings to be changed, sutures to be removed and drainage tubes to be adjusted. These were all jobs for the nurses. Some additional investigations had been requested which Richard would have to arrange. Paul was pleased that no further work had been generated for him, but still wished that Sir William should drink his coffee quickly and allow him get on with his other duties. With his mind very much on his meeting with Kate, he didn't want to be delayed at any stage of the day. A sense of courtesy and respect however, meant that all the team stayed until Sir William left to have his lunch.

Paul's afternoon operating list of minor operations, performed under local anaesthetic, went smoothly and by five pm, his days work complete, he was back in the flat, anxiously watching the clock, wondering what the evening would bring. It was two years since he had last been with Kate and scarcely a day had passed when he had not thought of her. He showered, put on his smartest grey flannels, blazer and tie and then, his heart pounding in his chest, he went to meet her at the Nurses Home.

Chapter Eleven

The Nurses Home was under the strict control of an exceedingly fierce 'Home Sister' who took her responsibilities very seriously! If she wished to leave the residency in an evening or at the weekend, Kate had to '*sign out*' and was required to '*log back in*' again before the 11 pm curfew, when the doors were locked for the night. The Home Sister was known to be protective of both the physical and moral wellbeing of her young charges! She particularly viewed young doctors with the gravest of suspicion. She had been known, on occasion, to personally vet members of that profession, and then formally advise them of the conduct expected of them, before allowing her nurses to accompany them on a date. Kate waved as she ran down the steps to meet Paul, apologising for being a few moments late. As always, she looked stunning, wearing a simple summer cotton dress and a white cardigan, her face smiling and glowing with health. Paul felt an overwhelming desire to take her into his arms, to hold her tight, to show her just how much he cared for her, and how much he had missed her. But such feelings had to be held in check. He did not know how things stood between them.

"Hello Paul," she said, as she gave him a quick kiss on the side of the cheek.

"Hello Kate. It's lovely to see you." Paul wondered if the kiss had any special significance or whether it was merely a conventional greeting between old friends.

He held the door of his dilapidated old Morris Minor for her.

Kate smiled. "Still the perfect gentleman, I see."

"Still the same old motor car," he replied, laughing.

They drove to the village of Babington some five miles away, to a pub that they had visited in the past. Paul had booked a table in a quiet corner of the room, a table at which they had dined previously. He hoped this would induce some happy memories.

As they sat and ate, the conversation was of inconsequential matters; comments on the weather, gossip about various members of the hospital staff and talk of life in the operating theatre. Kate laughed when told of Sir William's encounters with Esme Morris. She teased him about the state of his car but all the while, Paul remained anxious and ill at ease. He was reluctant to bring the conversation round to those matters that concerned him most; afraid of what he might hear. From time to time he glanced at Kate. She wore no rings on her fingers. Jewellery was not permitted when nurses were at work but surely, if she were engaged or married, she would wear a ring in the evening. What sort of husband would allow his attractive young wife to dine with an old boyfriend without a wedding band on her finger? Paul felt that there must be a chance for him after all.

Looking at her across the table, Paul wondered what it was about her that attracted him so much. She was of average height, slim with a neat figure. Wearing little or no makeup, she had a fresh complexion and rosy cheeks, no doubt the result of her love of the countryside and outdoor life. Her eyes were soft and twinkled when she smiled. Her face was framed with mousy brown hair tied with a ribbon at the back into a ponytail. In many ways, she was quite unremarkable, the sort of girl you could pass in the street and not really notice. But Paul loved her. He knew her to be a gentle, kind and caring person. She was ideally suited to be a nurse. She was at home on the ward, chatting to the sick, reassuring them and giving them confidence with a smile here and a kind word there. She always seemed to be at ease with herself, enjoying her work, undertaking her job without any fuss. Certainly she was not one to draw attention to herself in any way. Once again Paul cursed himself for being so stupid to have let her slip out of his life.

As the waiter cleared away the dessert dishes and brought the coffee, Paul wondered how to broach the subject that was so important to him, but as had happened so often when they had been courting, it was Kate, with her easy manner, who created the opening.

"That was a lovely meal, Paul. Just like old times. Thank you."

"It's been a long time," he replied, "and I've missed you."

"Yes," Kate agreed. "It has indeed been a long time and a lot has happened to me since then. I'm a bit older now and a little bit wiser too, I hope." She looked across at Paul and for a moment her eyes held his, "and yes, I've missed you too," she added softly.

"It must be two years," Kate continued, "since we last spoke. You were working at the University then. What have you been doing since?"

"I've been working Kate. There hasn't been much time for anything else. As you know, surgery is based on a detailed knowledge of anatomy, so I went to the university to work in the anatomy department. The pace of life there was gentle. I was even paid when the students were enjoying their long university vacations. Then I scratched a living doing G P locums until an SHO job became available at the Middleton Hospital. I worked there until I returned to the City General."

"I imagine you set a few hearts fluttering at the Middleton," Kate commented.

Paul smiled. "Perhaps one or two, but truly, it was such a busy job, there was little time for relaxation or socializing. I was on duty in the hospital on alternate nights and since two or three patients were admitted most nights, I was usually exhausted on my days off."

It would have been easy to blame the hectic workload at the Middleton for losing contact with Kate but, in truth that was not the only reason, or indeed the main reason. Paul felt the need to explain.

"I'm sorry I stopped phoning Kate, and sorry that I didn't make the effort to drive up to see you as often as I should. The truth is that from time to time, I spoke with your father on the phone. He was obviously very upset about your mother's illness and on a number of occasions stressed that you were fully occupied caring for her. Perhaps he thought I was trying to drag you away. Then he started to mention a young man called Peter. The way he spoke suggested that I was no longer your 'number one' and later of course, he told me that you were engaged to be married. I know I ought to have done more to keep in touch and I'm sorry that I didn't. But when I heard you were engaged, it no longer seemed appropriate. With a new man in your life, your future husband, I knew you wouldn't want me continuing to pester you.

Bitterness showed in Paul's voice when he spoke of Peter. He had been deeply disappointed when Kate had left the City General and transferred to the hospital in Kendal. He fully accepted the need for her to be close to her mother, who had developed breast cancer, but had been significantly hurt on learning that she had a new boyfriend. Paul had honestly believed that theirs was a special friendship, one that would stand the test of time, one that would survive a period of separation. It had been a bitter blow to hear of her engagement. Now though, he desperately needed to know whether Peter was still on the scene. Were the two of them still engaged? Kate had seemed pleased to see him and had readily accepted this invitation to dinner. There was no ring on her finger and she had not mentioned a fiancé, but that did not quell the anxiety that Paul felt.

There was a pause and then Paul blurted out the question that had been tormenting him, the question he had been afraid to ask, fearing what the answer might be.

"So are you still engaged, Kate, or maybe married?"

"No, Paul, I'm not, and I know that I owe you an apology. Frankly the engagement was a huge mistake. I never had any real feelings for Peter. Nor I think, did he have for me."

"Surely it's a little difficult to get engaged by mistake!"

"Then let me try and explain how it happened." Kate spoke quietly and calmly, not upset by the sarcasm in Paul's voice. "When Mum developed breast cancer, I felt I had to try and support her and my father. It was a particularly severe form of the disease and we knew from the beginning that the outlook was bleak. Mum had surgery, then x-ray therapy but sadly she continued to deteriorate as the cancer spread. As you know, Matron here at the City General was kind enough to arrange for me to continue my nursing studies at Kendal, but as Mum got weaker and weaker, I needed to be with her, to nurse her. I didn't want her to die amongst strangers in hospital. I wanted her to be in her own home, with her friends and family around her. So I left nursing altogether. Mum's last few weeks were particularly difficult. She had a lot of pain, despite large doses of morphine. Dad found it very difficult to cope, and when Mum died, he grieved terribly. He took it very badly. He became moody and depressed."

Kate's voice faltered as she spoke. She was clearly still upset at the loss of her mother. She paused and wiped away a tear before continuing. "During Mum's illness, Muriel Jones, one of our neighbours, was very supportive. She's a lovely lady, the widow of one of the local farmers. She helped me to nurse Mum, did the shopping and so on. For many years, Mum and Dad had been great friends of Muriel and her husband before she was widowed. Peter is their son. As a child, in the school holidays, I used to work on their farm and occasionally the two families took short holidays together. Mum had helped Muriel when she was widowed, and when Mum was dying, and she knew that she was, she was worried about leaving Dad on his own. Dad had never been much use about the house. He didn't understand how the washing machine worked, had never learned to cook or clean, and I think Mum wanted Muriel to continue to help and support him.

Anyway, within a year, Dad and Muriel were married. It raised a few eyebrows in the village as you can imagine, but I think it was for the best and I'm sure Mum would have approved. It was a quiet affair in the local Registry office. I was the bridesmaid and Peter gave his mother away. Peter and I have been friends since we were toddlers. We mucked in together on the farm in our school holidays, attended village dances and I suppose we came close again when his mother and my father were married. Looking back, it seems strange that Peter and I became engaged. Perhaps we were just fulfilling the expectations of everyone in the village. Muriel was certainly very keen on the idea; in fact, I suspect that she suggested to Peter that he should pop the question. Dad was delighted. I know Mum would have been pleased too and looking back, I suspect that may have had some influence on my decision.

It wasn't long though before both Peter and I realised we had made a big mistake, and decided that it wouldn't be sensible for us to get married. We were old friends, very good friends as it happens and we still are, but I don't believe that either of us truly loved the other, in the way that a married couple should. We have totally different ambitions and outlooks on life. Peter wants to stay in the village to build up his father's farm. He has grand plans for the farm and for the way in which the land should be developed. He's happy to be a part of the local community, but for me the village is claustrophobic. I want to spread my wings and see the world, but first I want to complete my nurse training. I just couldn't see myself as a farmer's wife, living in one spot for the rest of my days. At first, Dad and Muriel were unhappy that Peter and I had decided to go our separate ways, but now they both understand that we wouldn't have made each other happy. They realise that it was better for us to part, and continue to be good friends, rather than tie the knot and embark on an unhappy marriage."

For a while Kate was silent and pensive, as she reflected upon these events. Paul was relieved to hear that the engagement was over. He was delighted in fact to learn that Kate remained unattached, although he felt a strong twinge of jealously that someone else had been so close to her. He wondered just how close they had been, particularly had they been lovers, but was inhibited from pursuing such a personal matter.

"So do you still see Peter?"

"Yes, of course. When Dad and Muriel married, they settled in Dad's house. I like Muriel very much. She's a lovely person and very good for Dad. Peter lives on the farm. It's only a quarter of a mile away but he often goes to Dad's for meals, so I see him whenever I go home."

Again Paul felt that pang of jealously. Perhaps Kate noticed a change in his expression, for she added quickly, "We're just good friends Paul, like brother and sister I suppose. We made a mistake when we got engaged but we both recognised it, and so we split up. There are no regrets or recriminations on either side. So here I am, back at the City General, making beds, washing bedpans, emptying vomit bowls and back on the shelf just as before, with twelve months more training before I qualify."

"Well we can't have that, can we Kate? Perhaps you and I should spend some time together. Do you remember those long walks we had in the Lake District, the parties at the hospital, trips to the cinema and always the rush to get you back before they locked the door of the Nurses Home? We had some good times together. I should love to re-live those days."

"I should like that too, Paul. I should like that a lot."

Her simple words, sincerely spoken, filled Paul with joy. She still cared for him, still wanted to spend time with him. He looked at her, a warm glow in his heart, then reached across the table and took hold of her hand but Kate looked at her watch.

"Paul, I'm afraid it's getting late. I need to get back. Matron has been very good to me, allowing me to return to complete my nurse training. I can't afford to get into her bad books."

They drove back to the hospital. Paul parked the car in the residents' car park, across the road from the main building and they walked slowly back to the Nurses Home, hand in hand in silence. There was no need for words. Relaxed from the food and wine, greatly relieved to know that Kate was not only free but that she still cared for him, Paul was happy simply to be in her company, content to enjoy the moment.

Though largely oblivious of his surroundings, he noticed a figure running towards the hospital, someone he recognised. It was Roger Watkins, the SHO from the Surgical Three Unit.

"What day is it today?" he asked Kate.

"Wednesday. Why?"

"That's right. It's Surgical Three's duty day. I wonder what Roger is doing out of the hospital?

Then he remembered the day on which the switchboard had been unable to locate him, the day he had seen Mary Murphy on Roger's behalf on one of the medical wards, the occasion when his notes had been replaced.

"Is something wrong?" Kate asked.

"Sorry Kate. No, nothing's wrong. That was Roger Watkins. I rather suspect he should be in the hospital on duty. I was just wondering what he was doing out here."

Paul saw Kate safely back to the Nurses Home. They got there with five minutes to spare and he held her in his arms in the shadows, a little way from the front door. He loved this girl. Not a day had passed in the last two years when he had not thought of her, regretting that they had drifted apart. He remembered the hurt that he had felt when told by her father of her engagement to Peter, and the way he had thrown himself into his studies in an attempt to forget her. And now she was back. He wanted to be with her, to care for her, to protect her, to spend his whole life with her and he badly wanted to tell her so. The words came tumbling out of his mouth.

"Oh Kate you can't imagine how much I've missed you, how I've wanted to be with you, how I've needed to... "

But she put her finger to his lips. "Shush," she said, "there's no time now. Tell me later."

She gave him a kiss on the cheek, ran up the steps of the Nurses

112

Home, waved and was gone. Paul walked slowly back to his flat, feeling a wonderful warm glow. The evening had been a huge success. The two years of longing and heartache were over, the uncertainty that had haunted him since that meeting in theatre was gone. The future looked rosy. He knew with absolute certainty that Kate cared for him and felt confident that they would rediscover the happiness that they had shared before. This time, he vowed, he would not let her slip away, no matter what obstacles thrown in their path.

That night, alone in her room, Kate lay awake and reflected on the evening, particularly on her feelings for Paul. She wondered whether she was in love. She had dated boys when she had been at school, but only because that was what her friends did, and what they expected of her. But she didn't like the way that they grabbed her and dragged her onto the dance floor with a curt *'Come on, let's dance.'* She didn't like the way that they tried to kiss her at the end of the evening. She wanted to push them away. And she hated the sensation of their lips on her mouth. Her friends often said they were in love; that this boy or that boy was special. But a week later they had changed their minds. How, she wondered, did you recognize true love? What did it feel like? *'You will know it when it hits you,'* people said with a smile. What a pity, she thought, that it doesn't come with a luggage label attached!

But with Paul, she felt different. She remembered their first evening together, three years before. He had walked her back to the Nurses Home after that unforgettable trip to the cinema when he had fallen asleep. He had held her hand, but he hadn't tried to kiss her, even though she had wished that he would. It was to be a further three weeks before Paul plucked up the courage to do that and when he did, her heart had jumped so much that it had startled her. She liked his thoughtful manner. He was quietly spoken and considerate. Perhaps he was a little traditional in his ways, with old fashioned standards and values, but she liked that. It reminded her of her father whom she adored. She loved both her parents of course, but the bond she shared with her father was particularly strong. They had been a close knit family; open, with no secrets from each. All their various problems were discussed frankly around the dinner table. Then, tragically, her mother had been taken ill and it had quickly become apparent that she was not going to get better. Kate's instinct had been to be with her, to care for her. She had also felt the need to support her father and her younger brother who was still at school. She had been sorry to quit nursing, to leave Paul, but caring for her mother was more important and with the additional need to run the house, do the washing, ironing, cooking, and cleaning, there had been little time for regrets.

As her mother's illness progressed, Kate's life had become more and more difficult. Despite her training as a nurse, she had found it difficult to watch as her mother deteriorated, to see the flesh drop of her bones, to watch her suffer with pain and vomiting, and to witness her weakness and her helplessness as the end approached. And after her mother passed away, when she herself had needed comfort and support, her old family friend, Peter, had been at hand. She was grateful to him for helping her through those dark days but had never felt for him the feelings that she felt for Paul. She recalled vividly her surprise and delight when she had spotted Paul in the operating theatre a week or so ago. Lying in bed, her pillow held tight to her chest, she pictured him in her mind. With his dark brown hair, blue eyes, and his small snub nose, he was good looking rather than handsome, but it wasn't his looks that attracted her, it was something else, something intangible. She didn't know what it was, but there was something about Paul that was different. And whatever that 'something' was, it made him special in her eyes. She had often wondered what it must feel like to be in love, and for the first time in her life she thought she knew.

Chapter Twelve

Because Paul worked such long hours, time 'off duty' was precious, so when his first week's holiday arrived in early September, he was determined to make good use of it. Too often in the past, he had drifted the days away, catching up with his sleep, relaxing with friends and recharging his batteries by taking long walks in the country. On this occasion though, he had firm plans; there were some specific tasks he wished to address.

His first objective was to resolve a doubt that had arisen in his mind about his colleague from the Surgical Three unit. This was achieved very quickly. By checking the duty roster, he confirmed that Roger Watkins should indeed have been at work when he had chanced to see him, whilst walking Kate back to the Nurses Home. He presumed Roger had also been *'moonlighting'* when his absence had resulted in Paul being called to see Mary Murphy on the medical ward, a couple of weeks earlier. Once more he wondered whether this should be reported to Sir William or to the Professor, but again decided not to do so. There seemed little to be gained from rocking the boat.

Then some detective work was needed to investigate the fascinating case of the three boys whose wrists injuries had been sustained at the football match. Paul knew that if this hazard to spectators had not been recognised before, it would make an interesting article for one of the surgical journals. Academic articles were well regarded by hospital consultants. They helped juniors to gain promotion. Whilst working at the University, Paul had undertaken a study that had been published in an anatomical journal. His CV would be enhanced and his career prospects improved, if he could achieve a second publication.

Paul also wanted to find time to study for the Fellowship examination. Becoming a Fellow of the highly prestigious Royal College of Surgeons of England was an essential step on a trainee's surgical journey. The examination was taken in two stages. Paul had passed the first part, the major element of which was anatomy, whilst working in the anatomy department. There, to his great good fortune, he had actually been paid to study the subject. In the rarefied atmosphere of the university without any clinical duties or nights on call, there had been plenty of time to study. However, the second part of the exam was a far greater challenge. The scope of the syllabus was enormous. Candidates could be questioned on any aspect of a wide variety of different surgical specialties. Whilst working at the Middleton Hospital, and in his present post, Paul had seen many patients with abdominal problems but the exam covered areas of which he had little or no practical experience, such as orthopaedics, chest and cardiac surgery; everything in fact from broken bones to brain surgery, from trauma to transplantation. To succeed Paul also needed to know how wounds heal, and the manner in which the body reacts to tumours, infection or blood loss. Many aspiring surgeons attempted the exam but most failed. The pass rate was only 25%. It was a daunting prospect, not least because the 'on call' roster, severely limited the time available for study.

Finally, during his week off duty, Paul wanted to spend some time with Kate. Since hearing the wonderful news that that she was no longer engaged, he had enjoyed many happy hours in her company. They had reminisced about their previous romance and caught up on each other's activities during the time they had been separated. It was clear that they both regretted drifting apart. From Monday until Friday Kate would be working but she had invited Paul to visit her home in the Lake District at the weekend. He was looking forward to meeting her father and enjoying some fresh air.

Having satisfied his curiosity about Roger's rota, Paul's next task was to investigate the possibility of writing an article on wrist injuries. There was no prospect of a publication if the injury had been described before, so on the Monday morning he visited the medical library. He reviewed various orthopaedic textbooks and journals and was relieved to find that there were no previous reports of this problem. The next step was to discover whether any other youngsters had been treated at the City General with similar injuries. If they had, this was most likely to have occurred on those occasions when the largest crowds had attended football matches. This was not information that was available in the medical library, so Paul rang The Herald, the regional newspaper that was based in the city. He learned that the sports editor didn't arrive until three pm, and then worked through until midnight - something that Paul might have anticipated had he thought about the deadline for publication of a daily paper. However the editor's secretary sounded interested and suggested that Paul call again at four pm, explaining that the office was relatively calm at that time of day, but became increasing frenetic as the evening wore on.

The Herald's headquarters, where the newspaper was both edited and printed, was a large glass fronted building on Market Street, in the city centre. Paul found it without difficulty. The sports editor listened to his request for information and readily agreed to assist with the research. He truly could not have been more helpful. He showed Paul their comprehensive sports library, explained how information was catalogued and gave him a pass, allowing him access to the building as and when he pleased. He even offered the use of the newspaper's artist, to draw an illustration to show how the boys' wrists had been overstretched on the wall at the front of the terraces, by the weight of spectators behind them. All he asked in return was that Paul should write an article for the newspaper when his research was complete. In less than an hour, he had a list of all the dates within the last five years, on which attendance at the football grounds of the two local teams had exceeded 50,000.

Returning to the hospital, Paul went straight to the records department to review the notes of patients who had attended casualty within 24 hours of these matches. This proved to be far more time consuming; in fact, it took him the whole of Tuesday to complete the task, but it turned out to be a very fruitful exercise. The records yielded details of five further soccer supporters, all teenagers, who had sustained identical wrist fractures. Delighted with his progress, he went in search of Mr Potts and was encouraged to find that he was equally enthusiastic.

"I'm sure Lambert," he said, "that it will make an interesting article for one of the surgical journals. Clearly it's not a major academic breakthrough, but it's certainly relevant to orthopaedic and casualty staff. Editors are aware that their journals can be rather dry. They're always on the lookout for something a little light-hearted that will be of interest to a more general audience."

"That's good, Sir. I'll get to work on it at once."

"Hang on a minute Lambert," Mr Potts cautioned. "There are couple of things to consider before you go any further. You'll need to obtain the consent of the consultants who managed these youngsters. These are orthopaedic cases; they weren't admitted under my care. You can't write about another doctor's patients without their permission. But if you like, I'll do that for you. I'm sure they will agree."

"That's most kind of you, Sir."

"And it may be useful, if you let me read through the article when you've drafted it, before you submit it. I've written dozens of papers over the years. I'll make sure it's presented to the journal in an appropriate style."

Grateful for his enthusiasm and advice, Paul thanked him profusely.

The next day, after a pleasant evening spent in Kate's company, Paul sat down and in less than three hours, had written what he thought was an interesting article, which he entitled 'Soccer Supporter's Wrist'. It described the details of the injuries sustained, both by the lads that he had seen himself, and the cases which had come to light during his review of casualty records. Then, as before, he sought Mr Potts, to invite him to review the article as he had suggested.

"Yes," he said. "Leave it with me. I'll happily look at it for you. If I'm satisfied, I'll send it to the journal on your behalf. Publishing in medical journals is not always as straightforward as you might imagine. Occasionally a little skulduggery, or you might call it duplicity, takes place."

Unsure of his meaning, Paul asked him to explain.

"Well, Lambert, the journal is edited in London and it has been known for members of the editorial committee to steal a good idea. It would be very easy for someone to check if similar injuries were occurring at Wembley or Twickenham and then to write a similar piece to yours."

"But what would be the point, if my article had already been published?"

"You may be surprised but there are a number of ways in which they could publish an article first. They could easily delay yours, by asking for a more detailed analysis, or by requesting that it be redrafted. Somebody might be tempted to take advantage of a lowly SHO but they wouldn't dare take liberties with a senior consultant. Just leave it with me."

Once again Paul thanked him for his assistance, though considered that Mr Potts' concern about sharp practice was overstated. It was only much later in his career that he learned that some very unscrupulous things did indeed happen in the world of medical publication. At various times, pharmaceutical companies have published data biased in favour of their own drugs, or suppressed information about the side effects of their products. It has even been known for senior doctors, some with international reputations, to publish cases that are entirely figments of their imagination. And plagiarism regularly occurs.

Finally, well pleased with his progress, Paul settled down to do some serious swotting for the College examination. It had been extremely difficult to study at the Middleton Hospital, where he had worked every other night. Coming off duty after a 32-hour stint, was not conducive to digesting the contents of a surgical textbook! Occasionally he had tried to study, but his brain had refused to absorb new knowledge and catching up with sleep had been a greater priority. An additional handicap at the Middleton, had been the lack of any formal tuition. It had been an old fashioned apprenticeship, though Paul had actually learned a great deal, by listening to the consultants as they explained things on the wards, and by watching as they operated in theatre. However, as well as the practical side of surgery, there was a great deal of theoretical knowledge to acquire and for the rest of the week, he burned the midnight oil, all the while looking forward to spending a pleasant weekend with Kate.

When Friday evening arrived, Paul collected Kate from the Nurses Home. They drove sedately in his old car to her family home in Westmoreland, where she introduced him to her father. Paul immediately recognised the root of Kate's gentle personality. He too was quietly spoken, had a calm and easy manner and a warm personality.

"Welcome," he said, shaking Paul firmly by the hand. "I'm very pleased to meet you. Kate has often spoken of you, and I'm delighted that you will be joining us for the weekend."

"It's good to meet you too, Sir.

"Oh, for heaven's sake, Paul. Forget all that 'Sir' business. Please call me Ralph."

The family home was a small detached cottage, built in local stone, five or six miles north of Kendal, just off the road to Windermere. To one side, there was an acre of land, devoted entirely to vegetables. Behind the cottage, with its grey slate roof and small sash windows, the land rose gently across green fields, interspersed with wooded copses and the occasional white washed cottage. Beyond were fine views of the hills of the southern Lake District inviting discovery.

"I'm afraid that you'll have to put up with my cooking tonight, Paul," Ralph said. "Muriel is away, visiting her sister. She was sorry to have missed you."

"Dad is quite a chef," Kate commented. "He has learned a lot in the last couple of years. You just wait and see."

They chatted in the kitchen as Ralph prepared the food, then enjoyed a wholesome evening meal; shepherd's pie, with peas and carrots, followed by rhubarb crumble; all produce from Ralph's vegetable patch. It was accompanied by generous quantities of home brewed beer. Later, they worked as a team to wash and dry the pots and pans then, feeling mellow and satisfied, they relaxed in comfortable old armchairs, in front of a roaring log fire. As dusk descended, Paul found it wonderfully soothing to be in Kate's company, sitting and chatting in the cosy and peaceful parlour with its heavy oak beams, free from the responsibilities of patient care and away from the hustle and bustle of hospital life. Most of the time, he sat and listened as Kate and her father exchanged views and gossip. Kate spoke of her friends in the Nurses Home, patients she had nursed on the wards and things she had seen in the operating theatre. Ralph talked of local affairs and of matters that had been discussed at the village council, of which he was the chairman. He made no mention of Peter, Kate's former fiancé. Quietly, Paul observed Kate and her father as they chatted together. There was obviously a close bond between them, no doubt cemented by Kate's mother's illness and death. The relationship was not one of father and daughter but one of equals. Ralph asked for guidance on domestic matters, as a man might of his wife. Kate, in response, teased him about his somewhat old fashioned views on life. At ten o'clock, Kate produced mugs of coffee and some fruitcake that Muriel had baked, and with the prospect of a good weather the following day, they retired early.

In the morning, awakened by the delicious smell of bacon and eggs drifting through the bedroom door, Paul dressed and shaved quickly, then went downstairs to find Kate and her father preparing breakfast. Ralph greeted him with a warm smile.

"It really is a glorious day for a walk, Paul. Unfortunately, I shall be working in the pharmacy today, but if the weather is as nice tomorrow, I may join you. That is, provided you have no objection?"

"Of course we don't mind," Paul replied. "No doubt you know the fells round here extremely well. Indeed I was going to ask you if you had any suggestions for us today."

"Well I suggest you take the car to the top of the valley, and then tackle the Kentmere horseshoe. It will take you five or six hours but the views from the tops will be stunning on a day like this."

Kate though looked a little uncertain. "I'd like to take if fairly gently today Paul, if you don't mind. I didn't sleep too well last night and feel a bit tired."

Ralph looked up anxiously. "You're not sickening for something are you, Kate?"

"I'm not sure. I just feel one degree under, nothing very specific. I've struggled with a sore throat for the last couple of days and now I've got a slight headache."

"You've probably been working too hard at that hospital of yours," Ralph replied. "Take a couple of aspirins and let the mountain air blow the cobwebs away."

With freshly made sandwiches and a plentiful supply of water, Kate and Paul set off. As her father had remarked, it was a glorious day. There was a clear sky, warm sun and just enough breeze to prevent them from overheating as they climbed gently; initially through meadows, then through a wood and then out into open countryside above the tree line. As they gained height, the view got better and better. They looked down on Windermere, Esthwaite Water and Lake Coniston far below and even got a glimpse of Morecambe Bay in the

120

distance to the south. Paul had tramped these hills with Kate two years before. He knew her to be a proficient hill walker. She was fit and energetic and more than able to match him stride for stride. But today, she was quiet and she struggled up some of steeper sections. After a while, they stopped for a rest and a drink. Paul spread his rainwear on a carpet of heather and they lay back, side by side. Soaking in the view, with Kate at his side, Paul felt at peace with the world. It was an idyllic spot. Far below, the fields, some brown, some green, others gold with wheat ripe for harvesting, were patterned like a jigsaw by the dry stone walls, the result of centuries of hard toil by previous generations of farmers. Isolated cottages, small villages, copses and larger woods were laid out in the distant valley like some giant tapestry. They watched as a tractor, crawling like an ant, ploughed backwards and forwards across a meadow, gradually turning the green to a rich brown ready for the planting of an early winter crop. A kestrel hung high in the sky, then swooped down to hover nearer the earth, as it searched for some unsuspecting field mouse or vole; then disappointed, rose again and moved away to find another hunting ground. The sun was warm, the sky was blue, and there was a gentle scent from the heather. Paul turned to look at Kate, lying beside him and noticed a faraway look on her face, as if she were daydreaming.

"You're very quiet today," he said.

"Sorry Paul, I was just thinking."

He waited, wondering whether they were thoughts she wished to share.

"As you know," she continued, "when Mum was reaching the end, I gave up nursing and lived at home to be close to her; to care for her. It was tough. I don't mean physically hard, although at times it certainly was. It was emotionally exhausting. Even though I had nursed people with terminal illnesses at the hospital, it didn't prepare me for caring for my own mother. It was worse, of course, for Dad. He hadn't met it before and he reacted badly. It has taken him a long time to get over it. Occasionally, when I needed a break, Muriel would sit with Mum. I would come up here, to get away from it for a short while. Sometimes Peter would come too and we would just sit and talk."

Peter's name hadn't been mentioned for a week or more, but as soon as it was, Paul experienced a pang of jealousy. It hit him like a knife to the heart. He knew that it was unreasonable. He had been assured; indeed he fully accepted, that as far as Kate was concerned, Peter was in the past. But it was something that he couldn't control. It hurt him to think that someone else had been close to Kate.

"When I was up here, I was able to relax for an hour or two. Then I could start afresh with Mum. I find that being in the hills is very therapeutic.

"You obviously loved your mother a great deal," Paul commented, his hand in hers.

"Yes, I did. I loved her dearly and after she died, I would often come up here and just sit for a while, cry a while and recall all the good times that we shared as a family. It helped to ease the pain."

Paul looked into her face and saw tears welling in her eyes.

"I miss her terribly Paul. I find myself wanting to talk to her, to tell her about you and the good times we have together. I want to tell her about my nursing career, the things we do on the wards, the operations I see in theatre. Sometimes I need to ask her advice, and she's not there to guide me."

"And has it got any easier with the passage of time? Is it true that time eases the pain?"

"Yes, to some extent I suppose. Its well over a year since Mum died and it is getting easier. And it has helped that I've gone back to nursing. Doing something that keeps me physically and mentally active was certainly the right thing to do. At first, I felt the need to stay at home and look after Dad. He was distraught at the time, but then Muriel came on the scene. They had both been widowed and she's been very good for Dad. I didn't feel at all resentful when they married but afterwards, there were times when I felt like an intruder in my own house. At that stage, Peter and I spent a lot of time together. We had both lost parents and, somehow or other, we ended up engaged to be married, largely I suspect, because it's what Muriel and Dad expected. It was only afterwards, I realised what a mistake it was. So I decided to get away and resume my nursing career."

"So you broke it off with Peter?"

"Yes I did, but I think we both realised that it wouldn't have worked; that I would never have been able to settle down to country life as a farmer's wife."

"Were you close to him?"

"Yes. He's been a good friend for many years - and he was a very good friend in time of need."

"You must have been very close friends then."

As soon as the words were spoken, Paul realised they had been phrased, not so much as a comment, but more as a question, almost as an accusation. And they were leading into dangerous waters. Ever since he had learned about Peter, the matter had been pressing on his mind. But he hadn't meant to ask, afraid of what the answer might be. Kate had been lying beside him, gazing at the sky but now she turned towards him, propping herself up on one elbow. Her face, initially serious, creased into a slow smile.

There was a twinkle in her eye as she spoke. "I can still get married in white, Paul, if that's what you mean."

Paul reddened, embarrassed by his own clumsiness. "Look Kate, I'm sorry I didn't mean to pry. It's none of my business, it's just that......." He didn't know how to finish the sentence. There was a long pause, and he waited, knowing exactly what was coming. It was his own fault. He had taken the conversation into this intimate personal territory and now he would pay the price.

"Well Paul. What about you? Handsome young surgeon, single, surrounded by nurses, physiotherapists and radiographers; you must have had a few girlfriends in the last two years?"

"Yes, one or two," Paul admitted, "but nothing serious, nothing that lasted more than two or three weeks."

He had ducked the question, they both knew that and he waited for the follow up but for some reason, it didn't come. Perhaps she didn't want to know; perhaps it didn't matter to her. And why had he not told her? Was he embarrassed to admit to being a 25 year-old virgin? In truth, he was unable to explain it to himself. He didn't feel any shame. In many ways he felt pleased with himself, satisfied with his conduct. Of course, as a medical student and as a junior hospital doctor, there had been opportunities to lose the label, but he had passed them by. He knew that there were plenty of girls who would happily share a tumble between the sheets with a young doctor. He had seen them at parties, their intentions all too clear. He had heard colleagues boast of their 'success' the next day, though suspected that their accounts were frequently exaggerated. But he had chosen not to indulge. Certainly, he was reserved, shy by nature, but that was not what had held him back. It was simply that such girls held little attraction for him and his moral code would not allow it.

Five minutes passed and nothing was said. Both were lost in their own private thoughts. Paul was relieved to learn that Kate's relationship with Peter had not become physical. He wanted to reopen the conversation, to tell her that he too had shown restraint, but the moment had passed and he found himself unable to do so. For some reason, he was unwilling to admit to the situation, even to Kate. It was as if male ego demanded that by his age, he ought to have a string of 'conquests' to his name.

Finally, Paul sat up, reproaching himself that his lack of confidence had inhibited him from sharing an open and honest exchange with the girl he loved. "Come on Kate. If we're going to climb this mountain, we had better get moving."

"Paul, I'm sorry, but I need to turn back. I don't feel up to it."

Concerned, Paul looked at her. She looked flushed. He put a hand on her brow.

"You've got a temperature. How are you feeling?"

"My sore throat is getting worse and I'm aching all over."

"It sounds as if you are getting 'flu. Have a drink and we'll get you back to the car."

Kate was normally a good walker, who thought nothing of a 12-mile hike or a 3,000ft climb but she struggled to get home. They stopped several times on the way down to allow her to rest and she was very relieved when they finally arrived back at her father's cottage.

"I'm sorry to spoil your day Paul, but I'm afraid that I need to lie down."

He found some aspirins in the bathroom cupboard and gave her a couple with a drink of water, which she promptly vomited. She went to her room, and when he went to check on her 20 minutes later, she was fast asleep on her bed. During the course of the afternoon, he popped in several times to monitor her progress, but she appeared to be comfortable and remained asleep.

The rest of the day passed slowly, Paul drifting around without much purpose. He pulled up a few weeds in the vegetable patch, peeled some potatoes for the evening meal and waited for Ralph to return from work. Had he brought one of his textbooks with him, he would have done some revision but as it was, he could do no more than look at a couple of Ralph's pharmacy books, to read those sections that were relevant to surgical disorders.

When Sunday morning dawned, Kate said she felt a little better but ate no breakfast, had very little energy, did not feel like leaving the house and was certainly not fit enough to go walking. She argued that she didn't need anyone to stay to look after her, saying that there was nothing to be gained by Paul and her father remaining in the cottage all day. So the two of them went out walking. For an hour or more, they strolled along in a companionable silence, content to be in the fresh air and beautiful surroundings on another warm sunny day. Later they chatted. Ralph spoke of life in the village, of local characters and events, but it was noticeable that his comments were never negative or critical. He knew a great deal about the countryside, the farming calendar, rotation of crops and breeds of cattle and sheep. He spotted birds and animals that Paul would have missed; a fallow deer camouflaged in woodland, a kingfisher as it flashed low over a brook and swallows as they began their long flight to warmer climes for the winter. Without prompting, he spoke in his quiet voice with its soft Cumbrian accent, of his children of whom he was clearly proud. He acknowledged his gratitude to Kate for the sacrifice that she had made, when interrupting her nursing studies to support him when his wife was so ill. Although he clearly missed her after her return to the City General, he expressed support for her decision to return to nursing.

Paul learned that Kate had a younger brother, Lionel, who was studying pharmacy, following in his father's footsteps and planning, when he qualified, to join the family business. Ralph inquired about Paul's own background, his current job and future plans and although he made no specific mention of Paul's friendship with his daughter, Paul gained the impression that he did not disapprove. Paul found he liked him enormously. Although they were a generation apart in age, Ralph conversed with him as an equal, just as he did with Kate, something Paul found refreshing and which contrasted with the rather more formal relationship that he had with his own father.

Later in the day, when they returned to the cottage, Kate was up and dressed and looked a little brighter. They were both due back at work the next morning, so they decided to return to the hospital before it got too late, arguing that if Kate needed longer to recover, she could do so in the nurses sick bay, where there were staff to care for her. Although the weekend had not gone as planned, Paul was pleased to have met and enjoyed the company of her father. He was also aware that spending a couple of nights in his home had been an important step in his relationship with Kate.

After an uneventful journey back to the City General, Paul escorted her to the front door of the Nurses Home. Kate reported to the 'Home Sister' and was immediately placed in the nurse's sickbay, where she remained bed bound for the next two days. It seemed probable that her sore throat, headache and high fever would simply be due to 'flu and that she would soon be fit enough to return to work. Sadly this proved not to be the case. In fact, it proved to be something far more serious, something that would have a major impact on both their lives in the months to come.

Chapter Thirteen

During the following week, both Richard and Paul became increasingly angry with Mr Potts, albeit for very different reasons. The common thread was Liz. It was widely recognised within the hospital, that Mr Potts always appointed the most attractive female medical graduate to work as his house officer, irrespective of their performance as a student or in the final exam. He was also known to favour them when it came to the delegation of duties, but this preferential treatment was particularly noticeable with Liz. She was invited to join him in theatre when an assistant was not required, or to accompany him when he visited patients in their own homes, something that none of the other consultants ever did. All the while, Richard was left slaving away on the wards, doing the work of two people, covering for her absence. One afternoon, he took Liz to a medical lecture at a neighbouring hospital, and then invited her to stay for the dinner that was held in the evening. His regard for Liz appeared to extend beyond a desire to stimulate her academic interest in surgery. It was clearly more personal and that was what so antagonised Richard. The way that he spoke to her, the softness of the tone he used, the occasional hand on her shoulder and the casual arm around her waist, contrasted sharply with his curt manner towards the rest of the staff, and towards Richard in particular. Liz seemed flattered by the attention she was receiving, and gave no sign to suggest that Mr Potts' attention was unwelcome. The relationship between the consultant and his house officer seemed to be developing in an inappropriate manner, but it was not for Paul, or any of the other members of the team, to interfere. It was the subject of gossip, of course, within the hospital, but the general opinion was that Liz was quite old enough to look after herself. As the days went by however, Richard inevitably became frustrated and angry.

Paul's grouse with his consultant was that Liz, within a week of commencing her post, had complained that she was so exhausted that she was unable to undertake her casualty duties. Mr Potts had sympathised with her and *'invited'* Paul to deputise, an arrangement that was still ongoing. To many, it appeared that she had cleverly manipulated the system to her own advantage. Undeniably, the overnight casualty shift was exhausting and stressful. But it was the house officer's responsibility. The experience they gained, dealing with accidents and emergencies, was beneficial; it was an integral part of their training. If for any reason they were absent, perhaps because of annual leave or sickness, the other house officers were suppose to cover. But nowhere in Paul's contract did it stipulate that he should be first on call. His job was to assist and support the house officers should they need advice, not to deputise for them. In any case, it seemed to Paul that there was no legitimate reason why an additional locum doctor should not be appointed. There was however, nothing he could do about it. If the boss said '*do it*' – you did it. He was all-powerful and totally in control of your career. Cross your consultant and you said '*goodbye*' to surgery and '*hello*' to general practice!

And so it was, that at nine pm on their next 'admitting' day, quietly fuming, Paul walked to casualty. The nursing staff, of course, were delighted with the arrangement. Having a senior house officer working alongside them, instead of a newly qualified doctor fresh from medical school, eased their load considerably. An SHO, with the experience gained from having undertaken casualty duties on many previous occasions, was significantly more confident and competent. He knew which patients with head injuries could be sent home, which needed to be observed for a few hours, and which needed to be admitted. He was able to separate patients whose sprained joints could simply be strapped from those whose injuries required an x-ray. He was able to make a neat job of suturing lacerations and like all casualty officers at this time, had plenty of experience of removing splinters of glass from the faces of drivers and front seat passengers, who had gone head first through the windscreen in road traffic accidents. If the victim happened to be young and female, the job was performed under an anaesthetic in theatre but otherwise, it was a task for the casualty officer in the accident room. Having a more experienced doctor in the department also meant that patients were assessed and treated quickly. There were fewer grumbles from patients waiting to be seen and there were no delays waiting for a more senior doctor to arrive to give a second opinion.

A succession of minor injuries kept Paul busy during the course of the evening, helping time to pass quickly. By one am however, all the cubicles were empty, there were no more patients waiting to be seen and Paul retired to the tiny store room which served as the doctor's bedroom. Scarcely had his head hit the pillow, than the peace was shattered by the wailing of ambulance sirens, followed by the most tremendous racket coming from within the department. Without warning, ten to fifteen youths had arrived. Within seconds the place was in bedlam, as they rampaged around, running in and out of cubicles, shouting, swearing and being abusive to the nurses. A fight involving fists and beer bottles had broken out at one of the local nightclubs and a fleet of ambulances had brought the casualties to the department. The youths, who belonged to two rival gangs, were accompanied by some female camp followers, and all were clearly the worse for drink.

Paul's first impression was that none of the victims appeared to be significantly injured, indeed most seemed intent on continuing their battle in the casualty department, kicking, scratching and biting each other. Patients should always be seen and treated according to the severity of their injuries, the most serious being given priority, but no one was going to get any attention whilst the chaos continued. In vain, the nurses tried to separate those who were injured, from those who were not, but the uninjured refused to leave the department. They insisted that their mates needed their protection, whilst they were being treated. They continued to cause pandemonium, ripping posters from the waiting room walls, tampering with equipment and upsetting tables and chairs. One girl vomited outside Sister's office and one of the lads relieved himself in the reception area.

At night, the staffing of the department was limited to a sister, two junior nurses and the duty casualty officer, in this instance, Paul. Sister called the night porter, who quickly assessed the situation, decided that reinforcements were needed and rang the police. Within minutes, three burly bobbies arrived. At their appearance, the number of rioters immediately reduced; several melting away into the night. The police grabbed and restrained the remaining lads one by one, so that Paul was able to assess them. Those who were uninjured, or who only had slight bumps or bruises, were taken away by 'Black Maria' police van. They would be locked up for the night in the local police station and in the morning would appear at the city's Magistrates court, charged with being drunk and disorderly. Two girls, who appeared simply to be drunk, though in no fit state to go home, were placed in the observation area to sleep off the effects of alcohol. Of the others, all but one had minor injuries and the nurses stitched and patched their various cuts and scrapes, before they too were escorted away by the police. Only one young man, whose drowsy condition might have been due to drugs, drink or to a head injury, was admitted for observation. He would be re-assessed in the morning. Finally calm and order was restored, but it had taken the best part of two hours to sort it all out.

Paul was about to return to his bedroom, when he noticed that a 'genuine' patient had arrived by ambulance and was lying on a trolley in the cubicle at the far end of the department. A lady was standing at the door urgently beckoning to him, a lady whose face he recognised. It was Miss Mullins, who had attended previously with her pregnant cat and, surprisingly, she was again wearing the same colourful woollen 'tea cosy' on her head and the matching knitted cardigan.

"Hello, have you brought Kitty along again?" Paul asked.

"No, I haven't. I've come this time with my brother. He's desperately ill and he's been waiting hours to be seen." She sounded both angry and concerned.

"Yes, I'm sorry about that but I am sure you can understand why."

"Sadly I can," she replied, her face registering the disgust she felt, at the events that she had just witnessed.

It was immediately apparent that Miss Mullins' concern was entirely justified. Her brother was an extremely sick man with an acute abdominal problem. He looked drawn and pale; his skin was cold and clammy and he had a weak rapid pulse. Gasping for air, with a blood pressure in his boots, he was showing all the signs of an advanced state of clinical shock. The nurses placed a drip into his arm and Paul linked him up to an oxygen mask, before listening to his story. His mouth was so dry that he had difficulty talking, and most of the story came from Miss Mullins.

Paul learned that he had been vaguely unwell for the previous two weeks but had been reluctant to seek help. He was of the 'old school' and had not wished to trouble his own doctor. Then he had become constipated and had started to vomit.

"The smell of the vomit is awful, Doctor," Miss Mullins continued. "You would think it had come out of the other end. And he's had terrible abdominal pain, griping like labour pains."

This was another classic history of bowel obstruction and in a man in his seventies, like Mary Murphy, was almost certain to be due to cancer. He needed to be admitted, and after he had been resuscitated, required urgent surgery. Since Paul had to remain in casualty for the rest of the night, he rang Victoria to ask her to supervise Mr Mullins' care on the ward. It was after four in the morning when he finally got back to bed.

No sooner had he got to sleep, than the nurses woke him to see yet another patient. He looked at his watch and swore. It was ten past five. By nine am, he had to be up, dressed, shaved and fresh faced, ready to face another day's work, no doubt starting with the surgical exploration of Mr Mullins' abdomen. Unlike the yobs that had caused mayhem earlier in the night, at least this new patient was pleasant and polite.

John Collins was a man of about 30. He was accompanied by his wife. They quickly realised that Paul had been called from his bed. This was not altogether surprising! He had stubble on his chin, looked bleary eyed and had simply thrown a white coat over his pyjamas. They were immediately apologetic.

"We're sorry to disturb you, Doctor. We really don't feel justified in troubling you at this time of the night. We know that your job is to deal with major accidents and emergencies, but the note from our own doctor said to come here."

John went on to explain. "I've been troubled with indigestion for a week or so. I've been putting up with it, treating myself with milk and bicarbonate of soda. But it got worse, so earlier this evening, I tried to see my own doctor. The surgery is at his house you know, but there was a note on the door saying that there was no service until ten in the morning, and that anyone with a problem should come here. At the time, I didn't feel justified in coming to the hospital, but during the night, the indigestion got quite severe and I couldn't sleep. I took more milk but it didn't help. And I'd run out of the bicarbonate. That's why I've come to the hospital. All I need is some indigestion tablets or a white bottle. I had no idea that you would be in bed. I thought there would be a duty doctor working a night shift."

"There is," Paul growled. "It's me. I was on duty all yesterday and will be working 'til five this evening!"

Paul knew it was wrong to be angry with the patient. It wasn't his fault but he was furious.

"And who is this doctor who gives such an excellent service?" he asked sarcastically.

"It's Dr Clark in Chepstow Street."

Paul gave the patient an alkaline mixture and he and his wife went happily on their way, but Paul felt abused. He remonstrated with Sister.

"Why the hell should I have to see Dr Clark's patients in the middle of the night, simply because he's too bone idle to arrange a roster with his colleagues? Damn it, he's supposed to offer a 24-hour service but he absolves himself from all responsibility by sticking a note on the surgery door telling patients to come here. It saves him the cost of arranging cover, I suppose."

Sister tried to assuage Paul's anger. "It's no good getting het up about it, Paul. It happens all the time. Dr Clark is notorious, and he gets away with it because his surgery is just round the corner. He couldn't do it if his practice was five miles away."

"So he gets paid for giving a 24 hour service, never does any night calls and we pick up pieces, is that it?"

"That's about the size of it."

Paul was livid. It wasn't his job to be the casualty officer through the night. He was only doing it because Mr Potts was feeling sympathetic towards his precious house officer. It was already 5.30 in the morning and he had had virtually no sleep at all.

"Right," he said to Sister. "We'll see about that. What's his telephone number?"

"I'm not sure, but Bob on the switchboard will get it for you from Directory Enquires."

Two minutes later, Paul was on the phone. The phone rang and rang and rang before eventually a sleepy female voice answered.

"Hello," Paul said. Is that Mrs Clark?"

"Yes it is. Who on earth is that?"

"This is Dr Lambert, from the City General Hospital. May I speak with Dr Clark please?"

"Dr Clark is not on duty. He isn't taking calls tonight."

"So I believe. I'm sorry to disturb him," Paul lied, "but I've just seen one of his patients as an emergency in the casualty department. I need to speak with him about his management."

There were shuffling noises and gruff curses at the other end of the line, before finally a male voice answered.

"Hello, Dr Clark here. Who's that?"

"This is Dr Lambert from the hospital. I'm ringing to let you know that I've just treated a patient of yours, a man called John Collins. He has been suffering from mild indigestion. I've given him an antacid mixture, which should solve the problem. He saw the notice on your surgery door and attended casualty as instructed. I thought you would like to know, so that you will be able to continue his treatment."

There was a long pause; so long in fact that Paul thought he wasn't going to answer. Finally he spoke.

"You impudent young pup. A letter in the morning would have sufficed." Then the telephone receiver was slammed down.

With the savage satisfaction of knowing that he was not the only one whose beauty sleep had been disturbed, Paul retired to the hot and stuffy cubby hole that served as his bedroom but, too angry to sleep, tossed and turned until morning.

When his stint in casualty was complete and seething with rage and resentment at Liz, Mr Potts and the world in general, Paul left the department, to have a quick shower and shave. He passed the day staff, chatting cheerfully as they came on duty. They were fresh after their full, undisturbed night's sleep, whereas Paul was mentally and physically exhausted. Yet he still faced another eight hour day before he could rest. It was at times such as this, that he became fearful that he would make some dreadful mistake that would result in a patient's death. Further, there was a real danger that in the investigation that followed, no allowance would be made for the unacceptable hours of work and the chronic tiredness that numbed the brain. He might be held personally responsible when, in practice, it was the system that was at fault.

The day started with a visit to theatre to discover the cause of Mr Mullins' obstruction. Mohammed and Paul changed, donned theatre 'greens', caps and masks, then scrubbed and slipped into surgical gowns and gloves.

"Would you like me to assist you for this case?" Mo asked as they approached the operating table.

It was a generous offer, too good for a surgical trainee to refuse. There was no substitute for operative experience. Every opportunity had to be seized, no matter how exhausted you were.

"Yes, I would, thanks, so long as you promise to wake me if I fall asleep into the wound," Paul replied, half in jest.

In practice, there was no such danger. When Paul was operating, there was always more than enough adrenaline pumping around the system to keep him alert. In any case, he knew that Mo would be keeping a watchful eye on his performance.

When the abdomen was opened, it was quickly confirmed that the obstruction was due to a cancer. Sadly though, the tumour had grown into adjacent structures such that it was not possible to remove it. Worse, there was extensive spread to the other organs. Regrettably therefore, this cancer was incurable. Since bowel surgery and plumbing are similar, Paul was able to relieve Mr Mullins' blockage by creating a bypass. This allowed bowel content to escape from the distended loops of gut above the cancer, into the collapsed loops beyond. This would relieve the pain, vomiting and constipation which had been Mr Mullins' main symptoms. It was however inevitable, that even if he survived the operation, he would shortly waste away and die.

As the abdomen was being closed, Mr Potts entered the theatre. Never one to smile a lot, he looked distinctly stern.

"I see you're nearly finished here. You put the last few stitches in, Khan. I want a word with Lambert. In the surgeon's room now, Lambert!"

Conscious that the angry tone of the consultant's voice had caused the theatre staff to stare at him, Paul slipped off his gown and gloves. It was obvious that he was in trouble, but he couldn't imagine why. He was not aware that he had done anything wrong. Mr Potts was waiting for him in the surgeon's room and came straight to the point.

"Lambert, I've had Dr Clark on the phone. He says you rang him in the night and were extremely rude to him."

"Certainly I rang him, Sir," Paul protested. "But I was definitely not rude. In fact, I was at pains to be formal and polite."

"But you rang him in the middle of the night. What possible justification was there for that?"

Paul told him the whole story, confidently expecting Mr Potts' understanding and support. Everyone knew that the casualty department was for genuine accidents and real emergencies. It was not there for patients whose problems were minor. And certainly not there to allow a lazy GP to use the hospital to deputise for him, free of charge, without prior notice. Paul however, was sadly mistaken.

"I'm deeply disappointed in you, Lambert. You most certainly should have known better. Surely you understand that it's important to foster good relationships with our colleagues in general practice. Dr Clark is a senior practitioner; you are very young and inexperienced. There was no justification whatsoever for ringing him in the night, especially about a patient whose condition was not urgent. If you were unhappy about an aspect of Dr Clark's work, you should have shared your concerns with me, rather than taking the matter into your own hands. I expect you to show a great deal more maturity in future. You need to stay calm and consider things carefully, before you act in such an ill considered and irresponsible manner. You're not going to get very far in surgery, if you take such impulsive actions." A threat was clearly implicit in the consultant's words.

Unable to understand why Mr Potts should support a GP who so blatantly abused the system, Paul was amazed at the attitude his boss had adopted. To be criticised in these circumstances seemed grossly unfair, but he bit his tongue. He knew better than to argue with the consultant. Mr Potts looked at him expectantly, perhaps waiting for an apology, but if indeed that was the case, he was destined to be disappointed. There was a pause.

"Well, Lambert. What have you got to say for yourself?"

"Nothing Sir."

Mr Potts glared at his trainee but Paul was damned if he was going to apologise. Mr Potts looked as if he was going to continue the tirade but he didn't.

"All right, Lambert. This time we'll leave it at that, but don't let it happen again."

"No, Sir."

And with a final, "That will be all Lambert." Paul was dismissed.

Afterwards, Paul spoke with Mo, needing to understand why Mr Potts had sided with Dr Clark. Mo listened quietly, as he always did, and then offered a simple explanation.

"Consultants need to keep the local doctors happy. It's the GPs who send them patients, not just to their NHS clinics but also to their private rooms. That's where the money is. Popular surgeons can double their NHS salaries, if they can attract a lot of private patients."

"So," Paul said bitterly, "Mr Potts turns his back on abuse of his junior doctors, simply to keep the general practitioners sweet, and to line his back pocket."

Mohammed smiled sympathetically. "That's about it, Paul. That's the way the system works. I know it's not fair, but as I've told you before, it doesn't pay to buck the system. Don't imagine that you will change it."

Paul remained bitter about the reprimand he had received but was simply too tired to argue. Mo put a hand on his shoulder, "Cheer up Paul, I'll make you a cup of coffee. You look as if you need one."

***

Throughout the operation, Miss Mullins had been waiting anxiously in the side ward that had been allocated to her brother. From previous experience, Paul knew that breaking bad news to patients, or relatives, was never easy. Despite having done it many times, he always found it a difficult and unpleasant task. The words he used never seemed adequate to convey the sympathy he felt and no matter how carefully the words were chosen, or how gently they were spoken, he felt helpless to do anything, or say anything to reduce the inevitable distress that the message conveyed. Paul knew that Miss Mullins and her bachelor brother had lived side by side for 70 years, initially as children, later through their working lives and finally in retirement. They had never been alone, never had a period of separation. They had always been there for each other, running the home together, spending their holidays together and sharing each other's problems. Miss Mullins had no other family to support her. When the time came that her brother died, she would be on her own.

She rose to her feet when Paul entered the room.

"Is the operation over?" she asked, her voice tense and anxious. "Has he pulled through?"

"Yes, the operation is over," Paul replied quietly. "That's what I've come to talk to you about."

She saw the expression on his face and heard the sadness in his voice. "It's not good news doctor, is it?"

"No, I'm afraid it isn't."

"But he will be alright, won't he? Tell me that he will be alright."

Paul pulled up a chair and as gently as he could, explained what had been found at the operation.

Miss Mullins listened carefully and then asked, "So what does all that mean, Doctor?"

"I'm afraid it means that we haven't been able to cure your brother. We have managed to relieve the blockage, so provided that he survives this operation, his pain and vomiting will stop. But since he still has the cancer inside him, it means that he will get weaker and weaker. I'm afraid that we must expect that the cancer will win in the end."

Miss Mullins was fighting back her tears.

"So you mean he's going to die, don't you Doctor? How long has he got?"

This is a question that is asked many times, yet one that is extremely difficult for any doctor to answer. During the operation, Paul had seen the extent of the cancer at a single moment in time, but he didn't know how rapidly it was growing. Mr Mullins might die from complications of his surgery within hours or days, but equally, if he survived the operation, he might linger for 12 months or more. In the past, Paul had sometimes given a figure in weeks, months or years, but had come to appreciate that this was unwise. Too often his estimates had proved to be wildly inaccurate. Many doctors had the experience of giving a particularly gloomy prognosis, then having the patient come to see them year after year, brimming with good health. As often as not, the patient opened the conversation by remarking, with a huge grin on their face, '*I'm still here, Doc despite what you said.*'

"I'm afraid I really don't know the answer to that question," Paul said. "It might be anything up to a year or more, but you must realise that this has been a major procedure. Your brother is not a young man. He was extremely ill when he went into theatre. It will be a week or so before we know that he's safely over this operation."

There was a pause and then Miss Mullins started to reminisce.

"Frank's a lovely man, so kind and gentle. I couldn't have wished for a better brother. We've always been together. We went to the same school and we both stayed at home with our parents, even during the war. Frank was in a protected occupation, so he didn't have to serve. Dad died first and Mum followed soon after, but Frank and I stayed together in the same house. We looked after each other and of course, we looked after our cats."

It seemed best to allow her to continue talking, so Paul sat with her for ten minutes or so, as she consoled herself with her memories. She was of the 'old school', not one to show her emotions. There was no weeping or wailing, just a phlegmatic acceptance of what she had been told.

Finally, Paul asked if she had any more questions, knowing that many patients and relatives fail to digest bad news at the first time of telling. The information may need to be repeated, sometimes more than once, before it finally sinks in.

"No," she answered. "Not at the moment. Perhaps later."

"I'm afraid I must leave you now and get back to theatre," Paul said, "but one of the nurses will make you a cup of tea and sit with you for a while."

"That's kind, Doctor, and thank you for being honest with me."

Promising to speak with her again in a couple of day's time, Paul left to arrange a drink for her. Leaving the room, he felt emotionally drained. He found it impossible not to share, to some degree, the sorrow and grief that the exchange had caused. Miss Mullins and her brother had been lifelong friends. They had enjoyed a relationship as strong as that of any married couple. Her life would never be the same, and it was with considerable sadness that he returned to the theatre. For the rest of the morning, he assisted Mo as he completed the operating list, counting down the minutes until he could get 'off duty' and get some rest, little knowing of the drama that was about to unfold in the sick bay in the Nurses Home.

Chapter Fourteen

In theatre, most anaesthetists are able to find time for a drink (and to tackle the crossword in the daily newspaper), whilst an operation is in progress. Indeed, surgeons frequently comment that the toughest job for the anaesthetist is to stay awake when the patient is asleep! Surgeons though, are only able to relax for a moment or two between cases, as the anaesthetist wakes one patient and anaesthetises the next. These breaks allow time for a quick drink, whilst writing an account of the surgical procedure in the patient's notes. It was on such an occasion the next morning, when Paul was assisting Victoria that he took the opportunity to ring the nurse's sickbay, to enquire after Kate. He confidently expected to hear that she was on the mend, anticipating that as soon as she had recovered from the worst of the flu, she would be allowed to spend a few days convalescing at home with her father. She would not be welcomed back at work, until it was certain that she was no longer infectious and a risk to patients with whom she came in contact. The last thing the hospital would want was a flu epidemic on the ward.

It was the Home Sister who answered the phone, her voice grave.

"Dr Lambert, I'm so pleased that you've phoned. We've been trying to contact you, but understood that you were scrubbed in theatre. I'm afraid Nurse Meredith is no longer here. She was transferred to a medical ward earlier this morning. They managed to find a bed for her on Medical Two."

Paul felt a twinge of alarm. "Why was she transferred, Sister? Has something happened?"

"It seems that she was not at all well in the night. The Resident Medical Officer (RMO) was called to see her. I wasn't with her at the time, so I don't know exactly what he found, but he was sufficient concerned to ring Dr Mitchie, the medical consultant. He advised that Kate be transferred to one of his hospital beds."

Now Paul was really anxious. "But what do they think is the matter?"

"I'm not sure. It would probably be best for you to speak with the staff on the medical ward."

"Has her father been informed, Sister?"

"Yes he has, and he asked if you would be kind enough to phone him when you have had a chance to visit."

Putting down the phone, Paul wondered what on earth could have happened to Kate during the night that required her to be admitted to hospital. Essentially she was a fit and healthy young woman. The illness that she had suffered at the weekend, her tiredness, sore throat and headache were typical of a dose of 'flu. But presumably the RMO no longer thought that was the diagnosis. Perhaps she had developed a complication of flu, such as pneumonia. He certainly wouldn't admit a patient with simple flu to hospital. He would send her home as quickly as possible to avoid spreading the infection.

After a quick work of explanation to Victoria, Paul went straight to the medical ward and was allowed a couple of minutes with Kate. She was in a side ward and looked far from well. She was pale, sweating and feverish. Instinctively Paul's eye went to the observation chart at the foot of the bed, noting the raised temperature and rapid pulse rate. He asked why she had been admitted to hospital.

"It's because I've developed a problem with my knee. Quite suddenly last night, it became painful and swollen. It blew up like a balloon and Dr Barber, the RMO came to see me. He said that he didn't think I had 'flu at all. He discussed it with Dr Mitchie on the phone; at two o'clock in the morning would you believe. They decided to admit me to the ward for a few tests. They say that it's just a precaution, but I must confess that I do feel rotten. I'm tired, I ache all over and I've got no appetite or energy at all. And my knee really is very painful."

"What can be the matter with your knee? You didn't fall or twist it did you, at the weekend, when we were out walking?"

"No, not at all but Dr Barber says the swelling is due to fluid. They plan to take a sample of it later today, to see what's causing it."

It didn't make sense at all, especially as there was no suggestion of an injury. Paul wondered if perhaps Dr Mitchie thought the combination of fever and a painful knee was due to an infection, but if that was the case, why had Kate been admitted to a medical ward? If there was an infection in the joint; surely Kate would have been admitted to the orthopaedic ward.

Paul cast his mind back to his student days. Having studied surgery for the last three years, medical conditions with which surgeons were not involved had slipped to the back of his mind. But suddenly the penny dropped and his anxiety increased ten-fold. Kate had suffered from a sore throat for a week or more. She still felt ill, her temperature hadn't settled and now she had fluid on her knee. The physicians must be concerned that she had rheumatic fever. Paul had never actually seen a case and desperately tried to remember what he had been taught about the condition at medical school. He had a vague recollection that it was condition that developed after an attack of tonsillitis and, if his memory served him correctly, the disease could affect the heart, as well as joints. If Kate had rheumatic fever, her knee was not inflamed as a result of an injury or infection, but with a rheumatic process.

At that moment, the ward sister came in.

"I'm sorry Dr Lambert, I shall have to ask you to leave now. The porter has arrived to take Kate for an x-ray of her chest and a tracing of her heart. Later Dr Mitchie will be coming to see her, and she is going to have fluid drawn from her knee. I think it would be best if you visited again this evening."

He had politely been told that he would not be welcome on the ward that afternoon!

Until he heard of the deterioration in Kate's condition, Paul's main worry, selfish he knew, had been that Kate would recover quickly enough for them to spend time together during the next weekend. However, there was now far more to be concerned about, and later that morning, he paid a visit to the hospital library and sought Cecil & Loeb's authoritative Textbook of Medicine, all 2,500 pages of it. Rheumatic fever, he read, refreshing the knowledge he had acquired as a student, was a condition that developed after an attack of tonsillitis. Instead of recovering from the infection in the usual way, the fever continued. Then new problems developed. Paul's memory had not misled him. Other organs in the body could be affected, but most commonly it involved joints. Less common, though much more serious, was involvement of the heart. The damage caused could be permanent, leaving the patient with a lifetime of physical disability, unable to run or to climb stairs.

According to the textbook, the outlook was uncertain. Many patients slowly improved, but others were left with lasting damage to joints or to the heart. Unfortunately, since the cause of the condition was unknown, there was no specific therapy. The mainstay of treatment was prolonged bed rest, with aspirin and steroids to reduce symptoms. As he read on, Paul became progressively more gloomy, increasingly concerned for Kate. The disease often recurred, and even when the patient had recovered from their initial illness, problems could return weeks, months or even several years later.

Paul wondered whether he could have come to the wrong conclusion; whether it might be some other condition, but everything he read suggested that rheumatic fever was the correct diagnosis. The sore throat, the raised temperature and the swollen knee joint; it all fitted. It was difficult to believe that it could be anything else. Poor Kate, at best she was going to have to rest in bed for weeks and then convalesce slowly for months. At worst, she could end up with a heart problem that would permanently limit her activity. She would hate that. She loved sport and the outdoor life.

For the rest of the day, Paul tried to distract himself by focussing on his clinical duties. In the afternoon, he worked alongside Mr Potts in the outpatient department, seeing patients who had been referred by their GPs. Then he went to the ward to review the patients who had undergone surgery that morning. It was however, difficult to concentrate; such was his concern about Kate. Finally 7pm arrived, the time at which visitors were allowed on the ward and he went to see Kate, only to find that she had been heavily sedated and was sleeping soundly. The nursing staff had no news of her various investigations, so Paul sat at the bedside feeling impotent, desperately wanting to do something to help, but knowing there was nothing that he could do. The chart of Kate's pulse and temperature alarmed him. Her heart rate had risen to 110, even though she was sedated, and from his research in the library, he knew that this was a sure sign that the heart was affected. At one stage, she roused for a few seconds and seemed to recognise him, but promptly fell back into her medically induced sleep.

Desperate for information, he bleeped Dr Mitchie's house officer. He had not taken Kate's history or indeed examined her; protocol dictating that whenever possible nursing staff were treated by more senior doctors, but he was able to confirm that Dr Mitchie was confident that rheumatic fever was the correct diagnosis. Over the next couple of days, Paul received regular telephone calls from Kate's father, who was anxious to understand the nature and severity of his daughter's illness. The nursing staff had answered his inquiries formally and politely but he had learned little about her condition. Eventually, thanks to the ward sister's intervention, an appointment was made for him to speak face to face with Dr Mitchie. Mr Meredith, Paul had difficulty in thinking of him as *'Ralph'*, invited Paul to accompany him to the meeting. *'With two of us there,'* he had said, *'we should get a fuller understanding of Kate's illness'.*

The meeting took place in the consultant's office. As a student, Paul had never been allocated to study on Dr Mitchie's ward and despite having attended one or two of his lectures, he knew little of him. Perhaps in his early fifties, he was old enough to have significant experience and wise enough to be cautious with his words. Slightly built, prematurely grey, with round spectacles and a furrowed brow, he appeared to carry the cares of the world on his slender shoulders. After formal introductions, he started to speak of Kate's illness. There was a nasal element to his voice and he spoke quickly and quietly, using medical terminology that Mr Meredith, despite his background in pharmacy, struggled to follow.

"Our working diagnosis," he began, "is rheumatic fever. There isn't a definitive test for this condition, but Miss Meredith has sufficient evidence to make all other diagnoses improbable. We have a positive anti-streptococcal antibody, auscultatory and electrocardiographic evidence of cardiac disease, as well as the tachycardia and of course, the non-traumatic arthritis. No other diagnosis gives this combination of stigmata, so we are therefore, reasonably confident of the pathology."

Mr Meredith looked bewildered and asked if Paul had understood what had been said. Paul confirmed that he had and presumed, incorrectly as it subsequently transpired, that Dr Mitchie, having heard the exchange, would speak in simpler terms. Not for the first time, he worried about the communication skills of some of his medical colleagues. If this was the way that Dr Mitchie normally addressed his patients, few would be the wiser for speaking with him! The consultant however, instead of simplifying his language and addressing Kate's father, who was his patient's next of kin, proceeded to ignore him and instead, spoke directly to Paul. He went on to detail *'the sterile but inflammatory nature of the joint aspirate, the prolonged PR interval on ECG and the blowing systolic murmur heard in the apical area'*, words and phrases that meant absolutely nothing to Mr Meredith!

As the consultation was drawing to a close, Mr Meredith again turned to Paul and inquired if he had understood all that had been said, requesting that he explain it to him afterwards. The remark implied criticism of Dr Mitchie, but if the consultant was aware of it, he didn't show it.

Afterwards, Mr Meredith and Paul walked to the doctor's residency and sat together in the lounge. Paul explained that Dr Mitchie was as sure as he could be that Kate had rheumatic fever. It had started with tonsillitis but instead of just shaking it off, as would be expected in a healthy young woman, Kate had responded in an unusual way. Areas of inflammation had sprung up in various parts of her body, particularly her knee and heart. Paul stressed that usually things settled down but admitted that occasionally there could be some lasting damage. He hoped that Mr Meredith would not realise that this was a rather optimistic interpretation of Kate's problem.

"But surely," Mr Meredith said, fidgeting nervously in his chair, "antibiotics are available these days that will cure a bacterial infection."

"Yes, Kate is receiving penicillin, but that is simply to make sure the throat infection has gone. Her troubles now are not due to an infection, but a reaction to the germ that was present when Kate had tonsillitis; a reaction that no-one understands."

"But Dr Mitchie said that Kate was likely to stay in hospital for a month. I can scarcely believe that."

"The mainstay of treatment is bed rest. I'm afraid that there is no specific treatment."

"And how will we know if her heart recovers?"

"Kate will have ECG's from time to time, but the best guide is the pulse rate which is recorded on the chart at the foot of the bed."

There was a long pause as Mr Meredith digested this information.

"Poor Kate. She loses her mother and now this."

He looked across at Paul, his eyes moist with tears. "Paul, I'll come down as often as possible, but working single-handed and with a business to run, I can't possibly come every day. You will ring me regularly, won't you?"

"Of course I will, daily."

Together they walked slowly back to his car where, rather formally, Mr Meredith offered Paul his hand.

Paul watched him drive away, then turned and walked slowly back to his flat. It was true. Losing her mother was bad enough, but now she had the threat of a lifelong disability hanging over her. If she were to suffer permanent damage to her heart, she might be unable to pursue her career in nursing. For someone dedicated to caring for others, that would be a disaster. It didn't seem fair and Paul felt desperately frustrated. Despite all his medical knowledge, he was unable to do anything useful to help her.

***

The more attention that Mr Potts lavished on his attractive young house lady and the more that this was reciprocated, the more resentful Richard became. The change in his manner was obvious. Having previously been bright and cheerful, ready with a joke or light-hearted word, he became sullen and uncommunicative. He ceased to exchange pleasantries with other members of the team. He no longer participated in the irreverent repartee that enriched life in the doctor's residency and helped to make the long hours of work bearable. Attempts to engage him in conversation were generally met with a brooding silence. Mo, Victoria and Paul were very conscious of it, as were the two nursing sisters, but if Mr Potts noticed, he didn't show it. The consultant's habit of teasing Richard about his good looks, athletic build and the opportunities that he had to date pretty nurses, inevitably aggravated the situation. It wasn't clear whether Mr Potts was unaware that Richard and Liz were engaged, or whether he did know and was being

142

deliberately provocative. Whichever it was, it added to the tension that existed between the senior consultant and his young houseman. It was a surprise therefore, that whilst sharing tea and biscuits in the office after one particular ward round, Richard again raised the subject of the forthcoming cricket match.

"Have the consultants managed to raise a team, Mr Potts?" he asked.

"Yes, we have, albeit with the help of family and a few friends," his boss replied cheerfully. "I'm looking forward to it."

"No professionals I hope?"

"No. Certainly no professionals, but I've invited a couple of local GP's to join us to make up the numbers. I did ask Sir William if he would care to play, but he said his cricketing days were over. He did however agree to be one of the umpires. I should just mention though, that my son, Andrew, is extremely keen to get involved. He's only nine years old but already plays in the local under 11's cricket team. I'm sure that I can rely on you to respect his age and to treat him accordingly."

No doubt in an attempt to impress Sister Ashbrook and the nurses who were present, Mr Potts went on to boast of his cricketing prowess, just as he had done in front of the theatre staff. He described a match-winning innings that he had played for a local club team and hinted that he was also an accomplished bowler.

"We're looking forward to teaching you youngsters one or two of the finer points of the game," he added with a smile.

"We'll see about that," responded Richard, a challenging ring in his voice, and omitting the 'Sir', which junior doctors usually employed when addressing their consultants!

As the mood in the office was pleasantly relaxed, more so than was usual when Mr Potts was present, Paul took the opportunity to ask him about the article he had penned on the injuries sustained by the three lads at the derby football match. A fortnight had passed since Paul had given him the draft and, concerned that Mr Potts might have forgotten all about it, he was anxious to submit it to one of the surgical journals. A second publication would look good on his C V and would improve his chances of promotion. It might also make life easier at some future job interview. The article might catch the eye of one of the interviewers. It was always safer to speak on a familiar subject, and it left less time for interrogation on more difficult topics.

"Oh yes, Lambert, I should have told you. I sent it off to Marcus Langley, the editor of the surgical journal. He's a pal of mine; I've known him for years. We did our junior surgical jobs together in London. In fact, I rang him a couple of days ago to see what he thought of it. You will be pleased to hear that he liked it and has accepted it for publication. You should see it in the journal within the next month or so. Another string to your bow, eh?"

For Paul, this was excellent news. A second publication would undoubtedly increase his chances of promotion. However, only fellows of the Royal College of Surgeons were appointed as registrars. The next challenge therefore, the obstacle that loomed in front of him like a mighty mountain, was the fellowship examination. Until he overcame that hurdle and became *'Mr Lambert'*, instead of *'Dr Lambert'*, there would be no further job interviews. If there was any small consolation about Kate's illness, it was that her confinement to a hospital bed meant there was no temptation for Paul to socialise. It gave him the chance to get his head down and undertake some serious study.

***

When the next weekend arrived though, tired after a couple of disturbed nights, Paul felt jaded, depressed and was desperately worried about Kate. He found it difficult to concentrate on his textbooks and the date of the exam was rapidly approaching. Kate's knee was now a little less swollen but only because the medical staff had removed fluid from it for a second time. Her temperature had fallen at little, which was encouraging, but her pulse rate, despite bed rest, remained stubbornly over 100. It had not improved at all, indicating that the heart tissues were still inflamed. Desperate to hear some good news, Paul frequently questioned the ward staff but got very little information from them, simply the usual platitudes; *'She continues to be satisfactory. We are watching her closely. She will be with us for some time yet.'*

And so a long and anxious period ensued. Kate remained ill and confined to bed, other than for toilet purposes. Day after day, she lay in her side ward, pale and listless, running a fever and troubled with the arthritis in her knee. Later she developed arthritis in her wrists, and the observation chart at the foot of the bed continued to show her rapid pulse. Paul was allowed a short visit at lunchtime, which was not an official visiting time. He also went to see her each evening, sharing the time with her nursing friends and colleagues, who similarly wanted to wish her well.

Paul discovered that being a patient's friend and visitor was an enlightening experience. For three years, he had roamed the hospital as a doctor, a member of a clinical team, with a definite role to play, talking to patients, examining them and making decisions on their management. He had always tried to do his best for his patients, but had never questioned the organisation of the ward, believing it to be efficient and effective. As a visitor however, concerned for Kate's health and wanting the very best treatment for her, he saw the situation in a totally different light. The attention that she received seemed slow and cumbersome. On a ward round one afternoon, Dr Mitchie decided that the dose of steroid should depend on the result of a specific blood test. It would have been in Kate's best interests for the blood sample to have been taken immediately, but the house officer allocated the task to his next venepuncture round, which happened to be the next morning. Paul offered to take the sample himself, but this suggestion was politely refused. In due course, when the sample was obtained, it was placed in a rack in the treatment room, ready for the porters to take it to the laboratory at their next routine visit, which proved to be at lunchtime. His offer to save time, by walking the sample to the laboratory himself, was again declined. The system seemed grossly inefficient, yet when he reflected on the situation, he had to acknowledge that the service being given to Kate was no different to that offered on his own surgical ward.

As the days passed, it became apparent that the ward staff were beginning to regard Paul as a nuisance. Since he was in the hospital every day, he popped in to see Kate whenever he had some free time, not restricting himself to the official visiting hours. In due course a notice appeared on the door of her room, stating that *'no visitors were allowed without Sister's permission'*. When he requested that permission, it was usually declined with the words; *'Kate needs to rest'*. On hearing his protests that sitting at her bedside chatting would hardly tire her, Sister hid behind the nurse's standard defence; *'I'm afraid that is what the doctors have decided'*. Once more it was sobering to realise that what he was witnessing on this medical ward, was exactly the same as a visitor would experience on his own surgical ward.

Meanwhile, Kate was miserable. She was feverish, her joints ached and her head throbbed. With no energy, she was listless. She had no appetite and in any case, she found the hospital food unappetising. Trapped in her side room, she was bored. The days seemed endless. At times, she tried to read books and magazines, even attempted to study her nursing texts, but found it impossible to concentrate. She imagined that the worst aspect of punishment for prisoners must be boredom, especially for those in solitary confinement. At least she had nurses popping in from time to time to give her drinks, to change the bed, and to give her medication. She asked if she could be moved onto the main ward, where she could chat to other patients but this request was denied. Dr Mitchie wanted her to rest. And she was embarrassed. As a nurse, she wanted to care for others. She felt awkward and self conscious that the nurses had to do jobs for her. And worst of all; there was no end in sight. It was always *'We'll have to see how things go. We need to wait 'til your temperature comes down. Your pulse rate still hasn't settled'*.

Just as observing ward routine as a visitor caused Paul to question the efficacy of his medical practice, so Kate found that being a patient, made her see nursing from a completely different perspective. It caused her to reconsider much of what she had been taught at the nursing school, and what she herself had practised on the ward. She observed that on Dr Michie's round, much of the consultation took place between a huddle of doctors at the foot of her bed, leaving her feeling excluded. Subsequently, she had to ask Sister, or question the house officer, to learn what had been decided about her progress and treatment. Both Kate and Paul came to realise that their impatience with Sir William, their frustration at hearing his oft-repeated, long and detailed explanations was misplaced. Although it was tedious for his staff to hear the same explanations over and over again, they were greatly valued by his patients. It was an important lesson for them both. They both came to the conclusion that medical and nursing care would be improved if doctors and nurses were required to spend a few nights as patients on their own wards - to be on the receiving end for a change!

***

Whilst Paul was suffering as a visitor at Kate's bedside on the medical ward, so Miss Mullins was suffering at her brother's bedside on the surgical ward. Regrettably Mr Mullins was deteriorating rapidly. Although he had recovered from his anaesthetic, he had developed a troublesome chest infection. Sadly, with his extensive, untreatable malignant disease, there was only one way this story was going to end. It was inevitable that he would continue to decline, drift into a coma and slip away, probably within the next week or two. Unable to offer any treatment to slow the progression of the disease, the efforts of the staff were directed at making him as comfortable as possible; ensuring that he received adequate relief from pain, encouraging him to drink and turning him regularly in the bed to avoid pressure sores.

Miss Mullins was constantly at Frank's side, fretting over him and doing what she could to ensure that he was comfortable; fluffing his pillows, giving him sips of water or weak tea, and mopping his brow. Paul and Victoria spent time with her, explaining the nature of her brother's problems as gently as they could, stressing that she should prepare herself for the worst, but she seemed disinclined to believe them. She insisted that her brother had always been there for her, from the day that she was born, when their parents died and even through the dark days of two world wars. She was adamant that he would recover and be there to care for her into the future. She was quite unable to accept that her lifetime companion was going to die.

Mr Mullins was a quiet, reserved man. Just as he had accepted without complaint, the delay that had occurred when he had first presented, when the gangs of youths had run amok in the casualty department, so he accepted the current situation without comment or question. He did not ask what had been found at his operation, nor was this information volunteered to him. Paul wondered whether, in such situations, the staff ought to be more honest with their patients and offer the truth. Did patients really not want to know what the future held for them, or were they reluctant to ask questions because they were afraid of what the answers might be? And when held in ignorance, how often did patients imagine the worst, then spend their final days fearful of death or afraid of dying in pain? Surely such fear could be assuaged to some degree by a frank exchange and reassurance that relief from symptoms and professional support were available.

Paul recognised though, that there were occasions when the failure of communication arose, not from a reluctance of the patient to ask questions, but from the reticence of the staff. At times, difficult conversations were avoided because the staff found such exchanges stressful. Some doctors and nurses doubted their ability to give satisfactory answers to the questions they might be asked. Having received little or no training on how to approach the subject, they felt unable to find the right balance between honesty and hope; unable to give a patient a realistic assessment of the situation, without leaving them in a state of utter despair. And sadly, there were times when staff avoided these conversations because they knew that to do the job properly was extremely time consuming, and time was a commodity in short supply.

***

It was perhaps inevitable, that as the days slipped by, Kate began to feel depressed. Normally a lively and outgoing person, she became bored with her long confinement in bed, particularly as no end was in sight to her imprisonment in the side ward. One evening, she voiced her frustration to Paul.

"I am beginning to feel a little better and my knee is less sore than it was, but they won't let me do anything for myself. The nurses gave me

147

a bed bath today, embarrassing for them, humiliating for me. I could easily have walked to the shower room but they wouldn't allow it. And it's the doctor's party this weekend, isn't it?"

It was customary for the housemen to host a party every couple of months in the doctor's residency. To make for a particularly memorable occasion, Richard had arranged that the party should be held on the same day as the cricket match. Understandably he had chosen a weekend when the Surgical Five unit was not 'on call' for emergency admissions. The format for a successful party involved importing a generous supply of cheap alcohol, employing a local disc jockey to provide music, rolling the carpet back to provide a small area for dancing and, most important of all, publicising the event in the Nurses Home. For this evening and this evening only, nurses were allowed entry to the building. This was a cause of considerable concern to the formidable hospital matron, who regarded young doctors as devils in disguise, demons in white coats, predators from whom her nurses had to be protected. The parties were also a worry to the hospital management, who tolerated them with some reluctance. There had been occasions in the past, when too much alcohol had been consumed and a certain amount of damage to the residency (and to the reputation of the hospital) had occurred.

Paul had fond memories of the first party that he had attended in the doctor's mess. It remained indelibly imprinted on his mind. The lights had been low, the music soft and slow, and in the anonymity of the crowd, he had held Kate in his arms for the very first time. They had swayed in time to the music, moved as one and she had snuggled ever closer to him, her head on his shoulder, the soft curls of her hair against his cheek, the scent of her perfume intoxicating him. It had been the most wonderful feeling. It had felt like heaven and he had wanted the moment to last forever. Then disaster had struck; he had been called away to attend a case in theatre. He had only expected to be away for a short time, half an hour at the most, but had spent the next three hours assisting whilst Mr Potts undertook an emergency operation. Scrubbed at the table, unable to get a message to Kate, he had been reprimanded by Mr Potts for failing to concentrate and for clock-watching. By the time that the operation had finished and he was finally able to escape from theatre, the party was over. As a result of a misunderstanding, he had come to believe that Kate had spent the evening in the arms of another, when in fact she had taken the first opportunity to return to the Nurses Home. Sadly a rift had developed between them which, exacerbated by Paul's jealous nature, had taken two months to heal.

"Will you be going to the party, Paul?" Kate asked from her sick bed, before adding somewhat unconvincingly, "I don't mind if you do."

"No," he replied. "It's Surgical Three's weekend and Roger Watkins, their SHO, asked if I would swap weekends with him. He knows that you are ill and he's keen to go to the party himself. I agreed, provided that he covers Saturday afternoon so that I can play cricket. The match promises to be a lot of fun, and it will be entertaining to see how the consultants fare. With a bit of luck, one or two will embarrass themselves. I'll be working in casualty on Saturday evening when the party is being held. The arrangement actually suits me quite well since it will allow me to have an extra weekend off when you are better."

Kate smiled. "I will look forward to that, assuming that I ever get out of this wretched side ward.

And Paul was quite right - the cricket match did indeed prove to be highly entertaining. Events occurred that kept tongues wagging for many weeks to come!

Chapter Fifteen

The cricket match had not been formally publicised but thanks to the hospital grapevine, a sizeable crowd of staff, together with friends and relatives, turned up to enjoy the entertainment on a gloriously sunny, late summers afternoon. Believed to be the first such contest to be held in the history of the hospital, the match had been eagerly awaited, both by the players themselves and by many other hospital personnel, who were keen to watch the consultants in action, and to see how they would perform against their younger and fitter opponents. The venue was the park adjacent to the hospital. Built originally on land that had formed part of a wealthy merchant's country estate, the City General Hospital had started life in Victorian times situated amongst pleasant green fields. Over the years though, it had become surrounded by urban development as the city had expanded. Because infectious diseases, particularly tuberculosis, were rife at the time, it had been constructed as a series of detached three storey blocks. Glass corridors had subsequently been added, making it possible to move around the hospital without being exposed to the elements. Fortunately, the area immediately adjacent to the hospital had been preserved as a park for the recreation and enjoyment of the public.

The cricket match provided a fine example of the social cohesion that blessed the City General. It enjoyed a friendly community spirit; the hospital being a hub of social activity as well as a place of work. It was therefore no surprise to find that there were plenty of helpers willing to facilitate the game. Although the park had not previously been used for cricket, the hospital gardeners had levelled a rectangular area and put down a length of matting for use as the strip. They had not been asked to prepare the pitch, nor had they been paid to do so. They had done the work spontaneously and voluntarily, evidence of their good-natured loyalty to the hospital.

This community spirit was particularly in evidence at Christmas, when everyone went out of their way to create a cheerful atmosphere for patients who were unable to be at home with their loved ones. The porters brought Christmas trees to each and every ward, which the nurses decorated. For many, the highlight came on Christmas Eve with the visit of the nurse's choir. Without warning, the ward lights were dimmed and the nurses entered, two by two, in procession. They wore their white headdress and maroon capes, and each carried a shepherd's crook bearing a lantern. As the candlelight flickered round the ward and the carols rang out, a tear formed in many a patient's eye. On Christmas

Day, the catering staff came on duty early and roasted turkeys. These were carved by the consultants in the centre of the ward, and then served by his wife and family. Father Christmas provided a present for every patient, usually a bottle of beer for the men and some toiletries for the women. The Salvation Army brass band visited and played carols in the corridors. There were far too many players for them all to squeeze onto the ward but the warmth of their music reached every bedside. The staff also came together to perform the hospital pantomime, a very popular event, which was a wonderful opportunity for the junior doctors and nurses to poke fun at the consultants and the hospital matron. They took it all in good heart of course, indeed were affronted if they were not the butt of at least one good joke.

In the absence of a cricket pavilion, the teams gathered in two informal groups on the edge of the field. Many student nurses were present, eager to support the junior doctors who, in turn, were keen to impress with a display of their sporting prowess. There was quite a contrast between the teams. The junior doctors were aged between 23 and 35 and, with one exception, wore green theatre vests and trousers. The 'odd one out' was the only female member of the team, Victoria, the surgical registrar. The age of the consultant team ranged from 30 to 60 and again there was one exception, Mr Potts' nine-year-old son. They were of various shapes and sizes, sporting a motley selection of attire, some in regular cricketing whites, some in theatre greens, others in beach shorts.

There was much curiosity to see which of the consultants had been brave enough to play. Normally respected by virtue of their seniority and experience, many were liked and admired but one or two had become domineering and autocratic. Would they be shaken from their lofty perch and brought down a peg or two? And how would others fare, given their generous waistlines? Paul was pleased that Kate had been allowed to attend. The long days of forced inactivity were getting her down and she still had a slight fever and some residual bodily aches. To relieve the boredom, she had requested permission to watch the match. This had been granted, strictly on condition that she sat quietly and did not exert herself. Paul had wheeled her from her medical ward in a bath chair and she now sat, a red hospital blanket around her knees, with the other nurses in the junior doctors camp.

Paul looked across at the consultant group. He knew most of them but there were three or four unfamiliar faces, presumably local general practitioners who had been drafted in to make up the numbers. Leslie Potts was there of course, immaculately attired, his white trousers starched and pressed, wearing cricket boots and a white sweater. There was a club motif on both sweater and cap. Perhaps he was a good cricketer after all, Paul thought. Maybe his previous self-praise had not merely been the product of a big ego, a lively imagination and a desire to impress the nurses! By contrast, the Professor of Surgery, not the smartest of dressers at the best of times, had merely taken off his jacket and tie, tucked the bottom of his brown corduroy trousers into his black socks and donned a pair of white tennis pumps. Clearly not a cricketer!

Mrs Potts, together with her son and daughter, were amongst the consultants group. Paul had met the Potts family once before, when he had been the house officer on the unit. They had visited the ward on Christmas Day, when, as was traditional, Mr Potts had carved the turkey using the longest and sharpest knife that was available in the operating theatre; the one normally reserved for amputating limbs! Mrs Potts and her daughter had helped the nurses to serve lunch to the patients. Paul decided that propriety dictated that he should walk over to chat with her. She was a striking figure, tall and slim, with an exuberant and bubbly personality, quite a contrast to her dour and brusque husband. She shared her outgoing disposition with her son. His name was Andrew and he had been six years old when Paul had last seen him. With his mother's blonde hair, blue eyes and a cheeky grin, he had caused chaos on the ward within five minutes of arriving. He had brought two of his Christmas presents with him; a clockwork car and a football. The car, whose speed had disappointed on the lush lounge carpet at home, went like a formula one racer on the polished linoleum of the ward floor. It frequently disappeared under patients' beds or items of medical apparatus and in a flash, Andrew went after it, knocking over anything that stood in his way. Much to Sister's annoyance, his father had done nothing to curb his son's enthusiasm! After a drip stand and two commodes had been sent flying, their malodorous contents having been spread far and wide, Paul had taken him to the far end of the ward and set up two chairs to act as goal posts. Then he had acted as a goalkeeper, whilst Andrew had taken penalty kicks with his new football, screaming with delight with every goal that he scored. This was not a role included in Paul's job description, but it proved to be an effective way of preventing further damage to ward equipment!

On this occasion, like his father, he was correctly and smartly attired. Although only nine years of age, he was wearing long white trousers, cricket boots and pads. He was playing flamboyant strokes with his junior cricket bat, as Sir William, dressed in his umpire's white coat (no doubt borrowed from one of the housemen, then freshly washed and starched in the hospital laundry) tossed a ball to him underarm. As always, the senior consultant wore a fresh red rose on his lapel. Clearly Andrew was a *'chip off the old block'*, a showman in the making, like his father. Also standing with the consultants was Frederick Swindles, the obsequious secretary to the consultant's management committee. Paul had met him when being interviewed for his job at the City General. He too, had been co-opted as an umpire. He was a slightly built, insignificant, greying, middle-aged man, who tried to insist on being called 'Frederick', but was known to one and all simply as 'Fred'. In stark contrast to Sir William, he was wearing a crumpled brown jacket over a woollen cardigan, a shirt and tie of discordant colours and scuffed shoes. His life was spent at the beck and call of the consultants, not that he altogether resented this. He recognised that they despised and bullied him, but his association with them gave him a certain kudos within the hospital, that he reinforced by 'name dropping' at every available opportunity. Having started as an office junior, some twenty years before, he had been promoted over the years to his present post, but had never left the secluded security of the administrative department. Knowing how he loved to inveigle his way into the good books of the consultants, Paul doubted that the junior doctors would benefit from many of his umpiring decisions.

As Paul watched, Liz arrived and waved merrily to Mr Potts. Unsurprisingly, with his wife close at hand, he did not respond in kind. Instead Paul saw him stiffen slightly, and then half turn his back as he continued to chat with his consultant colleagues. Liz however, not appreciating that her presence was not welcome at that particular moment, waltzed straight up to Mr Potts and gave him a hug. For one dreadful moment, Paul thought she was going to kiss him. She didn't, but the familiarity of the greeting was unmistakably.

"Hello Leslie," she said brightly, beaming at him. "I've been looking forward to this match for weeks. I must say you really do look the part. I'm sure that you will play a starring role."

Her words jarred. House officers never addressed consultants by their Christian names. It was unheard of.

Mr Potts had no option but to respond. "Ah. Good afternoon, Dr Webb. I see you've come to watch the match."

"Yes I have, and I'm looking forward to it immensely. I'm expecting you to make lots of runs and take a few wickets."

"Thank you, my dear," responded Leslie Potts, the coolness in his voice unmistakable. "That's very kind of you to say so, but I think you are in the enemy camp. The residents' team is over there."

Paul had been chatting with Mrs Potts and both had witnessed the exchange between Liz and her husband.

"Who is that young woman?" Mrs Potts asked, her voice cold and prim.

"It's Dr Webb, one of the house officers," Paul replied, thinking it unwise to volunteer that the *young woman* in question, had been personally selected by her husband to be his house surgeon and had received a good deal of his personal attention since taking up her post.

"I see. Perhaps you would just excuse me for a minute, Dr Lambert."

But Sir William had also seen the exchange and showing creditable diplomacy, moved in to defuse the situation.

"Leslie," he said cheerfully. "I think we're about ready to begin the match."

Then to Liz he added, "Dr Webb, I believe Dr Hill is the captain of the residents' team. Could I trouble you to ask him to come across and we'll get the game started?"

With Liz cleverly despatched and Sir William engaging Mr Potts and his wife in conversation, the tension had eased by the time that that Richard wandered across to join the group.

"Now," said Sir William, "before we have the toss, can we have an agreement about the rules."

"What we would like to suggest," Richard said, "is that the match be restricted to twenty overs, with everybody except the wicket keeper bowling two overs. This is a friendly game and we want everyone to feel involved and to play an active part."

"Are the consultants happy with that arrangement?" Sir William asked.

Mr Potts nodded his agreement.

"Unfortunately," Richard continued, "we have a slight problem. Some members of our team are on duty but they are carrying their 'pagers' in their pockets. It means that there may be some coming and going during the course of the match. In fact, we are actually one man short at the moment. Dr Watkins has been called to see a patient in casualty, though he expects to be able to return shortly."

"I'm sure that will be acceptable," said Sir William, without referring the matter to his fellow consultant. And I see you have a girl playing for your team."

"Yes," responded Richard. We have struggled to get a full team and Miss Kent has agreed to make up the numbers. I hope that you have no objection, Mr Potts?"

"No objection at all. In fact, it should add to the merriment."

"Right," said Sir William. "Are we ready to toss?"

Both captains agreed, a coin was flipped and Richard duly won.

"Right," he said. "Since we're a man short, we will bat first and hope that when we come to field, we'll have a full team."

There was polite applause and a few catcalls from the spectators, as the consultants, led by Mr Potts took to the field, his son at his right hand. Professor Butterworth, the Professor of Surgery, now wearing wicket keepers pads over his corduroy trousers, looked even more incongruous than before. The cheering grew louder when Richard, who had many female admirers, took to the field, bat in hand. He looking determined and had a steely glint in his eye. Tony Myers, one of the medical house officers accompanied him to the crease. A trace of a smile crossed Richard's face however, when it became apparent that Mr Potts planned to open the bowling for the consultant's team. Richard's animosity towards his boss and his anger over Mr Potts developing relationship with his fiancée were widely known, not only by the resident doctors but also by many members of the nursing staff. Richard had made no secret of the fact that he regarded this match as his opportunity to gain some retribution. It seemed that the spectators were to be treated to a fascinating contest.

Mr Potts had claimed to have had significant success as a cricketer in his youth, both as a batsman and as a bowler. Paul waited with interest to see whether this self-confidence was justified. Stockily built, he delivered the ball with reasonable accuracy, at a good medium pace, off a shortish run. Richard though had a good 'eye', he was young and athletic and he swung his bat lustily, attempting to hit every ball out of the park. His cricket bat became a weapon with which to assuage his anger. The first over yielded four boundaries, two of them sixes. It was entertaining stuff, every blow being cheered by the crowd as the score rattled along. A look of grim satisfaction appeared on Richard's face.

Whilst Leslie Potts may well have been a reasonable cricketer in his youth, and still retained much of his cricketing skill, he had not retained his fitness. Before he had completed the second of his permitted overs, he was red faced and blowing like a steam locomotive. He did however have the satisfaction of getting the first wicket as Richard, attempted one blow too many, didn't quite middle the ball, and holed out on the square leg boundary. Mr Potts was ecstatic, appealing loudly to the umpire. When Fred's index finger was raised, he danced with delight. It was as if he had just won the £75,000 jackpot on Littlewoods pools. After only three overs however, the resident's score had reached 36 for the loss of one wicket, 30 of them coming from Richard's bat.

The first bowling change introduced an athletic looking man of about 35, one of the local general practitioners. It was later learned that he also played regularly for one of the minor counties! Unfortunately for the junior doctors, no one had informed him that this was a friendly game and he bowled fast and straight with devastating effect. The score of 36 for one, rapidly became 48 for four and one of the wickets to fall was Paul's. At school, he had enjoyed playing cricket, but had only been a rather average performer and was no match for this tyrant. He did manage to survive a couple of deliveries, even nicking one through the slips for a boundary, but then, more concerned with his own safety than protecting his wicket, completely missed a fast, straight full toss. He was comprehensively bowled. Having hoped to impress Kate, he was disappointed but she was suitably sympathetic, commenting later, that it was unworthy of the opposition to import 'professional' players into their team.

In the next few overs, the score crept up slowly but came to a complete halt when Leslie Potts Junior came on to bowl. Clearly imbued with his father's huge self esteem, he took a 20 yard run up, which he covered with impressive speed, only to come to a complete halt, when he reached the wicket for his delivery stride. Without the strength to propel the ball the full 22 yards to the other end of the pitch, the ball dribbled to a halt five yards short of the batsman. There was a suggestion, shouted from the ranks of the residents' supporters, that since the ball had not reached the batsman, it should be designated a wide, but Sir William, who was umpiring at the bowlers end, decreed otherwise. After three such deliveries, Sir William suggested to the batsman, that 'Potts Junior' should be permitted to bowl from a point a third of the way down the pitch. This was readily agreed, (not that anyone would have dreamed of disagreeing with the most senior consultant in the hospital), but even so, the ball only reached the batsman grubbing along the ground. Scoring was impossible and as a result, young Andrew was the only bowler to bowl two maiden overs.

After 12 overs, with five wickets down, the score had only reached 73, disappointing after Richard had given the team such a bright start. This quickly became 73 for six when Dr Mitchie held a sharp slip catch, off the bowling of Mr Keeley, the orthopaedic consultant. This brought Victoria to the crease. Strangely, of all the members of the resident's team, she was the most appropriately attired. She wore smart white flannels, a white shirt, and cricketing pads that actually seemed to fit her. Mr Keeley was a giant of a man; not less than six feet three inches tall, weighing at least twenty stones. It was easy to imagine him straightening broken bones, without the slightest difficulty. Red-faced, bull necked, and as broad as an ox, he looked as if he would be more at home in the front row of a rugby scrum, rather than on a cricket pitch. He towered over Victoria, who looked positively petite in comparison.

"Would you prefer me to use a tennis ball?" Mr Keeley asked from the bowlers end. It was genuinely a courteous question, in no way intended to be sarcastic. Clearly he had not seen the county badge on Victoria's sweater, nor had he noticed the rather professional way in which she asked the umpire for a middle and leg guard.

Victoria answered, firmly but politely, "That won't be necessary, thank you, Sir."

"OK," the bowler responded. "Then I'll bowl nice and gently."

"Just as you wish," came the reply.

The first ball was a slow long hop, well outside the off stump. It sat up invitingly, asking to be hit, and Victoria duly dispatched it, off the middle of the bat, to the mid wicket boundary. The crowd was stunned but reacted with surprise and delight. Mr Keeley looked a little bemused but said nothing as he ambled back to his mark. His second ball, another gently delivery, was again short, but this time on the line of the leg stump. Victoria rocked onto her right foot, swivelled and struck the ball sweetly along the ground to the square leg boundary. This time there was a roar of approval from the crowd. The third ball, noticeably faster than the first two, was a full toss. This was met with a firm straight bat and two more runs were added to the total. Victoria had scored ten runs off just three deliveries. The spectators were ecstatic, on their toes, scarcely believing what they were seeing, crying out for more. Mr Keeley though, was not amused. He started to bowl with the speed and determination he had shown against his male opponents. It made little difference. Straight balls were met with a solid defensive stroke and anything loose was dispatched to the boundary. It was a fascinating David and Goliath contest, Victoria cool and compact at the wicket, concentrating on every ball with admirable resolve; Mr Keeley, a giant in comparison, getting more and more angry, ever redder in the face, attempting to bowl each ball faster than the last, but only succeeding in getting wilder. One full toss whistled back straight over the bowler's head. It landed short of the rope but still reached the boundary for another four. The crowd loved every minute of it. The more bad balls he bowled, the more rapidly the score mounted. Victoria was not physically big, nor powerfully built, but her timing was immaculate. She simply used good technique and the speed of the ball to score at will. Although wickets continued to fall occasionally at the other end, Victoria's inning was chanceless and she had hit an undefeated 46 by the time the last over was bowled. She left the field to a standing ovation. The junior doctor's final score was 130 for the loss of eight wickets. Richard declared himself satisfied. He felt reasonably certain that this total was beyond the reach of the consultants.

Chapter Sixteen

During the interval between the two innings, there was a further demonstration of the community spirit which was such an attractive feature of life at the hospital and that bound the staff together. Just as the gardeners had voluntarily prepared a pitch for the match, so the catering staff had organised refreshments. Standing behind trestle tables that the porters had carried to the edge of the field, they smiled and chatted, as they served players and spectators with tea and plates of biscuits.

Roger Watkins, having dealt with his patient in the accident department joined the team. Unfortunately, just as he arrived, one of the other housemen was called away to attend to a problem that had arisen on the ward. With his team still one man short, Richard cast around for another doctor to make up the numbers but unfortunately no one was available. In desperation, he approached the 'camp followers' who were gathered on the edge of the field and asked for a volunteer. His appeal was immediately answered as one of the nurses pushed her way through to the front of the crowd.

"Yes. I'll happily join in." Inevitably it was Sue Weston.

Paul had been troubled by his feelings for Sue, ever since his initial encounter with her in the casualty bedroom, during his first week as a house officer. He had been reminded of it, when he had visited the medical ward to see Mary Murphy. He felt ill at ease whenever she was around. At one and the same time, she both attracted and frightened him. There was an earthy sexiness about her. It showed in the sway of the hips as she moved, the slight smile that played on her lips when she caught his eye and the husky voice and the innuendo in the words that she used. She was what some might refer to as '*common*' and over the years had acquired quite a reputation in the hospital. Rightly or wrongly, Paul felt that she regarded him as a challenge. Physically attractive though she undeniably was, he was determined to keep her at arm's length.

The resumption of the match was delayed for a few minutes to allow Sue time to change. When she reappeared, she was wearing theatre greens which, possibly by accident though probably by design, were several sizes too large for her. She had rolled up the trouser legs to avoid tripping over them, but could do little with the flimsy cotton top that occasionally slipped down over her shoulders in a revealing manner; not that she was the kind of girl to be in the least concerned by this. Her appearance drew appreciative comments from her new team mates, which was no doubt, exactly what she intended!

When the match recommenced, Professor Butterworth walked to the crease to open the batting for the consultant's team. Accompanying him was the GP 'ringer', who had taken three wickets in a couple of overs when the junior doctors had been batting. It quickly became apparent that not only was he a demon bowler, he was also a very accomplished batsman. Not so the Professor, who scarcely knew which end of the bat to hold. To the delight of the crowd, he swished enthusiastically at every ball that he received, completely missing most of them, all the while laughing heartily at his own incompetence. He was the beneficiary of two very dubious umpiring decisions, both given by Fred. The first was an appeal for 'leg before wicket', which looked fairly plumb, but there was no way that the fawning clerk to the consultants committee was going to give a decision against the Professor of Surgery. The appeal was turned down, almost before it was uttered. On the second occasion, the visiting GP, clearly accustomed to batting with players as nimble as himself, called for a quick single. The Professor, gasping for breath and lumbering like a carthorse, looked to be at least two yards short of the crease, when the wicket was broken. Again the appeal was emphatically rejected.

"Come on, play the game," muttered one of the housemen.

"Definitely not out", repeated Fred. "Professor Butterworth clearly regained his ground."

The Professor's charmed life continued. Once again the general practitioner, not having learned the lesson from the previous episode, turned a ball to square leg where Victoria was fielding. He called for a quick single. Victoria picked up the ball and threw it accurately to the stumps where Watkins caught it in both hands. The Professor was still halfway down the pitch. Unaccountably, the ball then slipped from Watkins hands, and he fumbled in his attempt to retrieve it. This allowed the Professor, now too short of breath to run, plenty of time to walk sedately to safety. Obviously Watkins, who worked on the Professor's ward, and was dependent on him for his next reference, did not regard it in his best interests to dismiss his boss! *'Why kill a goose that might lay you a golden egg'* he admitted afterwards! The Professor's reprieve however, proved to be short lived. A couple of balls later, his innings finally came to an end. Having missed most of the deliveries that he had received, he actually managed to put bat to ball, only to see the ball lob gently to be caught in the gully. The junior doctors wondered whether Fred would dare to call a much-delayed 'no ball', but he didn't. Instead he apologised to the Professor.

"I am most terribly sorry Sir, but I'm afraid you must be out this time."

The Professor however, wasn't in the least perturbed and, grinning from ear to ear, having enjoyed himself immensely, walked off the field to a generous round of applause.

Although the Professor had added little to the total, the GP at the other end was scoring freely. After a chanceless fifty, perhaps aware that there was a danger that he might win the match for the consultants single-handed, he started to hit the ball in the air, to give catches to the fielders. The first couple were dropped, but eventually Richard accepted a chance and the 'ringer' left. After only seven overs however, the score had reached 70 for the loss of only two wickets. The junior doctor's total of 130 was beginning to appear inadequate and Richard became visibly concerned. With little idea of the competence of the members of his scratch team, he looked around the field and then tossed the ball to Mohammed Khan, probably more in hope, than in expectation.

With the ball in his hand, Mo looked completely at ease. Standing at the bowler's end, he quickly reorganised the field, all the while spinning the ball casually from hand to hand. Then, walking gently to the wicket off a two-yard approach, he bowled a slow delivery that looped deceptively through the air, landed exactly on a length and then fizzed viciously off the matting toward the wicket. Paul thought at first, that the ball must have hit a bump to behave in such a fashion, but Mo repeated the trick time and time again and it quickly became apparent that this quiet unassuming man was in fact, an extraordinarily skilled cricketer.

"You've played this game once or twice before," Paul commented as they passed at the end of the first over.

Mo smiled modestly. "Yes," he said, "I used to play a little at school and at college. In fact, I once played for the Indian under 19's team, but that was a long time ago. I thought I'd lost the knack."

"Why didn't you have a bat?" Paul asked.

"This is the house officer's day," he replied, "a day for them to enjoy."

His second over was just as effective as the first, and as wickets fell, the consultant's score slipped to 82 for five. Things were looking brighter for the junior doctors. This appeared to be a good time for Richard to put himself on to bowl, to capitalise on Mo's success. However, for some reason he continued to hold himself back.

When the sixth wicket fell, Mr Potts strode confidently to the wicket to join Dr Mitchie at the crease, accompanied by some clapping and ribaldry from the spectators on the boundary rope.

"Show them what you are made of, Mr Potts, Sir."

"Let's see if you're as good as you say you are," cried a less charitable voice, safely hidden in the midst of the crowd.

Whether Mr Potts heard these remarks or not is difficult to say, but he did raise his bat and then his cap, in recognition of the applause.

When Richard saw Mr Potts coming to the crease, he brought himself onto bowl. Evidently he had saved himself for this moment. The last wicket had fallen to the last ball of an over, so Mr Potts went to the non-strikers end of the pitch and did not have to face Richard's first delivery. Surprisingly, Richard placed all his fielders half way back to the boundary, which gave Dr Mitchie an opportunity to score a single, more or less wherever he chose, which he duly did. Paul then began to understand Richard's strategy. With Mr Potts now on strike, he brought the fielders in close, clustering them around the bat. He then marched back for a 15 yard run, a venomous look on his face.

Richard's first ball to his boss was fast and straight, a 'yorker'. It was aimed directly at the consultant's feet. It carried with it, all the pent up anger that had built within Richard since he joined the unit. Mr Potts' instinct was his personal safety, particularly to get his ankles and toes out of the firing line. He managed to keep his bat on the ground to protect his wicket, but with both feet in the air and a startled look on his face, he gave a fair impression of a pole vaulter at the point of take off. The ball, travelling at great speed, nicked the edge of the bat, whistled passed the stumps and raced to the boundary. Richard appeared not to mind in the least that four runs had been added to the consultant's total. There was a look of savage satisfaction on his face. The next ball was equally fast but slightly off line. It whistled passed the batsman and the wicket, narrowly missing both, before being caught in the wicketkeeper's gloves. The fourth ball of the over was even faster than the previous two. Short in length, it rose off the pitch, passing within two inches of Mr Potts' left ear as he ducked out of the way at the very last minute. Up to this moment, the game had been played in a good spirit, everyone enjoying themselves in the sunshine. There had been a lot of light-hearted banter between the opposing teams and, whilst both sides were keen to win the match, everyone understood that the result was not of prime importance. Paul could well understand Richard's anger at the attention that Mr Potts had shown to Liz, but this display of aggression was misplaced. It would not impress Sir William, the Professor or the numerous consultants who were watching. Doctors were expected to demonstrate self-control at all times. Even if Richard did not intend to continue with a career in hospital medicine, perhaps preferring to work in public health or to practice in the community, he still needed a reference. The consultants had significant influence, and Richard was in the process of committing professional suicide. Besides, there was a danger that Mr Potts might get injured.

Paul exchanged an anxious glance with Mo, whose face echoed his concern. But Richard was blind to any such considerations. His next ball, a horizontal rocket, was aimed directly at Leslie Potts' midriff. He jumped sideways and only just managed to get his body out of the way in the nick of time. The ball brushed his shirt and flew into the hands of the wicket keeper.

Mo had seen enough. He called for the wicket keeper to throw the ball to him, and then walked to the bowler's end, to hand it to Richard. Quite a long discussion between the two ensued. To a casual observer, it might have appeared as if a captain and his bowler were discussing how a field should be set for a new batsman, but clearly this was not the case. Paul was not party to the conversation but understood exactly what was being said.

Then there was another development. It became clear that Mo was not the only one concerned for Mr Potts' safety. His wife, evidently overlooking, at least for the moment, the evidence she had seen of her husband's familiarity with his glamorous young house officer, came running onto the pitch.

"Leslie, Leslie, Leslie. You must put this on," she shouted, waving a cricketer's box high in the air. The spectators, who had watched Richard's aggressive bowling in silence, dissolved into gales of laughter and inevitably there were more catcalls.

"Got to protect the crown jewels."

"You might need that equipment later tonight, Sir. Better safe than sorry!"

"That will give Richard something to aim at!"

Mrs Potts ran all the way to the middle of the pitch and then handed this vital piece of protective equipment to her husband. The crowd loved it. Seeing a senior consultant loosen his belt, then slip the box down his trousers to protect his genitals in the middle of the cricket field, in front of so many young nurses, was a spectacle that became a talking point within the hospital for many weeks to come.

Richard bowled the remaining ball of the over in a more conventional style. It was slightly slower and directed at the wicket, rather than at the batsman. Mr Potts turned it to leg and took a single. In doing so, he passed Richard in the middle of the pitch. The two glared at each other but no words were exchanged.

There was a further interruption before the next over was bowled. Much giggling was heard from the nurses who, having previously been scattered around the boundary, were now huddled together in a tightly packed group. It was clear that something was happening amongst them that was causing great hilarity. Then, from the centre of the group, a 'flag' was waved in the air, which on closer inspection, proved to be a cricket bat to which was attached a generously proportioned black bra. It seemed that Mr Potts was not the only one to have adjusted their clothing, for Sue Weston appeared from the midst of this laughing throng, a huge grin on her face. Unnoticed, she had left the field of play, whilst everyone else had been watching Mrs Potts providing protection for her husband.

Meanwhile Richard had tossed the ball to Victoria and Mr Potts, having had a torrid time during Richard's last over, looked much brighter at the prospect of facing the female registrar. The field that Victoria set to bowl to Mr Potts was conventional in all respects except one. She placed Sue about four yards in front of the bat, where the consultant could not fail to see her. As Victoria prepared to bowl and Mr Potts took his guard, Sue bent forward into a crouching position. As she did so, her overlarge theatre top fell forward, revealing to the batsman gaze, Sue's neck, naval and everything in between. Leslie Potts was confronted by the sight of Sue's generously proportioned breasts. Victoria's first ball was slow and straight, and unsurprisingly Mr Potts, mesmerised by the sight of Sue's chest, completely missed it. The ball bounced over middle stump, missing it by a whisker. Unfortunately, the wicketkeeper, similarly distracted, also missed the ball, which slipped away for a couple of byes. Frankly, at this point, Mr Potts might just as well have forfeited his wicket and retired from the field of play, for he really stood no chance. He couldn't see the oncoming ball without seeing Sue's chest, and he couldn't see Sue's chest without being reduced to a state of paralysis. He continued to miss each delivery until one hit his wicket. Mr Potts left the field looking deflated. Meanwhile, Victoria and Sue celebrated together, their knowledge of the batsman's weakness and their exploitation of it, having been remarkably successful.

At this stage, the consultant's score had slipped to 98 for seven. It seemed likely that it would be a close match, and so it proved. Later, with four overs remaining, twenty runs were needed, and then eleven from the last two overs. When the ninth wicket fell, four runs were required from the last four balls. It was at this point, that Leslie Potts Junior came to the crease, his father at his side. Unfortunately for Paul, he was the bowler. Whilst Junior went to the crease and took his guard in a very confident manner, Mr Potts approached Paul.

"Andrew has really been looking forward to this game," he said. "It would do his confidence the world of good, if he were able to score a run or two." He put his hand in his pocket and for one dreadful moment, Paul thought he was going to produce a five-pound note. He didn't. Instead, he handed Paul a tennis ball.

"You will treat him gently won't you, Lambert." Mr Potts' words sounded like an instruction, rather than a request. Then he patted Paul on the shoulder and walked away, shouting '*Good Luck*' to his lad as he left.

Paul wondered what on earth he was supposed to do. He was twenty-six years old, reasonably fit and athletic, with only a nine-year-old boy standing between him and a win for his team. Yet he was also a surgical trainee, ambitious and eager for promotion and the obstacle between him and victory was the son of his boss. And his boss clearly wanted Paul to allow his son to '*score a run or two.*' Paul decided that the only appropriate course of action was to bowl very slowly, but reasonably straight, and let fate take its course. If Junior missed the ball and it chanced to hit the wicket, then that was just too bad. Paul thought it best to bowl underarm, then even if Andrew was bowled, at least it would appear that he was trying to oblige his boss. Paul though, was unaccustomed to the lighter weight of the tennis ball and his first delivery was far too gentle. It bounced three times before coming to rest at Junior's feet. He took a swipe at it, but only managed to return it to Paul along the ground. Now there were only three balls left and the consultants still needed four runs for victory. Then Paul had a brainwave, a moment of inspiration. A good strategy would be to let Junior score a single and then bowl the last couple of balls overarm, with a proper cricket ball, to the consultant at the other end. With this in mind, he pushed the fielders back, almost to the boundary and then threw the ball higher in the air, hoping that Andrew would hit it into one of the unprotected areas, where a single was perfectly possible. Unfortunately, however, he bowled far too high and a little too fast. The ball landed two thirds of the way down the pitch and then bounced clean over Junior's head. He waved his bat at it gallantly but it was quite out of his reach.

"Hey, you," Junior shouted at Paul, in much the same tone that his father used to address his staff, "that's not fair." Then he turned towards his father, who was watching eagle-eyed on the boundary.

"Dad, tell this man to bowl properly."

All eyes turned to Mr Potts to see what his response would be, but he was wise enough to say nothing. Meanwhile Sir William had signalled a wide for the last delivery. The consultants now needed three more runs to win and there were still three balls left. Once again, Paul tried to bowl a ball from which Junior could score a single. This time, the tennis ball reached him at just the right height for a gentle push, into any one of the spaces Paul had left for him to score. Paul was delighted. His plan was working. But Junior had other ideas. He opted for a wild slog. The contact of bat on ball was perfect. The ball sailed away off the middle of the bat, high into the air, clearly visible in the bright light against the cloudless blue sky. It flew straight into the hands of Mohammed Khan, the international cricketer, who was fielding on the square leg boundary. It was the simplest of catches but mysteriously, it slipped through his fingers, then bounced once, before crossing the ropes for a boundary. Four runs and a victory to the consultants, with just two balls to spare. Junior did a war dance of delight, and then, whooping happily and waving his bat high in the air, he ran back to his father.

"I did it, Dad. I did it, and we've won."

Ruefully Paul turned to Sir William, who handed him his cap.

"Well played, Lambert. Well played."

Then he looked Paul in the eye and smiled. "Surgery can throw up some difficult dilemmas, can't it?"

"It most certainly can, Sir."

Chapter Seventeen

After the cricket match, Paul wheeled Kate back to her sideward and then walked, somewhat reluctantly, to casualty. He had promised to swop duties with the Surgical Three SHO so that Roger Watkins was able to attend the doctor's party. Roger had been heavily involved it's organisation and was keen to return to the residency to oversee the final arrangements. Paul would have loved to attend the party too, but only if Kate had been able to enjoy it with him. His consolation was the knowledge that Roger 'owed him' time, that he could spend with Kate when she recovered, though how soon that would be, and whether her recovery would be complete, remained to be seen.

Although Dr Mitchie had allowed Kate to watch the match, this was only to break the monotony of her prolonged confinement in the side ward. He insisted that Kate should remain in hospital under his supervision and that she should continue to rest. Fortunately the swelling and pain in her knee was slowly improving and no new joint problems had developed but with her pulse still slightly raised, Paul was concerned that she might be left with some permanent heart damage. He desperately wanted her to recover quickly and completely; not least so that they could spend some time relaxing together. He recalled the weekend that they had spent at her father's cottage near Kendal. What a shame that could not be repeated now. With autumn fast approaching, the trees would be turning to put on their glorious show of colour before the onset of the winter frosts. For Paul, this was the time of year when the Lakes were at their magnificent best. The crowds that frequent the shores of Windermere and Derwentwater in summer have returned to their suburban homes, leaving the countryside calm and serene. In the early morning, a mist fills the valleys, then slowly melts as the sun breaks through to reveal the hills, some clothed purple with heather, others golden brown with bracken, reflected in the stillness of the lakes. It was an ideal time for walking; the ground still firm and dry, the air fresh and cool, the hills standing proud, preparing to withstand the snow and gales of the coming winter.

Kate was normally such an active and healthy person. She loved tennis, swimming and cycling. In the past, they had enjoyed long walks together in the countryside, followed by a drink and a meal in a friendly country pub. She would greatly miss these outdoor pursuits, if they were to be denied by a chronic weakness of her heart. Inevitably, Kate was bored and frustrated. Paul was able to see her every day but only for short periods, taking his turn with her other visitors. Kate was popular; she had many friends who wished to see her, particularly colleagues with whom she worked. Her father, of course, came at weekends, though his work in the pharmacy precluded visits during the week. If he was on his own, he slept overnight in Paul's flat; if with Muriel, they stayed at a local hotel. On one occasion, Dr Mitchie chanced to visit Kate one evening. At the time, Kate had six or seven friends in her room and a lively atmosphere had developed. Dr Mitchie disapproved. He didn't want Kate to get over excited, or over tired. As a result, another notice was pinned on Kate's door, this one stating that visiting was restricted to formal visiting hours and only two visitors were allowed in the room at any one time.

For a couple of hours, Paul worked in casualty alongside the Professor's houseman, a sensible young man called Malcolm. They were busy clearing a backlog of minor cases, when Mrs Brown arrived. She was in a state of collapse with a thready pulse, a barely recordable blood pressure and looking as pale as a ghost. Earlier in the day, she had passed a stool containing a large volume of fresh blood and she was continuing to bleed copiously from her back passage. Given her life-threatening condition, the first priority was resuscitation. After three years in hospital practice, collapse from blood loss was a situation with which Paul was quite familiar, and with Malcolm as his assistant, they fell effortlessly into the usual routine. They administered oxygen, inserted drips into both arms to replace fluid, whilst blood was prepared for transfusion. Initially Mrs Brown was barely conscious and unable to give any sort of history, but as she responded to the blood transfusion, Paul was able to obtain some information from her. She was 42 years of age and had recently come to the area to live with her sister, following a separation from her husband. He still lived with their son and daughter at the family home in Bristol. At first, the bleeding had been minor and intermittent. Then she had suffered a sudden, dramatic haemorrhage and had fainted. Her sister had dialled 999 and she had been rushed to the hospital by ambulance. Paul questioned her closely for any clues that might suggest the underlying cause of the bleed, but to no avail. She denied having had any previous bowel symptoms and said that prior to this episode, she had been perfectly fit and well. Sometimes such haemorrhages may be due to an abnormality of blood clotting, such as haemophilia, but Mrs Brown had never experienced any difficulties with heavy periods, or with excessive bleeding at the time of dental extractions.

Having denied any recent medical problems, Paul was surprised to find two fairly fresh scars when he examined her belly.

"One was for gall stones," Mrs Brown explained, "and the other was an operation for appendicitis."

"And did the surgeons in Bristol experience any problems with bleeding when you had those operations?"

"None at all; at least, none that they mentioned to me."

Paul asked Malcolm to ring the Bristol Hospital and arrange for the notes to be forwarded to them. Then to Mrs Brown, he added, "Which hospital was it in Bristol?"

"It was the Bristol Royal, but I doubt that you'll need the notes; it was all very straightforward."

The blood emerging from the back passage was bright red. This suggested that the site of the bleeding was close to the anus, so Paul used a short telescope to look for its cause. The examination was a failure; fresh blood obscured the view.

Paul suggested that the examination be repeated later in the evening, this time under an anaesthetic. If the cause of the bleeding could be located, it was likely that the flow of blood could be arrested.

Mrs Brown then made an unusual request.

"Doctor," she said. "Under no circumstances do I want my son or my husband to be informed of my medical problem. I don't mind if you talk to my sister or my daughter, but on no account should anybody speak with my husband or son. Is that quite clear?"

Paul explained to her that doctors were bound by an ethical code which included confidentiality, and that no information should be given to a third party without the patient's express permission. In saying this, he was aware that, in practice, this rule was often broken. If a patient's next of kin enquired about their condition, information was frequently imparted without permission being obtained. However, to ensure that everyone was aware of Mrs Brown's specific request, he attached a note prominently to the front of her case records. He was curious though, to know why this request had been made.

"My husband and I are getting divorced. We are going our separate ways and unfortunately my son has decided to side with my husband. If you were to meet them, they would probably express sympathy for me, but then start asking nosy questions about my condition, when in reality, they don't care for me at all. I would prefer to keep the details of my illness to myself, thank you very much."

She sounded quite definite, had clearly made her decision in advance, so Paul did not press the matter, nor did he seek to dissuade her.

As it happened, two road traffic accident victims then arrived, and a log jam of non urgent cases built up in the department. It became a question of 'all hands on deck', so it was actually Mo, rather than Paul who examined Mrs Brown in theatre later that evening. He told Paul about the findings the next day. When he had washed away the blood, he found a deep ulcer, just inside the back passage. He explained that most commonly this would be caused by a tumour, but this particular ulcer did not look cancerous. Uncertain of its cause, he had taken a sample for analysis. Then, with some difficulty, he had sutured the ulcer to control the bleeding.

For the rest of the evening Paul was kept busy, now working alongside David Jenkins, another of the housemen. He had come to undertake the dreaded overnight shift. Together they dealt with the usual run of Saturday night problems, including the occasional drunk, though fortunately there was no repeat of the level of disturbance that had delayed Mr Mullins treatment. Eventually the flow of patients slowed but it was one in the morning before Paul got back to the residency. He was ready for bed and hoping for an undisturbed night. However the chance of a full night's sleep was not good. Having swapped duties with Roger, he was now covering David. Not having worked with him before, he had no idea how experienced he was. This was always an awkward situation. If David were to phone him in the night asking for advice, since Paul was unaware of his clinical ability, it would be necessary for him to get out of bed to check things for himself. The alternative was to stay in bed, but then to lie awake, unable to sleep, worrying if all was well.

Loud music drew Paul to the lounge, where the residency party was in its death throes. The bar had been closed, most of the guests had already departed and one of the housemen was collecting glasses and emptying ashtrays. Two couples were wrapped in each other's arms, snogging on settees in the darker corners of the room and Sue Weston sat alone propping up the bar, a tankard of beer in her hand. She looked slightly the worse for wear, her little black dress rucked up, allowing a generous view of shapely thigh and ample bosom. Smiling to himself at the memory of Mr Potts dismissal in the cricket match earlier in the day, Paul turned on his heels and went to the bedroom allocated to doctors required to be 'on call'. No one occupied it permanently and it looked tired. It was sparsely furnished; a desk, one chair, a single bed and inevitably a small bedside table, upon which stood the telephone which Paul hoped desperately would not disturb him during the rest of the night.

Quite what time it was when Paul woke, he never knew, but suddenly he became aware that he was not alone in the room. Something or someone was moving towards him. Sitting up, he tried to focus through the gloom, and as his eyes gradually became accustomed to the darkness, he saw a figure standing at the side of the bed. It was Sue. Sue had never quite forgotten that morning in the casualty department several years before, when she had woken Paul on the pretence of offering him an early morning cup of tea. At the time, she had felt vaguely irritated by his rejection of her, but it had not worried her unduly. After all, there were plenty more fish in the sea. Afterwards, she had wondered whether it was Paul's personality to be cold and aloof, or whether his attitude had perhaps been due to a combination of shyness and inexperience. She had promised herself that one day she would find out; and that moment had arrived. With her inhibitions abolished by the alcohol that she had consumed in the course of the evening, she was determined not to let this opportunity pass her by.

"Hello Paul." Her voice was quiet, husky, and suggestive, her speech slightly slurred. "I've come to say 'hello' and finally I've got you on your own, all to myself. I've been looking forward to this moment for such a long time. But the wait will be well worth while – I promise you that."

"But I......"

She put a finger on his lips. "Shush, don't say a thing."

She smiled; a slow seductive smile. She moved closer, until she was no more than a stride away from him. Then, standing perfectly still, she fingered the buttons that ran down the front of her dress. Paul sat and watched, spell bound as she toyed with the top button, stroking it, caressing it, before finally undoing it. Then her fingers moved down to the next button. As each was released, her dress slipped, first from one shoulder then from the next, until it fell in a shadowy halo around her feet. Her eyes captured Paul's and again she smiled.

"I'm all yours Paul, yours to enjoy."

As she held his gaze, she slowly and deliberately slipped out of her bra and pants and stood before him naked, like a statue, Rubenesque. The faint glow of the streetlight through the curtains, shone on the prominence of her round hips and full breasts, shadows hiding valleys and clefts. Mesmerised, Paul watched as her hands languidly stroked her thighs and belly, cupped her breasts and teased her nipples. She was proud of her body, aware of its power, relishing the situation. She was beautiful, desirable and was offering her firm pneumatic body to him. Paul was hypnotised, a moth bewitched by a naked candle flame. Finally, after years of self imposed restraint, firm young flesh, warm and yielding was to be his. Unable to move, able only to watch, like the moth, he was fatally attracted; no longer in control of his actions.

Sue gazed down at him as he sat on the bed. His eyes were wide open; he looked startled, guilty, like a child caught in the act of stealing sweets. Now she knew. It was obvious to her. This was his first time. As a lover she was vastly experienced. To her sex was essential, the food of her life. She needed it regularly; be it a quick snack taken on the back seat of a mini late on a Saturday night or a five course banquet taken at leisure in a boy friend's flat over a long weekend. With the whole of the night ahead of her, she planned to take things slowly, to sate her appetite, to relish every moment, to enjoy herself.

She spoke, her voice no more than a whisper. "Well, Paul. Aren't you going to invite me to join you? You know that's what you want."

Entranced, and truly without conscious intent, Paul did something that he was deeply to regret. He turned back the bedclothes, only a few inches but it was as clear an invitation as it could have been, for Sue to join him. The slow seductive smile turned to one of victory. She threw back the sheets and blankets much further, so they were below Paul's waist. Then, in the same slow, unhurried and deliberate fashion with which she herself had undressed, she unbuttoned his pyjama jacket. He felt the light touch of her fingers, as she ran her hands over his chest. Her own body yearned to be caressed, to be stimulated, but Paul was paralysed, his arms frozen to his sides.

"Don't just look, Paul. Touch, feel, relax and enjoy. This will be a night for you to remember."

Paul reached tentatively towards her, a child wanting to touch but afraid to handle. She felt his clumsy hands on her breasts, fingers and thumbs, prodding as if testing the ripeness of fruit in a shop. It wasn't what she wanted, but no matter. She wasn't entirely a selfish lover; by morning she would have taught him how to please a woman. Gradually, Paul became bolder. He marvelled at the warmth and softness of her thighs, the silky smooth skin of her belly, and the firm mounds of her breasts.

His pyjama trousers were held in place by a white braided cord. Sue held one end delicately between finger and thumb and gradually pulled it towards the ceiling, enjoying the faint soft sound, as the knot became undone. Then her fingers continued their downward path. She ran a fingernail against Paul's skin, gently scratching sending waves of pleasure through his body. Then she saw the ugly scar on his lower abdomen and for a brief moment her nursing curiosity surfaced. Probably the scar from an appendix operation she thought, given that it had healed so badly.

Although she had promised herself that she would take her time, that she would pleasure him slowly, a sudden hunger demanded satisfaction. Abruptly, she placed a hand on each of his shoulders and thrust him back onto the pillow. Her face hovered over his, a look of triumph in her eyes. She kissed him full and hard on the mouth, her fleshy lips on his. It was the smell that brought Paul to his senses. It hit him as effectively as a bucket of cold water; the smell of her breath, the stench of stale beer and tobacco. He looked up at her face and saw the coarse skin, pock marked from teenage acne. Again her lips came down, cold, wet and suffocating. Her tongue entered his mouth, the foul smell converted to taste. Suddenly Paul was appalled. How had he allowed this situation to develop? Why hadn't he stopped her the moment she entered the room? He didn't want this girl. She was a slut and he was determined not to be another of her conquests. His mind shot to Kate, lying severely ill in a hospital bed, not 100 yards away and he felt deeply ashamed. Horrified at what had happened, his only thought was to escape. Roughly, he thrust her away.

"No," he stuttered. "I don't want this. Get out."

Her voice was soft and coaxing. "No, Paul. We've come too far. Relax, enjoy yourself." Gently she tried to push him back onto the bed, but his strength and willpower had returned.

"Out," he shouted. "Out, right now."

"What. Looking like this?" she mocked, sitting naked on the edge of bed. "I'm staying here."

"Like hell you are, you're going."

For a few seconds they fought, but Paul was much the stronger. He tossed her off the bed and she landed heavily on her backside on the floor. She rose to her feet, a woman scorned, in vicious mood.

"I'm bloody well staying here," she screamed, attempting to get back in the bed. "It's two in the morning. The Nurses Home is locked for the night. If you don't like it you can piss off. Not good enough for you, am I? Too full of sweet innocent Nurse Meredith, I suppose? A fat lot of good she is to you, half dead in a hospital ward."

With that Paul flipped.

"You're nothing but a tart. A cheap, nasty, drunken whore."

She raised a hand to strike him, but he pushed her away and she fell again onto the floor. For a moment there was silence.

"Well," she said, coldly. "This is where I'm spending the night." She jumped into the bed and pulled the bedcovers over herself. "You can join me if you wish; otherwise you can bloody well find somewhere else to sleep."

Blinded by rage, determined to get away, Paul quickly dressed, picked up his white coat and left the room, then stood in the corridor trembling with rage. Not just angry with Sue, but furious with himself.

He knew that he should have turned her out the moment he saw her.

He was horrified that he hadn't stopped her as she undressed and worst of all; he was deeply ashamed that he had turned back the covers, so clearly inviting her into his bed. How stupid he had been and how weak. But his overwhelming feeling was one of guilt. Guilt that he had failed to stick to the principles that had guided him through his adult life, but mainly guilt that he had betrayed his love for Kate.

Slowly it dawned on him that it was the middle of the night and he had a problem. He was on duty, he was required to stay in the hospital, but had no bed for the night. He wondered whether there might be an empty bed in one of the side wards. The night sister would probably not be too enthusiastic about the idea but might permit it, if she believed there was nowhere else for him to sleep. He could claim he had inadvertently locked himself out of his room. When Paul checked however, none was available; all the side rooms were full. Then it struck him that David Jenkins was working as duty houseman in casualty, his room would be available. So he went to have a word with him. Lying again about being locked out of his room, he offered to take over David's casualty duties, suggesting that he could spend the rest of the night in his own room in the residency. David of course, was delighted; relishing the prospect of sleeping undisturbed 'til morning. So Paul bedded down in the tiny room in casualty but scarcely slept a wink, not because casualty was busy, but because of his anger and shame.

The next morning, the moment that his casualty shift was complete, physically tired from lack of sleep and full of self-reproach, he marched back to the residency in determined mood, to throw Sue out of his room. But the room was empty; she had already left. The only evidence of the night's events were the crumpled linen on the bed, a lingering smell of tobacco and the words '*Piss off*' written in bright red lipstick on the mirror above the sink!

Feeling the need to cleanse himself, Paul had a long hot shower then, feeling marginally fresher, walked to the dining room for breakfast. Inevitably the talk around the table was of the cricket match and particularly of the party the evening before. Paul didn't see how anyone could possibly have the slightest suspicion that Sue had spent the night in the residency, but he was wrong. She was the hot topic of conversation on everyone's lips. She had been seen slinking out of the building at seven in the morning, still wearing her little black party frock. Everyone wanted to know where she had spent the night. They were particularly keen to discover who had benefited from her sexual favours? Amid considerable ribaldry and lewd comment, many suggestions were made. Since no one owned up, the mystery surrounding the event only served to inflame the conversation. To Paul's great relief, no one pointed a finger in his direction, and he kept as quiet as a church mouse.

From the discussion around the table, Paul learned that at the party, Sue and her boyfriend, one of the laboratory technicians called Terry, had a fearful row. Sue was accused of dancing too intimately with one of the doctors, Terry had felt slighted and a slanging match had resulted. At one stage, Sue had to be restrained from physically assaulting him. When Terry had walked out in a huff, Sue had retired to the bar, where she had spent the rest of the evening drinking heavily. However no one had seen what became of her when the party ended, and David Jenkins, the only one who knew that Paul had '*inadvertently locked himself out of his room,*' clearly saw no connection between that and the mystery of Sue's nocturnal accommodation.

Much relieved that no one suspected that he had been in any way involved; Paul left the breakfast table to begin another day's work, assisting Mr Potts and Victoria in the theatre. He had feared that Mr Potts might be angry that Richard had subjected him to a barrage of dangerous deliveries but found the consultant in an ebullient mood.

"Good match yesterday, Lambert, wasn't it? Good to see that the consultants have lost none of their sporting prowess over the years. I must confess that before the game started, I thought the advantage would be with youth, but I was pleased to be proved wrong."

Paul was not in the mood for light conversation. His mind was elsewhere, troubled with Kate's illness and wracked with guilt over the episode with Sue. And so much had happened since the match that he found it difficult to believe that it had only been played the day before.

"Yes, Sir, I thought the consultants did well." he replied, thinking it unwise to mention that the consultant's victory owed a great deal to the quick fifty runs scored by their 'imported' player, the one who had also taken three wickets in the space of a couple of overs.

Mr Potts obviously noted a certain lack of enthusiasm in Paul's response.

"You mustn't begrudge us our success, Lambert. It's the playing that counts you know, not the winning."

"Yes indeed, Sir." Paul replied, trying to sound a little brighter. "It was an enjoyable afternoon. Perhaps it should become an annual event."

"My son, Andrew would certainly welcome that. He thoroughly enjoyed himself. He hasn't stopped talking about it ever since. Particularly the way he scored the winning runs..... ." The consultant looked across the table at Paul, his eyes twinkling above his surgical mask, "... off your bowling I seem to remember."

It would have been churlish not to respond in kind.

"Yes Sir," he said. "He's a talented young cricketer and did very well. He obviously takes after his father."

Paul was rewarded by a questioning look from the theatre sister and hoped that the remark had not sounded too obsequious!

Fortunately the conversation then lapsed as Mr Potts gave his attention to the operation but as the procedure dragged on, Paul found it hard to concentrate. He kept yawning, his eyelids were heavy and there was a grave danger that he might nod off. On a number of occasions, he was reprimanded.

"Come on, Lambert. Keep that retractor in the right place. How can I see what I'm doing, unless you hold the bowel out of the way?"

"Sorry Sir, I was doing emergency duty this weekend and I spent most of last night in casualty."

He could have said, "Well when this case is over, go and lie down for a couple of hours. The rest of this morning's cases are only minor, Victoria and I can manage perfectly well on our own." But he didn't.

"Well just stay awake until this operation is over, for God's sake," was his unsympathetic reply.

Chapter Eighteen

Normally Paul enjoyed life on the surgical ward. It was hard work, of course, exacting work too, and the hours were long, but caring for patients was rewarding and the cheerful camaraderie kept him going. With the possible exception of Sister Ashbrook, the nursing staff were pleasant and helpful, and even she had been less prickly, since the episode with Jimmy McMillan and his dramatic collapse. That had boosted Paul's morale considerably and ought to have cheered him up, as should Mr Potts decision to reinstated Liz's night shift in casualty. That had come as a pleasant surprise and a great relief. It lightened his workload considerably. Quite what caused Mr Potts to have a change of heart Paul never knew, but suspected that his wife had in some way influenced the decision. She had witnessed Liz's overly familiar behaviour towards her husband at the cricket match and had probably demanded an explanation! Inevitably Liz called Paul several times to ask for his advice whenever she was on duty, but this was preferably to working through the night and seeing every patient himself.

However, throughout the next week he remained miserable, continuing to feel guilty about the episode with Sue in the *'on call'* bedroom. It played on his mind, distracting him when he was working by day and preventing him from sleeping at night. He recognised of course, that she had entered the room uninvited. She had stripped slowly, deliberately and provocatively in front of him. She had offered herself to Paul in the most blatant way, but his conscience would not let him forget that he had been the one who had turned back the bedclothes, indicating his willingness to accept her offer. How he wished that he had not done that. In truth, it was not the result of any conscious thought or decision. It had happened as if by instinct and yet he hadn't stopped her when she had unbuttoned his pyjamas. He had fondled her breasts, allowed his hands to explore her body. Why on earth had he allowed it to happen? He should have rejected her the moment he saw her. Had he done so, his mind would now be at ease, his conscience clear.

Then less worthy thoughts entered his head. He could have taken what was on offer. No doubt, others would have done so, without the slightest hesitation and with no subsequent self-recrimination. He could have relaxed and enjoyed discovering the pleasures of intimacy with real flesh, instead of giving rein to his imagination in the privacy of his room. It would have been easy to let Sue take the lead, as she surely would have done, to rid him of that innocence, that label, of which he was both proud and yet self-conscious, certainly unwilling to admit to his friends. In his heart, he realised that Sue was a tart, a slut, and had things progressed to their natural conclusion; he would simply have been another of her conquests, another of her one nightstands. No doubt she was stork proof, but he might very well have ended up with an unpleasant antisocial infection; at the time he had given no thought to any form of protection. But there was a more serious concern. What should he say to Kate? The question went round endlessly in his head. If he said nothing about the night's events, if Kate remained in total ignorance, she would have no reason to worry, no cause to be angry. There would be no risk to their relationship. The alternative was to tell her openly and frankly exactly what had happened, in all its atrocious detail, and hope and pray that she would see Sue for what she really was, and forgive him for a moment's weakness.

But suppose Kate did not forgive him. What if she broke off the relationship? Paul loved Kate. In her presence, he felt comfortable and relaxed. She lifted him when he was tired or felt low. She calmed him when he was anxious or angry, and she reassured him when he had self-doubt. They shared the same interests; their love of fresh air, the open countryside and high fells. He dared to think that maybe, just maybe, they might spend their lives together, though this was a dream that he had never been bold enough to put into words. He had lost her once. He couldn't bear it, if it were to happen again. Perhaps it was better to say nothing. Least said, soonest mended.

But what, Paul wondered, if Sue were to speak of it? What if Kate learned what had happened, not from him, but from her? Surely that would be worse. Kate would hate him for being deceitful. It was possible that Sue might keep quiet, given that she had been rejected and her advances spurned. She might curse him, maybe laugh at him for being stupid and old fashioned and then simply forget the whole sordid affair. But equally, she might feel angry, resentful, and even vindictive. She could take her revenge by talking about the episode, spreading it around the Nurses Home, even telling Kate. And if she did, she would surely not admit that at the last moment, Paul had rejected her. She would simply say that she had joined him in his bed. If that happened, would Kate, could Kate believe his account? He was simply unable to decide what to do, and all the while the guilt went round and round in his head.

***

"You look worried, Paul." It was Kate. As usual, Paul was sitting in

177

her side ward, troubled by his conscience, attempting, with little success, to concentrate on his books in preparation for the fellowship exam. He looked at her, weak and pale, supported on two pillows in the bed. Her chart showed that her temperature had finally returned to normal but her pulse rate, though much improved, was still slightly raised. Her face though, was calm and composed as always. Should he share his guilt with her, get it out in the open, explain fully and honestly what had happened, before she heard of it from another source? But he couldn't. He was simply too ashamed and too fearful of her reaction. He just had to hope that Sue would also stay silent.

"I'm sorry," he lied. "I'm just worried about the exam and of course about you."

"You needn't be worried about me, Paul. Dr Mitchie came to see me again today and said I was finally on the mend. He used his words cautiously as he always does, but provided there is no relapse in my condition, he doesn't think there will be any permanent damage to my heart. That's great news isn't it? And for the first time he suggested that I might be able to complete my convalescence at home. But even though I pressed him, he wouldn't give me any idea when that might be. He simply said that it depends on my progress. But it shouldn't be too long now."

"And how long do you think it will be, before you can come back to work?"

"Possibly after a further month, maybe six weeks. Again it depends on my progress. Matron has been very good about it. She has arranged that I drop back into the class below. It means that I will take my final nursing exam three months late. How soon do your take your exam Paul?"

"The written paper is in about four weeks. If I pass that, I have to travel to London for the clinical and oral exams. I'm dreading it. The success rate is only about 25%."

"But you passed your exams at medical school, and also the first part of the fellowship exam. And you have done hours and hours of revision."

"But the medical school exam has a pass rate of about 90%. They don't tell you at the time of course, but after they have invested five years and thousands of pounds in your training, they're not going to fail you. If you don't pass the first time, you invariably pass the resit."

Since taking that examination himself, Paul had worked as an invigilator and seen how the examiners assisted the medical students, encouraging them and guiding them to the correct answer. Quite the opposite was true in the final fellowship exam, where the bar was set very high, ensuring that only the very best candidates became fellows of the Royal College.

"The first College examination also has a high failure rate and you sailed through that."

"That's true, but I had a huge advantage. At the time, I was working 'nine to five' in the anatomy department with all the university facilities available to me. Others were struggling to revise in the evenings and at weekends, having been on duty for 60 or more hours each week."

In truth, the fellowship exam was a formidable hurdle. The syllabus was so wide-ranging, the standard so high, that unless you were superbly prepared, you would inevitably fail. Even if you knew the textbooks from back to front, to pass you still had to be lucky on the day, when facing the examiners in the oral exam.

"And can you take it again if you fail?" Kate asked.

"Yes you can, but it's expensive and I really need to succeed. I can't apply for promotion until I get my fellowship. If I don't pass, I shall probably remain an SHO for the rest of my days!"

The bell rang to mark the end of visiting time and Paul trudged back to his flat, guilt and worry bearing heavily on him. Once again he opened his books in an attempt to study, but although his eyes scanned the pages, his brain was otherwise engaged. Recognising that he was wasting his time, he retired to bed and tossed and turned fitfully before finally managing to find sleep.

***

The next day, Paul was able to spend some time with Anne Brown and got to know her better. Mo's handiwork with needle and thread, suturing the ulcer, had successfully arrested the bleeding and as a result, her condition was much improved. The colour had returned to her cheeks and her observations had remained stable, enabling her intravenous drip to be discontinued.

She was a slim lady with a bony angular frame, who looked as if she had lost weight recently, although this was something she strenuously denied. Her face, with its prominent cheek and jawbones, crowned by dark hair prematurely streaked with grey, carried a pinched, tense and unsmiling expression. She appeared to carry the cares of the world on her shoulders. It was noticeable that she did not mix easily with the other patients on the ward, and was usually to be found sitting on her own by her bed. She seemed withdrawn, being difficult to engage in conversation. It is probably unwise for junior surgeons to attempt to diagnose psychiatric conditions but Paul suspected that she was

179

depressed as a result of the break-up of her marriage and the difficult relationship with her son.

Unfortunately, on the day she was due to go home, she bled again. On this occasion, the volume of blood lost was not life threatening but nevertheless; it necessitated a two-pint blood transfusion and a return trip to the operating theatre. This time it was Victoria who undertook the procedure. She thought the ulcer looked deeper and a little more ragged than had been described previously by Mo. Again there appeared to be no obvious reason why it had developed. The sutures that Mo had inserted previously had disappeared, so Victoria re-sutured the area to arrest the haemorrhage, before returning Mrs Brown to the ward.

Mr Potts normally conducted his ward rounds in a brisk and businesslike fashion, rarely spending more than two or three minutes with any patient but on his next visit, he spent a considerable amount of time with Anne Brown. He liked his juniors to introduce patients to him with a brief summary of their condition, no more than the bare facts of the case. He rarely questioned patients himself, but on this occasion he interrogated Mrs Brown personally and in considerable detail. It was obvious that her condition caused him concern, partly because of the threat that the haemorrhage posed to the life of a relatively young patient, but also because of the lack of any diagnosis. Without knowing the cause of the ulcer, it was impossible to be rational about the treatment.

Attempting to resolve the mystery, Mr Potts inquired about Mrs Brown's general health and bowel habit. Finding himself unable to add anything to their existing knowledge, he tentatively asked questions that might suggest a rarer cause of the rectal ulcer. Had the patient participated in any unusual sexual activity?

"My husband and I live apart. We're getting divorced."

"That doesn't quite answer my question, does it?" said Mr Potts persisting with his line of inquiry.

"The answer is still no," snapped Mrs Brown.

"Have you travelled to any exotic tropical countries?"

"My husband always puts himself and his job before me. We rarely have holidays. And now that I have to fend for myself, there is scarcely enough money for the clothes I stand up in, never mind any thoughts of foreign travel," came the angry retort.

Concerned that the patient might have an abnormal bleeding tendency, such as haemophilia, Mr Potts inquired, as both Paul and Victoria had done previously, whether there had been any excessive blood loss when she had her babies, or at times of tooth extractions. But try as he would, he could add nothing to their existing knowledge.

Back in the office after the ward round, Mr Potts again raised the puzzling case of Anne Brown.

"Khan, you say that the ulcer doesn't look like a cancer at all?"

"Not at all," replied Mo, "and we now have the laboratory report on the sample I took for analysis. The pathologist says there is nothing to suggest that this is a tumour; indeed nothing to suggest any diagnosis at all. The changes seen under the microscope are entirely non-specific."

"If it's not a cancer, the only other common cause of an ulcer in the back passage is chronic constipation. A lump of stool as large and hard as a cricket ball can get stuck in the rectum. Sometimes that can cause pressure on the lining and result in an ulcer."

"But in this case Sir, when we did the telescope examination, apart from the blood, the bowel was completely empty. And the patient has been moving her bowels entirely normally between the episodes of bleeding."

Mr Potts turned to Paul. "Have you run tests to look for abnormalities of blood clotting?"

This was a question that would normally have been directed to his house officer. In recent weeks though, since the day of the cricket match in fact, his attitude towards Liz had cooled. He had required her to restart her overnight casualty duties, for which Paul was very grateful, but had also started to ignore her on ward rounds. He avoided speaking to her unless it was absolutely necessary. As a result, tasks that would normally be allocated to her, were now being given to him. Paul delegated them to Liz as soon as Mr Potts had departed of course, but it was irritating. It wasted time and risked confusion.

"Yes, blood clotting has been checked twice," Paul replied, "and both samples were entirely normal."

"And what about tests on the stool to look for abnormal infections?" Again the question was directed at Paul.

"They have been repeated and everything is totally normal, Sir."

"You say her two abdominal operations were performed in Bristol. Have you got the notes from the Bristol hospital?"

"Yes. They arrived this morning. She had two operations in Bristol. The first was to remove the gall bladder, although it seems that she didn't actually have gallstones, just a little inflammation of the gall bladder. The second operation was undertaken because she was getting a lot of abdominal pain. Numerous tests were performed to try to ascertain its cause, but all were normal. Eventually it was thought that she might have a grumbling appendix. The appendix was removed but there is nothing in the notes to suggest that she bled excessively. On both occasions, she was discharged from the hospital in standard time."

"Actually," Paul added, "she's got quite a thick set of notes from Bristol. As well as her two operations, she had a lot of investigations for severe headaches. She was due to have more tests but these were cancelled when she moved up here."

"Well," said Mr Potts, "we don't have a diagnosis to explain this ulcer and that's a real concern when she bleeds so heavily from it. The trouble is that I can't think of any other investigations that would help. We shall just have to hope that she doesn't bleed again and that the ulcer heals. But one thing you might do Lambert, is to speak with her husband and see if he can throw any light on the matter."

Again this was a task that should have been given to Liz. It crossed Paul's mind to suggest this to him but, wary of the consultant's short fuse, he wasn't bold enough to do so. Unfortunately, it seemed to Paul that whether Liz was in Mr Potts' good books or out of favour, extra work came his way!

"There's a problem there, Sir," he replied. "Mr and Mrs Brown are getting divorced. She has specifically instructed that under no circumstances must we impart any information about her condition to her husband or to her son."

"How very odd," Mr Potts commented. "Of course we must respect her wishes but it should be possible to speak with him in general terms, without giving away too many details of her illness. Simply ask him whether he can shed any light on the matter."

Sister Rutherford joined in the conversation. "Mr Brown rang the ward earlier today to inquire about his wife, saying that he intended to travel to visit on Saturday. In the circumstances, it may be best if Mrs Brown doesn't see Dr Lambert speaking with her husband."

She turned to Paul. "If you like, I'll catch him when he is leaving after visiting time and you can speak with him on the other ward."

As Mr Potts left the office, a worried look on his face, he made a final request. "Let me know if there are any further developments, day or night, especially if she should bleed again. That would give me a chance to see this ulcer for myself."

It was clear that the mysterious case of Anne Brown was of considerable concern to him.

Chapter Nineteen

At the very time that Mr Potts was conducting his ward round and worrying about Mrs Brown's mysterious illness, a conversation was taking place in the Nurses Home that was dramatically to affect Paul. Two of Kate's best friends, Sally Cummings and Claire Wells were locked in a deep discussion in the room that they shared. All three had left school to train as nurses at the same time. Kate though, had slipped behind the others because of the time that she had lost when she was away caring for her mother. Despite that, they had remained good pals, usually socialising as a group and sharing each other's problems. Many of their colleagues laughed at their friendship for they seemed an unlikely trio. Kate was quiet and conscientious, taking her nurse training seriously, whereas the other two were full of fun, usually passing their exams by the skin of their teeth. They were frequently called before Matron and reprimanded for some minor misdemeanour. Now though, they sat gravely on the side of the bed, hands around their knees, deep in thought.

Sally frowned. "You've heard about Paul, I suppose?"

"Yes, I have, and it saddens me." Claire replied. "At first, I thought that Sue was making it up but she's adamant that the story is true. Her roommate says that she didn't sleep in her bed that night and Sue has been telling everyone that Paul has a scar at the base of his willy. She would scarcely be able to do that if it wasn't true."

"I really am surprised at Paul," Sally responded. "I would never have dreamed that he would be disloyal to Kate."

Claire though was less sure, having recently been let down in a similar fashion. "He's a man, isn't he? They're all the same. Show them a flash of knickers and they go weak at the knees. They follow like pet dogs, their tails wagging, their tongues hanging out drooling. And everyone knows what Sue's like. She would take great pleasure in ruining someone else's romance."

"I don't suppose that Kate knows yet."

"No, and I hope that she doesn't get to know."

"But she's bound to find out. It's all round the hospital. Everyone is talking about it."

"Do you think she ought to be told?"

"Yes I do. If Paul is going to behave like that, she needs to know before she gets more deeply involved with him. Besides it isn't fair on her to be stuck in that sideward, whilst everyone outside is gossiping about her behind her back."

"I suppose that's right. But who's going to tell her?"

"We are, together, this evening when we visit her."

"She's going to be very upset. She dotes on Paul."

"True, but surely its best that we tell her. She would be even more upset if she were to hear it from someone else?"

***

As the days passed, Paul's feeling of guilt over Sue's nocturnal visit slowly diminished. He managed to persuade himself that, while he ought to have shown Sue the door the moment he saw her, at least his moral code had exerted itself before the situation had got completely out of hand. At times, he even congratulated himself on managing to say '*no*' in the face of great temptation, albeit at the very last moment. Inevitably his conscience troubled him whenever he visited Kate, but she had remained blissfully unaware of the incident and, at least initially, it appeared that his decision to keep quiet was justified.

Gradually though, Paul came to understand that this happy state of affairs was not destined to last. His suspicions were first aroused when he realised that he was the subject of gossip and speculation on the hospital 'grapevine'. It wasn't any single event that raised the doubt in his mind, rather a succession of apparently unrelated events. One of the staff nurses on the ward asked him if he had '*recovered from the party*', with a smile on her face and a twinkle in her eye. Then a group of student nurses went into a huddle, whispering and giggling when he passed them in the corridor. But his worst fears were confirmed when he rang the medical ward to enquire after Kate's progress. The orderly who answered the phone, declined to give him any information. Instead she informed him that the ward sister wished to speak with him.

"Dr Lambert, Kate is not receiving any visitors today," she said.

"Why, Sister?" Paul enquired. "Has something gone wrong?"

"No," she said, speaking rather formally. "Nurse Meredith continues to make satisfactory progress but she has asked that you don't visit today."

"Why on earth not?"

"I don't know the full story but I believe it's something to do with the doctor's party."

Paul's heart sank. His worst fears had been realised.

"But I need to explain to her."

"I'm sorry, Dr Lambert. Nurse Meredith is adamant about the matter. At present, Dr Mitchie is well pleased with the improvement in her condition and we can't risk upsetting her."

184

"But Sister....."

"No, Dr Lambert. You will not visit her today." She put down the phone.

Mortified, Paul put his head in his hands and cursed. He cursed Sue Weston for being a whore and cursed the hospital grapevine for spreading malicious gossip. He cursed himself for his weakness and his decision not to have been open and honest with Kate. Why hadn't he told her about the events himself? But how had the story got out? There could only be one answer. Sue Weston herself. Enraged, he ran to her medical ward to confront her, only to find that she wasn't there. From the ward staff, amongst further sniggering and furtive glances, he learned that she had gone on a week's leave.

He tried to be rational. Only two people knew exactly what had happened that night in the 'on call' bedroom, Sue and he himself. But at least David Jenkins and the nursing staff in casualty could confirm that he had deputised for David for most of the night. Certainly he had lied to them, inventing the story about locking himself out of his room, but at least there were people who could support part of his story. If Sister on the medical ward would not allow him to visit Kate, she might allow David to visit. He could tell Kate that, whatever she might have heard, he had in fact spent the night working in casualty.

He immediately paged David and joined him on his ward.

"David, I need a quiet word with you. Is there somewhere where we can be alone?"

David looked surprised. "Certainly. There's an empty side room here, we'll use that."

"Look," Paul began, "it's about the night of the party."

David's face immediately broke into an enormous smile. "Yes, I've heard all about that. It's all round the hospital, you dirty old dog."

Then he looked rather more serious. "I must say Paul; I was surprised when I was told about it, especially with Kate ill at the moment. I wouldn't have expected it of you."

"David, please tell me what you have heard?"

"Well basically, that you took Sue Weston back to your room that night. Everyone's talking about it."

"David, that's not what happened."

"Well that's the story that everyone believes."

"And where did the story come from?"

"Apparently from Sue Weston herself. She's been telling everybody about it, both on the wards and in the Nurses Home."

"But David, if you remember, I relieved you in casualty that night. I know I told you that story about locking myself out of my room, but that wasn't true. Sue came to my room when I was asleep. The door wasn't locked and she simply walked in. She had drunk far too much. She wouldn't leave. That's the real reason I had to find somewhere else to sleep."

David looked thoughtful. "So you and Sue didn't have a ding-dong that night." He smiled. "I suppose that if you had, you wouldn't have left that nice, warm, plump body of hers, to come and deputise for me in casualty!"

"Certainly not. And now Kate refuses to see me. She obviously believes I've been unfaithful, which simply isn't true. David, please, on my behalf, go and see her. I'm desperate. I love Kate. I couldn't bear it if anything came between us."

"And what do you want me to say to her?"

"Just ask her to see me. Tell her that the hospital gossip isn't true. Say that I deputised for you in casualty that night and the nursing staff can confirm that."

"Alright Paul. I'll try. I'll slip along and see her this evening."

But when evening came, David wasn't able to see Kate. There was a large notice on the door of her side ward stating that '*No visitors are allowed without Sister's permission*'. And when David spoke with the Sister, he learned that only Kate's closest nursing friends were allowed to visit, and he was turned away.

Later that evening, Sister Ashbrook phoned bearing more bad news.

"I'm sorry to trouble you Paul, but Mr Mullins died rather suddenly an hour ago and his sister is extremely agitated. I thought she understood that he was expected to die, but she seems very angry. In fact she wants to lodge a formal complaint. I realise I ought to ask Liz to talk to her, but since you have had dealings with her before and are a little more experienced, I wondered if you would mind coming to the ward to see her."

Having already had several conversations with Miss Mullins, helping her to understand the nature of her brother's illness, Paul couldn't understand why she should be angry. He had told her repeatedly that there was only one way that this illness would end. Upset yes, grief and shock yes, but why anger? And why should she wish to complain? Mr Mullins had been beyond cure from the moment that he presented in casualty. His cancer had spread throughout his abdomen. There was nothing anyone could have done to prevent his death. However he recognised that she was a spinster, that she had led a quiet life, living throughout in the shelter of her brother's care, so he resolved to be sympathetic and try to understand what was upsetting her.

Entering the office and pulling up a chair, he sat down facing Miss Mullins. Sister was at her side, the inevitable cup of tea on a table nearby, but Miss Mullins was ignoring both. She was sitting bolt upright, head thrust forward, her face taut and angry. Paul opened with the familiar condolences with which doctors and nurses are so familiar, so practised.

"I'm so sorry that your brother has died and on behalf of all the staff here, may I offer you our sincere condolences? I know that you and your brother were very close, that you've spent a lifetime together and I'm sure that you will miss him enormously."

But Miss Mullins was not impressed. Paul had marked her as a gentle soul, tolerant and mature, but she came at him angrily, like a foxhound, running wild, scenting blood.

"It's just not right, Dr Lambert, it's not right at all. My brother Frank was the kindest of men, always the perfect gentleman. He was good mannered and generous. He spent his life doing good deeds, helping others. He worked for charity, giving freely of his time. The way he was treated was appalling."

"Look, I'm sorry you feel like that," Paul began, "but I'm afraid that his cancer was so advanced at the time he attended the hospital, it was inevitable that it would overcome him. There was no therapy that could have cured him. It's a shame that he slipped away rather suddenly today, but in some ways that......"

But Miss Mullins interrupted, tense, red faced and now shouting. "I'm not talking about his medical treatment; I'm talking about what happened in casualty."

Taken aback, not understanding what she was referring to, Paul looked blank.

"All those horrid louts; shouting, swearing, running about, breaking medical equipment, chasing the nurses. And those tarts with their short skirts; collapsing on the floor, vomiting because they were drunk, whilst my brother had to wait. And he was so ill, so desperately in need of medical attention."

Paul felt a surge of relief, when he realised that she was not angry with the care that she had received from the medical and nursing staff. He recalled all too clearly the chaos that had existed in the casualty department, on the night that her brother had attended. It had taken two or three hours and the presence of the night porter and the police before order had been restored. It was undoubtedly true that on that occasion, patients had not been treated in accordance with their clinical needs. Mr Mullins would certainly have received pain relief and fluid replacement much sooner under normal circumstances. The priority at the time had

187

been to regain control of the department.

As gently as he could, Paul explained that the casualty staff are bound to treat everyone who attends the department; people from all walks of life, be they young or old, rich or poor. The staff treat honest upright considerate people like her brother. But they also have to deal with louts who, intoxicated by drink or drugs, prevent the doctors and nurses from caring for genuine patients with serious, indeed life threatening conditions. Miss Mullins however, her anger unabated, continued to vent her grievance.

"Frank never hurt a fly. He was such a quiet gentle man. He worked hard all his life, always putting others before himself. He never offended anyone. He tried not to consult his doctor with trivial complaints. He had even tried not to trouble anybody with this problem, despite me pleading with him to seek medical advice. And on the one occasion that he needs help, he has to play second fiddle to those drunken yobs."

She was distraught, but deciding that his best strategy was to allow her to vent her anger, to release all the frustration that had been locked within her, Paul let her continue to rant, which she did for several minutes. All the while, tears rolled freely down her cheeks. Clearly she and her brother had lived a quiet sheltered life. They had no concept of what life could be like in a city centre on a Saturday night. To have such a graphic demonstration, at a time when she was stressed and in need of help and support, had been an enormous shock.

Gradually she calmed, slowly managing to gain some control of her feelings, though she continued to sob quietly, Sister Ashbrook's arm now round her shoulder. Eventually she composed herself and looked at Paul, her face still wet with tears.

"I know it's not your fault, Doctor. I shouldn't be shouting at you. I do see that the nurses had no option but to attend to the troublemakers first, but my Frank was so desperately ill, so badly in need of medical attention; it just seems so desperately unfair."

"I don't disagree with a word you've said, but regrettably not everybody lives their lives as you do. I'm just sorry you had to find out like this."

It seemed that her anger had burned itself out and conscious that there were other duties waiting for him, Paul moved the conversation on.

"Is there anything that you want to ask about Frank's medical treatment, Miss Mullins? Is there anything that you don't understand?"

"No thank you, Doctor."

"Then I'll leave you to have a chat with Sister. I'm afraid that when someone dies, there are one or two formalities that require attention. She will be able to explain them to you. But do tell me before I go, how are Kitty and her kittens?"

Finally he got a tearful smile from her.

"She's fine, thank you. She had three kittens, if you remember. We gave two of them to friends and kept the prettiest for ourselves. She is quite a big cat herself now. We decided to call her 'Mags' as she was born at St Margaret's maternity hospital."

***

Kate sat alone in her room. A book lay open in front of her but she was unable to read. She was devastated. Sally and Claire had broken the news to her as gently as they could. Then they had tried to console her. At first, Kate had been disinclined to believe them, but when told of Paul's ugly scar, she had been forced to accept that it was true, even though she had never seen the scar for herself. Kate knew all about Sue Weston's reputation. It was general knowledge in the Nurses Home. She knew she was loose, that she took her pleasures as and when she chose, but she never thought that Paul would have been taken in by such a cheap woman. Kate had been so certain that Paul was different. His behaviour towards her had always been impeccable, beyond reproach. He was respectful and retiring. He wasn't forward or familiar, particularly where girls were concerned. And he was shy; it had been their third date before he had plucked up the courage to kiss her! She honestly believed that he cared for her – that he loved her. And her father had liked him too. When they had left the cottage after the weekend in the Lakes, as her father had kissed her goodbye, he had quietly whispered in her ear, *'Paul seems to be a nice young man'*. She knew it was his way of saying that he approved, and Kate had always believed her father to be a good judge of character. How wrong they both had been.

She was still sobbing quietly when the night sister popped in, doing her late evening round. She laid a hand on Kate's. She had no need to ask what the problem was. Everyone knew.

"I've made you a nice hot drink," she said, "and I'll leave you a couple of sleeping tablets. A good night's sleep will do you good. I'll pop back later to see that you've settled."

But after the sister left, Kate stayed awake brooding. She had believed that Paul was someone who could become her partner for life. There had never been any talk of marriage, setting up house together or raising a family. But when they had discussed where Kate might work

189

after she completed her nurse training, or what Paul's next move might be if he passed the Fellowship exam, there had always been an unspoken assumption, an acknowledgement that they would do things together. She felt that they had so much in common; they shared the same interests and the same moral values. Bitterly she repeated the words to herself; '*the same moral values*' and now this. How could he?

Suddenly the door burst open and Paul marched in without knocking. For two long days, his unhappiness had distracted him from his work by day, and prevented him from sleeping at night. Finally, he had determined that he would see Kate. No diktat from the nursing sister, or anybody else, was going to prevent him. Kate looked up, startled by his sudden appearance.

"Kate, we have to talk," he said.

"There's absolutely nothing to talk about. You might as well leave right now. I don't know how you have the nerve to come bursting in here, after what you've done."

"And what am I supposed to have done?"

"Spent the night with Sue Weston."

"Kate, I did not spend the night with her." Paul spoke the words quietly, slowly and deliberately, trying desperately to stay calm.

"But she says you did. She's told everyone in the Nurses Home. She's deliberately told all my friends." Kate was hysterical, her words coming out in a rush. "How could you? How do you think that makes me feel?"

"Kate, I repeat, I did not spend the night with her. She's telling lies."

"You're the one telling lies. I know because she was seen creeping back into the Nurses Home early the next morning."

"Kate, listen to me. Please give me a chance to explain. Sue did come to my room that night, but she didn't sleep with me. I tried to get her to leave but she wouldn't go. I spent the night in the casualty department because there was nowhere else for me to sleep. I told David Jenkins that I would do his duty for him. He went back to the residency whilst I stayed working in casualty until morning. The nursing staff will vouch for me."

"But what was she doing in your room? You don't deny that she was in your room?"

"No, I can't deny that, but please Kate; let me tell you what happened. If you remember, after the cricket match there was a party, but I didn't want to go. It would have been no fun without you. I agreed to swap duties with Roger. You knew about that arrangement. It meant that we could have an extra weekend to spend together when you were better. All evening I worked in casualty. By one in the morning, everything was quiet, so I went back to the residency. I did look into the lounge to see if the party was over and Sue was there, looking slightly the worse for wear. I didn't speak with her and most certainly did not invite her into my room. I left and went to bed."

"But she's telling everyone that you spent the night together, and you admit she came to your bedroom."

"Yes, she must have seen me and then followed me. She came into my room and made it quite clear that she wanted to make love. I tried to get her to leave, but she refused to go. She said it was too late to get back into the Nurses Home, that the doors would be locked. So I left her there. But then I had nowhere to sleep. I asked the night sister if there was a side room that I might use, but they were all occupied. So I went back to casualty, told them that I had locked myself out of my room, and spent the night there working."

There was a long pause. Paul desperately hoped that Kate would believe him, though he was acutely conscious that he hadn't told her the full story. She looked at him, a forlorn expression on her pale face. But Paul could not look her in the eye; his gaze slipped to the floor. Kate reached out and held his hand in hers.

"Paul," she said her voice quiet and earnest. "Paul, look at me. Is that the whole story? I need to know. If we are to spend our lives together, I need to be able to trust you. We need to be able to trust each other. Is that the whole story? Is that really all that happened?"

Suddenly Paul's heart leapt. She had been bold enough to put into words what had been in his mind for many months. She had been brave enough to say what he had been afraid to ask. But how was he to respond? Suddenly, the outcome of this exchange had become of critical importance. He could easily say that he had already told her the whole story, not mention that Sue had been naked, that he had run his hands over her body and allowed her into his bed. No one could prove otherwise, he thought, unaware that Sue's knowledge of his scar was evidence to the contrary. But if he were to do that, where was the trust, where was the honesty upon which to build a permanent relationship? So he told her the whole story, in every detail, expressing his sense of shame and the guilt that he now felt. Yet curiously, he found it a relief to be able to talk of it, to get it out in the open. A weight was taken off his shoulders and he felt better for it.

Kate listened in silence. "So you didn't make love?" she asked quietly.

"No," he said, "we didn't."

"And that's the whole story?"

"Yes, that's the whole story."

"And you say that Sue landed like a sack of potatoes on the floor?"

"Yes she did; very heavily on her backside."

Kate smiled. "I wish I'd been there to see that."

"If you had been, I don't suppose Sue would have been there as well."

"No I suppose not. Thank you for being honest with me Paul. If people go on spreading Sue's lies, I shall just tell them to ask Sue how she came by the bruises on her bottom, then everyone, including Sue, will understand that I know the truth."

For some time, they sat hand in hand at the bedside. Paul felt hugely relieved to have told Kate the truth, but also elated, not simply to have her understanding and forgiveness, but to hear her say that she wished to spend her life with him. How ironic that Sue, vindictively trying to break their relationship, had actually brought them together.

"Kate," he said. "A moment ago you mentioned spending our lives together. That's something that has been in my mind for weeks now. I've been trying to pluck up the courage to suggest it. I love you and I want us always to be together, if you'll have me that is."

"Is that a proposal, Paul? I'm a poor catch at the moment, stuck in this side room."

"But you're on the mend. It's only a matter of time until you fully recover and Kate, yes, it is a proposal. Please say that you will marry me?"

"Yes, Paul, I will. Nothing would give me greater pleasure."

Kate was wrapped in Paul's arms in a warm embrace, when the door opened and the night sister reappeared. Her face expressed surprise and anger; her voice was severe.

"There's a notice on the door, Dr Lambert that says '*No Visitors.*'

Kate answered on his behalf. "It's alright Sister. It was put there at my request but it can be taken down now. And I can give you back these two sleeping pills. I plan to sleep well tonight."

Chapter Twenty

At a stroke, Paul's engagement to Kate cleared many of the doubts and anxieties that had been troubling him and he was filled with a sense of great optimism. Congratulating him, Kate's friends spoke of her caring nature and warm personality, adding to his joy and pride. Even Sister Ashbrook remarked what a fortunate young man he was, to win her hand! It appeared that at last, fortune was beginning to smile on them, for other events followed that were equally welcome. As if by magic, Kate's pulse returned to normal, all her aches and pains melted away and within a week, she was allowed home, albeit on the strict understanding that she rested in bed for three hours every afternoon and avoided strenuous physical activity.

The next weekend, Paul drove up to Kendal, once more staying in Ralph's delightful stone cottage. Paul took the opportunity to ask him formally for his daughter's hand in marriage. Kate was amused by this gesture, which she regarded as being extremely old fashioned. Her father laughed out loud.

"Paul, for heaven's sake, if Kate has said '*Yes*' there's nothing I could possibly do or say to stop her! But I do whole-heartedly approve and you both have my blessing."

They readily agreed that they should be married within a few months, for which Paul was grateful. Although he would never have dared to admit it to Kate, Sue Weston had aroused emotions in him that had long been suppressed, emotions that were in need of expression. And there were times were Kate's kisses were so passionate, that he was in little doubt that a similar fire burned within her.

To add to Paul's optimism, there followed developments at the hospital that opened up the prospect of promotion. After a number of unsuccessful applications, Mo was appointed as a consultant in the North East. His elevation was long overdue and the folk living in the Tyneside area were indeed fortunate that such a conscientious and competent surgeon was coming to serve them. Professor Butterworth's registrar was then appointed to fill Mo's position, which meant that a registrar post fell vacant. However Fellowship of the Royal College was a prerequisite for application. If Paul were to pass the exam, which was imminent, he could and would apply. He recognised that, realistically, there was little chance of being appointed, since there were other SHOs in the hospital who were senior to him. His application though, would be a public declaration of his intent to progress as a surgeon. It would put him in the frame for any subsequent posts that fell vacant.

Gaining entrance to the College of Surgeons however, was a formidable challenge, as indeed was entry to the other royal colleges such as those of paediatrics and obstetrics. Although Paul had studied diligently, his apprehension increased and his confidence diminished as the date of the exam approached. The examination was held in London at the Royal College in Lincolns Inn Fields. It involved assessment on two separate days, three weeks apart. The first hurdle was the two written papers, each of three hours duration. Only if performance was judged to be satisfactory were candidates invited back for an appraisal of their diagnostic skills at the bedside and for a viva on operative technique. Surprisingly, there was no assessment of actual operative skill, the misguided assumption being, that if you were able to describe how an operation was performed, you were actually capable of doing it. This was as crazy as granting a driving licence to a learner driver, without actually seeing them behind the wheel of a car!

The examiners were eminent surgeons, often professors from Great Britain with the occasional overseas examiner. To ensure fairness, they worked in pairs and were not permitted to examine anyone with whom they had previously had contact. Candidates were examined anonymously by number and not by name.

Paul was not relishing the prospect of the trip to London, for the capital was not his favourite city. It was not that he disliked the people who live there; it was simply that he associated London with stress and anxiety, interviews and examinations. This aversion originated from his unsuccessful application for a place at the medical school of one of London's oldest and most prestigious teaching hospitals. At the time, as a rather naive and unsophisticated sixth form schoolboy, he was making his first trip to the city. His train had arrived at Euston station an hour and half late, thanks to a signalling failure at Crewe. Then there was a further delay on the Northern Line of the Underground. In an attempt to make up time, he ran the last quarter of a mile to the medical school, through wind and rain, arriving hot, breathless, wet and agitated. After trouble finding the department where the interviews were to be held, he had no time to compose himself, before he was ushered into an oak panelled committee room, still wearing his wet gabardine. He came face to face with two very distinguished looking, elderly gentlemen, whose faces were just as severe as those of the unsmiling figures depicted in the gold framed portraits on the wall behind them. Presumably they were past consultants of the hospital, now long dead and no longer able to terrorise aspiring young doctors such as Paul.

The older of the two regarded Paul over the rim of his half moon glasses. His thin white hair, lined face and gaunt appearance suggested that it might not be long, before he too was immortalised in a framed portrait! He spoke in a clipped, high-pitched, wavering voice.

"Now what have we here?" The use of the word 'what' instead of 'who', together with the tone of his voice, suggested that this was less of a question addressed to Paul, so much as a comment to his colleague.

He peered at the papers in front of him.

"I suppose its Johnson, is it?"

"No Sir, Lambert."

"Bamber, did you say?" he responded, a hand cupped to his ear.

"No, Sir, Lambert," Paul replied, speaking a little louder, and as clearly as he could.

"Did you say Lambert? You really mustn't mumble, my boy. You should learn to speak more distinctly."

"Yes, Sir, Lambert,"

The old man looked down again and made an amendment to the notes in front of him.

"I see. So you're Peter Lambert, Rupert Lambert's grandson from Winchester, I suppose. How is your grandfather keeping these days? Does he still do a spot of fishing?" He turned to his colleague. "Rupert and I were at college together in the old days. We played a lot of rugger together. Did you know that we were both in the team that won the intercollege shield?"

"No Sir, I'm Paul Lambert from Accrington."

The elderly gent frowned and consulted his notes again.

"If you're not Peter Lambert, you should be Johnson, David Johnson. What are you doing here?"

A doubt entered Paul's mind. He had arrived at the last minute in a fluster. Was it possible that he was in the wrong place?

"I applied for a place at the medical school, Sir. Your secretary took my name and escorted me in here."

The interviewer who had addressed him but had, as yet, failed to introduce himself, conferred with his equally anonymous colleague. With unfashionably long grey hair that hung down in untidy strands over his collar, and wearing a velvet jacket and a red and white spotted bowtie, Paul marked him down as a retired psychiatrist. He was possibly a couple of years younger than his partner, but still looked to be nearer eighty than seventy. Then the older man spoke again.

"We were expecting to see Johnson next; I really don't understand what can have happened. Applicants are supposed to come in here in alphabetical order, but I do see there is a 'Lambert' on our list."

There was further conferring and more shuffling of papers. Paul felt a growing irritation. It seemed reasonably obvious to him that Johnson had either cancelled or been delayed, and that Lambert was the next name on their list.

"So you're Lambert are you, from Accrington? That's in Lancashire, isn't it; somewhere north of Manchester?" From the grimace on his face, and the sideways glance at his partner, Paul gained the impression that, in his mind, Manchester was the limit of the known world, beyond which civilisation ceased to exist!

Paul nodded.

"And you aspire to study medicine here?" he questioned, managing to instil a tone of incredulity into his voice. He regarded Paul's windswept hair. Then his eyes swept over his wet raincoat, which was dripping water to form a small puddle on the polished parquet floor. He sniffed quietly as he noted Paul's trousers, damp from the knee down and his best black school shoes; the ones that he had cleaned, brushed and polished so assiduously before leaving home, but which were now mud splattered and scuffed.

He sniffed again. "Well Lambert," he said, disapproval evident in his voice, "if you wish to be considered for a career in medicine, I must advise you that medicine is a respectable profession. We expect a certain minimum standard of dress and behaviour. Our patients expect us to be appropriately attired at all times. The purpose of these interviews is to ensure that we only admit the right sort of chap. You do understand that, I suppose?"

"Yes, Sir," Paul replied. "I do apologise for my appearance. Unfortunately, my train was delayed. It has been quite a rush to get here, and it is raining rather heavily outside."

"Our patients also expect us to make contingency plans, to ensure that we always fulfil our appointments. You should have travelled down last night, shouldn't you?"

"Yes, Sir," Paul replied. He could have countered this criticism on the grounds of expense but decided that any further attempt to justify himself would be counterproductive.

With that, his aged assessor sniffed again, jotted some notes on the pad in front of him, then turned to his colleague.

"I don't think I have any more questions for this fellow Charles. Is there anything that you wish to ask?"

The younger of the two geriatrics eyed Paul quizzically, as a cat might eye a mouse, wondering whether to kill it straightaway or to have some fun before doing so. He decided on the latter course.

"Tell me Lambert, what's life like up in Accrington?"

Paul was at a loss to know what to say. He had never been in such a situation before and had received no guidance on interview technique, either from his parents or at school. When trying to predict the questions that he might face, he had anticipated that there might be reference to his academic record, his interests, sporting activities and hobbies. He thought perhaps they might ask his reasons for wishing to study medicine, but not about life in Accrington.

"Well Sir," he managed to reply after a longish pause, "It suits me well enough. I'm happy there. But it's the only place that I have lived; I really have nothing with which to compare it."

"Happy in Accrington, eh? Surely not." The interviewer looked across at his colleague, smiled sadly and then turned back to Paul.

"Perhaps that shows a certain lack of ambition," he commented. "Have you given any thought to moving, perhaps to study in Manchester or in Liverpool for example?"

"I have ambitions to study medicine in London, Sir," Paul replied stiffly, angered by the tone of the question.

"Ah yes, but should those ambitions not be realised, would Manchester or Liverpool suffice?"

It was obvious that he was being told that his application was unsuccessful. They had taken one look at him, heard his North Country accent and decided that he was not suitable for their prestigious teaching hospital. The interview continued for a further two or three minutes during which time, they ascertained that there was no opera, ballet or concert hall in Accrington, before they politely showed him the door. Why, Paul wondered, had they had bothered to drag him all the way down to London for an interview, if they were going to dismiss him so abruptly?

The gathering dusk, a developing fog and the continuing rain added to his gloom as he left the hospital, and turned back towards the tube station. As he did so a huge road sign confronted him. It showed a large black arrow pointing up the road along which he was walking. In the most enormous letters was written 'THE NORTH'. That just about sums it up, he thought. Go back where you belong young man, London is not for you.

***

Paul's second trip to the capital had been to sit the first part of the fellowship examination. It too had been a challenge, and not merely due to the rigours of the exam. At the time, he had been employed as a 'demonstrator' at the University. There were half a dozen such posts, the main responsibility being to teach basic anatomy to students of medicine and dentistry. It was an ideal stepping-stone for an aspiring surgeon, since the exam was essentially a test of anatomical knowledge. The pace of life at the university was slow, there was no evening, night or weekend duty and Paul was actually paid more for a 40 hour week, than he had received for working 90 hours a week in his previous job as a houseman!

Over the years, an association had developed between the young doctors in the department and a certain Mrs McNamara, who ran a boarding house on the Mile End Road, in the east end of London. Mrs McNamara was always pleased to welcome them, frequently making the exaggerated claim that over the years, she had provided bed and breakfast accommodation for most of the surgeons in the country. The snag was that Mrs McNamara had a daughter called Bessie, and it was her mother's ambition to have a surgeon as a son-in-law; her intention being that, sooner or later, she would manage to marry Bessie to one of the young doctors who came to stay. Paul had been warned about this in advance and advised to be on his guard. Inevitably he had been curious to meet Bessie, though rumour had it that she was a pleasant enough girl, though somewhat plain and simple.

Mrs McNamara's three-story house, built in red brick, was situated in the middle of a terraced block, its front door opening directly onto the street. It looked unpromising from the outside, but inside it was warm, bright and cheerful. Mrs McNamara was a likeable, homely, buxom woman. She greeted Paul with an apron round her waist, flour on her hands and a welcoming smile on her face.

"You must be Dr Lambert," she said. "Do come in and make yourself at home. I'm just baking some scones. You shall have one with a cup of tea, the minute you've unpacked."

Aged between forty and fifty, with a dumpy figure and a round and jovial face, crowned with dyed blond curls, she wasted no time in introducing Paul to her daughter.

It was immediately apparent that Bessie was pathologically shy. She stood, ill at ease with her head bowed, her hands tightly clasped in front of her, clearly uncomfortable in the presence of a stranger. She was however, not unattractive, with her mother's rosy cheeks, if perhaps a little on the plump side.

"Well, say '*Hello*' to the young doctor, Bessie."

"Hello," whispered Bessie, her voice almost inaudible, eyes still glued to the floor.

"Bessie wants to be a nurse, don't you Bessie? Tell the young doctor you want to be a nurse, Bessie."

"I want to be a nurse," she muttered, her lips scarcely moving.

"That's good," Paul said, as brightly as he could. "It's a very interesting job. Very worthwhile too, helping people when they're sick. Have you applied to join a nursing school?"

There was silence.

"Well, tell the young doctor what you've got to do Bessie, to get into nursing."

This instruction was greeted by silence, so Mrs McNamara spoke on her behalf. "Bessie has to pass her 'O levels' first, haven't you Bessie? She struggles a bit, Doctor, especially with her maths."

Paul glanced again at Bessie. She looked to be 20 or 22 years old, surely a bit old to be taking GCE's.

"No doubt the young doctor will help you this evening, by giving you a bit of private tuition."

Paul remembered the warnings he had received about Mrs McNamara's intentions. He cut in quickly. "Actually, I was hoping to do a bit of last minute studying myself, Mrs McNamara. I've got my exam tomorrow."

"But I'm sure you can squeeze in half an hour after supper and Bessie will be ever so grateful." Her mother spoke decisively, leaving little room for manoeuvre.

Paul was trapped but before he could protest any further, the door opened and a lad of about four or five entered.

"Oh, this is our Jimmy," Mrs McNamara said. "Jimmy, say '*Hello*' to the young doctor."

Whereas Bessie was shy and retiring, Jimmy was bright and cheeky.

"Hi, Doc," he said, as he went straight through to the back room. He emerged a moment or two later with a large slice of bread smothered in strawberry jam, much of which was already smeared around his mouth.

Paul wondered which of these two women was his mother. It could have been either of them. He waited to see which he would call '*Mum*' or whether perhaps, he would refer to one of them as '*Gran*', but he used neither word. Most of his sentences began with the words '*I want*'.

Mrs McNamara proved to be a fine cook and when the dishes had been cleared, after an excellent dinner of lamb stew and apple pie, Bessie and Paul sat down side by side at the table. Mrs McNamara produced an arithmetic book and suggested some exercises. They started with some problems based on simply multiplication but Bessie remained painfully shy and monosyllabic. It quickly became clear that she had no aptitude for maths and had no chance whatsoever of obtaining an 'O level' in the subject. Nor was she in the least interested in learning. Paul asked if she had started work.

"No, not proper work."

He enquired further.

"I help out as an assistant at the nursery where our Jimmy goes each day."

As soon as the nursery was mentioned, she became quite animated and talked freely about her role and about the children for whom she cared. They ranged in age from babes in arms to five year olds. Quite spontaneously, she described several amusing incidents that had occurred whilst she had been working there. It was clear that she thoroughly enjoyed the work and probably had a natural aptitude for it. Bessie's academic ability, or lack of it, meant that she would never gain entrance to a school of nursing. It seemed to Paul that she would be far better advised to train as an auxiliary or nursery nurse. Later he said as much to her mother. Mrs McNamara was not aware of the distinction between state registered nurses (SRNs) and enrolled nurses (SENs) and was interested to learn that enrolled nurses did not need such high academic qualifications. Paul explained that they were not allowed to administer drugs, or undertake some of the more complex nursing procedures. None the less, they did extremely valuable 'hands on' work, caring for the sick and were very much appreciated by patients. Furthermore, they could choose to work with children if they so wished.

The next day, after an early breakfast, Paul thanked Mrs McNamara for her hospitality and left for the examination hall, but not before he had been asked if he had enjoyed Bessie's company.

"Very much thank you. She's a pleasant girl," he said, politely and honestly, "and I expect that she would do very well in the right sort of nursing."

"That's good," beamed Mrs McNamara. "When you come back in a week or two, you could take Bessie to the pictures. You would like that, wouldn't you Bessie?"

Before Bessie had a chance to reply, Paul interjected. "I shall only be coming back for the oral exam, if I pass the written papers today."

"Oh, you will back," said Mrs. McNamara confidently. "All my young doctors come back."

Chapter Twenty One

The following Saturday afternoon, Paul was watching sport on the television in the residency, when Sister Rutherford rang. She had successfully manoeuvred Mr Brown into the office on the male ward, without his wife's knowledge. He was waiting there to speak with Paul. He seemed a pleasant man, perhaps in his early forties, his anxious face and general demeanour suggesting genuine concern for his wife, who was perhaps a year or two older. He was eager to know the cause of her troubles. Paul had to inform him, that he was unable to answer his questions, since his wife had specifically instructed that no information was to be released about her medical condition, either to him or to his son. He explained, with regret, that he was bound by the hospital's code of confidentiality.

Mr Brown's response was somewhat muted. "I suppose I'm not surprised. It's the sort of thing she would do."

He went on to confirm that he and his wife were getting divorced, stating that no third party was involved, but that the love that they had once shared, had simply melted away over the years.

"We just appear to be drifting apart. I don't seem to be able to do anything to please her these days. Don't get me wrong, Doctor; it's not that I hate her or wish her ill. In fact, I'm sorry she's poorly now, but we can't go on as we are. We're simply no longer compatible. That's why we have agreed to go our separate ways. Our children are grown up and independent. They can see what has happened to us and they understand. I was talking it over with my son only this morning. He thinks we should get on with the divorce straightaway, make a clean break of it. But I really don't feel that would be the right thing to do whilst she's ill, particularly now that she is in hospital. But we will have to get the divorce finalised one day. We'll go ahead with it when she's better."

As Mr Potts had suggested, Paul asked whether Mr Brown could throw any light on his wife's illness. But since he was unaware of the nature of the problem and as Paul was not at liberty to inform him, unsurprisingly, he wasn't able to add anything useful.

Paul scarcely had time to return to the residency, when Sister Rutherford rang again. This time it was to inform him that Mrs Brown had produced another heavily blood stained stool. Given her track record, this almost certainly meant a further trip to theatre. Remembering how ill she had been when she was originally admitted to hospital, Paul undertook the now familiar steps to resuscitate and transfuse her, but recognised that senior advice was needed. Officially, Mo was not 'on duty' but knowing that he was already familiar with Mrs Brown's problem, Paul asked the switchboard operator to try to contact him at home, and when informed of the situation, Mo readily agreed to return to the hospital.

Mrs Brown continued to bleed and by the time Mo arrived, her condition had deteriorated further. Together they put up a second drip and ordered more blood from the laboratory.

Mo looked concerned. "I'm going to ring Mr Potts to see if he's available. He may or may not be around this weekend but he did say that he wished to be informed, if there were any further developments. He's been very worried about Mrs Brown and she really is a mystery. This will be her third operation and we still don't know why this ulcer has developed. Mr Potts hasn't seen it for himself yet. He may have some ideas as to what's causing it and what we might do to cure it. There's a real danger that she will bleed to death, if we aren't able to solve the problem soon."

Whilst Mo went to the phone, Paul stayed with Mrs Brown. She wanted to know what was planned to stop the bleeding. Paul backpedalled.

"I'm not sure at this stage. We're hoping to have a word with Mr Potts but I presume that the ulcer will have to be stitched again. I'm afraid that it's likely to mean yet another operation."

Mo returned. "I managed to speak with Mr Potts. He's looking after his children at the moment whilst his wife is shopping, but he expects to be here in about an hour. In the meantime, he wants us to organise an anaesthetist and obtain consent for a further telescopic examination. He thinks that a further trip to theatre is inevitable.

A couple of hours later, Paul watched as Mr Potts examined the ulcer but, like Victoria and Mo before him, he was unable to suggest what had caused it to develop. The ulcer was now wider and deeper than it had been before and it continued to bleed furiously. All Mr Potts attempts to arrest the flow of blood were unsuccessful. It was with considerable regret that he decided that in view of the continuing life-threatening haemorrhage, he could see no alternative but to remove the rectum. Showing great surgical skill, he then performed a complex two-hour operation, which resulted in the removal of Mrs Brown's back passage and the formation of a colostomy; a permanent opening on the abdomen through which her bowels would function. In future, the stool would be collected in a plastic bag, supported by a belt that she would wear around her waist. As the stoma was being formed, Paul was acutely aware that when speaking with Mrs Brown before the operation, he had only obtained her permission for an examination by telescope and suturing of the ulcer. It was true that the small print at the bottom of the 'consent' form, gave the surgeon licence to do '*whatever necessary*' but very few patients bothered to read the whole form, indeed most signed the form without reading any of it. Paul believed that if the surgeon were to write '*removal of head and all limbs*' on the form, the majority of patients would happily sign it without a second thought. In this case, with the ongoing bleeding, there had been no alternative to creating the stoma but it was going to come as a devastating shock to Mrs Brown when she learned of it.

***

Fortunately, the first few days after Mrs Brown's major operation were free of any complications. Heavily sedated and confined to bed with her abdomen bandaged, she was blissfully unaware of the nature and complexity of her surgery. Under Sister Rutherford's motherly supervision, the nurses on the ward were caring and compassionate to all their patients. Inevitably though, particular patients, in view of their individual circumstances, received especially sympathetic treatment and Mrs Brown was one, because of her relative youth, her difficult family circumstances and her unfortunate medical problem.

As the days passed, the need for pain relief and sedation diminished and she became more alert. She was noticeably brighter and more cheerful than she had been before her operation. She seemed to revel in the care and attention that she received from the nurses. She also started to engage more freely in conversation with the other patients on the ward. One day she spoke with Paul about her plans for the future. She had originally trained as a teacher and although she hadn't worked since her marriage 20 years before, she was now considering returning to that profession, possibly in a part time capacity. She thought that as she was effectively starting life again as a single woman, teaching would raise her status, give her independence and offer financial security. She appreciated that since her sister had a young family, she couldn't live with her permanently. She contemplated renting a small flat close by. At no stage in the conversation, did she make any mention of her colostomy, or the effect that a stoma might have on her plans. This caused Paul some disquiet and afterwards he went to discuss the matter with Sister Rutherford, to seek her advice and guidance. He presumed she had met this situation several times before.

"Sister, Mrs Brown has just been speaking of her plans for the future, but she never once mentioned her colostomy. In fact, she doesn't seem to realise that she has one. I presume that she hasn't been told yet."

"No, she hasn't Paul, and it's been worrying me too. I had a similar conversation with her yesterday. The fact that she has a stoma doesn't preclude any of her plans of course, and most folk, especially the younger ones, adapt to the new situation really well. The vast majority lead full active lives."

"I appreciate that, although there will still be some hurdles for her to overcome. What do you suggest? Do we just wait until the colostomy starts to function? Surely that would come as an awful shock to her. Wouldn't it be better for us to make the first move; informing her and preparing her in advance?"

"Undoubtedly it's best to tell her in advance and frankly, the sooner it's done the better. At the moment, she's more cheerful and positive than she was before her operation; that will certainly help when she's told. Are you free now?"

Paul had no other pressing tasks, so together they walked down the ward, pulled the screens round Mrs Brown's bed and drew up two chairs. As they sat, Paul glanced across at Sister Rutherford and she looked back at him. Neither of them had thought who was going to open the conversation and there was a momentary pause. Mrs Brown looked anxiously at each of them in turn, no doubt wondering why they had come to see her, sensing that they had some bad news to relate.

Hesitantly, Paul began. He explained that when she had gone to theatre for the third time, Mr Potts had tried to stop the haemorrhage, by stitching the ulcer in the manner that had been successful on the two previous occasions. He went on to say that, unfortunately this had proved impossible. The heavy bleeding had continued and Mr Potts had decided that the ulcer would have to be removed, together with the length of bowel upon which it was situated. Paul emphasised that there had been no other way to stop the profuse bleeding, which would certainly have been the death of her, had it been allowed to continue. He then explained that since her back passage had been removed, it had been necessary to allow the stool to exit the body by another route, in other words to perform a colostomy. He paused, wondering whether she understood what a colostomy was, but she had obviously heard of this operation.

"That's the 'bag' operation isn't it, Doctor?"

"Yes," he said, grateful that she already had some understanding of a stoma. "The bowel now ends on your tummy wall. Your motions will appear there and will be collected in a small plastic bag. You will need to wear a belt around your waist to support the bag."

To Paul's surprise, Mrs Brown's anxious expression melted away and she began to look more relaxed. He presumed that she had not fully understood the full significance of what was being said. Wondering whether to plough on and give more detail, Paul looked across the bed to Sister, hoping for guidance. She seemed instinctively to understand his dilemma and took the initiative.

"Obviously you will be with us for a week or so yet," she said, "so there will be plenty of time for us to tell you more about it. We'll show you the bags and belt, and explain to you how they work. There are one or two 'tricks of the trade' you will need to learn, but we won't let you go home until you've got the hang of it."

"So that means I'll have to come back into hospital for another operation, doesn't it?" Mrs Brown still seemed relaxed about the situation, even managing a smile, apparently unruffled by the thought of more surgery.

Paul realised that he hadn't made the situation completely clear.

"No. We're not planning any more surgery."

"So the plumbing just goes back to normal on its own, does it? That's very clever."

"No," Paul said quietly. "I'm afraid that you don't have a back passage any more. It isn't possible for us to return the plumbing to normal. The colostomy, the artificial opening, is permanent."

Such a possibility had never entered her head and the revelation shocked her. A look of horror crossed her face, initially disbelieving, then frightened and angry.

"But why? Why has he done that to me?" her voice, previously composed, now halting and strained.

Sister moved from her chair, sat on the bed beside Mrs Brown and put an arm around her shoulders whilst Paul repeated his previous explanation of the necessity to remove the back passage. Again he emphasised that this had been the only way to stop the bleeding, which otherwise would have led to her death. He stressed that such a step would not have been taken, unless it had been absolutely necessary.

Mrs Brown, though, didn't hear a single word that was being said, as she sobbed inconsolably.

Paul remained seated as Sister continued to comfort the patient. He knew that there was little further he could usefully do or say; yet was conscious that it would be awkward to walk away and leave a patient in such distress.

Sister broke the silence.

"Dr Lambert, I'll stay here with Mrs Brown for a moment. Would you please ask one of the nurses to come and join me?"

Gratefully he slipped away confident that Sister Rutherford and her team would do their very best to comfort and console the patient, aware that they were much better equipped for the job than he.

***

The surgical journal was published monthly so as each edition appeared, Paul went expectantly to the hospital library to see if his 'Soccer Supporter's Wrist' article had been published. He had seen other doctor's CVs and had frequently noticed the phrase, *'publication in progress'*. This might mean that a good piece of research had been undertaken, an article had been submitted to an academic journal, then accepted by the editor and was simply waiting to appear in print. However the phrase might equally mean *'I have written a research article, but have yet to persuade the editor of a journal to accept it'*. It might even mean *'I have a vague idea for a research project but have yet to do anything about it'*. Interview panels were wise to such tricks. They only gave credit to research that had already been published. If Paul's article were actually to appear in print before he applied for his next post, his chance of success would be greatly improved.

Finally the day arrived when, on one of his regular trips to the library, he glanced through the index of the journal and saw it. His article was in print. Delighted, he turned to the appropriate page and there it was; a bold heading and the diagram, illustrating how the wrist could be overstretched on a football barrier. Then his eye fell on the names of the authors listed under the title; *'Soccer Supporter's Wrist' by Leslie Potts, Consultant General Surgeon, James Keeley, Consultant Orthopaedic Surgeon and Paul Lambert, Surgical SHO'*. They had stolen his paper! They had relegated him to third author. His initial delight turned to anger and dismay. He had been the one who had seen and treated the patients in casualty. He had spotted the potential for an academic publication. He had done the research, both in the medical library and in the newspaper offices. He had linked the injuries to the size of the crowd. He had written the entire article, yet the consultants had claimed the credit, having contributed nothing to the publication. He had only mentioned it to Mr Potts out of courtesy. Damn it, there was no justice at all.

Then it suddenly dawned on him why Mr Potts had volunteered to submit the article to the editor of the journal. The sly old fox wanted the credit for himself. Yet what could Paul do? The paper was now in print. He could scarcely get it republished with himself as sole author and most certainly he couldn't remonstrate with his boss. That would be surgical suicide. Once more, the vulnerability of his position as a junior doctor struck him, dependant as he was on his consultant for career advancement. Without his support, it would be pointless to apply for a registrar post, even if he were fortunate enough to pass the fellowship exam.

As usual, when he needed advice or guidance, he went to have a chat with Mo Khan, expressing his disappointment and disbelief at Mr Potts' behaviour.

"You really shouldn't be surprised, Paul. Mr Potts needs publications just as much as you do."

"Why? He's a consultant already. He doesn't need them. And in any case, surely he's not entitled to steal my ideas."

"Your ideas Paul, but not your patients. You saw them in casualty, but at the time you were working for Mr Potts. He carried the overall responsibility for those patients, even though you saw them on his behalf. He's the one who carries the can if you mismanage them. And don't forget, it was the orthopaedic staff who took over their care. They were the ones who reduced their fractures and then followed them up in their clinics. Mr Keeley has every right to have his name on the paper. Besides, if you had submitted the article as a single author, as a junior doctor, it may not have been seriously considered. But if it bears a consultant's name, with the authority that implies, it's less likely to be rejected. But I do agree, it would have been more generous if they had placed you as the first author."

"But why does he need more publications?"

"Because he wants the kudos and because he's working towards a merit award."

Not knowing what this was, Paul asked him to explain.

"Consultants get a basic salary for the work they do in the hospital. That includes being 'on call' on urgency days and weekends, but if they do extra work, work that is deemed to be 'meritorious', they receive a merit award. It involves making a contribution that is beyond the normal call of duty, maybe doing research, or pioneering a new clinical service. The award comes as a supplement to their salary. There are several levels of award, and they can significantly increase a consultant's basic salary. A tiny handful of consultants, those with the highest level of award, are practically able to double their salary."

"So I do all the work and they get the credit," Paul commented bitterly.

Mohammed smiled. "I'm afraid that's how the system works, Paul. I've told you before, as a junior doctor, you have to accept the system as it. You won't change it and if you try to buck the system, the system will simply turf you out. You just have to hope that when you apply for your next job, Mr Potts remembers that he owes you a favour."

Paul was subsequently to discover though, that when he duly applied for promotion, Mr Potts did remember. However, it proved not to be to his advantage. Amazingly, he actually used the publication as a weapon with which to severely castigate him!

Chapter Twenty Two

As it happened, the Fellowship examiners did call Paul back for the second part of the College exam, but not wishing to be the subject of Mrs McNamara's matchmaking, he elected to stay in a large city centre hotel. This proved to be a bad decision. The cost was prohibitive, the hotel impersonal, the food unpalatable. The only member of staff with whom he spoke was the receptionist, who gave him the key to a hot and stuffy room on the 4th floor. The room was situated on the front of the building, overlooking traffic lights at a major road junction. Paul was kept awake half the night by heavy lorries, as they ground to a halt, then crashed their gears as they set off again. With hindsight, he would have been far happier in the homely atmosphere at Mrs McNamara's, even if this had meant accompanying Bessie to the cinema.

As he travelled south on the train, sitting gloomily by the window, every mile taking him closer to London and the rigors of the final examination, Paul reflected on the challenge that lay ahead. He was about to have his clinical skills assessed, face-to-face by examiners, who were the most senior and eminent surgeons in the land. He was to be grilled on patient management and to have a specific interrogation on operative technique. The 75% failure rate was daunting and he knew of numerous surgical trainees who had failed, many of them more experienced than he was, and whose knowledge and clinical acumen he envied. Some had failed more than once. The range of topics on which the examiners could question candidates was immense; anything from toenails to tonsils, from trauma to transplantation and horror stories abounded of examiners who deliberately tried to unsettle the candidates. In this respect, Victoria and Mohammed had been extremely helpful. They had arranged mock vivas for Paul, testing him on a wide variety of subjects and warning him of some of the tricks that the examiners were known to play.

An examiner might say, '*I want you to imagine a young man, say 22 years old, who has fallen off his motor bike and broken his ankle. Tell me how you would manage him.*' If you started to describe how the ankle injury should be treated, the examiner might immediately interrupt, sounding shocked. '*This man is lying in the middle of a busy main road. Wouldn't you move him to a place of safety first?*' So you would start again; '*Having moved the patient to a place of safety, I would immobilise the leg by splinting it and...*' Again the examiner might butt in. '*Are you seriously suggesting that you move this patient, without checking for other injuries? He might have broken his neck.*

You could paralyse him for the rest of his life, if you drag him across the road.'

The safest thing was to assume that the patient was found in the middle of the road and describe each and every step from first aid to transport to the local hospital and wait for the examiner to become impatient.

The game could be played in many forms. If, for example, you were asked how to remove a patient's appendix, it seems natural to commence by saying: *'I would make an incision two inches long, in the lower right abdomen, centred on McBurney's point,'* at which moment the examiner might comment, somewhat sarcastically, *'don't you think that the patient might appreciate it, if you anaesthetised him first?'*

"Yes Sir, sorry Sir," you would reply. *"With the patient anaesthetised, I would make a two inch incision, centred over ......"*

There could then be a further interruption.

"Wouldn't you put an antiseptic on the skin first, or are you deliberately trying to give the patient a nasty wound infection?"

'Yes, Sir,' you would correct yourself, trying to keep a cool head, *'with the patient anaesthetised and having painted the skin with a suitable antiseptic solution, I would make an incision.....'*

And so it would go on.

On the other hand, if in answer to the original question, you said, *"with the patient anaesthetised, I would paint the skin with an antiseptic solution, wait for it to dry, put drapes around the operation site and then make an incision...."* the examiner was likely to stop you in your tracks, saying, *"yes yes, yes. I wouldn't expect you to plunge your knife into a patient who was wide awake, would I?"*

Similarly, if it became apparent to the examiner that you knew the answer to a question, he would move quickly on to a new topic, or perhaps go off at a tangent, *"now tell me who McBurney was?"* All the while, they were searching for a weakness in your knowledge. It was designed to unsettle you, to see if you could cope under pressure. To succeed, you needed to stay calm and avoid becoming rattled.

As part of the examination, each candidate was required to take a history and make a diagnosis on a genuine patient. You counted yourself fortunate if you were allocated a patient who was articulate and had a reasonable command of the English language. Luckily most of the long suffering patients who agreed to be used for these examinations, in return for a modest remuneration, had told their stories so often, to so many different candidates, that they had them off pat. If asked, they might even disclose their diagnosis. Care needed to be taken however, for it was not unknown for patients to mislead a candidate, having been instructed by the examiners that, if they were asked such a question, they should lead the candidate astray. They might for example, say that they had renal colic due to a stone in the kidney, when in fact they had biliary colic due to gallstones.

As it happened, Paul's first case was straightforward. The patient was a man in his 40s, who had a stomach ulcer and had vomited blood. Paul had managed many such patients on the ward and had seen operations performed for stomach ulcers. He knew that his answers on this subject were satisfactory.

"Reasonable," said his examiner, grudgingly. "Now let's see how you fare with something quite different."

He passed Paul an ophthalmoscope and invited him to inspect a patient's right eye. This was most unusual, for although the fellowship exam was wide ranging, problems with eyes were generally agreed to be too complex for general surgeons. Eye surgery was the one specialty excluded from the syllabus. Aspiring eye surgeons faced their own specific exam. Furthermore an ophthalmoscope is not an easy instrument to use at the best of times and in this instance, was made more difficult because the light in the room was quite bright, causing the patient's pupil to be constricted. Opticians usually put drops in the eye, to dilate the pupil, before they attempt an examination. Nonetheless, Paul was able to see the retina and had the most amazing piece of good fortune. He immediately knew, without the slightest doubt, exactly what the diagnosis was, not because he was a brilliant student, or because he had read about it. It was simply that an identical case had been presented at an educational meeting at the City General less than three weeks before. It was an extraordinarily interesting condition that follows an eclipse of the sun. The retina, the highly sensitive tissue upon which we depend for our sight, was swollen and inflamed. This was without doubt an 'eclipse' burn, a thermal injury resulting from the patient watching an eclipse of the sun. Just as the sun's rays may be focussed by a glass lens and cause a piece of paper to burst into flames so, if someone looks directly at the sun, the lens in their own eye will focus rays onto their retina and cause a burn. Although an eclipse of the sun occurs somewhere on the earth's surface every 18 months, it only occurs in any particular locality every 200 or 300 years. This injury therefore was incredibly rare; one which the majority of ophthalmologists never see in their entire careers. The examiner invited Paul to describe what he could see, which presented no particular difficulty. He was most certainly not going to admit that he had chanced to be shown an identical case so recently!

"What do you think might have caused it?" the examiner asked.

Playing along, Paul replied. "May I have a look at the other eye, Sir?"

"Why would you wish to do that?"

"To see if it has a similar injury."

"Let me tell you then," said the examiner, not wishing to waste any time, "that the other eye has an identical problem. What do you think is the diagnosis?"

"The only condition that I know that can cause damage like this to both eyes is a thermal injury resulting from the recent solar eclipse," Paul said.

The examiner was amazed. He could not contain his pleasure. He beamed with delight and actually shook Paul by the hand.

"Well done, young man. Well done indeed. I'm not supposed to tell you this, but you are the only candidate today to have made the correct diagnosis."

Confident that his performance so far had been satisfactory, grateful for his good fortune and with the praise of the last examiner still ringing in his ears, Paul sat and waited for his final viva, an interrogation on operative technique.

The examiner appeared to be rather young to be undertaking the role, scarcely old enough to be a consultant, but he smiled in a friendly fashion when Paul met him. He was accompanied by an older surgeon. He would not be asking any questions but would be involved in allocating a mark at the end of the assessment. None of the examiners wore name badges. Nor was it their custom to introduce themselves to the candidates, so Paul had no idea who they were or where they worked.

"You seem to have made a good impression with the patients that you examined," said the younger of the two, looking at the scoring card that followed the candidates through the exam. Were those general surgical cases?"

"One was a stomach complaint and the other was a patient with an eye problem," Paul replied.

"Right, well let's see what you know about orthopaedics."

Inwardly, Paul groaned. He had never worked on an orthopaedic unit and had no practical experience of the specialty. His answers would have to be based on what he had read, rather than on what he had seen. Further, despite many hours of study, he hadn't found time to read a standard textbook on the subject. His knowledge was based entirely on notes written for the guidance of junior doctors at the Middleton Hospital. The senior orthopaedic surgeon there was a small fierce Scot called Alexander McAllister. He had a short fuse and ran his department with a rod of iron. He had very definite views on the treatment of bone fractures and had written these down in the form of rigid rules, in a fifty-page handbook, known locally as 'McAllister's bible'. The junior staff were expected to follow these instructions to the letter and woe betide anyone who failed to do so. Even if the result of a patient's treatment proved to be disastrous, Mr McAllister would not criticise his staff, provided that the directives in his 'bible' had been followed. However, if they were not followed, it didn't matter that the patient made a wonderful recovery from his injuries, he came down on them like a ton of bricks

"A young man has been involved in an accident and has fractured his femur," the examiner asked Paul, "tell me how you are going to manage him."

Remembering what Mo and Victoria had taught him about examination technique, Paul asked where the accident had taken place.

"Well, it doesn't really matter, but for the sake of argument, let's say that he fell off a ladder whilst pruning trees."

"Sir, firstly I should make a general assessment, particularly looking for any evidence of an injury to the head or neck. I would want to make sure that it was safe to move him. Then, I would----"

But the examiner did not want to waste time by allowing Paul to describe basic first aid.

"No. This young man is in your casualty department. His xray shows a simple fracture of the shaft of his femur and he has no other injuries. Tell me how you would manage his fracture."

"I should apply a Thomas splint, Sir."

The examiner looked more than surprised, he looked startled.

"Would you indeed! And tell me, how would you apply this splint?"

So Paul told him, word for word, step by step, according to Mr McAllister's 'bible'.

"Making sure that the patient had adequate pain relief; I would place the broken leg into the metal frame of the splint, and then apply traction with cords attached to a weight that I would hang over the foot of the bed."

"And is that really what you would do?"

The question seemed designed to put a doubt into Paul's mind. He assumed it was a ploy to unsettle him.

"Yes, Sir," he said, trying to sound definite.

"And tell me; just how long would you keep this splint on?"

"For three months, Sir, until the fracture had healed."

"And you would keep this young man in hospital for three whole months? Unable to go to the loo, unable to have a bath or a shower?"

The examiner sounded incredulous, as if he couldn't believe the answers that he was hearing. Anxiously, Paul cast his mind back. Could he be mistaken? Was this really what 'McAllister's bible' said? But he was certain that it was.

"Yes, Sir," Paul answered, though an element of doubt was now showing in his voice, a doubt that got ever stronger as the examiner continued with this line of questioning.

"And the patient would be off work for this period, I suppose. I wonder if his job would still be there for him when he recovered. And what do you think would happen to his muscles whilst he was immobilised for such a long time?"

"Since he would not be using his muscles, there would be considerable wasting," Paul replied. "He would need physiotherapy afterwards to restore them."

"In the splint, the patient's knee would remain in one position for the duration. What do you imagine would happen to his knee?"

Paul thought for a moment. "I suppose it would stiffen. Again he would need physiotherapy."

"Yes, it would. Let me tell you that if a joint remains fixed in one position for a prolonged period, fibrous bands develop across the surfaces of the joint. Physio will probably break down most of them, but it's likely that some permanent stiffness will result. He would also get arthritis in later life."

The examiner's voice had lost its tone of surprise and incredulity. It was now matter of fact. Paul became aware that he was no longer being examined; he was being given a lecture. The management he had suggested was clearly wrong; his recollection of the instructions in the 'bible' obviously incorrect. His memory had failed him. Perhaps the Thomas splint was used for fractures of the neck of the femur, not the shaft, or perhaps it was used for fractures of the shin. Paul could no longer be sure. He would have to check when he got home.

There was a pause and then Paul was asked an unexpected question. "Tell me young man, where did you train?"

After Paul had told him, he commented, "Well, I sincerely hope that I never have the misfortune to break my leg when you are on duty there!"

He turned to his colleague, "Do you have any questions for this candidate?"

There was a sad shake of the head. "No, I don't. What a shame. He had clearly done well until this final viva."

All parts of the examination over, Paul left the college and staggered down the steps onto the street, oblivious to the other candidates milling around. He aimed a kick at a pigeon that was pecking at some litter on the pavement. He missed and the bird flew off, screeching angrily. It landed barely ten yards away then turned and looked back at him mockingly. Blindly, he wandered across the road into Lincoln's Inn gardens. A cyclist swerved to avoid him, then shouted abuse as he peddled away. Paul sat on a bench, put his head in his hands and closed his eyes. He felt utterly wretched. The last examiner had torn him to shreds, brutally exposing his lack of knowledge of orthopaedics. And up to that very last interrogation, he had performed well. He had thought that he had a good chance of success. Yet at the very last hurdle, he had failed. All the hard work, all those hours of revision, all to no avail. It had been a calculated risk attempting the exam without having worked on an orthopaedic unit. Now he would need to leave Surgical Five and get a job in that speciality before sitting the exam again. But there were other specialties of which he had no practical experience, urology for example and children's surgery. And if he gained experience in orthopaedics, Paul thought bitterly, he would probably fail on a urology question at his next attempt.

Chapter Twenty Three

The candidates had been told that they would be informed of the results of the exam at six o'clock in the entrance lobby of the college. Paul collected his overnight bag from the hotel where he had left it that morning, then considered what he should do. He was sorely tempted to go straight home. He could easily take the underground to Euston station and then catch an early train north, but some bloody-minded impulse made him decide to have his failure confirmed. Unable to settle, he walked the streets, wondering what the future held. What a shame about that final question. If only it could have been about an abdominal operation, perhaps one he had seen on Surgical Five. Had he passed, he could have applied for a registrar post. There were others senior to him of course, with whom he would be in competition, people such as Roger Watkins. They would be appointed because of their greater experience. But even if he were not successful with his first application, at least the consultants would know that he was no longer just plain '*Doctor*' Lambert. They would realise that he was a serious contender for some future post. Regrettably, his failure meant that he would now have to tread water, juggling his long hours on duty with even more revision, before retaking the exam.

As he drifted along, killing time, with no particular destination in mind, his thoughts turned to Kate, thankfully now recovering well. She was convalescing at home, and taking gentle walks in the countryside, as she regained her health and strength. Paul imagined her sitting in front of the log fire in the parlour of their cottage, chatting with Muriel and her father, whiling away the hours. It had been agreed that she could resume her nursing duties within a couple of weeks and she was eagerly looking forward to it, just as he was looking forward to having her close at hand. She had been so patient whilst trapped in her hospital side room and so understanding of Paul's need to spend time studying. Had he passed, his reward would have been to spend more time with her and to plan their marriage. Then perhaps, they would be the ones chatting in the evening in their own home. It was a wonderful prospect.

"Just the two of us?" Kate had asked, when Paul spoke to her of his dream of a life together.

"Well perhaps just the two of us for the first year or so, while we get used to living together," he had replied.

She had smiled at that, knowing exactly what was in his mind.

He wondered whether they should proceed with their marriage plans anyway. His feelings for Kate were getting stronger all the time, as he

216

felt sure, were hers for him. They both felt frustrated by their restraint. It was becoming increasingly difficult to control natural emotions. Having to revise and then retake the exam during their early married life would not be ideal, but surely it would be preferable to staying single. But would that be fair on Kate? If a young surgeon is to succeed, he has to make sacrifices, which means that his wife has to suffer as well. Why should a wife accept a husband who is away from home every second or third night; a husband who then comes home irritated and exhausted and is unable to socialise because he has to study? No wonder so many medical marriages ended in divorce.

As Paul walked the streets of London, he realised that there was an alternative course of action, one that was very appealing. He could turn his back on surgery. He could easily make a comfortable living in some 'nine 'til five' branch of medicine; one that did not require any further qualifications. Then his evenings and weekends would not be spent studying. He could just take life easy and settle down with Kate. They could enjoy each other's company and raise a family. After his experience earlier in the day, it was an attractive and tempting prospect.

The trouble was that if he were to be honest with himself, he had to acknowledge that he enjoyed surgery. He was happy working on the Surgical Five unit. There was a good spirit amongst the team of doctors and nurses. He was proud of the work that they did, and proud of what they achieved for their patients. They accepted that the hours were long and that the work was arduous, but it was immensely satisfying and subconsciously, Paul suspected that they all enjoyed the appreciation that was shown to them by their patients. And the 'buzz', the thrill, that he experienced after successfully completing an operation was, at times, intoxicating. There was certainly much that he would miss, if he were to turn his back on surgery now. Previously, during his short surgical career, he had never considered these matters, but it was now clear that they were questions that needed to be addressed. And they weren't questions that just affect him. Just as he enjoyed working as a surgeon, so Kate loved nursing. She wanted to continue in the nursing profession when she qualified. That needed equal consideration. They would have to have a serious discussion when he got back.

Suddenly Paul glanced at his watch. It was 5.30. Wandering aimlessly around the streets, he had been daydreaming. Looking around, he saw that he was on the embankment, close to the Houses of Parliament. He consulted his street map, and then set off briskly back to the college.

Back at Lincoln's Inn, there was quite a crowd waiting for the results, perhaps 70 or 80 in all. 150 applicants attempted the exam twice a year, so presumably the rest had failed the written paper and had not been invited for the practical assessment. They gathered in the entrance lobby, a wide chamber, through which Paul had passed earlier in the day. To one side, a broad staircase led up to the surgical museum, where all manner of diseased organs were available for study. Full-length portraits of previous presidents of the Royal College hung on the walls. All were adorned with the richly embroidered robes that denoted their high office. In the centre was the largest portrait of them all; that of Lord Moynihan, father of the college.

There were no seats in the hall, so everyone stood as they waited for an announcement to be made. It had been a long demanding day; Paul doubted that many had slept well the night before. The candidates were tired and quickly grew restless. Many had trains to catch, if they were to get home for the night. Conversation was sparse. They were largely strangers to each another, having come from different parts of the United Kingdom and it seemed, from many different parts of the world. The wait continued until, with the huge grandfather clock on the end wall about to strike 6.30, the head porter appeared through the door of the museum on the first floor. Slowly descending, he positioned himself half way down the staircase, immediately in front of Lord Moynihan's portrait. He had a single sheet of paper in his hand, detailing the names of the successful candidates, the young surgeons who would become fellows of the college. What was written on that sheet would alter lives. Some, flushed with success, would get the green light to continue their chosen career and seek promotion. Others, who had perhaps attempted the exam repeatedly but who had failed yet again, would turn their backs on surgery and seek employment in another branch of medicine. Others would hide their disappointment, settle down to further revision and attempt the exam again. And when Paul's failure was confirmed, what would he do? The truth was that he really didn't know!

From his position on the stairs, the head porter had no need to request silence, or to ask for attention; all eyes were already looking up at him expectantly. He stood tall, square shouldered and smiled down on the candidates below.

"Gentleman," he announced, although there were in fact, two ladies present. He spoke slowly in a deep sonorous Scottish voice. "The Council of the Royal College of Surgeons of England are pleased to offer fellowship of the College to the following candidates. I shall call the numbers of the successful candidates in groups of ten. Those whose numbers are called should proceed through the oak door adjacent to the clock, where they will be invited to meet the examiners and partake of a glass of sherry. He paused. "To those whose numbers are not called, I offer my sincere condolences. You have not been successful on this occasion. You are free to leave, but are welcome to return to the College to attempt the examination at some future date."

Again he paused. There was absolute silence as the candidates waited to learn their fate; their careers hanging in the balance. This moment was the culmination of years of surgical training and months of intense study.

Then, in his firm, clear voice he announced, "Candidates whose numbers are two, four and nine."

From amongst the crowd, three young men walked towards the oak door at the end of the lobby, and those identified by a single figure number that had not been called, filed dejectedly to the exit. The head porter waited until the room was once more still and quiet, before he spoke again.

"Numbers 13, 15, 17 and 18. Again there was a pause as four candidates walked forwards and six others, heads down, slipped quietly away.

Paul had been examined as number 63 and the suspense was agonising. Surely the numbers could be read out all at once. Why prolong the tension unnecessarily?

"Numbers 22, 25, 26 & 27."

After each group of numbers was called, there was a delay of at least a minute as the successful candidates, relief and joy written large on their faces went forward. Others, downcast, some muttering oaths, left the building. And so it went on, the room gradually emptying and always the delay for quiet to be restored before the next group of numbers was called. The head porter went through the 30's, then through the 40's.

"Number 56." There was a gasp, a communal in drawing of breath as it became apparent that only one of that group of ten candidates had been successful.

Again the porter delayed; the wait unbearable. Now feeling slightly nauseous, aware of his heart pounding in his chest, Paul closed his eyes and waited for his fate to be confirmed.

"Numbers 61, 63, 64, 68 & 69"

For a moment, Paul stood in shock, frozen to the spot, disbelieving. Had he really called number 63? Surely not. After that last interview, it was impossible for him to have passed. But number 63 had undoubtedly been called. Curiously, he didn't feel exalted; he simply experienced a huge wave of relief, as if an enormous burden had been lifted from his shoulders. In a daze, and half afraid that someone would chase after him, to apologise and explain that number 63 had been called in error, he joined the successful candidates as they edged towards the end of the lobby.

Paul had given no thought as to what to expect behind the oak door. He might have imagined a waitress, perhaps wearing a smart black uniform and a white apron, holding a silver tray laden with glasses of sherry, one for each of the successful doctors. Or possibly a line of senior surgeons, the examiners, ready to shake him by the hand and compliment him on becoming a fellow of the college, but it was neither of these. He found himself in a small, windowless, oak panelled room. It was already crowded with those whose numbers had been called and who had entered before him. The room was alive with emotion as joy and relief spilled out. The new fellows chatted excitedly, congratulating each other, shaking the hand of folk they had never met before and might never meet again; many, like Paul, scarcely daring to believe that they had been successful.

Despite what they had been told, there was no sign of the examiners or the glass of sherry that they had been promised. Instead they appeared to be in a queue, at the head of which, was an administrator sitting behind a small desk. For a few moments Paul was mystified, but the explanation was quickly communicated down the line. They were being invited to write a cheque to cover their first year's College subscription!

As Paul waited, it struck him that everyone in the room was male and that the vast majority were 'white'. When sitting the written papers some three weeks before, most of the candidates in the examination hall had been overseas graduates, mainly Indian, Pakistani or Ceylonese, with a sprinkling of African doctors. He could not believe that the bar was set higher for such doctors. There were two obvious explanations. The written papers required four essays to be written in three hours. Any doctor whose first language was not English, would be at a grave disadvantage, particularly in understanding the different approach needed when answering a question such as "*describe the.........*" as opposed to "*discuss the ....*". The other explanation lay in the postgraduate training available in different hospitals. 'Home grown' doctors tended to work in University and teaching hospitals, where opportunities for learning were greater and the ratio of doctors to patients was higher. The majority of overseas doctors were employed in district general hospitals.

On reaching the head of the queue, Paul saw that the clerk actually had his full name 'Paul Andrew Lambert' on his printed list. This finally dispelled his fear that number 63 had been called by mistake. He completed an application form, which required him to '*uphold the honour and traditions of the esteemed college'* and to abide by its rules and regulations. He also signed a cheque, despite knowing that when the cheque was presented, he would be overdrawn at the bank. No doubt, at the end of the month, he would receive a sharply worded letter from his bank manager, reminding him of his financial responsibilities! Finally, he passed through a door at the far end of the room and entered a large informal lounge, where a smartly dressed waitress offered him the glass of sherry that had been promised. The room was crowded; the examiners mingling freely with the new fellows. Paul noted that, as well as the examiners, several members of the college council had joined the party, including the President, who looked splendid in his colourful robe. They had probably been attracted by the prospect of a free drink, to which Paul's cheque would doubtless have contributed! To his surprise, he spotted Sir William amongst the crowd. Paul had not seen him during the course of the exam, nor had Sir William told him that he would be there. He came bounding over, a huge smile on his benevolent face.

"Congratulations, Mr Lambert," he said laying heavy emphasis on the '*Mister*' and clapping Paul heartily on the back. "May I be the first to congratulate you? Well done indeed. Not that I didn't expect it, you understand."

Still shell-shocked, Paul expressed his amazement at his success.

"Yes, I heard that you had a difficult time. In fact, there's someone here who would like to have a word with you."

He led Paul through the throng and introduced him to the examiner who had grilled him about the management of a broken leg, not four hours before.

"I believe that you two have already met," he said, "but let me introduce you formally. This is Professor Bates from Oxford. Professor, this is Paul Lambert, the SHO on my unit."

The Professor held out his hand. "Congratulations, young man. This is a very important day in your life, one that you will probably never forget. Perhaps you find it difficult to believe that you are actually standing here now."

"I am, Sir. I was certain that you would be the one to fail me. It was obvious that I was totally mistaken about the use of a Thomas splint."

"You were indeed completely wrong and Mr Adams, who was examining with me, was adamant that you should fail. But I thought that I knew the reason why. You may remember that I asked you where you had trained. When you told me, I guessed that Mr McAllister had taught you. It left us with a quandary. Should you be failed because you had been taught outdated techniques? Twenty years ago, your answer

221

would have been perfectly acceptable; indeed it would still be acceptable now, in places where modern surgery is not available. But these days, such fractures are treated in theatre by open fixation. The patient becomes ambulant and goes home within a week.

Mr Adams and I could not agree how we should proceed, whether you should pass or fail. So it was discussed at length during the examiners meeting this evening. That is why there was a delay before the exam results were posted. Even at the meeting there was disagreement. Some said that you should be more widely read; that you should not accept evidence from a single source. Others argued that the syllabus was so wide, that to do that would be impossible. In the end, it was decided to discount that particular viva and judge you on your performance in the rest of the exam. So here you are."

With that, he excused himself and left Paul chatting with Sir William. The college 'freshers' and the examiners continued to mingle for a few minutes longer and then, as if by common consent, the two groups separated and Sir William and his fellow examiners slipped away to have dinner in the college dining room. Conversation between the successful candidates soon flagged and Paul left, passing through the now deserted lobby, where the drama of the head porter's announcement had taken place. Out on the street, in the cold fresh air of an early winters evening, Paul's feeling of numbness and shock melted away, to be replaced by one of glorious delight. He ran joyfully to Euston station and found a telephone box. Kate must have been waiting by the phone. No sooner had it rung, than she answered.

"Hello Kate, this is *Mister* Lambert speaking......."

***

The next day, on the unit, Paul was greeted as a conquering hero. There was genuine delight at his achievement, both amongst the nursing and the medical staff. Mo produced a bottle of sparkling white wine. Sister handed round slices of homemade cake and Sir William made a speech, reminiscing about the day that he had become a College fellow. He finished by presenting Paul with his new name badge: 'Mr Paul Lambert, Surgical SHO'. Such celebrations were one of the attractive features of life on Surgical Five and were a frequent occurrence. They were held whenever there was a reasonable excuse; perhaps when a member of the team gained promotion, or when one of the nurses got married or left to have a baby. They were enjoyable events and had the added benefit of being good for staff morale. Even more enjoyable was the party held in theatre when Kate returned to work a fortnight later. The previous weekend, Paul had driven to her father's house, stayed overnight, and then driven Kate back to the hospital the next day. On this occasion, there were biscuits and cakes, but no alcohol. The best they could manage was fizzy lemonade, but Paul was delighted to feel the warmth of the welcome given to Kate and to see how pleased everyone was that she had recovered from her prolonged illness.

That evening, Kate and Paul had their own private celebration. They dined at their favourite restaurant and then returned to the flat for coffee. Relaxing on the settee, they spoke of their future life together. They imagined the home that they might have, the holidays that they would enjoy, the places they would visit and the children that might bless their marriage. For the last two months, Paul had frequently been close to Kate, but always in public, either in her side ward in hospital, or at her father's home. It had been a long and intensely frustrating period, having her so near, being able to see her, to talk to her, yet being unable to hug and kiss her, to express in a more physical way, the urgency of his feelings for her. Now, in the privacy of his flat, he held her in his arms. It was a delight to hold her close, to stroke her face, to run his fingers through her hair, to feel the warmth of her body next to his, and thrilling to feel the way in which she responded. Kate knew exactly how he felt.

"All the time I was trapped in that side ward Paul, I was waiting for this moment. The more ill I felt, the more I closed my eyes and dreamed of moments like this. It was what kept me going."

"And let me tell you Kate, it wasn't easy for me either, seeing you night after night in that pretty little night dress of yours, but having to keep my distance. Many is the time that I had an urge to jump into bed beside you!"

As they spoke, Paul's hand slipped beneath her blouse. Kate reacted with passionate kisses but as he grew ever more bold, she stayed his hand.

"We must try to wait," she said, though there was little conviction in her voice.

As the hands of the clocked approached eleven, the hour at which the Nurses Home was locked for the night, Paul was acutely aware that the door to his bedroom was only three short steps away. It required all his self control to walk Kate back to the Nurses Home.

In the shadows, she held him close once more and as they kissed goodnight, she whispered, "Paul, I'm not sure how long I can wait. We must get married soon," before slipping from his arms and into the nurses residency. Whether they could or would wait, Paul was not sure, but he decided that it would be sensible for him to brave a potentially embarrassing trip to the chemist.

Chapter Twenty Four

When Anne Brown realised that her stoma was permanent and that she would have to wear a 'belt and bag' for the rest of her life, her mood changed dramatically. She became sullen, withdrawn and showed a deep resentment towards all the medical staff. Her animosity was particularly marked towards Mr Potts and there were embarrassing moments on his ward rounds. Whenever he arrived at her bedside, she turned her back. She wouldn't look at him and declined to speak with him. Worse still, she wouldn't acknowledge the existence of her stoma, ignoring the nurses when they tried to teach her how to manage it. She refused to touch the bag herself; she simply called for the nurses to sort things out whenever the colostomy needed any attention, as it frequently did.

Her physical recovery however, continued to progress satisfactorily. Within a further week, she could have been discharged, had she not continued to refuse to have anything to do with her stoma. She wouldn't even look at it, let alone handle it. Sister Rutherford and Victoria both had long discussions with her. Another of Mr Potts' patients, a married woman who had adapted well after a similar operation, came to speak with her, to demonstrate to her that someone with a colostomy could lead a full and active life; but it was all to no avail.

Then the story took another twist. Sister Rutherford rang Paul, concern in her voice.

"Paul, I'm afraid that Mrs Brown is bleeding again. I'm not certain, but it appears to be coming from her front passage."

"Probably just her period, Sister," Paul said, remembering that she was only in her 40's.

"Actually I don't think so. It doesn't look like menstrual flow and it's not her time of the month. Fortunately the bleeding is only slight, but perhaps you could come and have a look when you have a minute."

Sister's words did not cause Paul too much concern. *'Common things occur commonly,'* as Sir William regularly reiterated. This was likely to be menstrual blood or perhaps a little seepage from the wound where the rectum had been.

When he next visited the ward, Sister Rutherford joined him at the bedside. She showed Paul Mrs Brown's nightdress and the sheet from her bed. It was true; the stains did look like pure blood. He inspected the wound but this was almost fully healed. There was nothing to suggest that it was the source of the problem. Perhaps the blood was coming from the front passage after all.

Mrs Brown's general condition was good but aware of her previous track record, Paul took the precaution of setting up a drip and checking that blood was still available, should she need another transfusion. Sister suggested that Mrs Brown should insert a tampon and wear a separate pad over the wound. Then if there were to be any more bleeding, at least they would know where it was coming from.

Half an hour later Sister was on the phone again.

"Paul, there's no blood on the pad but there's a lot more blood on the tampon and it looks fresh."

It was time to seek more senior advice and Paul discussed the situation with Victoria over the phone.

"I just cannot believe that this can be explained by an abnormality of blood clotting," she said, speaking quite slowly, as she considered how this latest problem should be handled. "She's just had major surgery. Her blood clotted perfectly normally throughout the operation but to make absolutely sure, you had better get another sample to the lab. Perhaps you could speak with one of the consultants there and see if they can offer any advice. Ask them if there are any rare disorders that wouldn't have shown up on the tests that we have done so far. Also see if you can get one of the consultants to come across from St Margaret's. If Mrs Brown now has a gynaecological problem, we're going to need their advice. I presume you've organised the observations, the drip and the blood?"

Paul assured her that this was so and she rang off, with a request that she be informed should there be any significant changes in Mrs Brown's condition.

Later that afternoon, Paul happened to be in the office when Mr Phillips, a consultant from St Margaret's, entered to record his findings in the notes after he had seen Mrs Brown. Paul had already had a long conversation with the experts in the laboratory, who had been unable to shed any light on the situation. They were adamant that there was no evidence whatsoever of a disorder of blood clotting. It was both puzzling and extremely worrying.

"Lambert," Mr Phillips began, "I believe you are the SHO here. May I have a quiet word with you and with Sister? In private if I may," he added, looking meaningfully at two student nurses who had been working at the desk. Sister took the hint and asked them to leave. Mr Phillips crossed the room and closed the door.

"As you know, Mrs Brown is bleeding from the front passage," he said, "and when I took a look inside, it's fairly obvious why. There are numerous scratch marks on the lining of the vagina."

"Scratch marks?"

"Yes, multiple scratch marks, some of them quite deep. It's as if somebody has been playing noughts and crosses in there."

"And how have they got there?"

"That's what we have to find out. I've told Mrs Brown that I need to examine her more thoroughly. I've said that she will need to travel to St Margaret's tomorrow to see me in my clinic. I would be grateful Sister, if you would arrange an ambulance. Whilst she's there, I'll talk to her and examine her again in a cubicle. That will create an opportunity for my staff to search everything she brings with her. It would be helpful if she travelled light. Whilst she's away from this ward, I suggest that you make an exhaustive search of her bed, her locker and all her belongings."

He paused, considering the strategy and then added, "I suppose that there's a danger that her neighbours here might see you going through her things whilst she is away. They might not like what you are doing, so perhaps it would be a good idea if you were to move her into a side ward tonight. But do give her the opportunity to take all her belongings with her. If I'm right with my diagnosis, she doesn't need a gynaecologist, she needs a psychiatrist."

The next day the plan was put into action. They waited until Mrs Brown had departed and then began a thorough search of the side ward, into which she had been moved. Twenty minutes later, they were about to abandon the search, when Sister found what they were looking for. It was a four-inch metal nail file, whose end had been sharpened to a point. It had been concealed by being taped to the underside of one of the metal bars of the bed. Paul rang Mr Phillips to tell him of their discovery, and learned that the staff in his clinic had found an identical object, hidden in the lining of her handbag. Finally the picture had become clear. She had inflicted the vaginal wounds on herself. Presumably the rectal ulcer was self-inflicted too. No wonder the sutures that Victoria and Mo had placed in the ulcer had come adrift and with hindsight, not surprising that the laboratory could find no evidence of a blood disorder or any abnormality when they examined the samples taken from the ulcer.

Mr Phillips commented that he had seen one such case before, in a young woman who was newly married. As a result of the scratches, she bled every time she had intercourse, which alarmed her husband. She had used it as a device to avoid intimacy.

Paul discussed the news with Sister Rutherford.

"But why should she do such a thing?" she asked.

"I can only assume that she has a mental health problem. We're going to need advice from the psychiatrists," he replied.

Paul's immediate reaction was one of anger. Anne Brown's bizarre and irrational behaviour had caused the whole team a great deal of anxiety. For weeks they had worried as they tried to discover the cause of her ulcer and prevent her from bleeding to death. Yet all the time, she had been deliberately deceiving them, pulling the wool over their eyes. But how dramatically her plan had backfired. As a result of her actions, the poor woman had undergone major surgery. She now had a colostomy. No wonder she had been so upset when she learned that the stoma would be permanent. That must have been devastating news for her. For the rest of her life, she would live with the result of her lies and deceit, with a daily reminder every time that she emptied the bag. Surely she must be severely mentally disturbed to harm herself in this way. Paul wondered if this was attention seeking behaviour, self-loathing or possibly a curious attempt at suicide. No doubt the psychiatrist would be able to tell them.

Then he had a sudden moment of enlightenment and broke out in a cold sweat. It dawned on him that he actually knew why she had harmed herself; that all along he had held the key to unlock this mystery, though he hadn't had the sense to realise it at the time. All too clearly, he now recalled what her husband had told him. He was unwilling to proceed with the divorce until his wife was restored to health. He wasn't prepared to go through with it, whilst she was ill. That was why she had done it. She was trading on his good nature. As long as she was ill, she could cling onto the marriage. Paul cursed himself for not appreciating the significance of the information he had been given. Perhaps if he had shared this knowledge with Mr Potts, the colostomy operation might have been avoided.

He rang Victoria to tell her that Mr Phillips had solved the mystery that had worried and puzzled them for so long. Tentatively, he also sought her guidance as to whether they should inform Mr Potts of the latest developments at this stage, or whether it might be better to tell him on the ward round the next day.

She thought for a while before replying. "We don't need his medical advice at the moment, so I think we'll leave it until the morning. She's made a fool of all of us. The boss is not going to be best pleased."

There was always a slight tension in the air when Mr Potts was on the ward. It wasn't simply that his ward rounds were more businesslike than Sir William's, or that his natural manner was brusque. It was that there was a sharp edge to his tongue. Any error, real or perceived, on the part of his junior staff, earned a brisk reprimand. Inevitably they were concerned how he would react, when told that self-harm was the cause of Mrs Brown's troubles. They decided that it would be best to inform him of the latest developments in the office, before they ventured onto the ward, arguing that it would be difficult to tell the full story at the beside in Mrs Brown's presence. Rather cautiously Mo raised the subject.

"Mr Potts, since you were here last, we have made some progress in the case of Mrs Brown, mainly thanks to detective work by Mr Lambert and Sister Rutherford. As a result, we now have a much clearer understanding of her problem. Perhaps Paul, you would like to explain."

Briefly, Paul informed him about the episodes of vaginal bleeding, the deep scratches that the gynaecologist had discovered, and the subsequent discovery of the sharpened nail files.

When he had finished there was a long pause; the staff apprehensive, fearful as to how the consultant would react. The silence was finally broken by Mr Potts.

"Damn and blast her. She's taken us all for a ride and she's made me feel like a complete idiot. I've taken away her rectum, given her a colostomy and she's nothing but a bloody nut case."

"But she's still ill, Mr Potts," Sister Rutherford said, rather tartly.

Mr Potts echoed the sentiment that had been expressed by the gynaecologist. "Maybe she is, Sister, but she needs a psychiatrist, not a surgeon."

Paul knew he had a confession to make and thought that the sooner he got it over with, the better.

"I'm afraid Sir that all the while, I've had a bit of information about Mrs Brown that I haven't mentioned before, because I didn't appreciate its relevance. But I now believe that had you been informed, the problem might have been solved earlier. You may remember that you asked me to speak with Mr Brown, to see if he could shed any light on his wife's illness. During our conversation, he mentioned that he wasn't prepared to divorce his wife whilst she was ill. Presumably that's why she has been harming herself. Whilst she was ill, she felt confident that he wouldn't divorce her. I'm sorry I did not tell you earlier."

Mr Potts looked thoughtful and there was another long pause. It was a relief to Paul when he spoke again.

"Don't worry Lambert. Perhaps there was a clue there, albeit a tiny one. I'm afraid that I've missed some much more obvious ones."

Paul looked up surprised. Mr Potts explained.

"A middle aged woman going through a difficult separation and divorce, estranged from her son. Two operations in Bristol within the last year, at which no definite pathology was found. Multiple attendances at the hospital with headaches, but always with negative investigations. And a set of notes four inches thick for a patient who is basically healthy. The signs were there if only I'd thought about them."

He stopped and thought for a moment. "Have you told her that we now know what she's been up to?"

"No," Paul said, "but since both nail files have been removed, I'm sure she will have realised."

"You say that she's in a side ward now? You had better keep her there until she's discharged. And since she's made a monkey of me, you'd better keep her out of my way. And Lambert, get the psychiatrist to see her."

There remained the problem of the patient's attitude to her stoma. Clearly the subject needed to be discussed with Mr Potts but it seemed that he was washing his hands of Mrs Brown. Paul decided not to raise the matter. It was a problem that Sister and the junior staff would try to resolve later. Except that they were not allowed the time to do that. The psychiatrist reviewed her and to everyone's amazement declared that she did not have a psychiatric disorder. When Mr Potts heard this, he stated bluntly that there were patients on his waiting list who were more deserving of a hospital bed and promptly discharged Mrs Brown to a convalescent home.

Chapter Twenty Five

A couple of days later, an event occurred that completely shattered the confidence that Paul had gained from his success at the fellowship examination. It all started when Professor Butterworth's registrar was promoted to fill the post vacated when Mo left to take up his job in Newcastle. This appeared to be good news, for it created a vacancy on the Professorial unit for which he applied. Paul knew, of course, that he was too junior to have any real chance of being appointed, others with more experience would be applying, but it did offer an opportunity to gain some useful practice of being interviewed. Since he was not expecting to be successful, he was not unduly apprehensive about the selection process. He felt quite relaxed as the day of the interview approached. Indeed with his wedding to Kate a mere three weeks away, he had more important things on his mind.

He was invited to attend the administrator's office at two pm. Arriving with 15 minutes to spare, he found three other applicants already waiting in the anteroom. One was his old nemesis, Roger Watkins, the SHO from Professor Butterworth's Unit. The others were an overseas graduate who had travelled from Sheffield, and an Englishman from Leeds.

As usual, little consideration had been shown to the candidates. All four applicants had been instructed to attend at exactly the same time, despite it being known that each interview could be expected to last at least 30 minutes. Waiting was inevitably stressful. Paul made some polite but rather formal conversation with the Indian candidate, a man called Mr Bhattacharjee. He had qualified as a doctor in Bangalore but had undertaken his postgraduate training in the UK. He was at least six years senior to Paul. Although he had no publications to his name, he had extensive experience in a number of surgical specialties. He had been a fellow of the Royal College for no less than five years. There were rumours that, in a pretence at political correctness, overseas graduates were sometimes invited for interview, even though there was no serious intention that they be appointed. Paul wondered whether Mr Bhattacharjee was a case in point. Generally teaching hospital consultants liked to train home grown doctors. It was the peripheral hospitals that employed large numbers of overseas doctors, nearly all from commonwealth or ex-commonwealth countries. The man from Leeds was less communicative, but introduced himself as Jonathan Worrall. He was two years senior to Paul, had held a fellowship for eighteen months and was clearly a serious contender for the job.

In due course, Fred entered the waiting room. It was the first time that Paul had seen him, since he had umpired the 'consultants v juniors' cricket match. Paul smiled at the memory of the dodgy decisions that he had made, when he had declined to give the Professor out! At least he wouldn't be involved in any decisions today – his role was purely administrative. Having informed the candidates that they would be called to meet the panel in alphabetical order, Fred invited Mr Bhattacharjee to follow him into the interview room, leaving Paul with Roger and Mr Worrall. Paul looked across at Roger but he studiously avoided Paul's eye. As the minutes dragged slowly by, they sat in silence, but a burning anger and resentment grew in Paul's head. Internal candidates held a definite advantage, since the consultants in the hospital already knew them. If the two external candidates didn't get the job, Roger most certainly would. Superficially Roger and Paul's CV's were similar. They had both qualified from the same medical school, had both undertaken similar posts at the City General Hospital, but having qualified 12 months before him, Roger had some significant advantages. He had more experience and therefore his competence in theatre and on the wards was greater. He had passed the fellowship examination six months ahead of Paul and was currently working on the Professorial Unit. Professor Butterworth would be keen for a member of his own team to be promoted. No doubt he had written an excellent reference for Roger. Yet Paul knew him to be dishonest and to lack any sense of conscience or responsibility. It would be grossly unjust if such a man were to be rewarded.

Much of Paul's anger though, was directed at himself. He knew that Roger had slipped out of the hospital when on duty, probably more than once. He knew that Roger had removed Paul's notes from Mary Murphy's file and substituting his own. Yet Paul had done nothing about it. If he had possessed the courage to expose Roger, to inform the Professor of his dereliction of duty, his prospects at this interview would have been enhanced. But he had been too timid. He had been scared of being labelled a troublemaker and afraid that he would not have been believed, knowing that it would have been Roger's word against his own. Now there was a price to be paid for his silence. In his heart, Paul recognised that with the Professor supporting his own man and with two experienced external candidates in contention, he personally had little chance of success. That didn't worry him but he would be furious if the job went to Roger.

The time dragged, but eventually Fred escorted Mr Bhattacharjee back into the waiting room. His interview had lasted 40 minutes, suggesting that he was indeed a serious contender for the post. It was unlikely that his interview would have lasted so long, had he been there solely to give an appearance of political correctness. Fred then invited Paul to meet the panel. The candidates had not been informed who would be conducting the interviews but it was logical to suppose that the Professor would be present, since he would be responsible for supervising and training the successful candidate. This supposition proved correct. He was one of a three-man panel. They were sitting behind a large oak table, strewn with various papers, presumably the application forms and references of the four candidates. Paul was delighted to see Mr Potts sitting alongside the Professor. He felt certain that his own consultant would support him. Paul had worked hard on his unit, not made too many mistakes and it was just possible that Mr Potts might feel that he owed Paul a favour, having named himself as first author on Paul's article in the surgical journal. Paul had also obliged him at the cricket match. He had bowled gently to Mr Potts' son and allowed him to score the winning runs for the consultant's team, though it was highly unlikely that such a trivial incident would have any influence on the important matter of an appointment to the Professor's unit!

The third member of the panel was a man of about 45, whom Paul did not recognise. Unlike the two surgeons, who wore grey suits, he was casually dressed; brown corduroy trousers, a chequered shirt open at the neck, and a woollen cardigan with large leather buttons down the front. With his beefy red face and tousled hair, he looked as if he would be more at home relaxing in a country pub with a pint of ale in his hand, rather than judging Paul's fitness to advance up the surgical career ladder. Fred introduced him as Dr Williams, a lecturer from the Department of Philosophy who was representing the University. He seemed to be a strange choice to be selecting a surgical trainee.

Professor Butterworth commenced the interview by asking Paul about his publications.

"Lambert, I see from your CV that you have written a couple of research papers. You seem to specialize in interesting titles. The first though, would suggest that it should feature in the Titbits magazine, rather than in the reputable British Anatomical Journal."

Paul smiled. The paper was entitled 'Sensation of the Female Nipple'. The co-author of the paper, a consultant who was an expert in diseases of the breast, had suggested this title, knowing that it would provoke comment at interviews. 'Give a paper an eye-catching title,' he had advised, "and you are more likely to get it published and you are bound to be questioned about it at interviews. It's easy to talk on a subject which is familiar to you and it leaves less time for more difficult *questions.'*

Paul explained that whilst working at the university, one of the surgeons in the city had approached the anatomy professor with a problem. A number of his patients had complained that their nipples had lost all feeling after their breast operations, presumably because the nerves to the area had been cut during surgery. He wondered whether, by making his incisions in a different place, he could avoid this complication. The professor decided that the problem could be solved by undertaking a detailed examination of the area, on the cadavers that were studied by the medical students. He therefore set Paul the task of identifying these tiny nerve filaments and, by painstaking dissection, tracing their path to the nipple.

"And did your findings result in a different surgical technique?" the Professor asked.

"Yes, they did," Paul replied, "and subsequently none of his patients developed numb nipples." *'Numb nipples'*, he explained, had been an alternative title that they had suggested for the research paper but the editor of the Anatomy Journal had rejected this. It did however bring a smile to the face of Paul's interviewer!

"Do you feel that this was serious research? Do you think it important for women to have sensation in their nipples?"

Paul looked carefully at the Professor, trying to judge whether this was intended as a serious question, but there were no clues in his facial expression. He remembered though that the Professor was a dour Yorkshire man, not known for his sense of humour. He decided it was wisest to answer the question with a straight bat and a straight face.

"It was because of complaints from patients, who had lost sensation in that area, that the study was undertaken, so yes, I believe it is important. There should be fewer dissatisfied patients in future."

There was the faintest smile on the Professor's face.

"A very diplomatic answer," he said. "Now tell me about this second publication, the one about wrist injuries."

Normally Paul would have been delighted with such a question, which again invited him to speak on a topic upon which he was well informed. It would probably be of some interest to the Lecturer in Philosophy as well, but Paul had some anxieties. The idea for the paper had been his. He had been the one who had done the research in the newspaper library and the one who had reviewed hundreds of casualty records. But Leslie Potts, whose input to the article had been negligible, appeared as first author. He had relegated Paul to third author. Yet here he was, sitting in front of Paul, waiting to hear what he had to say. Paul was aware that his answers could lead him into dangerous waters, and so it proved. Quickly he described the injuries that the three lads had sustained at the football match.

"Very interesting," said the Professor, "and I presume Mr Potts encouraged you to investigate whether this mechanism of injury had been described before."

There was an awkward pause and Paul hesitated before answering.

"Well no, Sir. Actually I decided to do that myself."

"And what happened next?" enquired the Professor.

"Well I looked to see whether similar injuries had been treated in this hospital previously and to investigate whether there was a correlation with the size of the crowds at the matches. I discovered that these injuries were quite common when the attendance was in excess of 50,000."

"And you did all that yourself?" queried the Professor.

Again Paul hesitated, knowing that it was perfectly fair for him to take the credit for his initiative, yet anxious not to upset Mr Potts.

"Well yes, I did." he said.

"How interesting," commented the Professor. He looked sideways at Mr Potts, who had the grace to look a trifle sheepish.

"So who actually wrote the article?" was the Professor's next question.

"Well I drafted it, and then Mr Potts was good enough to polish and correct it," Paul said, pleased to be able to suggest that his consultant had provided some input, despite the fact that they both knew that Mr Potts had not altered a single word! "Mr Potts also sought comments from the orthopaedic surgeons and gained their permission to publish the article."

Having initially been pleased that the subject of his publications had been raised, Paul now wished that the Professor would move on. Unfortunately he didn't and Paul's situation rapidly got worse.

"Well it certainly makes an interesting article," said the Professor. "And I presume that you reported your findings to the Football Association?"

"The Football Association, Sir?"

"Yes Lambert, the Football Association."

"No, I didn't Sir," Paul said, wondering why he should expect the Football Association to be involved.

"Perhaps you informed the police?"

Paul's silence and the doubt on his face indicated to the Professor that he was at a loss to understand the question.

The Professor frowned. "What was the purpose of recording this injury, Lambert?"

"I thought it would be of interest, Sir."

"And look good on your CV perhaps." This was spoken more as an accusation than a comment.

Paul could not deny this. Everyone in the hospital service recognised that in a highly competitive speciality such as surgery, the stronger your CV, the better your chance of promotion. Surely the Professor, with his academic background, would acknowledge this.

"Well yes, I suppose so," he said.

"Tell me Lambert, why did you undertake your investigation on the nerve supply of the nipple?"

"Because patients had complained that their nipples became numb after surgery," Paul replied, suddenly realising where these questions were leading.

"Yes," continued the Professor, "and by undertaking the research, by demonstrating that if surgeons changed their technique, numb nipples could be avoided, you helped the patients. In this case, you have identified a cause of injury at football matches. It must be expected that injuries of this kind will continue to occur, unless the design of the grounds or the management of crowds change. The Football Association and the police are responsible for public safety at football matches, yet you have done nothing to inform them. How many more broken wrists do you think there have been at football matches, how many more boys have suffered pain and disability, since you identified the problem?"

Without waiting for a reply, the Professor added to Paul's discomfort. "Have you taken the trouble to find out if such injuries are occurring at rugby grounds too, perhaps at Twickenham, when large crowds gather for rugby internationals?"

Paul had to admit that he hadn't.

The Professor then proceeded to give Paul a short but formal lecture on the reasons for research; stressing that advances in medical knowledge should immediately be followed by consideration of the way in which patients may be benefitted. Then he looked Paul straight in the eye.

"Lambert, the reason for research is not simply to publish an article in a medical journal, so that it looks good on your curriculum vitae."

Paul had to concede that this was absolutely correct. The research had been interesting. It had been accepted by a surgical journal, but he had completely missed the purpose of the study. He had done nothing to bring the matter to the attention of the appropriate authorities and had given no thought to preventing such injuries in the future. There could be no doubt that the Professor's criticism of him was fully justified.

There was a pause in the interrogation and it seemed to Paul that he was being given the chance to comment.

"I do appreciate now that the Football Association should have been informed, Sir. I will correct my omission."

Again there was a short silence and gloomily Paul reflected on what had happened. A discussion on wrist injuries ought to have been his strong suit; an opportunity to present himself as an astute observer, a diligent researcher with an active mind. Instead it had turned into a disaster, merely revealing a selfish motive for the study and a desire for self-aggrandisement. However, the thought occurred to Paul that perhaps he was not the only one at fault. Neither Mr Potts nor Mr Keeley had suggested contacting the authorities!

If the interview so far had been a disaster, it was rapidly to deteriorate further, as the Professor invited Dr Williams from the Philosophy department to continue the interview.

"Why did you decide to become a doctor, Mr Lambert?" It sounded strange to be addressed as *Mister* Lambert. The hospital consultants invariably referred to their juniors simply by their surname, just as Paul's teachers had done at school.

This was a question normally encountered by sixth form students, when they applied for a place at medical school and one for which there was a fairly standard reply.

"There were many different reasons, Sir. Obviously it's a stimulating career with job security. It also offers the chance to interact with people from many different backgrounds but essentially, it's because it offers the opportunity to help others."

"Yes, that's right," he responded. "A doctor is greatly privileged because he is able to help others." He spoke slowly and quietly, suggesting that great thought had been given to the choice of every word.

Paul presumed he was continuing the theme of wrist injuries and thought that a further apology was required.

"Yes," he said, "and I'm sorry that I didn't take steps to prevent similar problems occurring in the future."

"So," Dr William's continued, "if medicine is about helping others, what would you do, as a surgeon, if you became aware that you had a weakness, perhaps ignorance of a specific condition, or a lack of skill with a particular operation?"

"I should try to remedy the deficiency, Sir, either by studying textbooks or by seeking advice from a senior colleague."

"Yes, that right." As before, his voice was quiet, the delivery slow.

It was almost as if he were thinking aloud.

"And suppose you spotted a deficiency in the work of a colleague. What steps would you take in that situation?"

"Well again, presuming that patients might suffer as a result of the deficiency, I would take steps to rectify the situation."

"And do you think that would be a difficult thing to do?"

Paul thought for a moment. "Well if it was a junior member of staff, perhaps a house officer, I don't think it would be difficult at all. After all, in my present post, I have been helping and advising house officers for a year or more."

"But suppose it were someone more senior? A consultant, for example?"

Paul paused, not knowing quite how to answer. It was something that he had never considered. The consultants were like Gods. They were all powerful. No one questioned consultants. Dr Williams seemed to understand Paul's dilemma and probed more deeply.

"Well let us say, just for the sake of argument, that you saw Mr Potts, your own consultant, doing something that you were absolutely certain, beyond any doubt at all, was hazardous to patients?"

With the question posed in such stark terms, the answer was obvious.

"Well," Paul replied, "if there was no doubt that what was happening was harmful to patients, it would have to be reported. The bottom line must be the safety of patients."

"And to whom would you report it? With whom would you share your concerns?"

Again this was a question Paul had never considered and he answered with some hesitation.

"I suppose I would report to Sir William, as Mr Potts' senior colleague."

Then Dr Williams leaned forward a little, and his slow, quiet and thoughtful words took on an extra edge. Paul became aware that Professor Butterworth and Mr Potts were watching him closely.

"Let me ask you another hypothetical question, Mr Lambert." Was it Paul's imagination, or was there the slightest emphasis on the word 'hypothetical'?

"Let us suppose that it was not Mr Potts, but someone you knew well, perhaps a colleague to whom you felt loyalty, who was neglecting his duties, putting patients at risk. What action would you take in those circumstances?"

Paul looked sharply at Dr Williams. Was this really a hypothetical question? Surely they didn't know that Roger had left the hospital when

238

he was supposed to be on duty. But the required answer was clear enough.

"If patients were being put at risk Sir, the matter would have to be reported."

"Yes, that's right. So, let us summarise. You say you would report a colleague if you were certain that a patient's care was being placed in jeopardy. You've said that you would even be prepared to report your own consultant. Then tell me, Mr Lambert, if it came to your attention that a fellow senior house officer was in the habit of visiting a nightclub when he should be on duty, and perhaps you even ended up deputising for him to cover his back, what should you do?"

They knew. These questions were not hypothetical at all. The panel had conspired to lead him into a carefully laid trap from which there could be no possible escape. His surgical life was over, just as surely as that of a fox trapped in a corner staring down the barrel of a farmer's shotgun or facing a pack of hungry hounds. All they had to do now was to pull the trigger, dismiss Paul from his job and put him out of his misery. With hindsight, even the Professor's questions on preventing further injuries at football matches had been part of their strategy. With total clarity, Paul saw that he had utterly failed in his responsibility, both in his duty to spectators at football matches and to hospital patients when turning a blind eye to Roger's behaviour. To avoid danger to patients, such obvious neglect ought to have been reported; yet Paul had failed to do so. There was nothing he could do or say to rectify the situation. He had just told them, that his first and only consideration was the safety of patients, regardless of the situation, even if it were the behaviour of his own boss that was putting patients at risk. But his past actions contradicted everything he had said. He had revealed himself to be weak, morally corrupt and a blatant liar.

It was Mr Potts who broke the silence. Quietly he asked, "For Heaven's sake, Lambert, why didn't you tell me? For Watkins to leave the hospital without informing anyone, without even arranging cover, was a highly irresponsible and dangerous thing to do. A patient might have collapsed and died because of his absence."

It was a perfectly rational question to ask, but one to which Paul struggled to find any reasonable response. In reality, the answer wasn't simple. There had been many different considerations; concern that he might not be believed, fear of being labelled a trouble-maker and a reluctance to be the cause of another's downfall. With hindsight however, none of these considerations justified putting patients at risk.

"Well?" demanded Mr Potts.

"I'm truly not certain in my own mind Sir." Paul answered meekly.

"I did consider reporting it; indeed I discussed it with a colleague, but I suppose I was afraid of rocking the boat. I do realise now that I should have acted differently."

"With whom did you discuss it?"

"I would rather not say, Sir."

Dr Williams and the Professor exchanged a glance.

"All right, fair enough."

"Look Lambert," it was the Professor who took up the theme, "I do appreciate that when placed in such a position, there are many factors and pressures to be considered, but at the end of the day, as a doctor, your first consideration must be your patients. It is no good simply paying lip service to it, but then acting in your own best interests or those of your colleagues. If you find yourself in such a situation again, apply the 'newspaper test'."

Paul looked blank, so the Professor explained. "Ask yourself how a national newspaper would report the story, if a patient died because a doctor absented himself without arranging cover. And imagine what the paper would say about those who knew of the danger but turned a blind eye, allowing it to continue?"

A heavy silence filled the room. The interview panel looked stony-faced. Paul sat with head bowed, severely chastened. He knew that he had failed in his duty as a doctor, that any chance of promotion had evaporated and that his days as a surgical trainee were probably at an end.

Eventually it was Fred who spoke, addressing the interview panel.

"Do you have any more questions for this candidate, gentlemen?"

"No. That will be all," replied the Professor.

But Mr Potts then added, "Lambert, stay behind after the interview. We shall need to have another word with you."

Paul's interrogation was over and he returned to the anteroom and fell into a chair, his distress obvious to the other candidates.

"By God, you look shell shocked, Paul," Roger remarked, a self-satisfied smirk on his face. "They must have given you a rough time. You look as if you have been run over by a steam roller."

"I have," Paul said bitterly, and so will you be in the next ten minutes, he thought.

Whilst Roger was being interviewed, Paul reflected on the motives that had guided him through the previous six months. He was forced to acknowledge that his driving force, when researching the injuries sustained by the football supporters, had been selfish. The truth was that he had been motivated to write the article purely to enhance his CV. He had wanted to improve his prospects at job interviews and to promote his own career. It had never occurred to him that he had a responsibility to reduce the chance of future casualties, by communicating the danger to the authorities. It was also true, that had his prime consideration been the welfare of patients, he would have informed on Roger, ignoring any risks to himself. And yet, paradoxically, even after his failings had been so forcibly demonstrated to him, Paul still considered himself to be a caring person and a conscientious doctor. He worked tirelessly for his patients on the ward and derived great satisfaction when operations were successful. He never went off duty leaving jobs for others to complete. As a result, he frequently continued to work, long after he was supposed to be off duty. In that sense, he did put patients first. Yet he had failed the sterner test. He had failed to see the bigger picture. It had cost him this chance of promotion and would probably result in him getting the sack.

Unsurprisingly, Roger's interview proved to be considerably shorter than Paul's, and when Roger emerged, he marched straight across the room, tight lipped and angry and left, slamming the door behind him. Paul was soon to learn that he had been dismissed, news that he received with mixed emotions. There could be little doubt that his punishment was deserved, yet despite that, Paul felt some sympathy for him. Without a reference, his career in surgery was at an end; he might even struggle to find employment as a doctor in any capacity. But Paul was also aware of a sense of relief, that he had not been the one to have precipitated his downfall. Had he reported Roger for his dereliction of duty, Roger's demise would have weighed heavily on his conscience. Yet that is precisely the load that he would have been expected to bear, had he become a whistleblower.

After Watkins left, Mr Bhattacharjee and Paul sat in silence whilst Mr Worrall met the panel. His interview lasted 45 minutes. Then the three applicants waited for Fred to come and formally announce the name of the successful candidate. After ten minutes, Paul considered walking out, but Mr Potts had instructed him to stay. Paul was already in enough trouble without disobeying his consultant. 20 minutes become 30 minutes, which became three quarters of an hour and still Fred had not appeared.

As the waiting continued, Paul became more and more concerned. Since it would be impossible to appoint Watkins in the light of his unacceptable conduct, the panel had to make a straight choice between Mr Bhattacharjee and Mr Worrall. They were such different candidates that it seemed unlikely that it would take very long to make a decision. Paul concluded that the delay must be caused by a discussion about his failings. His action, or rather his inaction when he knew Watkins was

241

neglecting his duties, was to be his downfall. Anxiously, he waited and wondered what his punishment would be. Would he be dismissed or was it just possible that he might escape with a severe reprimand?

Over an hour passed before Fred finally appeared.

"Mr Worrall, the interviewing panel would like to meet you to offer you the post of registrar."

Then, turning to Paul, he added, "When the panel has spoken with Mr Worrall, they want to have a further word with you, Mr Lambert." How ominous those words sounded.

The successful candidate went back to meet the panel, a smile of relief on his face. Paul didn't have long to wait before Fred returned.

"Right Mr Lambert," said Fred. "The panel will see you now."

Paul re-entered the room with a heavy heart, fearing the worst. He stood by the chair which he had occupied whilst his failings had been so brutally dissected and exposed. For a moment, there was silence in the room before Dr Williams spoke.

"Do take a seat, Mr Lambert." As before, he spoke quietly and very deliberately.

"Mr Lambert," he said. "We have spent the last hour debating how best to proceed. It was only this morning that we learned that your colleague, Mr Watkins has been in the habit of visiting nightclubs whilst on duty, and that you were not only aware of it but on occasions, covered for his absence."

Paul looked at him enquiringly, wondering how they had come by this information, curious to know who had informed them. It was the Professor who read his mind.

"No," he said, paraphrasing Paul's earlier remark. "I prefer not to say who it was, but I do need to ask if you were you complicit in the arrangement?"

"Most certainly not," Paul protested vigorously. "On a couple of occasions, Mr Watkins couldn't be found. The staff on the switchboard, knowing that I live on site, asked me to help, which I did. But I do assure you that nothing was arranged in advance."

"We have discussed this situation at length," the Professor continued. "Watkins behaviour was clearly unacceptable, as it was when he altered the records of some of my patients, something else we only learned today. We have therefore decided that it is no longer appropriate for him to continue working at this hospital. We have also considered your situation very carefully. I'm sure you now realise that when you became aware that Watkins was neglecting his duties, you should have informed us. However, it appears that you covered his absences, working in your own time without complaint, for which I personally am grateful. They were my patients and I carry the responsibility for them. We also recognise that you failed to inform on your colleague through a sense of loyalty, albeit that your loyalty was gravely misplaced. Reports that we have received suggest that, apart from this disturbing incident, your progress in surgery has been encouraging. We feel that you cannot fail to have learned from this experience and therefore we have decided that this sad episode should not prevent you from continuing your surgical training. As you will already have surmised, Mr Worrall has accepted the registrar post that was available today but of course similar posts will fall vacant in the future. We hope, indeed we expect, that you will apply and in due course be successful."

Paul's mind was in turmoil as he struggled to come to terms with this sudden change in his fortune. At the start of the afternoon, he hadn't expected to be appointed. At the end of his interview, it was certain that he would not. Indeed he thought it possible, perhaps probable, that he would be dismissed. Now, the Professor was 'expecting' him to be promoted to become a registrar in the foreseeable future. Paul didn't know what to do or say. He should have smiled, apologised again for his failings, perhaps promised to work diligently until the next registrar post fell vacant, but numb with shock, he just nodded. It had been a roller coaster of a ride and he was having difficulty in taking it all in.

The mood in the room had been serious, almost sombre, but Dr Williams decided it was time to lighten the atmosphere.

Smiling, he said, "Mr Lambert, you must understand that no-one goes through life without making mistakes. I do; so does Mr Potts, even the Professor. We wouldn't be human if we didn't err from time to time. What we must do though, is learn from our mistakes. I recommend that you reflect on recent events, learn the lessons and then move on."

As he left the room, Paul reflected that this was exactly the same advice that Sir William gave to his staff when mistakes were made with patient care on the ward.

Chapter Twenty Six

Not wishing to be disturbed during the interview, Paul had arranged cover until 6 pm. With thirty minutes to spare, and needing some time to reflect on the afternoon's events, he wandered into the park adjacent to the hospital. Much had happened since the cricket match had been held there. Away from the busy main road, with few people around, it was quiet and peaceful and as dusk gathered, he sat on a bench and looked at the hospital buildings. From the outside, they appeared solid and tranquil but inside, during the course of the afternoon, emotions would have been experienced, every bit as dramatic as his own. Some patients would have been informed that their illnesses were incurable; that their cancer had spread beyond the scope of surgery and that their lives were coming to an end. For them, there would be no second chance. Others would have learned that they had been to the brink, that it had been 'touch and go' but that their operations had been successful; that they would live on. No doubt they would offer thanks for their reprieve, and determine henceforth to lead their lives to good purpose. Like them, Paul had been given a second chance. He wasn't sure that he actually deserved it, but as Dr Williams had observed, he would learn from this episode. He would be wiser as a result. He resolved that from this moment onwards, the 'well being' of patients would be his only consideration.

Further thoughts on the matter were interrupted by the shrill sound of his bleep. It was his old sparring partner, Sister Ashbrook.

"Is that you, Paul? I've just had the theatre on the phone. They need to know what cases are planned for tomorrows operating list. I know it's not your job but Dr Webb, that flighty house officer of yours, is nowhere to be found. And we also have some problems on the ward. Frank Gibson can't pee and Fred Barlow still hasn't moved his bowels despite those suppositories Sir William inserted yesterday. He really is bunged up. You'll probably need to do a manual removal on him! And old Tom Tennant's intravenous line has failed again. Why you doctors can't make a drip last for more than 24 hours, I shall never know. You'd better get up here as quick as you can and sort them out."

Paul sighed. It had been a long, eventful and sobering afternoon. It had changed the way he looked at himself and had forced him to reassess his priorities. It had caused him to make a firm resolution about his future conduct but it seemed that life at the City General would continue just as before. Once more it was time to return to the grindstone.

"OK Sister," he said. "I'm on my way."

That evening, all his responsibilities on the ward fulfilled, he returned to his flat for supper. Kate joined him, as she now did on a regular basis. With the fellowship examination safely negotiated, he no longer needed to spend long evenings with his head in a textbook or surgical journal. Spending time with Kate was infinitely more pleasant. He had already given her a brief account of the afternoon's interview on the phone, but was now able to discuss it with her in more detail. He tried to explain how he felt. Although delighted that the Professor *'expected him to be successful in some future interview'*, he felt bruised after the painful dissection of his character. His motives for choosing surgery as a career had been challenged and it had left him deeply troubled. He loved surgery. It was stimulating and exciting. Being able to locate disease within a patient's body and then use the technical skills he had acquired to remove it, was exhilarating. To restore health to an ill and anxious individual and return them safely to their family was extremely rewarding. Successfully completing an operation was like a drug. It gave him a 'buzz'. It induced a heady feeling of pride and well-being. He desperately wanted to believe that his motive for pursuing a surgical career was solely to help others, but the events of the afternoon suggested otherwise. His love affair with surgery, and the personal satisfaction that it gave him, had been the cause of his misguided decision to keep quiet about Roger's misdemeanours. He had not wanted there to be any risk to his own career. It had blinded him. It had prevented him from seeing that it was not a question of whether he liked or disliked the work; the only thing that mattered, was the potential that surgery had to benefit others. His motives had not been purely altruistic; in major part they had been for self-fulfilment.

Inevitably Kate was sympathetic, commenting that it was widely acknowledged that Paul was conscientious; that he worked hard for the patients in his care. He was the first to arrive on the wards in the morning and the last to leave at night. In his heart though, Paul knew that his interviewers were right; he had let himself down badly. In failing to report Roger's absences, he had ignored a grave risk to patients. One of the Professor's patients might easily have collapsed and died whilst Roger had been absent from the hospital - and Paul would have been equally to blame.

Later in the evening, some of Kate's nursing friends dropped round for a drink and a chat, but Paul was not in the mood for light conversation, even though the main topic was his forthcoming marriage, now just three weeks away. Originally they had planned a quiet affair but had come to realise that this was simply not possible, given the number of friends and family that they had. The girls chattered gaily about dresses, shoes, flowers and other wedding paraphernalia, but Paul was distracted. He produced some snacks and dispensed the drinks but contributed little to the conversation. As the clock approached eleven, Kate's friends departed in time to return to the Nurses Home before the doors were locked for the night but Kate lingered. For a while they sat on the settee, wrapped in each other's arms.

"You were very quiet tonight, Paul. No second thoughts about the wedding, I hope?"

"I'm sorry, Kate. No, it's nothing to do with the wedding. That can't come fast enough for me. It's just that I can't believe how stupid I've been. Looking back now, it all seems so obvious. I can't understand why I didn't do the right thing. The interview panel really roasted me - and they were fully justified to do so. The Professor and Mr Potts must think me an absolute fool."

"But they suggested that they have you marked for promotion."

"Yes, they certainly said as much, but I wonder if they will still feel the same way, when they have had a chance to reflect more fully."

For a while they sat in silence but it was impossible for Paul to feel down with Kate at his side. His troubles melted away when he held her close. The feel of her soft hair against his face delighted him. The gentle touch of her fingers on his cheek thrilled as did her lingering kisses. The warmth of her body exited and aroused. The sensation was heavenly, unlike anything he had experienced before; and he wanted it to last forever. He desperately needed to let her know just how much he cared for her, how he wanted always to be at her side. But he struggled to find the words to express the depth of his feelings, or to do justice to the intensity of his love.

For a moment he held her away from him. "Kate, you have no idea how much ....."

But she put a finger to his lips. "I do know. And you have no idea how much I love you."

Lost in each other's arms with passions aroused, time flew, and as Paul's hands wandered unchecked and ever more boldly, so the hands on the clock marched steadily on.

"Have you seen the time?" he whispered.

"Yes, I have. The Nurses Home will already be locked for the night."

The warm smile on Kate's face told Paul all he needed to know. In that moment, all their inhibitions were lost. They shared a burning desire to express the love that they felt for each other, in the most natural of ways. They covered the few steps to the bedroom, shedding their clothes as they went. At first hesitantly, nervously and awkwardly, but subsequently driven by a wild passion born of months of restraint, they broke the covenant that had, for so long, existed between them.

Afterwards, relaxed, naked but without shame, Kate lay in Paul's arms, her head on his chest. A wonderful sense of peace enveloped them both. For some time, no words were spoken, each lost in their own thoughts. They had taken their love to a new level and in doing so, Paul was certain that they had cemented their relationship for all time. They were no longer individuals; they were as one. From now on, they would make their journey through life together; they would face the world with confidence, whatever obstacles were thrown at them.

Paul raised himself on one elbow and looked down at Kate. Her eyes were closed, a soft contented smile playing on her lips.

"No regrets?" he asked, brushing back a strand of hair that had fallen across her cheek.

"Only that we waited so long," Kate replied, drawing Paul down to her with an urgency that surprised and excited him. "In fact, I think we have some catching up to do."

Message from the author

Writing this novel has allowed me the pleasure of reminiscing about days gone by, as often as not with a glass of wine at my elbow! I hope that you have enjoyed reading it. Should you have any questions or comments about it, or about life on a surgical unit in the 1960s and 70s, I should be pleased to hear from you. I can be reached via the 'contact' tab on the website **www.petersykes.org**

Points for discussion

- Would you prefer to be a patient of Mr Potts or Sir William?

- 'Surely a patient is better served by a doctor troubled by a degree of self doubt?' Do you agree?

- Do you regard Paul as being caring and compassionate or arrogant and ambitious?

- Why was Paul unable to admit that he was a virgin?

- 'Such impressions are usually made at first encounter and once made rarely change.' Do you agree?

- 'Without feelings, you will never be a good doctor.' Do you agree?

- 'The vulnerability of his position struck him, dependant as he was on his consultant for career advancement.' How true is this in the workplace today?

- In what ways is the life of the modern junior doctor different to Pauls?

- Does chastity before marriage have any place in modern society?

Lightning Source UK Ltd.
Milton Keynes UK
UKOW05f0433281113

221997UK00003B/32/P